WHICH WAY HOME?

HESTER'S HUNT FOR HOME • BOOK TWO

LINDA BYLER

Good Books

New York, New York

WHICH WAY HOME

Good Books books may be purchased in bulk at special discounts for sales promotion, corporate gifts, fund-raising, or educational purposes. Special editions can also be created to specifications. For details, contact the Special Sales Department, Good Books, 307 West 36th Street, 11th Floor, New York, NY 10018 or info@skyhorsepublishing.com.

Good Books is an imprint of Skyhorse Publishing, Inc.®, a Delaware corporation.

Visit our website at www.goodbooks.com.

10 9 8 7 6 5 4 3 2 1

Library of Congress Cataloging-in-Publication Data is available on file.

ISBN: 978-1-68099-124-6
eBook ISBN: 978-1-68099-135-2

Cover design by Koechel Peterson & Associates, Inc., Minneapolis, Minnesota

Printed in the United States of America

WHICH WAY HOME?

TABLE OF CONTENTS

CHAPTER 1

Night was coming on.

All around her the thickets turned to shadows, the crickets' song heralding the approach of darkness when the light would fail her. She'd need a place to rest or at least stay still. Alert, perhaps, but definitely still.

Now more than ever, she needed every ounce of her Indian heritage. Was "heritage" the right word? Or was that knowledge simply in the blood that flowed through her veins? Had she been born with the Indian way?

She guessed "heritage" fit more with the Amish, the people who found her when she was only a few days old. Or was it weeks? She would never know. She only knew that she was a full-blooded Lenape who was found by a white Amish woman. The Amish brought her up, these plain people who migrated from Switzerland to avoid religious persecution.

This afternoon, after a long-overdue confrontation, Hester had packed a few possessions in her haversack and left her family and the prosperous farm, built by their years of hard labor and good management in the wooded valley of Berks County, Pennsylvania. Her father's affections for her had ignited her stepmother's jealousy, until the situation escalated to the point of misery for Hester, Hans, and his new wife Annie.

Now Hester was on her own. She had always roamed the familiar forests of her childhood. Her own special rock, a large, flat limestone, jutted from the steep incline on the mountain where she spent entire afternoons. She went there as often as she could for some solitude, away from the ten siblings born after Kate had found her one morning by the spring. She loved the hills, knew the way of the forest, and was instinctively adept with a slingshot and a hand-crafted bow.

But now this was different. She had no large stone house to hold its protective arms around her at night. There was no fireplace, no cookstove. She no longer had a home.

Hester Zug had gone to school for a short period of time, but letters and numbers got all mixed up for her like a pot of vegetable soup. She could decipher some words, enough to get by, but numbers she had no need for. What she couldn't grasp in book-learning, she made up for by knowing the forest and developing acute skills with her weapons.

She stopped. Everywhere on the darkening hillside, there was laurel, thickets of it. Underbrush, tangles of vines, sharp blackberry shoots—almost impossible to navigate—stopped her ascent. She had wanted to reach the crest of this sharply inclined ridge, but since night had darkened the path, she would stay where she was. Lowering the haversack from her back, she sank to the ground, then rolled to one side to tear at the brambles that pricked through her skirt. She pulled the cork from the handled crocking jar, took a few greedy swallows of water, and replaced the cork. She had found no spring, no creek, so far.

Through the deepening gloom, she kept looking for a bed of pine needles, knowing her chance for a night's rest increased if she could lie on that natural carpet. But finding none, she'd have to make do. Leaping to her feet, she bent her back and rid the ground of stones, thorny bushes, any obstruction that would bother her during the night. Then she spread the cleared area with dead grasses, leaves, anything to cushion her night's rest.

Her stomach growled, and her whole body felt pinched with hunger. Sleep would be long in coming if she ate nothing. Reaching into the sack, she pulled out a long, flat piece of deer jerky, inserted one end into her mouth and tore at it ravenously with her teeth. She swallowed before the section was properly chewed, struggling to make it go down before tearing at it once more. The salt and grease increased the natural flow of her saliva, so she slowed down, chewing longer with relish before trying to swallow.

She disciplined herself. She would need that in the coming days. Another sip of water and her evening meal was complete. She would have loved a warm bucket of water to soak her feet and wiggle her toes, to slosh about extravagantly as she used a bar of homemade lye soap to scrub the dirt from under her toenails.

In summer, Hester was always barefoot. She detested the restriction of shoes, especially those heavy shoes from the traveling cobbler. Her mother allowed her to wear homemade moccasins, light and supple, at home, but to go to Amish church services, she was made to wear the cumbersome leather ones. Her feet were calloused, the healthy blue veins showing through the brown of her skin, capable of walking over any terrain. She wore no shoes now.

In her haversack, she had packed a pair of moccasins, one shortgown, more dried meat, and the journal of recipes from the old Indian woman. It was filled with directions for making the medicines and herbal remedies, the Indian knowledge of healing which she had entrusted to Hester before her death. That was it, except for the slingshot, a knife, and a ball of twine. She would need the sturdy string to make a bow.

The slingshot would serve her well for small animals, but before winter arrived, she would need to kill larger animals. She would need the skin of the deer. She would also need a shelter first, though many miles would need to separate her from her former home before she put something up that could be easily spotted.

She had no idea where she would go. She was headed east and perhaps a bit to the south. She had heard of the great blue waters, the Atlantic Ocean, and wondered how long she had to walk before she came upon it. For now, she knew there would be an endless string of hills, valleys, and rivers, all covered in woods. These were Penn's Woods—Pennyslvania—where William Penn had signed a treaty and worked constantly to maintain an unsteady peace with the Indians.

She figured Hans would try to find her. He'd stomp around for miles, his face flushed with fear and the fever of his longing. Hester's mouth was a compressed slash in her face. Her large, half-moon eyes were flat with disgust, clouded with remembering her own sense of innocence through the years when all the signs of his hidden torment had eluded her.

He'd send Noah and Isaac, his oldest sons, to find her, the sons born after Kate had discovered Hester, a newborn crying at the spring. The sons he ignored, so taken was he with Hester from the first day he held her in his arms.

Noah and Isaac had come to expect their father's neglect. They had each other. They sat beside their father in church, swinging their bare feet, content to be with him and unaware of his lack of attention, not knowing they needed a father's love.

They thought fathers always loved daughters more. Until they grew in age and stature. Their outward obedience had served its purpose. But an inward seething pot of rebellion, a fire stoked by Noah's intelligence as he absorbed the supposedly well-hidden thoughts of his pious father, only grew. Hester didn't know about this.

But Hester was confident that Hans would not find her. He was not taught well in the ways of the wild. He thrashed around through the woods with his heavy workboots, awakening or alerting every shy creature for miles. Sure, he was a hardworking farmer and a good manager, but he wasn't worth a lick at tracking or shooting.

He posed no threat. Besides, Hester knew he would not leave his wife for any extended period of time. He held his status in the community close to his chest like a priceless treasure, tending it lovingly.

Hester felt a fresh wave of hatred. It boiled through
her veins, a foreign thing. She had never hated. She knew
dislike, annoyance, irritation, but nothing like this. She
had learned from her Amish community to be honest
about her weaknesses, her sins. But how should she re-
gard her father, who was held in high esteem by his fellow Amish? She imagined him wearing some kind of rich
robe of righteousness, while inside he was crawling with
maggots of lurid thoughts and consumed by wrong de-
sires not yet acted upon.

Hester was past the age of twenty, but how far, she
wasn't sure. She had come to believe that her own simple mind had failed to grasp what more intelligent girls
would have seen years before. She had accepted the faith
of the Amish. She had been baptized and had become a
member of the church, promising to live for God since
being saved by Jesus Christ. She had vowed to denounce
the devil.

Yes, she had promised. She knew that the hatred driving her was wrong. She could not realize the promise of
heaven when she harbored such intense dislike of Hans
Zug, her father.

Hester was beautiful, and for that she took no credit.
She was created in near perfection by God alone. A gift
that might have been a blessing had turned out to be a
curse, or so she thought. It was many things—the way
she carried her tall lissome figure as graceful as a dancer;
her thick, straight, jet-black hair; her dark eyes containing a myriad of lights; her small, straight nose; her full,
perfectly curled lips, behind which a set of brilliant white
teeth would occasionally appear. When they did, it was a

delight to anyone who beheld her, so pure, so total was her charm. And so achingly guileless.

Many young men had been enamored, smitten by the young Indian woman. William King from Lancaster, tall, dark, taking her hand to accompany her to supper at her father's wedding to his second wife after the death of his first. Padriac Lee, the young man who poled travelers across the river on his raft, his red hair and easy Irish charm the source of her daydreams. But nothing had ever come of either one's attention. Hester had always been elusive.

Too many times she was labeled an outsider because of her Indian blood. She had developed no real relationships outside her family. Even her friendship with other Amish girls was sparse, cold, restrained, and reluctant. Now here she was, alone in every way.

She wondered how long it would take until hatred separated her from the God she believed in. Or might God understand the intensity of her disgust? Hester understood well that to be forgiven, she had to forgive. But an overriding sense of hate, and the resentment she carried for having to leave the home she loved, ruled her.

She was born an Indian. Her very being was of the Lenape tribe. The Amish called them *faschtendich*. Sensible people who roamed the forests of Pennsylvania, taking care of the land and worshipping the Great Spirit. But don't get on their wrong side. They don't forget, Hans always said.

Hester twisted her body until she lay on her side, drew up her knees, placed both hands beneath her cheek, and closed her eyes. A shiver ran along the top of her shoulder and slid down her back. The night air was cooling down. Well, there was nothing to do about that. She had no quilt, no blanket to ward off the chill of the settling dew. She drew her knees up farther.

The crickets and katydids kept up their night music, but Hester didn't notice. At home, with the upstairs window open, the same sounds sent her off to sleep every night. She knew the call of the screech owl, the barn owl, and the night hawk, the yip of the foxes, as well as the baying of the wolves.

She shivered at the high, primal scream of the wildcat, hoping she'd never encounter one alone in the wild. Noah had. He said they were shy creatures who would slip away unnoticed much of the time. When they were hungry or threatened, they were dangerous, however, so Hester learned to keep her eyes and ears on high alert when she was alone during the day.

The trees overhead hid most of the stars, but a few twinkled like friendly beacons between the leaves. As far as she could tell, there was no moon. She'd put a notch in a soft sapling branch every day to record the moon's rising as well as waning.

Small scurrying sounds reached her ears. Little night creatures snuffled their way through the thick undergrowth, she knew. Mink would be slithering about, their long, thin bodies sleek and supple. Bright-eyed deer mice rustled as quietly as possible, their lives dependent on the ability to escape the largest creatures.

Hester swallowed, thinking of a squirrel or rabbit cooking over a spit, the hot fire roasting the dark flesh to perfection. She'd find some blackberries in the morning.

Sleep would not come. She was cold. Sitting up, she reached for her haversack, pulled out the clean blue dress, and spread it across her legs. Removing the remaining items, she draped the heavy sack across her shoulders. Ah, that made all the difference. She couldn't believe a summer night could turn so cool, when at home, upstairs, it was so uncomfortably warm. The last thing she remembered was one star wishing her good night from its perch on the lacy pattern of leaves above her.

She woke with a start. The sound of crashing underbrush assaulted her senses. She lay perfectly still. The sound of her heart swelled in her ears, the thumping in her chest painful, as if it would increase its beating until it exploded.

If she got to her feet, she'd be no better off. The thicket, the thorny branches, the laurel, all the undergrowth would not allow her to run. She estimated the time it would take to gather her things and attempt to crawl through the heavy growth. Rolling her eyes, she estimated the distance to the nearest tree. She knew if it had low enough branches, she'd be able to draw herself up out of danger, but what if there were no branches she could reach? Then she'd only be revealing herself.

She thought of the white-tailed deer. The old bucks, the wise ones that grew the biggest antlers, often eluded hunters by bedding down in impenetrable undergrowth, especially laurel. She'd stay.

She estimated the cracking of twigs to be a few hundred yards off. Not close. If it was a large animal, it would have to be a bear, and a very careless one at that. No deer made that amount of ruckus while moving through the forest. A cat was even quieter.

Humans? Was Hans on her trail? She knew she was capable of leaving little or no sign of travel, especially in her bare feet. He would not be able to track her. He was far too clumsy.

Noah? Or Isaac? Real fear gripped her whole body like a vise, clenching her insides until bile rose in her throat. She fought it down, swallowing repeatedly.

Realizing that Noah would be able to follow her crowded her like an onslaught of defeat. She knew his way. He was her brother. As children, they roamed the woods, the surrounding hills their playground. Hester taught Noah where the redbirds built their nests and where the squirrels hid their cache of nuts for the coming winter. She taught him how to track an animal by pointing out one leaf turned on its underside, one section of bark peeled unnaturally from the side of a tree.

But would Noah accompany Hans? With all the hidden drama, this sordid battle of Hans's nature, would Noah be perceptive enough to grasp the underlying truth of what was happening? As she lay in the undergrowth, Hester reasoned that Noah was someone she was barely acquainted with.

He was her brother, her playmate. But after their mother passed away and a stepmother entered their lives, Noah became a young man she no longer understood. He grew to towering heights, his shoulders widening into thick, powerful muscles that could fell a tree much quicker than Hans could. Rarely did he speak, and he never acknowledged her presence.

Sometimes Hester imagined he was a mute, perhaps deaf or not quite right, harboring a brain disease.

Or perhaps he simply disliked her because she was an Indian. She didn't know. She supposed if Hans ordered Noah to accompany him to find Hester, he would obey.

She could not go back. There were no options there. The breaking of small branches drew closer. Hester curled herself in a fetal position, completely motionless. Had she made the wrong decision?

Suddenly, the crashing stopped. Hester's heartbeat was the only sound, the steady, dull thumping in her ears and in her chest. Had it been an oversize, clumsy black bear that had bedded down for the night? These bears were the reigning authority over a vast area of Pennsylvania's mountains.

Would he catch her scent? The air was from the southwest, behind her, the way it mostly was on warm summer nights. The bear, as she now called the noise, was a bit south of her perhaps to the east, which meant she would be downwind of him. He would not catch her scent readily.

As she lay, hope infused her, along with the realization that all would be well after all. Black bears were fat and lazy in summertime, gorging themselves on berries and the fish that would be spawning thickly in the clear, gray-green waters of the many streams that flowed to the Susquehanna. The bear would go to sleep. And at the first streak of wan daylight, she'd be on her way, skirting the laurel by a wide margin, giving the bear plenty of territory.

When the crashing sound resumed and she heard the frustrated, whining sound of her father's voice, it did not penetrate her understanding at first. She thought the bear had spoken. But when she heard Hans' high-pitched yell calling to Noah, then to Isaac, she knew he was after her. He had so much power over his grown boys.

A great calm enveloped her, folding around her neatly like a freshly washed quilt ready to be put in the cedar chest. She'd stay. They wouldn't find her in this thicket. Hans hated pushing his way through any brambles, often saying that nothing in a mess like that was important enough to put yourself through the pain.

She calculated the distance between them. Perhaps a hundred yards.

On they came now. Hester remained in the same position. Thoughts of being taken back to the farm entered her mind. She could go if she had to. She'd go. But she would walk all the way to the bishop's house. John Lantz was a kindly man, stooped and aged, wise and loving, the best man Hester knew. She'd tell him about Hans. Bring down the golden castle of his pride.

Then, just as quickly, she knew that was an impossibility. Hans had done nothing wrong. His denial of wrongdoing would be accepted long before anyone would take her word. He actually had never acted on his thoughts.

Hester began to shiver, then to shake uncontrollably, her teeth chattering and clacking together, a riptide of her fear overtaking her. The sound of breaking twigs, the scuffling of leaves came closer. Would they be able to smell the fresh earth where she had torn briars away, moved stones and branches? Noah might, or Isaac, but not Hans.

Another shout. So close, Hester brought the tips of her fingers up to cover her ears, pressing in on them so hard they hurt, as if that course of action would shut out the men.

"Noah, *shtup*!" There was no answer except for the stillness, the ceasing of breaking twigs.

"There is no possibility of Hester traveling through this laurel," Hans said, his voice high with irritation, fatigue, and anxiety, a voice Hester knew well.

Someone continued on, making less noise. They were so close. How could they see to move? They must have had lanterns, or perhaps only torches.

Then Hester heard breathing. Only when she took her fingers away from her ears did she realize how close either Noah or Isaac had stumbled. Another long silence, and then Hans directed his boys to retrace their steps.

The space of a few heartbeats seemed like an eternity. She heard level, even breathing, the raking aside of thorny branches. She did not move a muscle. If she were found, she'd have to go. But she'd devise another plan. Reasoning, calming herself as best she could, Hester remained motionless. Then she heard the breaking of the underbrush, the stillness as the breathing went away.

Hans bawled out another order to Isaac as the three men made their way down the side of the ridge, leaving Hester weak and so powerless she thought she might die of sheer relief. She remembered to thank God with one small, German prayer from her childhood, which made her feel a bit as if she should be caught and hung for treason. For how could she hate Hans and thank God?

Did God hear the prayers of someone like her? Or did he look upon her with mercy, understanding her plight? She didn't know. She only knew that she needed to increase the distance between her and Hans as fast as she possibly could.

The racing of her heart would not allow her to relax, so she lay awake under the dark canopy of trees, trying to devise a plan. Should she avoid settlements? Or find a group of people and blend in among them? She had heard of the large community that started in Lancaster County east of her. Acceptance there seemed out of the question. Everywhere she traveled, she'd be an Amish Indian. An oddity. If she chose to dwell among civilization, she would have to desert the ways of the Amish. She'd need to stop wearing her muslin cap at least.

Weary, her thoughts upsetting, she decided to take one day at a time. Surviving was the most important thing. She'd travel fast, getting as many miles away from Berks County as possible. That was the best solution.

God would provide, or at least she hoped he would remember to look after her, walking through the wilderness in her bare feet without her muslin cap and with a heart filled with disgust for her father.

CHAPTER 2

WHEN THE FIRST STREAKS OF PINK LIGHT SEPA-
rated the dark blue and gray of the early-morning sky,
Hester was on her feet, the haversack bulging on her
back, her eyes searching for the best route around the
laurel. She was strangely exhilarated. She stepped out,
moving swiftly as the light strengthened. She could see
pine trees now, but who could have known they were
there in the fast-fading light of evening?

She skirted the laurel, making her way over rocks and
around thickets, but steadily up the side of the incline.
On top, she ate some of the dried deer meat, drank sparingly of the water, and made her way quietly down the
opposite side.

She guessed there was a creek, perhaps a spring, at
the bottom of this ridge. She was surprised to find only
a deep gouge containing layers of old leaves. A perfect
place to sleep, but that time was not now. The sun was
rising, a hot, red, shimmering orb of heat. Flies droned
everywhere; bees hovered by the raspberry bushes.

Raspberries? Excitement pulsed through her veins when she realized how thick the raspberry canes stood along this small clearing. The purple berries grew profusely. Hester walked rapidly, plucking greedily at the sweetest berries. She lifted them to her lips, gobbling them like a starving bear. She ate until she could hold no more, thinking how berries satisfied hunger and quenched thirst at the same time.

That day, she calculated she'd walked a distance of fifteen miles. It was only a guess, but she knew she was in country she'd never seen or heard about. Tonight she'd start a small fire. But first, her water was all gone. She needed to find a stream. On top of the mountain, she'd figured there'd be a spring somewhere, but she'd been unable to locate one.

She knew the book of Indian medicines contained directions about how to find water using the forked branch of a peach tree, but those trees weren't around, and besides, she wasn't certain it would work.

She made her way down the mountain, clinging to small trees to lower herself. Thirst spurred her on. Her tongue was dry and heavy, her lips parched. She should have brought more water, should have known it was the dry summer season, and that water might not be as easy to find as she'd imagined.

A snake slithered across a flat rock, scaly and dry and brown. She was not afraid of snakes, finding them to be shy as long as they were undisturbed. The backs of her legs ached from the rapid descent, but she tried to ignore the pain, knowing the most important thing at the moment was to find a source of water.

The steep mountain leveled off a bit; the trees grew larger and farther apart, as if they received more nourishment to grow to this resplendent size. Hester smelled the river long before she saw it. It smelled of sulphur and iron and moisture. It smelled of mud and wet grass and dragonflies and butterflies. She increased her speed, her breath coming in gasps. Her mouth was painfully dry, her throat on fire. Ahead, the trees thinned even more.

Remembering caution, she slid soundlessly from tree to tree, her large eyes searching her surroundings for any sign of human habitation.

The clearing was surprisingly hard to get through, the thick grasses overgrown by wild rose bushes. Her feet were bleeding by the time she slid down the muddy bank of the river, plunging into the clear, brownish-green water like an otter and submerging her tired body completely. Then, rising to the surface, she cupped her hands and drank deeply, over and over, until the fiery thirst was gone.

She wished for soap. She rinsed her hair, clambered up the bank, and shook herself like a dog, then inhaled the pure, wet air, the pleasurable sensation of being without thirst. She felt alive, in control of her situation. What did she want for supper? Fish or wild game?

Schpeck and Sauerkraut? Stewed chicken and carrots?

Hester smiled, remembering the long plank table and the great bowls of food passed around to the thirteen hungry people. Saliva pushed into her mouth. She swallowed.

Efficiently then, she took stock of her situation. She'd have to stay beneath trees and away from the clearing. There was no sense in being a sitting duck. Why be free picking for unsavory characters? Or for bears that decided they had had plenty of fish for the summer?

She found a natural alcove with the trunk of a great tree at her back, the upturned roots of a fallen one beside her. It was perfect, shielding her from sight and protecting her from animals. All she needed was a roof.

No, that was not possible. She had not put enough distance between herself and her family. She must stay rational, no matter how homey this natural little wonder appeared to her. She set about piling soft materials into a small hollow. She found grass, soft bark from the fallen pine tree, moss, and wonder of wonders, great sheets of old bark that she could peel from the dead tree. Perfect for a sleeping cover.

Squirrels chirred from the tree branches, so she bent swiftly, retrieved her slingshot, found a smooth stone by the river, and let fly an expert shot at the nearest, especially saucy one. Triumphantly she picked up the nice, fat, gray squirrel, one of the biggest she'd ever seen.

The round, orange sun was hovering just above the mountain to the east when Hester cleared a small area, then gathered dry leaves and very small dry twigs. She found a healthy hickory tree and pulled off the lowest, small branches. Then she began to rub them together, squatting on her haunches above the small pile of dry leaves.

She'd often done this and had shown Noah and Isaac the way of it. There was a trick to attaining enough friction, in the proper span of time, with the right amount of dry leaves to catch those first few sparks. But now she was hungry and tired, and her arms felt soft and pliable when she had rubbed for only a minute or more.

She continued, faster and faster, her shoulders hunched, her teeth pressed together as she concentrated on starting a fire to cook the squirrel.

She could not stop the friction to check how hot the branches were becoming. Her breath came in rapid puffs, and the muscles in her arms knotted, sending up spasms of pain as her fingertips heated up. Good. Faster now. Only a while longer.

A thin, white plume of smoke curled up from the peeled hickory branch, followed by a few orange sparks. Hester moved her hands even faster. More sparks fell on the dry leaves. A gray curl of smoke blackened the edge of a leaf, then another. Still Hester's hands flew back and forth, as more sparks showered on the dry leaves.

Suddenly a bright orange and yellow flame danced to life. Quickly, she flung the hickory branches to the ground and sifted dry leaves over the small, orange flame. Her eyes lit exultantly when the flame grew large, licking greedily at the dry twigs Hester placed on top.

As soon as the fire was started well, she surrounded it with stones, then fashioned a spit from green branches. Taking up her knife, she cleaned the squirrel with a few expert slices, then cut off its head, legs, and tail, drawing the skin down and away from the carcass. She impaled the prepared squirrel on the green branch, hung it low above the now crackling fire, and lay down on the bed she had made for herself to wait hungrily until the meat was done.

As the shadows lengthened across the river, the trees' reflections became longer and darker, the water no longer friendly the way it had been with the sun glinting on it. When sun shone on water, it created light, like ice. Sometimes the light was blue or yellow or clear, but it always brought light and joy to Hester, no matter if the day had turned into drudgery.

She wanted to stay here by the river always. She picked the hot meat off the bones, crunching it with her fingers and in her mouth. She ate every scrap of meat, sucking it off the tiny, fragile bones, then chewing a few of them and eating the small bits of marrow. Marrow was life-giving, filled with iron and other good minerals, so she ate every morsel she could find.

She threw what little remained of the squirrel back into the fire, took a long drink of the tepid river water, and settled herself comfortably for the night. The river ran silently toward the east. Only occasionally, Hester heard the splash of a leaping fish in the distance. A loon called its ribald laughing sound. Another answered, then another. Bats wheeled and drove through the evening sky, marauders after every flying insect. Mosquitoes buzzed in Hester's ears. She slapped at them, then drew her hair across her ears to keep them away.

Exhaustion filled her mind and her body. Sleep overtook her, and she knew nothing more until the first light of dawn played across her brown face.

She scratched the red coals back to life, added dry twigs and small pieces of wood, then went to the river to wash.

The day was cool and fresh, the grasses hanging heavy with drew. Her bare feet were soaked by the time she reached the river. She stood on the bank of the slow-moving water, stretched her arms over her head, and caught the light of the sun's first rays, as tenderly warming as the heat from the fireplace on the winter mornings of her childhood.

She caught a fat, slow, brown carp beneath a tree root with her bare hands, a skill she'd developed along with her brothers. She cleaned the fish, grilled it fast over the hot fire, and ate all she could hold. The fish was not very tasty, but Hester knew beggars can't be choosers, as Annie would say. She did not know when she would eat well again. She considered spending the day catching fish and drying them, but then thought better of it. She needed to keep moving as fast as possible.

She continued along the riverbank until she found an area of the river that appeared shallow. She began to pick her way across, her bare feet feeling for rocks that were sharp or holes that appeared unexpectedly. There was nothing in her sack that could not get wet if she needed to swim, except for the volume of Indian medicines. She could not have it destroyed by water or stolen. Nor could she lose it. The book contained the only wisdom she could use to make her way in the world.

She would apprentice to a midwife. Or a doctor. She'd figure it out, once she had put enough distance between her and Hans Zug.

She reached the opposite side without mishap and kept moving straight up the mountain without looking back. She knew she would not find a cleared spot again like the one where she had spent the previous night. She had covered the area with grass and rocks so that every trace of the fire was gone. She had put the large piece of bark back on the tree. No one could tell that it had been pulled off and served as her cover. Even someone following her would not know.

A cold chill chased itself up her spine. She looked back over her shoulder. The morning light barely penetrated the covering of leaves, leaving the mountainside dark and wet with the night's dew. She glanced over her shoulder again. She stopped, caught her breath, then resumed climbing. Up, up, she went as the sun rose, too, heating the side of the mountain. Perspiration broke out on her forehead and trickled down her back, yet still she climbed, her steps long and even, her breathing hard but steady.

She looked down the way she had come. Why couldn't she shake the feeling of being followed? She stopped, turned slowly in a half-circle, and assessed her situation, trying to calm herself. There was nothing but rocks, trees, bushes, and the usual mountainous terrain. Nothing out of the ordinary. A blue jay called its raucous cry, but that did not necessarily mean anything. It was big and bold like blue jays are, leaders of the bird world, or as they imagine themselves to be, crying out about everything, even a big, green, walnut letting loose and crashing to the forest floor. She climbed on, then stopped to uncork the jug of water and swallowed large, thirsty gulps, before stopping herself.

Now on top of the mountain, she laid down her sack of belongings and looked for a tree with low branches. She swung herself up, hand over hand, pulling herself from branch to branch until she came close to its top. She had found a panoramic view of the river and could see down the way she had come. Perhaps this would take away her unsettled feeling. The sun was white hot, the air shimmering with heat and humidity. Falling away as far as she could see were tree-covered mountains and hills, like little bumps of green—the dark green of the pines, the lighter green of oak, maple, hickory, ash, and chestnut, the pale green of locust—all these millions of trees.

Hester had no idea how much a million was, or a thousand, for that matter, but she figured it would take an awfully long time to count them all.

Her eyes located the small clearing, the edge of the forest where she had slept. For a long moment she kept her eyes on that spot, never moving them. The grass was pale green, almost yellow. Along the edge of the sparkling brown river, the cattails were darker. Absolutely nothing appeared to be moving. She was probably too far away to tell.

She checked the branch below her, ready to descend, then looked one more time out over the trees below her. A part of the pale green grass had a dark spot. One she had not noticed earlier. A rock?

As she watched, the dark spot moved toward the river, then stopped. Hester knew it was not a black bear or a deer. It was a man. Who, she could not tell. Her eyes narrowed as she evaluated her situation. He may not be following her at all. He might just be a traveler, too, searching for a way across the river like she was. She had no reason to be alarmed.

She had a long running start away from him if he was following her. He'd have a hard time keeping her trail, as far upriver as she'd gone away from the shallow water. Confident now, she climbed slowly out of the tree, dropped to the ground, and landed squarely on her feet. She picked up her haversack and continued down the other side of the mountain.

By late afternoon, she was hot, tired, and hungry. She found two creek beds filled with rocks and small, yellow, locust leaves that drifted down from tired, dry trees. But not a drop of water. She drank sparingly, just enough to keep the misery of thirst at bay, and kept walking fast.

She picked her way among rocks now, coming to a hill covered with dead, fallen trees, where sharp limestone rocks were piled one on top of the other. The place appeared to be cursed, as if nothing green were blessed enough to grow there.

She stopped. The heat waved and shimmered, a thing alive, pressing down on her head and her lungs, burning her back with its power. Her whole body cried out for water. She uncorked the jug, took a swallow of the warm river water, then forced herself to put the cork back in its place.

Bent on all fours now, she crept along the rocks, her feet shaping themselves to the formations, her hands steadying her progress. When she came up over a rise, she gasped. So this is what happened. Lightning had struck, starting a fire. From blackened stumps and gray ash, tender green trees were emerging from the burned ground. The rocky area had stopped the raging fire.

Hester walked through the acres of destruction, wondering at the power of God, the way nature reinvented itself. She found a perfect pink rose growing on a vine that wound its way around a black tree stump. Stopping, she bent to pick it, held it to her nose, and inhaled deeply. This beauty among ashes. It was so lovely Hester could hardly bear the thought, the pink rose so alone, lighting the destroyed world with its presence.

She found a narrow cave beyond the burned area. She wanted to stay for the night, but there was no water, so she continued on her way with long, even strides that ate up the ground. She followed the side of a ridge, then turned downward, hoping to find a creek or a spring—just a trickle of water. She thought of Hans's springhouse, the cool, wet interior that housed the cold, creamy milk, mint tea, ginger beer. She had to find water.

She calculated the distance she'd come. Probably ten miles since morning, but that was only a guess. She hoped she had traveled far enough that anyone who searched for her had given up.

The light faded now. She lifted her face to look at the sky and saw black clouds rolling and tumbling. The wind rustled the leaves above her head.

Hester did not try to find shelter. She sat beneath a sparse old tree and lifted her face to the glorious, wind-driven, pelting raindrops. The flashes of lightning and ear-splitting claps of thunder evoked no fear in her. She cupped her hands and caught the pure, clean water, licking it up like a dying animal.

She winced when hail bounced off her head, then covered herself as best she could with the coarse haversack. On her hands and knees, she raked crazily at the small bits of ice, stuffing them into her mouth and chewing them to pieces. She could not get enough. Shivering, she kept swallowing, opening her mouth to the driving rain that followed the hailstorm.

The trees bent and swayed. Lightning flashed in jagged streaks across the sky, followed immediately by loud claps of rolling thunder. Not once was she afraid. This was the way it was. Nature punched and bounced itself around upstairs, throwing lightning down with fiery swords. But in all that clatter, the gift of rain followed,

saving withering fields of corn, assuring anxious housewives another chance at preserving enough vegetables
for the coming winter.

Her thirst slaked now, Hester remained beneath the aging tree. She thought of looking for a sapling so she could
strip the bark and gnaw the tender inside lining like a rabbit, but she was afraid her stomach would rebel because
it was so empty. The last thing she needed was to get sick.

She was cold, shivering, and so hungry she decided to
eat a whole strip of the jerky. She had to keep moving.
The storm was a big help, the way it would wash away
her tracks, but she could not relax or become sloppy or
inattentive.

She filled the crockery jug full of water from the tumbling little brook that appeared in the crevice between
two steep banks. Heartened, she walked swiftly along
the dripping forest, thunder grumbling in the distance.

The land was leveling out now, becoming almost flat.
She climbed another tree and was amazed to see a large
clearing just ahead of her. Would there be people living
close by? Her steps increased then, until she was panting
a little, so eager was she to see what was in the clearing.
A house? A town?

She ran shaking fingers through her long, unkempt
hair. She looked down at her torn skirt, the blackened
front of her shortgown, and decided to change into
her clean one. Raking her hair back from her face, she
snapped a piece of string from the ball in her haversack,
then tied it securely. Washed clean by the rain, Hester
decided she was presentable, just in case she did stumble
onto another person. Or people.

She walked eagerly now, realizing the happiness she would feel in meeting anyone—a family, perhaps, or a couple alone. She traveled the entire length of the clearing, her head swiveling, searching, without seeing one building or a small soul. Well, so be it then. She'd likely find a spot to spend the night, then kill a small animal for her supper. She was not thirsty, she was reasonably clean, and she still possessed enough strength to care for herself.

She'd start a fire, although that thought gave her a scare, but only as long as she let it. The man by the river was very likely uninterested or unaware of her presence. Probably both.

In the shelter of the trees, she repeated the previous night's ritual, although this supper was even tastier. The clearing popped with healthy, brown rabbits barely smart enough to hop away at the sight of her. She ate the succulent, browned meat, made a mild, tasteless tea with catnip from the meadow, then fell into an uncomfortable, restless sleep. The ground was wet and dripping. Her only cover was the sodden haversack and her soiled shortgown.

During the night, every fox and coyote in the mountains must have come down to the clearing to hunt rabbits. The yipping and barking and squealing were enough to wake the soundest sleeper. Finally, wet, uncomfortable, and chilled, Hester got up, poked the coals of her fire to a small flicker, then set the crockery jug on a hot stone to heat the catnip tea.

Sitting cross-legged, she lifted her face to view the vast panorama of stars in the night sky that was washed clean by the afternoon's hailstorm. Every one of those stars looked as if they had had their faces scrubbed, they were so bright and shining.

Alone in the vast universe without the base creature comforts she had always taken for granted, Hester sensed a wild elation growing in her chest. Her senses were freed like an eagle in flight, and her spirits soared. Ah, yes. "They that wait upon the Lord shall renew their strength; they shall rise up as eagles."

"Here I am, God. Please look after me. Amen." One star blinked, smiled, and bowed to her.

Chapter 3

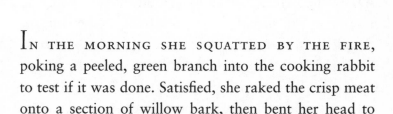

In the morning she squatted by the fire, poking a peeled, green branch into the cooking rabbit to test if it was done. Satisfied, she raked the crisp meat onto a section of willow bark, then bent her head to blow on it so it would be cool enough to eat.

Ravenous, she ate in great, tearing gulps, her strong, white teeth ripping the meat away from the bones. It was good even without salt. She tested the wild artichokes roasting in the fire, rolling them gingerly before popping a section into her mouth.

After she had eaten, she packed the haversack, set it aside, then kicked dirt on the fire, replacing the natural order of growing grasses as best she could. She lifted her face to the sun and walked toward it. East. Always east.

In long, loping strides, she covered the clearing and entered the surrounding forest. Her strength bolstered by the rabbit cooked over the fire, she was tireless. The air was crisp and clean without the pressing humidity.

The day passed the way the previous two had. She climbed ridges, then slid down the opposite side, hunger and thirst her only company. She found pokeberries, wild leeks, and a few tart strawberries that made her mouth pucker. Later on, a stomachache forced her to sit beneath a tree to rest. The wild creatures watched her approach, then slid noiselessly into the underbrush and behind fallen logs.

The sun had already dropped behind the high mountain ahead of her, the shadows lengthening to create a long twilight on the west side of the mountain. As usual, she was thirsty. She knew the best place to find water was at the base of the mountain, so she'd stay on this side for the night. She searched as long as the light befriended her, then stopped in defeat. Well, she'd survive till morning. If there was no water, she'd just rest for the night. Her stomach felt as if it would cave in, shutting off her airways with its deflating. There was nothing to do for it.

She did find a patch of liverwort. She knew the flat-leafed herb grew only in moist places, so she bent her back and spread her fingers through the crumpled edges of the leaves. The earth beneath the herb was damp, but not wet. She looked for a sturdy green branch, shaved the tip to a digging tool, then walked downwind to a place where the slope fell into a crevice.

Here she began to dig, repeatedly inserting her hand to feel for moisture. Her tongue clung to the roof of her mouth, her head buzzed with fatigue. When blisters formed on her palms, she pitched the pointed stick angrily to the ground and flopped down on the forest floor. But she did not give into the weakness of women. She did not cry. She merely gave up, fixed a bed of leaves, and dropped off into a fitful sleep. The sliver of moon that rose above the trees gave no light. It just hung in the sky above the endless green of the forest, a slice of peace and tranquility, a small thing of beauty, completely unnoticed by the sleeping Hester.

Another morning brought thirst like cotton fibers in her mouth. She thought of digging deeper, then looked at the angry red spots on her hands where the water-filled blisters had popped, leaving the tender skin exposed and burning.

The sun already dappled the way as she hauled the haversack on to her shoulder and set out. She would not attempt this mountain, even if it was a low one. She would walk north until she found water.

She tried not to think of water. Or tea, or any cold, frosty drink from the springhouse. She swallowed, then swallowed again. She coughed, a dry, rasping sound that surprised her.

When she broke out of the forest to a clearing lush with yellow tangled grasses, raspberry bushes, thorny wild roses, burdock, thistle, and locust seedlings, she stopped, sniffing the air warily. This field may have been tilled at one time.

She remembered Theodore Crane, the schoolmaster, telling her how the land reclaimed itself after settlers moved on. One of the most invasive plants were wild rosebushes, their roots multiplying underneath the thick, unkempt grasses. They and the locust seedlings.

Warily now, her thirst forgotten, her large, dark eyes roved the clearing, searching for buildings, piles of stone, split rail fences, any sign of human dwellings.

She stood as still as a stone. Nothing moved except the strands of loose hair that straggled across her forehead and the black eyes beneath them. She sniffed, then turned her head to sniff once more. Yes. Unsurprised, she caught the faint smell of woodsmoke. Turning back the way she had come, she glided noiselessly to the safety of the trees.

She'd skirt the clearing, remaining hidden. She would watch. She moved stealthily now, bent forward, dashing from tree to tree, lifting her head to breathe deeply. Ah, yes. The smell of smoke. She was surprised at the sharp sensation of homesickness. She smelled the smoke that had curled down from the stone chimney even in summer, when the cooking and baking needed to be done.

How her stepmother grumbled on humid mornings when the smoke hung over her laundry, infusing the spotless, sweet-smelling linens with its earthy scent. She conjured up the thought of breakfast cooked in cast iron kettles over the fire—fried corn meal mush with dried beef, plenty of eggs, and thick slices of good bread spread with churned butter. And all the water she could drink in the redware tumblers.

She felt lightheaded now. The forest spun, tilted to the right, then at a crazy angle to the left before righting itself, allowing her to keep moving. The smell of smoke was sharp and suddenly acrid. She froze when the deep baying of a hound dog began. Another voice chimed in. The high-pitched wail ended on a much higher note, stopped, then began all over again.

Hester's eyes searched for low branches. She found some pines, swung herself up into the lowest one, and climbed rapidly, her bare feet curling around the scaley extension, the pine tar harsh to her nose.

When the hounds' baying increased to a frenzy, she peered beneath the bough of the great evergreen to find the source of the woodsmoke far below to her left. A small gray house built of logs, with a weathered roof made of split shingles and covered in heavy green moss on the north side, stood at the edge of the clearing. Like a humble, squat soldier, it presided over the tangle of weeds and brush that covered the clearing. There were no out buildings, no barn.

The house had a porch on the gabled end to the north, where the cool shade of summer provided a place of comfort away from the blazing sun. A small section of the porch contained an uneven pile of firewood, stacked, but not efficiently. A stump in the yard hosted an axe sunk into its top, along with various articles that didn't appear useful.

She spied the hounds. Skinny, ungainly creatures, their bawling mouths wide, their lolling tongues waggling as they howled, their noses turned in her direction.

A door slapped open, then shut. A stout man appeared, but he was too far away to determine his age or the color of his clothing. He yelled something unintelligible and the hounds slunk away, their tails curled beneath them, cowering.

Hester remained in the tree as the man went back into the house, slamming the door shut behind him. She weighed her options. Her thirst became the deciding factor. She would ask for a drink, ask to have her jug filled, then move on fast. She'd risk being attacked by the hounds.

She lowered herself, branch by branch, until her feet hit the soft bed of pine needles. Shrugging her shoulders, she adjusted the haversack and stepped out of the forest, thirst taking the place of common sense.

As she had hoped, the shrill baying of the dogs brought the man to the door immediately, yelling orders in a language Hester did not understand. As before, the dogs slunk away, lowered their bellies, and crept beneath the porch. Startled, the man watched her coming across the edge of the clearing. He waited, a thick hand on the rough post supporting the roof of the porch.

A few bare spots held back the soiled tufts of grass among the rusted junk and various tools that spoke of times when someone tilled the soil. A few bones, lengths of string, pieces of bark, and clumps of dirt, rocks, and leaves littered the area surrounding the cabin. As she drew closer, she saw the man's beard was flecked with gray, the mustache drooping above it gray as well, yellowed, and uncut. His hair was long and tied back with a thong of rawhide, his clothes of undetermined origin, color, or cleanliness. Hester guessed his age to be around fifty, perhaps close to the age of her father.

Her words were a croak, unable to be understood. Hester tried to clear her throat but was unsuccessful. She stopped and pointed to her dry mouth, her pride pushing back the desperation she felt.

"Wal, wal."

The man's eyes were kindly, crinkled in a weather-beaten face. Eagerly, Hester watched him turn, go into the cabin, then emerge with a large metal dipper with a long curved handle, precious water dripping from it like diamonds. Muttering like a person gone mad, Hester reached for it, lifted it to her lips, and drank sparingly before lowering it.

His eyes approved, then he spoke to her in a foreign tongue. Hester did not reply. She lifted the dipper and swallowed once more.

"Where?" he asked.

She shrugged. He watched her savor a few more swallows, then turned and motioned her to follow. But she remained on the porch, standing uncertainly against the post, still cradling the dipper, greedily possessing it.

He came back out and offered her a crust of dark bread and a piece of soft cheese. His hands were darkened by hard work or soil, the nails black around the outer edges. A sour smell, an aura of soiled clothes and unwashed skin, surrounded her, making her shrink away, her eyes lowered.

"Don't be afraid." His words were halting and heavily accented.

When Hester lifted her eyes and saw his kindness, his will to please, she reached out and took the food from him. She gulped the coarse, nutty-flavored bread, washing it down with insatiable gulps of water that ran down the sides of her chin. She ate the soft cheese that tasted a bit moldy.

She handed the water dipper back to him and he refilled it, watching as she slurped thirstily. He brought more bread and cheese, which she ate ravenously.

She would not sit down or enter his house. In halting English, she told him she must move on. She had learned to speak it in school, but her time there had been so short and often sporadic, so that she had to concentrate to come up with the right word.

"Where you going?"

"I don't know."

"Why?"

She shrugged.

He invited her to stay. He said he would not harm her. She did not believe him. She stepped off the porch and bent to pickup her haversack, meaning to be on her way.

His voice behind her stopped her. "You need water. I will give you more bread."

She turned, hesitant.

"Come."

She followed him inside. At first, the dim light disoriented her, but she soon made out the shape of the fireplace, a table and chair, a bed in the corner, unmade. The logs inside were brown, not gray or weather-beaten like the outside. There were mounted deer antlers, skins stretched from peg to peg, and a shelf containing dishes and heavy pans. A few rumpled cloths covered with dirt lay in front of the fireplace.

Hester smelled the aroma of cooking and saw the black pot above the red coals. Her mouth watered. She watched the man warily, unable to scale the wall of suspicion. Mistrust left her pacing the room like a caged animal.

He brought a brown parcel and held it out to her, his eyes watching her face. "Take it."

She did, quickly, before he changed his mind. She turned to place it in her sack, then straightened, ready to go.

"You want soup?"

She nodded.

"Sit."

He hurried to draw up a chair, then cleared the bullets and skins away from her, leaving the table bare. Going to the fireplace, he ladled the thick, brown soup into a bowl, then placed it carefully on the wooden table. He brought a pewter spoon, as big as a tablespoon.

The soup was thick and rich, with a flavor she couldn't identify. She raised her eyebrows and pointed to the dish. "What is it?"

"Turtle."

Hester nodded. She had made soup from the gummy, white flesh of the snapping turtles from the pond in the lower field. It had to be boiled for hours, until the thick chunks turned into threads, then flavored with fresh herbs, carrots, and leeks. This was good. It filled Hester with strength, giving her a bright, new start, returning energy that had flagged to the point of exhaustion.

"Thank you," she said.

"More?"

She nodded gratefully.

He filled the bowl a second time. Smiling, she emptied it, then reached down to lift the haversack.

He stepped forward. "I want you to stay."

She shook her head. "I must go."

"Mountains all, if you go north."

She stopped, but kept her back turned.

"East, land will be flat. Towns. People. Lancaster."

She turned, despairing. "No. I don't want."

"Go north."

"No."

"West. No Lancaster."

She watched his face closely. She did not want to re-trace her footsteps. Neither did she want to be among her people, the Amish. It was unthinkable. They would not accept her, an Indian. She hesitated.

"Stay," he said.

She turned to watch his face. Still kind. Still open, honest, without cunning.

"You my daughter. I have one. She die. Wife die. In river when it is high."

"What river?"

"The Susquehanna."

"Am I close?"

He nodded.

Her mind worked fast. She would get to the river and away from the mountains. She would meet her people, the Lenape. They were by this river. She had to leave.

His sad eyes followed her for days. She could have stayed, but she knew it was unreasonable. How long would she remain his daughter? As long as Hans had her for his daughter?

There was no use courting temptation. She knew many lonely trappers, who, shunning society, took Indian women for their wives, but that was not for her. Maybe someday, if she lived, she would be glad to be a wife to one of these men, for she was nothing of value. Her skin was the brown color of the Lenape. That would never change. So she was close to Lancaster County and William King. How many ages ago had she harbored enough sense of well-being to imagine the handsome, dark-haired youth one day asking for her hand?

No, she would go to the Susquehanna, the river of her people. Determined, she turned south. She walked fast now. The land was flat with many creeks, some of them dry, but always there was another. The thirst she had experienced the first four days of her journey had not returned.

She kept walking south through forests and over small hills and ridges, but no tall mountains presented the endless challenge of finding water. For this she was grateful.

She fashioned a bow from the sturdy branch of a willow tree. She spent one whole day making arrows from sharp stones, twine, and straight, green branches which she peeled with a knife. She slung the bow across her back, carried the arrows, and resumed her journey.

Her eyes roamed the world around her, constantly searching for danger, watchful of small changes in the appearance of harmless trees and underbrush, observing clearings for any harm.

One day she noticed the first curling of the leaves. She felt the chill in the air at night. Locust leaves were beginning their dizzying spiral to the forest floor. Soon the large leaves of the oak and chestnut and maple would follow, turning the brown-hued forest into a world of vibrant color, the foliage taking on a blaze of glory before dying.

Winter would come riding in on the winds of hoarfrost and icicles, bitter elements she'd find hard to withstand alone. If she did not come upon her people by the Susquehanna and chose to reject Lancaster County altogether, would she be able to survive by herself? Adrenaline rushed through her veins. A greater challenge had never presented itself. Now it was served up on a platter of sheer fear. She shivered. She would need a shelter. She was hardly capable of building one alone.

And so she planned, her thoughts keeping her company as she traveled. She practiced her routine well. Evenings were filled with the chore of staying alive. She had become more experienced in starting fires. She learned to let the coals become hotter, without flames bursting from them, when she roasted animals. The meat was more edible and not as blackened and stringy.

She learned to roast wild yams, simply tossing them into the fire, then juggling them in her hands until they cooled. She gouged out the insides and ate them with crisp, wild garlic, sliced. She found chives and fennel and tucked them into her haversack so she could season roasted pheasant, whose meat she found fit for any dinner table.

When she came upon a wild crabapple tree, she wished for a pot to simmer the fruit in water, cooking it into applesauce. She thought that if she could find mallow, she would sweeten it. She had no pot, however, so she learned to eat what was possible and not wish for anything she could not have.

Sometimes she sang songs of the Amish church, the slow, mournful plainsong in German verse. Other times she merely walked, clicking off her strides in long sharp steps that ate up the ground.

She smelled change in the air. She smelled mud and the rolling brown water of the Susquehanna, she believed. Had she skirted Lancaster County entirely?

Excitement sluiced through her, tingling in her stomach. Would she find her people living in long, low houses covered in bark? She imagined the smell of cooking fires—and belonging to people of her same color.

Eagerly, she pressed on. Between the trees, she sensed movement now. Water? Her steps became soundless. She held her breath. Lowering her body, she peered from

beneath a fir tree. Before her lay a sight she had never
seen. A clearing so large she could not define the end
of it. There was no river, no mud. Only the rattling of
wheels as a team of four horses pulled a harrow, its teeth
tearing up the moist, brown soil, preparing the land for
a fall crop.

Hester lowered her head and laid her cheek on the
floor of the forest, letting the rich, earthy scent comfort
her as disappointment and exhaustion consumed her.
She had stumbled directly into the settlement she was
determined to avoid.

Mein Gott, she whispered. Now what? She would be
mocked, turned away. Back in Berks County, life was far
different. There, she had been accepted as a newborn,
a crying foundling saved by the lonely, childless young
woman who had been her mother. Could she stay here
somehow? Perhaps she could, with her vast knowledge
of herbal remedies and cures for sick people. Winter was
coming on.

She watched the horses' heads bobbing up and down,
their great hooves coming down, lifting up. She saw the
farmer guiding the horses as they pulled the wooden
plow through the ground, the iron piece cutting through
the soil and releasing its rich, earthy smell. The ache of
remembering was more than she could bear. She was a
young girl again, her white cap strings waving delicately, her face lifted to the sun, her legs strong, her bal-
ance complete, as she stood on the plow, the smell of
disturbed earth rich and sweet to her senses.

She wanted to retrace her steps and rid herself of the
burden of survival, of making decisions on her own.

Would she be defeated if she returned? Could she speak to her stepmother, try to reason with her father?

Perhaps if her face was disfigured, or if she became handicapped, she would be safe. All she wanted was to live within the sturdy protection of the stone walls of the great house and eat the food that always appeared three times a day—a wonderful thing, until now never fully appreciated. And so she cowered behind the veil of the forest, homesickness, fear, and doubt her only companions.

CHAPTER 4

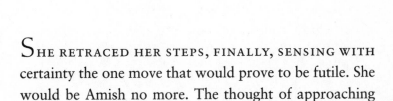

SHE RETRACED HER STEPS, FINALLY, SENSING WITH certainty the one move that would prove to be futile. She would be Amish no more. The thought of approaching the man with the plow was terrifying. She knew he would see her as an Indian, not a member of his own plain sect.

She had debated within herself. The Pennsylvania Dutch she spoke might convince him, but if *he* did not accept her, there were hundreds more who would not. Outwardly they would perhaps say they did, but they would not with their hearts. They would warn their sons. The German heritage should stay pure.

So she slipped into the forest, her only home. She walked aimlessly now, without caring. The land was almost flat except for an occasional rise, a small slope, a hollow. The trees were sparse where logging trails crisscrossed through the bush. She smelled woodsmoke, spied gray, weathered buildings and soft yellow ones, where the lumber was so new it had not yet aged.

Dogs barked. The lowing of cattle sounded unexpectedly. She heard voices in the distance. She imagined she was making her way through Lancaster County and would soon reach the great river, the Susquehanna. When the heat of the afternoon waned, Hester knew she would have to exercise much better surveillance, now that she would spend the night so close to other human beings.

She heard the barking of a dog in the distance. Realizing this might be her biggest challenge yet, she zigzagged through the dense, green forest. She could make no cooking fire. She would conserve her energy and drink very little of the tepid water in her jug. Earlier than she normally did, she prepared a bed of leaves and moss behind a large, uprooted tree, where the residue of past years had blown beside it, leaving a comfortable place of rest.

A chipmunk streaked across the log, then turned to watch her with bright eyes, its tiny cheeks bulging with a cache of nuts, the fruits of its energetic foraging. A garter snake slithered soundlessly through the leaves, its small eyes alert, the wee tongue lashing out repeatedly. A bumblebee droned past, then came to rest on a white flower, the columbine that grew profusely in low areas.

Perhaps she could find a few berries, so she heaved herself to her feet and was off in search of anything to ease the emptiness in her stomach. She soon found it was too late in the season for berries of any kind, but she came upon a tangle of wild grapes. They were turning purple, although most were green. She would have been cautious, but her hunger was a driving force. She pulled the clusters from the sturdy vine and devoured them, her thirst and hunger both easing as the sour juices puckered her mouth.

Sometime during the night, Hester awoke, a fire in her stomach. She rolled onto her side, drew up her knees, and shivered with the cold and the clawing pains in her abdomen. Too late she realized her mistake.

She remained by the log all that night and into the next day until her body had rid itself of the unripe fruit. Twice she had fainted from the scourge of pain. She cried aloud for water, her body dehydrating as her stomach expelled its contents. She lay by the log, finally deciding she would probably die because she could not bear the pain. She was too weak to sit up. Too weak to travel in search of water.

In the afternoon, the pains subsided and she slept. Jolted awake, she struggled to sit up, alarmed. The forest floor spun crazily, tilting at impossible angles, but she stayed erect until the dizziness passed.

She pushed herself to her feet, then sagged against the log, finally willing herself to move. Stumbling through the forest, her thirst a clenching fright, she weaved from left to right, her dizziness directing her feet. Then she smelled water. She had reached the great river!

With her remaining strength, she surged forward, her tongue cleaving to the roof of her mouth. Again, like her hunger for the grapes, her thirst overrode the restraint she needed. Breaking through a line of trees, she came upon a meandering waterway, a wide, sleepy creek. On its banks, green willows, turning yellow with autumn's approach, swayed above the deep, grey current. Rocks jutted from shallow places where the cool water ran against them, rippled around the obstructions, and sang merrily on its way.

Hester slid down the bank, her foot collided with a rock, and she was thrown into the water like a fish. Uncaring, with her thirst taking away any sense of danger, she sat on the pebbly creek bottom, drinking and drinking, then becoming as sick as before, her stomach resisting the onslaught of cold water.

She did not smell the cooking fires or the dogs or see the longhouses. She simply lay on the banks of the creek, heaving, wet, and too sick to care. They took her haversack and burned the contents in their cooking fires — including her cherished volume of remedies from the ancient Lenape woman. She was too sick to save it. The fat women that found her by the creek trundled her wet, feverish form home to their settlement, washed her, and dressed her in a warm dress made of soft, pliant deerskin, with colorful beads woven into an intricate design all over it.

They washed her hair with the herbs and flowers that they grew, while gabbling and laughing. They shooed the men and children away when curiosity drove them into the longhouse where Hester lay, barely conscious. They gave her bitter medicines, and she slept so long she didn't know how many nights she lay in the hut, or how many days.

She dreamed of Kate, her mother, dressed in white. She dreamed of white, blinking stars and lovely pastures where Lissie and Barbara beckoned to her. She dreamed of Hans, strong and mighty, shouting at her. And always on the outskirts of her subconscious, in an area she could not quite penetrate, the voice of someone she had known, someone she recognized but could not remember.

When she awakened fully, it was nighttime. Hester lay on her side, able to look around with one eye. The beating of her heart in her chest was loud in her ears, like drums that came from within. She rolled on to her back and stared wildly at the ceiling. A roof. A low bed of coals in a hole in the ground. Muffled sounds of breathing. Dark shapes of various sizes. A smell. A scent of animals, food, earth, skins, an overwhelming odor of something she could not name.

Someone had rescued her. She ran her hands along her body, touching the foreign garment. Her fingers found the beadwork, felt the texture of the deerskin, and knew. She had the explanation for the smell, the bed of coals. She was with the Indians, her people.

Fear overrode every other emotion. Her people were talked about as savages. Uncivilized. Uncouth. She had not been raised the way they lived. She wanted Kate, her soft, clean touch. She wanted wooden floors, lye soap, hot water, clean bedding, scrubbing brushes, white laundry strung on lines, flapping in the breezes.

But she was here now. Here in this building constructed in the way of the Indians, her birthplace. Every terrifying bit of gossip filtered through her mind—the massacres, the scalpings, the Amish women's tongues wagging endlessly with gruesome tales of the savages.

Not here, though. Not in Lancaster County and the surrounding areas. William Penn had lived peacefully among them, trading woolen blankets for the precious wampum and teaching them to cook in heavy cast iron pots.

Hester relaxed, breathing in the scent of the skins beneath her. The heavy robe covering her could hardly have been from a deer, its bulk weighing her down like the good, warm sheep's wool of home. The skins had an earthy, dry, smell. Not rancid, but surprisingly pleasant.

She reached her left hand out, but drew it back in alarm. She was not on the ground. She sat up in the heavy blackness. Her eyes searched the interior of the dwelling, but all she could be sure of were the holes in the ground where red coals glowed softly, illuminating only a bit of the darkness around them.

So she was on a raised platform, higher than her bed at home, it seemed. She was aware of the company of sleeping people—deep breathing, an occasional snoring sound, a cough. Someone stirred. It seemed as if the movement came from above her, but she couldn't be sure. Darkness did that sometimes, turning the world every which way.

An animal snuffled from outside the wall to her right, then moved off into the night. A child whimpered and began to cry, but the sound faded away quickly, either because of its mother's care, or because it had gone back to sleep.

Hester rolled on her back, snuggled deeper into the skins that kept her warm, and tried to go back to sleep. But she was awake for hours, her thoughts tumbling endlessly as she wondered what she should do or where she should go. Perhaps she should stay with winter coming on. She could adapt, if they would receive her.

In the first gray light of morning, Hester awoke, her eyes wide. Directly above her was a row of saplings bound together with long ropes made of bark. Slowly, she turned her head to find that she was lying on a raised platform, lashed to the sturdy poles that supported the domed roof of the Indian dwelling, the longhouse.

She raised herself on one elbow, making no noise. What she saw was incredible. She had never been in a house this large with so much open space. First she saw the number of poles on both sides of the structure. They held sleeping platforms—one lower one and another above it—the entire length of the longhouse. Raised mounds of skins dotted these platforms where the Indians lay sleeping.

She supposed if there were no barn, no cows or sheep or pigs, there were no chores to do. So perhaps they all slept later than Hans or Annie did.

As the light became stronger, her eyes focused on many items strung from the poles of the platforms. Bows, quivers made of reeds or skins, baskets made of different materials, beads, gourds, cooking pots.

The floor below her was bare, yellowish-brown earth, dry and compacted by the many feet that walked over it.

Flat rectangular stones held stone bowls with heavy pestles. Bags of dried corn sat beside them. She had heard that corn was the staple of the Indian diet.

When a grunting sound came from close-by, Hester lay back down in a flash. Feet hit the ground and lumbered past. The hide by the doorway was pushed back and then flapped down with a soft swish as the footsteps faded away.

Another set of feet thumped the hard earth floor, followed by another. A low tone of voice reached her ears, but Hester did not understand anything that was said. The words were garbled, as if they were swallowed, the sound of syllables she had never known existed.

Cooking fires were stirred into flames as more of the Indians awakened. Some squatted by the fire; others went outside immediately. A baby's thin, high wail sounded through the gray light.

Should she get up? Offer to help? Her heart beat rapidly as the full knowledge of finding herself in this situation confronted her. She had no reason to believe they would hurt her, and no reason to think they wouldn't.

She was gathering courage to rise when she became aware of breathing directly beside her. Her eyes flew open. Two woman stood looking down at her. The fat one, her eyes glittering black in the folds of her dark face, her small mouth moving as the words tumbled from it, pulled the heavy robe off from her shoulders. Loud exclamations and finger pointing followed. The younger woman reached out to touch Hester's hair and her eyes, then tugged gently on her nose, her eyes revealing her intrigue.

Words tumbled over one another, every one as foreign as the next. A few children came to peer at Hester like bright-eyed mice, half hiding behind their mothers' skirts.

The fat woman began motioning with her hands. Hester understood that she wanted her to come, so she threw back the heavy robe, which she now saw was buffalo, swung her legs over the side, and stood on her feet. The longhouse tilted to one side and spun crazily, so she held on to the pole beside her until the dizziness passed.

The beckoning continued, so Hester followed both women to the deerskin flap hanging over the door, bending to follow them outside into the crisp, fall morning.

The longhouse was built close to the banks of a creek, a slowly moving one that wound among the willows, deep and clear and quiet.

The women motioned for her to follow until they stood on the creek's banks where the tall, green, willow branches swept the earth like giant dusters, swaying slowly in the shivery little breeze. Hester watched suspiciously as they urged her with their hands to bathe in the creek. The fat woman motioned to the east where the sun had already risen, then to Hester to remove her deerskin dress.

"No. No."

Hester shook her head, her arms wrapped tightly around her waist. She had never undressed for anyone to see. Once a month—more often in summer—she and her sisters and brothers had bathed discreetly one by one in the great agate tub behind a heavy blanket in the farm house, all using the same scalding hot water. They had always been taught that bodies were to be covered, from their necklines to the soles of their feet. It was shameful to see even a bare ankle exposed.

The fat woman's eyes glittered with anger. She spoke to the younger one, who made more motions for Hester to bathe in the creek, pointing to the sun.

Why the sun? Suddenly it dawned on Hester that they wanted her to bathe each morning. Surely not. She refused again, shaking her head with even more conviction.

With lightning speed, they reached for her in one motion, lifted her and swung her down the bank. Hester felt the rough scrape of the willows before the cold waters

of the creek washed over her. She had never been under-
water before. Creek water filled her nose and her mouth
and poured down her throat. Instinctively, she flailed her
legs and arms as she propelled herself to the surface, her
mouth opening, gasping, and gurgling, before she felt
herself slide under the water again.

There was a fire in her chest as her lungs strained for
oxygen. The muddy water, churned up by her struggling,
filled her nostrils. Again, she rose to the surface, desperately sucking in air, only to choke and gag on the creek
water.

She had heard about going under a third time, heard
enough about people drowning. She lunged once more,
kicking out with her feet, her arms slapping at the water
that threatened her life.

One toe hit a stone. She threw herself in the direction
of it, found a toehold, and then another. Gasping, with
water streaming from her nose and mouth, she lifted
her face above the surface of the water, grabbed the life-
saving branches of the willow tree, and hung on with an
iron grip.

But when she floundered up the wet, slippery bank
and heard the women's raucous laugh like mocking
crows, anger consumed her. She had almost drowned
in that cold creek, and there they were, slapping their
knees, bent over with the force of their scornful laughter.

Lowering her head, with her breath coming in short
forceful bursts, Hester threw herself, catching the fat
woman by surprise. A powerful cuff sent her wobbling
sideways down the slippery bank and into the creek. The
younger woman was prepared, but Hester grabbed her

by her shoulders, easily overpowered her, then rolled her down the muddy bank after the other one.

She stood, breathing hard, her feet planted apart, feeling more alive than she ever had. Perhaps it was the near-drowning, perhaps it was fear, but she shivered with her newfound power. All of her life someone had ruled over her, bent her will to their own, including her brothers, Noah and Isaac. Once, when they had fought to gather the most walnuts, Hester had gotten angry. She kicked Noah's bucket over, scattering all the walnuts into the tall grass. He had wrestled her to the ground, held her hands behind her back, and cuffed a sound blow to her shoulder. She bit his hand. Surprised, he yelped, then looked at her as she raised herself from the ground, her eyes flashing dark fire.

In his eyes was an expression close to pride, or was it admiration? It was a new light. He had walked away, and things were never the same between them after that. It was as if he practiced the Amish way of shunning her, then, which often bound her to a great and stifling sorrow.

Now she watched as the two women sliced expertly through the water like large, dark fish, scrambled out, and came steadily toward her. Hester stood firm, her hands curled into fists, ready to roll them down the bank another time. But they were laughing. They punched her arms playfully, flexed their own muscles, stroked her hair, and made a fuss about her face, her strength, lowering and raising their eyebrows as they garbled away in the foreign tongue.

They took her into the longhouse, dried her, and then threw woolen blankets about her shoulders. They

cooked corn cakes on a thick, flat stone and brought
her meaty stew, steaming hot, in a maize-colored gourd.
They hung around as she searched for a spoon or a fork,
all the while making motions for her to eat.

Gingerly, with one thumb and forefinger, she fished
out a portion of dark meat, her fingers burning. Quickly,
she deposited it into her mouth, her lips an O, as she
breathed in and out to cool it. She nodded, smiled, and
licked her fingers, which brought a happy shout from the
women.

The meat was rich and salty. Eagerly, she grabbed another chunk, cooled it, and chewed hungrily. The corn
cake tasted like unsalted mush, which it was, she reasoned. She dipped it into the stew, which brought more
happy shouts of approval.

She guessed she was a hero now, or a princess, the way
the children adored her, touching her face and her arms
like inquisitive little chipmunks, and every bit as cute.

A bright-eyed papoose hung from its cradleboard securely fastened to the supporting pole along the bunks.
Hester wanted to free him from the confines of the leather
rope that bound him to the flat board so she could cud-
dle and hold him the way she had held Kate's babies. She
knew it was the Indian way to keep them confined till
they were seven or eight months old.

The men came into the longhouse, their height and
powerful builds frightening. She had never seen a man
without a shirt, so she kept her eyes downcast to the
earth floor. A conversation ensued, the fat woman flapping her hands, pointing, and finally laughing. Bright,
flat eyes focused on her.

She could not know how perfectly beautiful she appeared in the half-light of the longhouse. More than one of the men watched her, already planning a marriage ceremony in their hearts. One of the older ones could speak passable English. He squatted by her side. She turned her eyes to him, finding his black eyes expressionless, his nose hawkish, his black hair greased and tied back with braided thongs of rawhide. She did not look at his bare shoulders or his chest, it was too shameful.

"I Naw-A-Te."

Hester nodded, then said, quietly, "Hester Zug."

"You come?" He waved his arm, questioning her whereabouts.

"Berks County Amish settlement."

He lowered his fine eyebrows and closed his eyes as if trying to remember, then nodded slowly. "You live here with us? No?"

Hester kept her eyes lowered, shrugging her shoulders.

"We are the Conestoga. The last of the red man in Lancaster. All our brothers have gone west." He threw his arm disdainfully in that direction, as if the west was a loathsome destination.

"We stay. Conestoga our water. We are here. Mine."

Hester nodded. She understood his need to portray the ownership of this allotted space. She knew the Indians were constantly driven west as settlers poured into this region of Lancaster.

In the waning autumn, Hester stayed with the Conestoga Indians on the banks of the sleepy creek named for them. The days were golden and filled with light, the dusty air alive with the sounds of rasping black crickets.

Brown grasshoppers catapulted themselves from the tall grasses as her feet approached.

She helped harvest the Three Sisters—corn, beans, and squash—in the vast garden. She loved the work, falling easily into the steady rhythm of the season, reminding her of harvest at home on the farm.

She became accustomed to her early-morning bath in the cold waters of the Conestoga. It was such a new and unusual ritual, but now one she relished, submerging herself in the invigorating waters before starting her day. She found the term "*dreckichy* Indians" to be quite untrue. They were not unclean, the way she had believed them to be. In fact, the infrequent bathing done in Amish homes was likely less clean, in spite of the Indians' earthen floor and the skins.

She learned to scrape and dry buffalo, deer, and mountain lion skins. At first she had found it a revolting chore—the stench overpowering—but she kept on scraping with a flat, sharp piece of limestone and eventually, got used to the smell.

The wild animals sustained the tribe. They were their clothing, their food, their tools. The large shoulder blade of the buffalo was lashed to a straight branch with willow bark, which functioned as a sturdy shovel, turning soil in the garden. The smaller shoulder bone of the deer was turned into a hoe in much the same way.

Hester marveled at the ingenuity of these people. And when the golden days of autumn turned into the bitter winds of November, she was grateful for the shelter of the longhouse.

CHAPTER 5

WHEN ONLY A FEW CRISP, BROWN LEAVES RE-
mained on the oak trees, the air turned into a wet cold
that penetrated the skins she wore as she went about her
work. Hester knew snow was not far away, so she hurried, scraping the buffalo hide stretched on the upright
frame on the lee side of the longhouse.

The men had been on a successful hunt, ensuring food
for the coming winter months. A celebration of dancing
and eating had followed, the children alive with renewed
energy and joy, waving the bean-filled gourds gleefully.

Now the women must hustle. The snows were hovering over them, spurring them into action, or at least
those who were willing to perform their assigned duty.

The fat woman was named Clover, in English. They
all had Indian names in three syllables. When Hester
couldn't pronounce some of them, Naw-A-Te gave her
their English names.

A young woman named Beaver, who Hester imagined
to be about her own age, did not enjoy work of any kind,
wandering off or shirking her duties whenever she could.

Today Beaver was cold, cross, and lazier than usual. She cowered beneath two woolen blankets, her teeth chattering, her eyes boldly challenging the older women to do something about her lack of working.

Soon jabbering arose. Clover walked over, carrying her large, round form like a barrel on her stocky legs, her face like a thundercloud. When she lowered her face directly in front of Beaver, a tirade followed, finished by a smart thump on the side of her head. Beaver fell sideways, sent up a heart-rending yowl, and then became silent.

Hester shifted the sharp limestone to her left hand and kept on scraping the white membranes away from the buffalo skin. She glanced sideways at Beaver, who lay perfectly still. After a while, Hester could see she was sound asleep.

A younger woman, named Otter Run, came over to Beaver, crouched in front of her, then put the back of her hand to Beaver's forehead. She jumped back and began an excited tirade of words to Clover, who immediately laid her palm on Beaver's cheek. "I, yi, yi, yi, yi!" she yipped shrilly.

Together, they bundled Beaver off into the longhouse, put her to bed, and returned to the chore that needed to be finished before the snow began to come from the east, driven hard by the first icy blast of winter.

Clover did everything she could, but Beaver became deathly ill, her fever spiking in the evening until she writhed and gabbled, pointing to the hallucinations that tormented her. They covered her with heavy woolen coverlets they had received from the settlers, traded with the precious wampum, and still her teeth chattered from the cold. Sometimes she flung the covers from her miserable body until she shivered from the cold yet again.

Hester desperately longed for her book of Indian remedies. She could see these Conestogas did not have the knowledge and wisdom of the old Indian woman of the forest in Berks County. They danced around Beaver and shook various rattles and gourds to drive away evil spirits. They concocted many different herbs with vegetables and meat dishes and brewed teas, but nothing seemed to help.

They allowed Hester to try plasters made from onion, mustard, and wild garlic, which seemed to soothe her rasping cough. When angry red pustules appeared on Beaver's feverish skin, Hester knew what was wrong but kept the knowledge to herself. When the pustules turned yellow with pus, she bathed the thin form with a mixture of warm water and soothing spearmint.

Hester lay awake when the young child Corn Mouse came down with the same symptoms. She had to do something. She rose from her sleeping bunk and woke Naw-A-Te by shaking his heavy body relentlessly. He followed her past the sleeping tribe, through the flap of deerskin that served as a door.

The thin layer of snow dusted the earth the way Kate used to dust her cakes with granulated sugar. A sliver of white moon hung in the cold, black sky, surrounded by the blinking stars of early winter. Hester's breath was a white vapor as she spoke. "Naw-A-Te, you must bring a doctor. The little one has the same disease as Beaver. It is smallpox. They will die."

For a long time, Naw-A-Te remained as still as stone, his face shadowed by the night and the waning moon. Straight and tall, unhurried, he stood. Finally he spoke. "When all else fails, we go back to the Creator. We return to the earth from which we were made." He remained standing, his face in the shadows.

A thin wisp of woodsmoke curled from the hole in the rounded roof of the longhouse. Across the frosty lowland, a screech owl sent out its high rattling sound. It was answered by another.

Hester spoke. "I have heard of the smallpox. Indians die. It is given to them from the white people."

Again, Naw-A-Te remained mute. Hester watched his face. When he spoke, his voice was rough. "Which is worse? To die from the sickness, or to be driven from our land by the white people? The time is coming."

Hester spread her hands. "But you have to do something. Many will die," Hester cried. "They will die soon."

Naw-A-Te grabbed her shoulders roughly. The move was so sudden, his fingers digging into her arms so powerfully, she gasped and turned her face away, thinking he meant harm to her.

Slowly, his grip lessened, becoming tender. The tall Indian gently drew her against him. Hester heard the beating of his great, stout heart beneath her cheek. The deerskin he was wearing was soft and pliant. She was strangely moved by this gesture. She felt bound to him by a kinship, a bloodline that spoke the same language.

"It is well. It is good you are here."

Hester stayed very still.

"We are the few ones. They will not let us live. Soon they will kill us. Or drive us away."

Hester drew back. "But you don't know!" she cried.
"I know. My heart knows."

Sadness so thick it choked her crept into her soul, and she bent her head and wept. She cried for the Indians, for their ways that would eventually be lost. She cried for the unfairness of life itself. A small part of her railed against God for allowing these two cultures to meet in this blessed, rich land, completely unable to exist side by side.

The white man's goals were the opposite of the red man's—to clear the forest, cultivate the land, grow in knowledge, invent new things, while constantly moving forward for wealth and earthly gain.

The Indians were content to roam the forest, holding the trees and animals sacred, believing that they were given to them by the Creator. They did not understand the passion for wealth and power, the greed to own land. They fanned their fires with the wing of a wild turkey for hundreds of years. They grew corn, beans, and squash, content with the earth's gifts. If a week or a month went by in sunshine, and the grass grew brown with drought, they watered the corn, but made no effort to innovate or change the course of nature. For it was inseparable from the Creator.

When Naw-A-Te spoke softly, Hester listened. "You come to us with your beauty. You will live. The Creator has made you. The white man nurtured you as a small baby. Now he has a plan for you." Hester stayed very still.

They returned to the longhouse and their own bunks, each falling asleep, comforted in the still, frosty night.

Hester tended to the sick all that winter. Beaver died late one night with Hester holding her thin, cold hand.

The ceremony for the dead was performed, a foreign thing, the spirits and animals conveying Beaver's spirit to the Creator. Many of the children became ill. Mothers squabbled, the tension thick and filled with static.

A storm blew in from the northeast. Naw-A-Te held up one hand with three fingers spread out, showing there would be three months of snow. The young braves hunted on snowshoes to replenish the meat supply, dragging in thin, starved deer. But there was plenty of dried corn and beans, dried fish, and berries.

Often Hester walked along the Conestoga Creek, her legs encased in heavy leggings, her skirt sweeping over the snow. She filled her lungs with the fresh, cold air, watched the cardinals and chickadees flit from the snow-laden bushes and trees, and saw fish lying silent and dormant beneath the ice.

She remembered skating on the creek in Berks County, sliding around with boundless energy after being cooped up in the stone house too long. She scooped up a handful of snow and tossed it into the air, remembering snow fights with Noah and Isaac. Lissie was too young to do much harm, but like a buzzing fly, could become bothersome, sometimes having to be dealt with by a good face-washing with snow.

Would she ever be able to return to her childhood home? Would she ever have a home of her own? Two of the young Conestoga men had asked for a marriage ceremony, but so far, she hadn't been able to bring herself to accept this strange way of life.

In her own mind and heart, she wanted a husband, her own man, to love and to cherish, but she'd come to accept the fact that this wasn't possible for her among the Amish in Berks County. Here with the Conestoga, it was possible, but her whole being shrank from it. The communal living, the sleeping arrangement, the sharing of life with so many was not the way she imagined her future. And yet, what other choice did she have?

The snow drifted down through the tree branches as the wind moved them back and forth. Little gray birds flitted from one snowy branch to another, their busy little chirps lifting her spirits. She watched a brown rabbit strip the bark from a green sapling that was almost covered with deep, powdery snow. The rabbit eagerly chewed the tree's soft inner lining.

She was hungry, her stomach hollow and empty, but the corn and beans were rationed now. Naw-A-Te had spoken the evening before, saying the worst storms were still to come.

Sighing, she stopped, breathed deeply, then turned to go back the way she had come. She walked slowly now, her legs pushing the snow away with a soft sh-sh-sh, the cold finally penetrating her feet. She did not exactly want to return to the smoky interior of the longhouse, but she had nowhere else to go.

Lifting the deerskin flap, she went inside, her eyes adjusting to the gray half-light, the pungent smoke of the cooking fires. She sat cross-legged, watching Clover string beads on a sinew, then took up the dried reeds herself and began to weave a basket the way Clover had taught her.

The little ones were coughing. In a corner, Running Bear worked on his arrows, precisely carving another sharp head. He looked up, his piercing black eyes in his ruddy face boring into hers. Quickly she looked away and began weaving faster, the reeds moving through her fingers smoothly.

She felt him beside her before she actually saw him. He nodded to her to follow him outside.

Hester shook her head. He frowned and refused to move. He picked up the basket she was working on and moved it aside. She watched as his hand came down to take hers. He pulled gently. She looked up at him, his dark, dark eyes beckoning to her. How long could she keep saying no?

From the opposite wall, Clover looked up and giggled, holding her hand to her wide mouth. Soon enough, Hester would be prepared to become Running Bear's wife. Soon she would begin the wedding dress.

When the Chinook woke Hester one mild night, she felt a joy in her heart again, a sensation she could barely recall, a forgotten illusion. Had she ever been happy?

She would have to leave or marry Running Bear. The decision was hers, but she knew it had already been made. It would not be long now. After the scourge of smallpox, there were only seventeen remaining. The children slipped away, one after another, except for four of them.

Death among the Indians was understood the way other hazards and unfortunate happenings of nature were accepted. There was a sadness, but a soft, gentle receiving of what the Creator had done, an uncomplaining yielding of something they had once possessed.

Hester had cried for Beaver, but alone, in the privacy of her bunk. She was in awe of the loving acceptance she witnessed, so completely in tune with the Creator. Death was a passing, a turning of the wheel.

So many things among these people were good, but so many things were wrong. In the spring, when the thaw came, she would slip away. She would survive. She had done it before.

The snow melted into the earth, turning the banks of the Conestoga into a quagmire. The interior of the longhouse was dense with the lingering smoke of cooking fires.

Running Bear killed an elk, a huge antlered animal that had miraculously survived the deep snows. The people ate ravenously, tearing at the stringy meat like dogs and gnashing their teeth as grease dripped from their chins and fingers, staining their shirt fronts. They leaped and danced. Running Bear fell into a stupor, his head lolling like a broken doll.

Hester was seized with horror when the chanting began. Would this mean she would be given to him, the brave hunter? Her breath came in quick gasps. She looked around wildly. Darkness had fallen, which meant she could slip away unseen. A great cry rose from the feasting when Naw-A-Te stood, holding up both arms and calling for silence.

Hester did not wait. Slowly, as if she wanted to step outside for only a short time, she moved toward the door while every eye was stayed on Naw-A-Te and his upcoming announcement. Silently, like the smoke that disappeared through the hole in the roof, she slipped through the deerskin. Her heart racing, she stayed just out of sight, straining to hear what the eldest among them would say.

There was the distant sound of drumming. Had they already begun their celebration? No. Naw-A-Te was speaking. Distracted by the sounds in the distance, she could not hear his words.

She slipped to the ground and pressed her ear to the wet earth. The unmistakable sound of hoofbeats shook the ground. The full realization of the oncoming riders hit her like a sledgehammer. With a small cry, she raised her head, then sprang to her feet with another. Running at full speed, she immediately disappeared into the evening light as a posse of men from the town of Lancaster bore down on the lone Indian village.

They waved torches in orange flashes of destruction. Hoarse, hate-filled cries carried through the wet woodland by the creek.

Hester ran, zigzagging among the trees, finally hitting one with her bent knee. Pain exploded through her head as she fell to the ground. She heard the cries of the men, and then the hopeless wails of the Indian women. The torches had already lit the longhouse, an eerie orange glow placing each tree in silhouette.

Hester clung to a tree, her knee a throbbing appendage now. She must run. She must. The baying of a hound dog behind her sent her into a mindless dash. She felt no pain from her knee as she crashed through underbrush, weaving in and out of trees. The toe of her moccasin caught on a grapevine, and she was flung to the ground. Her head snapped back with the impact. She bit down on her tongue, tasting blood.

The hound gave its eerie, high-pitched howl, sending chills of fear up her arms. Through the dark, behind her, she heard more than one dog coming. She'd never get away.

The night was filled with orange light as the long-house went up in a roaring inferno, and the cries of the Indians mixed with those of the men who took them captive.

Hester looked back once, then turned sharply to the left. She slid down the muddy bank of the Conestoga Creek, lifting the branches above her head before succumbing to the mind-numbing cold of the snow-fed waters. She could not stay in water this cold. She would freeze. But she dared not get out, either. The dogs would lead the posse to her.

After a while her legs became numb, completely without feeling. When wave after wave of drowsiness overtook her, she knew she would freeze, so she had to take her chances with the dogs. The instant she dragged herself out of the frigid water, she knew she'd made a mistake. The baying began immediately, rising to a high pitch she could only describe as horrible. She ran on legs she did not know were there. Her only goal was to widen the distance between her and the dogs.

On they came. To the right now. She veered left. She became aware of thundering hooves and waving red torches bearing down on her. Still, she continued running.

The torches illuminated a pile of blackened brush. Bending low, she dived straight for the tangle of branches and weeds, then lay flat on the ground, panting, as the dogs and riders closed in. She kicked with all her strength, as the skinny, spotted dogs pushed their snouts through any available opening.

The horses slid to a stop. She smelled sweat and leather, heard the horses' nostrils quivering as their breaths came rapidly. Men dismounted. They flailed the bushes with their rifles, calling out to one another, their voices high with excitement. "Got 'em! Got 'em!" one man kept yelling in a strained, whining tone.

Hester stayed where she was, alternately kicking the dogs' noses and slapping at their jaws. She put up such a fierce fight that it took two men to drag her from her hiding place. One dropped his torch, which sizzled out in the cold, wet earth when she bit down on a hairy hand as hard as she could, sinking her teeth into the fleshy thumb.

Its owner howled a high-pitched screech of pain and anger. Hester felt an explosion of pain in her head as the man brought down the butt of his rifle, and mercifully, darkness took the world away.

Billy Ferree was nosing around the livery stable on Water Street in the town of Lancaster, much too late at night for a schoolboy to be out and about. He found out most of what was going on when the men came out of Carpenter Tavern and tried to hitch their horses to their buggies, which sometimes they did successfully and sometimes they didn't. When they had had too much brown ale, Billy offered his services. He had already squirreled away a plentiful stash of coins in the wooden box beneath his bed.

Tonight, though, he'd hid. That bunch of Indian killers coming through the door was enough to make him pop off and jump into the grain bin. He saw them dump a sack behind the bin where the straw was kept. Billy figured like as not, it was a dead Indian, which gave him the woolies.

He'd heard they were gonna get rid of Indiantown, the last of the Conestoga Indians' villages. Too many of the townspeople did not want them red men skulking about. Harmless, they were, in Billy's opinion, but then an eleven-year-old boy with a thatch of carroty hair couldn't go up against town council.

He waited. Some of the oats in the bin had gotten between his shirttail and his trousers, itching him terrible. He figured he'd better not scratch till that gang was gone.

Slowly, he raised his head above the top of the bin. His gray felt hat drooped and hung in all the wrong directions, the holes in the crown sprouting red hair. Beneath the floppy brim, his blue eyes rolled to either side of the stable before he slowly pulled himself up. He scratched heartily, then sucked in his stomach and shook both knees back and forth to rid himself of the stray oats.

He thought he'd better check on that sack of Indian. Looking back over his shoulder, he tiptoed softly to the spot he reckoned they'd dumped it. He didn't want to be too loud in the presence of the dead. He reached up and took off his hat, letting his red hair fall loose. It went every which way, as long as it was and uncombed.

Cautiously, with thumb and forefinger, he drew back the sacking. Oops. Feet. Wrong end. Softly, he tiptoed to the opposite end and pulled aside the sacking. He bent down to peer very closely in the weak, flickering light from the oil lantern swinging from the beams.

He whistled, a soft whoosh of astonishment. Boy, oh boy. This was no ordinary one. Had to be a girl. She was still as death, so he guessed she was gone.

He kept looking though. Just looking and looking, and thinking what a waste of life. A girl this pretty. A huge dark blue bruise. They'd walloped her good.

When a soft moaning sound reached his ears, he jumped so hard his teeth whacked against one another. He bent his ear to the girl's chest and heard the steady thud-thud of the faint heartbeat. Well, this was one for Ma, no doubt. If he could get her out of here, leastways.

CHAPTER 6

The soft moaning sound was followed by another. The head turned a wee bit to right. Straw was getting stuck in her hair, so he brushed it off with his dirty little fingers. He'd run home and get the wagon if she woke up. In the middle of the night, no one would know, and if they did catch sight of him, they'd think he was hauling feed for the horse.

She turned her head, getting more straw in the heavy wet tresses. Billy brushed it away, tenderly. He talked to her then. He told her she should try to wake up if she could 'cause his ma could watch out for her real good. Her name was Emma, Emma Ferree. She was a widow. Enos Ferree died from the lung fever. Now Emma took in any weak or poor or starving person, but she'd never taken a dead one yet, so far as he knew, so she better wake up.

When her eyelids fluttered, he stayed right where he was and kept on talking. When she looked out from between those black eyelashes and groaned, he lowered his face and asked her to repeat that sentence, please, that he hadn't rightly heard just what she meant.

He kept on, patiently trying to bring her to consciousness, but in the end, he decided to run the whole way home for the *seck veggley* (sack wagon). When he got back, he stopped at the tavern door and pounded on it with his fists until the black cleaning man came to the door, his eyes rolling up white into his head, he was so scared. "Come and see this awful-lookin' girl that got dumped in the alley," he begged him.

He obliged Billy, but could only assure him that no, she weren't dead, at least not yet. He said, "Laws, Laws, Laws a mercy," over and over so many times that Billy didn't know why he was calling on the law now. It wouldn't help much, seein' as she probably wouldn't be living till morning.

Billy trundled off down the deserted street with his burden covered in sacking, his step jaunty. But he was a frightened boy whose heart was knocking against his rib cage like a pigeon that wanted out.

Billy lived in a group of houses called Lancaster Townstead, located about a mile from the Conestoga Creek. James Hamilton, a socially prominent lawyer, laid out the plans for the town. Local folks thought Hamilton was foolish, planning the town so far away from the Conestoga Creek with no other good waterway. It was hilly and hampered, too, by the large Dark Hazel Swamp. Mostly German people lived there, and in time they overcame the less than friendly environment, creating businesses, and putting up row after row of wooden houses along the streets.

These Pennsylvania Dutchmen from Germany claimed that they didn't understand the fee the township required for them to live there. So they left their rents unpaid, their stoic, unchangeable ways driving the property owners to distraction. They said they'd paid enough rent the day they occupied their lots and refused to pay more. They were required to build a substantial house within a year, made of wood, with a good chimney, among other requirements.

Hamilton reasoned that if he kept out unskilled lower classes, the town would prosper with merchants, builders, and other professionals. Lancaster Townstead became a thriving community in the mid 1700s, with well-laid-out streets lined with lots and houses built to accommodate the mostly German population.

Emma Ferree's ancestors may have been French, but she'd say she was as "Dutch as they come" and proud of it. She was an extremely short, portly woman, her small feet propelling her stocky legs through the rooms of her house in a floating motion, her wide, gathered skirts brushing her scoured oak floors, her dark hair tucked beneath the white *haus frau* (housewife) cap she always wore. Her eyes were mostly hidden beneath puffs of flesh resembling good bread dough, but her bright, glinty gaze missed nothing, her eyes darting back and forth, often filling with quick tears of sympathy.

Beneath her homespun housedress, behind the row of fashionable buttons, her heart beat quick and sure, burdened only with the unfortunate circumstances of her people, which meant every person she encountered. She took in the sick, the beggarly, the cold, and the hungry.

She handed coins to the poor and ladled out her thick bean soup to anyone who was in the need of sustenance.

That was the main objective in her life, now that Enos was gone, may he rest in peace, she always said. For Enos had been a good man, following the plow and working the land until his knees wouldn't take it anymore. Emma persuaded him to purchase a lot in the town of Lancaster, and he set up a successful peddling business, buying cheese and butter from the country folk, then distributing them to the townspeople.

Oh, she missed Enos terrible, so she did, but she stayed busy and kept her grief at bay. Billy was not hers, he was *aw gnomma*. She never could bring herself to part with the three-year-old waif with the flaming red hair. A young Scottish girl, her husband killed on the front line of the never ceasing French and Indian War, with three little ones, two of them younger than Billy, and no way to support herself, had lived with Emma until she ran off with a British huckster, taking the two youngest and leaving Billy.

That was all right with Billy, who stuck to Emma like a small burr from the day she'd wrapped her soft, warm arms around him and kissed the top of his dirty red hair. He had been much like a bad case of lice to his tall, skinny mother, driving her to madness with his antics, his red hair, and his temper. All he knew from his mother was constant scolding, followed by stinging slaps across his face or shoulders or backside. He attached himself to Emma, and that was that. He never missed his mum, called Emma "Ma," and went right ahead with his life as if nothing out of the ordinary had ever occurred.

From the tavern, Billy pulled the wagon through the wide tracks made by horses' hooves and carriage wheels. The night was damp and cold, the light gray from the few sputtering gas lamps on iron posts. The snow hampered his progress, but he persevered, both hands curled around the iron handle of the wagon, his sack-covered burden lying perfectly still, a bag of feed by all appearances.

He was slogging his way up Water Street, then he'd turn left on Orange Street and right on Mulberry to the second house on the left. He leaned forward, his gray, felt hat pulled down to the tops of his eyes and over his large ears, his red hair bouncing with each tug.

The streets were quiet at this hour. The houses lined the streets like strict Quakers, tall and dark and silent, not even one welcoming orange glow from a black, rectangular window. That was all right with Billy. Coming home past midnight with a sack of feed might raise a few questions, as if he'd stolen it from the livery. The only thing that kept Billy on the straight and narrow (which was wider for him than for some) was the thought of being clamped in those formidable stocks on the square in front of the County Courthouse, where thieves and pickpockets, liars and frauds were stuck for days, while jesting onlookers made fun of them or threw tomatoes or eggs at them. Billy was afraid if that happened to him, and he couldn't get out to avenge himself, he'd explode from his fiery temper. So he better watch out, he reasoned.

He stopped the wagon by the front doorstep, dropped the handle, and pounded on the door with his fists. He waited, then pounded again, harder, looking over his shoulder. When the door creaked open and his ma peered around the flickering yellow light from the candle flame, he was weak with relief.

"Ma. I got us someone needs help."

"*Ach, du lieva. Grund a velt!*" As usual, Emma exclaimed in Dutch, set the candle down on the half-round, wooden stand in the hallway just behind the heavy oak door, and lumbered down the stone steps to peer beneath the sack on the *seck veggley*.

"*Mein Gott in Himmel*, Billy, now what have you got? A dead one, sure. An Indian. Oh, *mein Himmlischer Vater, ich bitte dichi, hilf mir.*" She was half praying, half crying, and her ever-present tears were already pooling in the soft folds beneath her eyes. She stroked the black hair and lifted the white face for further observation beneath the weak light of the gas streetlamp.

"*Ein maedle, Ein shoe maedle. Oh, du yay. Du yay.*" She wrung her hands, helpless in the rush of love and pity that consumed her.

"Ma, you need to shut up now," Billy said, not unkindly, but looking furtively over his shoulder, feeling keenly the possibility of being stuck tightly in those wooden stocks.

Emma hoisted the girl's shoulders in her capable hands as Billy lifted her feet. Grunting and exclaiming, Emma's breath coming in short puffs of steam in the gray, damp night, they hoisted the girl up the steps and into the candlelit hallway of the house.

Carefully, they lowered her onto the multicolored rag rug. Emma straightened, her chest heaving beneath the yoke of her linen nightgown, one plump hand going to her breast as if to control the thumping of her heart.

Emma whisked the sack away and rolled it into a ball, the dust from the feed wafting to the floor. She'd deal with that later.

Billy held up the candle as Emma bent over the cold, inert form clad in deerskin. Her hands and feet were blue with cold; blood had congealed and dried on her legs and hands. Billy was used to seeing injuries and starved folks, but he'd never seen a mess like this. The girl had been pretty, but the one side of her forehead was bulging with a huge blue-black bruise, oozing blood, the texture like sausage. Her eyes were hidden behind the gross swelling, her nose widened with the fluid that seeped from her injury. Her lips were chapped and bleeding, although much of the blood had dried black.

"*Ach, mein Herr Jesus, Du Komm.*" Praying now, Emma felt the need of her *Gott*. Hardly ever did she feel in need, as she capably tackled ministering to the wounded just as she handled the rest of her life.

Tenderly, she used her fingers to examine the wound and feel the cold limbs. They traveled over the young woman's body, searching for more injuries, broken bones, open wounds. Clucking her tongue against the roof of her mouth with small sounds of sympathy, she finished her inspection, straightened, and began to bark orders.

She lit two lamps in the kitchen. Then she stirred up the fire in the fireplace, added a hefty, split log, and swung the black, cast iron kettle over the fresh flames. She moved rapidly with single-minded purpose to the sitting room, there lifting the heavy, warm coverlets.

Then she was back in the kitchen, yellow with lamplight and the flickering flames beneath the pot of hot water. She spread the coverlets by the fire, then together they laid the girl on the soft warmth, so gently, so carefully. Billy put a down pillow beneath her head, and Emma drew up the heaviest coverlet to her chin.

While the young woman slept, they poured warm water into a crockery bowl, shaved lye soap into it, then dabbed at her wounds. Billy silently took a homespun cloth, patted the scratches on her feet and legs with it, then applied the comfrey leaves from the warm water in another bowl.

They worked together efficiently. They'd done this many times. When the wounds were sufficiently cleaned they applied bandages. Emma administered the smelling salts, wafting them back and forth beneath the girl's nose. When she did not stir, Emma bent to lay an ear on her chest, nodded, and kept waving the evil-smelling salts. Shaking her head, she sat back.

"She gonna make it?" Billy asked, his eyebrows raised.

"We should get her awake." Grimly she shook the thin shoulders, but her head wobbled back and forth on the pillow like a rag doll. This was beyond Emma's knowledge. She looked at Billy and then at the door, as if she were trying to decide.

Finally she went to the tall cupboard by the opposite wall, took down a redware bowl of tea leaves, placed them in two cups, then dipped boiling water from the pot over the fire with a long-handled copper ladle. She poured some water in each cup, then handed one to Billy who took it silently, wrapping his cold fingers around the heavy mug. He lifted the jar off the white cone of sugar, but Emma was too fast for him as she reached for the shears and clipped off a chunk of the expensive sugar. Her German frugality allowed her only a small snip for herself and a small one for Billy.

"Ma, that ain't enough for half a cup."

"*Ich glaub. Ich glaub.*"

Billy had to be satisfied with the hot semisweet tea, but was heartened when Emma set a cloth-covered bowl of biscuits and a small crock of jam beside him.

"So no, Billy. *Sage mihr.*" In fluent German, Billy told his story, relating his forays into the livery down by the tavern. Emma shook her head with consternation, blaming herself. She was far too easy on the boy. He should be at home in bed, not allowed to tramp about the streets, and certainly not near the tavern. But she knew about his stash of coins, knew, too, that he would aid her work in helping the poor, so how could it be so bad? That Billy had a head on his shoulders, so he did. He always had. The way his mother batted him around, it's a wonder he had a grain of sense.

She looked down at the bruised, sleeping girl, then to Billy as if he could help her make a decision. She spread her third biscuit with *hulla chelly* and licked her fingers well, the sweet preserves sustaining her flagging spirits. "Billy, *vass sagsht?*"

Billy shrugged as he looked down at the girl.

The lamps burned steadily, a waste of expensive oil. Heaving herself to her feet, Emma lowered her face and pursed her round lips, giving a hefty, whistling blow, extinguishing the lights.

"Let's try and get some rest, Billy. I'll check on her every hour, all right?"

The heat and the scalding hot tea were making him drowsy, so he nodded. Lifting the mug, he emptied it, placed it back on the table, and went upstairs to bed, unbuttoning his knee breeches as he went.

It was the pain in her hands and feet that woke her. At first she was aware of a ripping, tearing sensation, an awful thing she could not overcome. She moaned and turned her head, but an explosion of pain stopped her from doing anything. When she went to lift her hands to her head, giant pincers of pain gripped every finger. She tried to cry out, but found she had no voice.

She held very still, as wave after wave of tingling pain coursed through her feet and up her legs. She shivered with cold. She could not remember anything and had no idea where she was. She was terrified, suspended between a place she could not remember and a void she could not grasp. She had no focus and no sight, only the clawing, ripping pain in her feet and hands.

Slowly, she became aware of a persistent yellow light, a flickering through the blackness of her torment. She would open her eyes. It took all the strength she had, like lifting two huge stones.

The pain in her head exploded into something so white and hot she could not tolerate it. She whispered, then moaned. She tried again to open her eyes. This time, before the pain overtook her, she saw the source of the flickering yellow light. A fire.

She receded into unconsciousness, a blessed place of knowing, of feeling nothing at all until the painful sensation in her feet brought her unwillingly to the frightening knowledge that she was alive. All she knew was that she was somewhere between certainty and a vast area she knew nothing about, as if she were hurtling through a dark tunnel without end.

With her entire being and the full strength of her will, she tried to focus, to find a foothold somewhere. Painful as it was, she lifted both eyelids, willing herself to find an object, something nearby that would help her make sense of this unbearable hurting in her feet and hands.

A fireplace. A floor. Relief flowed through her veins. A floor. A wooden floor. She knew what that was. She knew the fire. A wetness ran down the sides of her face and she knew why. She knew she was crying. She knew her name now. Hester Zug.

When the rustling of skirts came near, she closed her eyes. When she heard the voice of someone saying words in German, she wondered if she was at home in the large stone house in Berks County with Hans and Annie. She wanted to see Lissie and Daniel and all the little children. She wanted to talk to Noah and Isaac the way she always had before they shunned her. *Ach! Ach, du lieva*, the crooning continued, mixed with prayers and pleadings, all in the Pennsylvania Dutch Hester knew so well.

She tried to tell this person about her pain. Her mouth opened, then closed and opened again, but she could not speak. She felt tender hands and willed them to her feet.

A squawk of recognition sounded from the region of her worst pain, now. *"My grund! Die fees. See Fa-fieer."* Over and over, she heard the exclamations about her feet being frozen. Then a slap, and the loud voice of the speaker berating herself. *"Dumkopf, Vot a dumkopf!"*

Steps retreated hastily, a loud, urgent calling ensued, and then another person joined the Pennsylvania Dutch–speaking woman. Together, they placed her hands and feet in cold water. The pain worsened, and Hester cried out, then bore it uncomplaining. She knew about frozen toes and fingers, and so she allowed the work that Emma and Billy were doing.

They gave her a shot of Enos's home-brewed whiskey or tried to, but with Hester unable to swallow, they wiped away the dribble from her chin, and what fell on the pillowcase, and gave up.

Her feet were still frozen but tingling with a milder sensation. And when the morning light shone through the windowpanes, Hester was able to focus her eyes, despite her swollen eyelids.

She saw a strange, round woman, wearing the English cap favored by the non-Amish. She saw a boy with riotous, long hair the color of fire and copper. She saw a kitchen, a fireplace, a cupboard and plank table. She could read a few words of a stitched sampler on the wall.

She remembered God, the hand that delivered her to this house. She thanked him softly.

They brought warm water now, further decreasing the pain in her thawing limbs. She tried to let them know how she longed for water to drink. They brought a bowl with a rag and let her suck it greedily for the cool water. As she swallowed, she choked and coughed, grimacing from the pain in her head. But her thirst was so strong she continued to work her throat muscles, finally receiving life-giving water into her body.

She told them her name in halting whispers. She learned theirs—Emma and Billy Ferree. These weren't

Amish names. Or Indian. Hester was confused. The woman spoke Dutch. Why was she not Amish?

It took far too much effort to ask, so she closed her eyes and slept. She slept for days, waking only to drink water.

It was early one afternoon when she finally awoke, her senses clear, her mind refreshed. She still lay on the oak floor, in the kitchen by the fire.

When Emma found her awake, she threw her hands in the air and yelled for Billy, who, she'd forgotten, had gone to school. "*Guten morgen, guten morgen!*" Emma kept repeating. Then she proceeded to heat water, thinking she could finally get this poor, striking girl out of that Indian dress made of deerskin. She could just picture the lice and fleas that must be crawling all over Enos's mother's best sheep coverlet.

When Hester tried to sit up, she couldn't make it the whole way, lying back down twice before she could stay erect. The pounding in her head increased each time, but she remained sitting upright, propped by the pillows Emma placed against the back of a chair.

Emma washed her hair when Hester felt up to it, gently but thoroughly, and more than once. She bathed her like a small child, dressed her wounds, and put her in a heavy linen nightshirt that had been Enos's. She put his woolen socks on her feet and made a warm, honey-sweetened porridge with milk, feeding it to her by the spoonful and talking the entire time.

When Billy came home from school about two hours late, she scolded like a hen whose eggs had been snatched from beneath her. But Billy didn't seem bothered by it, merely eating a slice of bread, tearing off the crust, and watching Hester, curiosity plastered all over his face.

"Hester. Hester Zug," Emma said. "Amish settlers in Berks County found her, an Indian baby at the spring close to the log house where they lived."

Billy's eyes lit up, recognition shining from their depth. "You're like me!"

Hester smiled, a small widening of her mouth that caused her eyes and nose to feel stretched, it had been so long since they had been exercised in this way.

"Your second mom better than the first?"

Hester shook her head.

"Well, you ain't got a thing to worry about no more. Ma's the bestest there ever was."

Hester watched Billy's face, his natural kindness as beautiful as a wild rose or a sunset, a reflection of the good in humankind. But she wondered what Theodore Crane, the schoolmaster, would say, if he heard that grammar.

CHAPTER 7

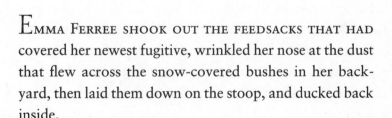

EMMA FERREE SHOOK OUT THE FEEDSACKS THAT HAD covered her newest fugitive, wrinkled her nose at the dust that flew across the snow-covered bushes in her backyard, then laid them down on the stoop, and ducked back inside.

It was cold, too cold to hang out clothes, but the sun was bright, the air was fresh, and she wanted to wash those union suits, both hers and Billy's. When long underwear got to itching, it was time to wash it.

She filled the gray wooden tubs, shaved lye soap into one, dumped in a pile of light-colored things, and began to stir with a well-worn wooden stick, swirling the thick, heavy undergarments around and around. The small room off the kitchen was thick with steam as she took up the wooden washboard and began to rub, her upper arms flapping in time to the furious scrubbing she gave the items she was washing.

Why, she'd sat beside Rhoda Denlinger down at the church house on Sunday and endured all that itching in silence, until she declared there must be insects in unreachable areas of her outerwear, as well her as underwear. She was in so much misery during the service she hardly heard a word the minister said, and all that week it seemed as if her soul needed food, which she couldn't find just by reading her Bible.

It was the way John Evans spoke, so true, so pleading. It just filled her soul with grace. And now she'd have to go hungry all week, where spiritual food was concerned, all on account of her insect-infected clothes.

She wrung the cumbersome garments with hands turned red from the hot water, then wrapped up in a too-small shawl, tied on the *vesh pettsa sock*, threw a heavy scarf across her head, took up the basket of washing, and ventured briskly into the frigid morning.

She shook out Billy's union suit and had just pegged it firmly to the line when a deep voice shouted her name. That dreaded voice was the very reason she didn't wash her long underwear more often.

Turning calmly, she answered in what she hoped was a level voice, her mouth flat, her face expressionless. "Why, Walter Trout." She didn't say it with a twinge of welcome or excitement, not even a smidgen of gladness. She meant to convey just a simple recognition, albeit grudgingly — as, Oh, there you are, and I wish you weren't.

"G' day to ya, Emma! Wonderful morning! Wonderful!" The beaming man on the opposite side of the fence could only be described as vast. His face was wide and florid, alive with color and good humor, his shoulders, back, and stomach twice the size of any other man. He wore no coat or hat. His pink head was circled with a

U of gray hair, as if a squirrel had taken up permanent residence around his noggin.

Emma was in no mood to take his sugary description of this frigid winter morning, when she was just about to hang up her undergarment shift which he could easily examine. So she turned her back, bent and picked up the basket, and returned to her washing, slamming the door unnecessarily.

Nosy, overfed man. If he'd stop eating all that tripe and liverwurst. Well, she was not hanging out her shift. She'd dry it inside. It dripped all over the clean floor, so she waited till he had himself back inside, then scuttled out the back door, her head lowered. She looked neither left or right as she brought the wooden clothespins down hard on the offending garment now hanging on the washline.

She had just reached down to retrieve a petticoat when a stentorian voice made her jump all over. She nearly dropped the garment, took a deep breath, and turned. Her supply of good Christian patience was awfully low, the way she'd missed most of John Evans's sermon, but being the kindly person she was, she said smoothly, "Why yes, Walter?"

"So, then, neighbor. Had a bit of a goings-on the other night, heh?"

"I don't know what you're talking about."

"Billy had a load of something or other on the sack wagon."

"Oh, that. Yes, yes, that."

"What was that?"

"Oh, that. Well, yes, it was that."

"What was it?"

"Well, don't you know what a sack wagon's for?"

Oh, he hadn't meant to offend her. Of course, a sack wagon was for hauling sacks. He thought that's what it looked like. He smiled widely, and the squirrel around his head moved upward a few inches, making Emma shiver, it looked so real.

He hung his florid face above the fence, like a red full moon, she thought grimly, and told her she had nothing to fear, he understood if she hauled things in her sack wagon that were not sacks. Then he giggled in the most obnoxious manner. Emma gave him a stare that surpassed the frigid morning air and said if it was all right with him, she'd be pleased if he stayed to his own business, thank you.

She went back inside with what she hoped was a courteous, regal walk. But Walter Trout saw the hat she was wearing backward, the hairpins hanging dangerously close to leaving her head altogether, then saw her nearslip on the icy doorstep. A resounding laugh came from way down in his rotund belly as he shook his head from side to side, thinking of the delightful Emma Ferree.

Hester was surprised to find Emma's angelic demeanor changed into one of red-faced fury when she finished the washing. Did she dislike that chore so thoroughly? Hester decided to offer to do the washing. She had always loved it, even in winter when her fingers became so cold she had to blow on them.

Emma hung up the clothespin sack, clapped her hands a few times, then ladled hot water into a mug, added tea leaves, cut a large square of molasses cake, and chewed methodically.

Hester sat by the fire in a worn rocking chair lined with coverlets. The bruise was not large, her dark eyes no longer slits in the purplish swelling, although she still faintly resembled a burst piece of fruit, in Billy's words. She watched Emma in silence.

Suddenly Emma burst out, "Some days I long for the farm. The idea of being townspeople may have appealed to me at one time, but this thing of hanging out my shifts for the nosy next door neighbor to see just *gricked my gase*!"

It hurt Hester's head to laugh, but she had to, the body-shaking sound rolling out of her before she could stop it. "Oh, that felt good to laugh," she said, breathlessly. "Kate used to say something 'got her goat'!"

Emma nodded, then reached for the pewter knife, measured another large square of the sweet, brown cake, and plopped it happily on her plate. "Tell me about Kate. Tell me about Berks County. Have you ever been to Philadelphia?"

Hester talked, slowly at first, then faster, as if she wanted Emma to see the woods and the stone house, Kate and the sweet babies that arrived so soon after they found her as a tiny newborn. She told her about Kate's dying, the ensuing misery when she was replaced by the hawkish Annie, how Noah and Isaac shunned her, and the reason she left, leaving her fate in God's hands. The reason she left, she said, was Annie's mistreatment of her. She never mentioned Hans.

Why? It made her head hurt to think about Hans, for she still wrestled with self-blame. He had been good to her. He had provided a home, shelter, food, a way of life. It was Hans who showed her the discipline of the Amish, the way of the cross. Could she always blame her leaving on him alone? Some things were best left unsaid. The whole thing made her tired, made her head ache.

Emma watched the battered Hester gimlet-eyed, missing very little. Who was this girl? What was behind the sadness in her swollen black eyes?

The good food Emma placed on the plank table nurtured Hester's body and spirit in the winter days after their talk. Billy came and went the way a ray of sunshine slips between puffy, gray clouds, illuminating a room with its brilliance. His red hair waved and straggled about his head like copper-colored flames. His blue eyes shone with mischief, curiosity, and an appetite for life that only small boys possessed.

He often wolfed down his evening meal, then roamed the streets of Lancaster Town, as he called it, claiming ownership to far more than he could in reality. He was the bearer of news, gossip, truth, and untruths. He soaked up tidbits like a dry sponge, then poured it forth at every evening meal, the only meal they ate together.

Tonight, Emma had made *Hootsla*, a quick, filling dish that Hester had never tried. Emma had cut stale bread into cubes, toasted them in butter in a heavy skillet, then poured a mixture of beaten eggs and milk over top. She had also made *Schmierkase* from the whey stored in the cold cellar, a spreadable cheese Kate had sometimes made. Hester bent her head to her plate of nutritious food and ate every morsel.

Emma watched her with satisfaction, noticing the color of her dark skin as the bruises healed. She could see Hester's unusual beauty emerge, the fine contour of her high cheekbones becoming more prominent.

"Hey," Billy said.

Hester carefully spread the remaining cheese on a slice of bread before looking at Billy, who was energetically shoving a crust of bread along the rim of his plate, the way Hans had taught all the children at home.

"They're saying." He paused until Emma stopped chewing and gave him her full, undivided attention. "They're saying there's no Indian safe in the town of Lancaster. Nary a one."

Hester held very still, absorbing the words, fighting down the panic.

"You know they got only thirteen of them at the jail-house. They're saying some men from Harrisburg want rid of 'em. Just wanna bushwhack them out of Pennsylvania entirely."

Hester nodded. She understood Naw-A-Te's words now. She could still feel the frosty air and see the sickle moon of that haunted evening. Yes, her people were leaving. Had left. Or been killed. Well, they'd done plenty of killing themselves, the settlers' hearts quaking with terror as they heard tales of the marauding Indians on the western frontier. A heavy sadness followed these bits of news, darkening Hester's life like an angry black cloud that hid the sun's face, whenever the threat was mentioned.

"So, you better not go out till this thing blows over," Billy finished, sticking a knife into a quivering custard pie before jerking the handle up and down like a saw.

"Now watch it there, Billy." Emma looked up from her *Hootsla*, her eyebrows lowered as he maneuvered the shaking pie onto his plate. "You have half of a pie there."

"The other half is for you."

"Hester?"

Billy eyed her, then said she didn't eat pie, like as not.

Hester laughed, but the sound was hollow, a false tinkling sound like a distant cowbell that someone was shaking foolishly.

Her thoughts churned, disturbing the normal flow of her mind, wondering, watching Billy's young face. If she was not safe here with Emma, would she ever be safe anywhere? Or safe, perhaps, but unwanted?

A part of her wanted to rise from the table, gather a few belongings, and be on her way, but on her way to where? Back to Hans and Annie? The days stretched before her, dark and mysterious, swelling with gigantic questions, unanswered now.

She had one thing, and that was her faith. God would protect her, go with her. Hans had taught her this. The imperfect Hans. How could she believe a word he said after he betrayed her with his well hidden ardor? Could she continue to believe in a God presented by Hans?

Naw-A-Te was true. He was faithful. He could press her head against his chest, and she could hear the steady beating of his heart, and nothing seemed wrong. If Hans would have tried the same gesture, it would have been vile, revolting. Should she have stayed and married Running Bear? Wen-O-Ma? A visual image of his face, slick with grease, was as real and as repulsive as ever.

Emma Ferree finished her pie, sat back, and watched the display of emotions, fanned by her troubled thoughts. Well, if she had anything to say, this battered Indian girl would suffer no more if she could help it, and she fervently believed she could. A fierce, protective feeling welled in her chest. Hester had suffered enough.

Emma's eyes narrowed shrewdly as her brain churned with possibilities. She'd have to let go of her pride and have a talk with that fat Walter Trout. She would find a way.

Walter had just tucked into a delightful stack of buckwheat cakes soaked in butter and drizzled with maple syrup, a large white cloth stuck in his collar to protect his shirt, when there was a rapid knocking on his back door. Thinking how unusual that was, he became a bit hasty, heaving his oversize body from his kitchen chair so that he knocked over his coffee.

Letting it go, he clucked mournfully at his loss but hastened his bulk to the back door, pulling it open and waving an arm with a flourish when he saw who it was. Emma Ferree!

She brushed past him, saying pointedly, "Take your bib off."

He clawed at it hastily, the red of his face turning to an alarming shade of purple as he rolled the cloth between his fingers, unsure if he should tell her it was not a bib but a cloth napkin which the gentry always had at their disposal. What would a German know about napkins?

So he drew himself up to his full height of five feet and five inches and told Emma in clipped tones that it was not a bib but a napkin. She answered tartly that he could call it what he wanted but it was still a bib.

She walked into the kitchen ahead of him, eyed the stack of buckwheat cakes, and to her horror, her mouth began to water. She swallowed. She had never seen better-looking buckwheat cakes.

She pulled at the ladder-back chair. Instantly, Walter rushed to her side, pulled the chair out, and asked her to be seated, but found he could not push the chair at all after she was on it. He observed the ample pile of skirts on each side of the chair and pretended not to notice when she bumped the chair up to the table herself. "Now, then, Emma Ferree, could I interest you in some buckwheat cakes?"

Emma swallowed. My, from down here they looked even better. "Perhaps you could," she said pointedly, feigning disinterest. But when he served her a stack of three cakes dripping with butter and a coating of syrup, made her a cup of tea, and handed her a cloth napkin, she didn't have the slightest idea what to do with it and laid the thing beside her plate.

So that Emma wasn't as high up as she thought. But he enjoyed her obvious delight in the buckwheat cakes and didn't mind when she licked her fingers, then brought up a corner of her apron to wipe her mouth. Such rosy cheeks, so well rounded, he thought. What a healing of his sad heart for her to grace his table.

She asked the favor of him. Did he not own land outside the town? Down by the Amish somewhere? Near Coatesville?

Yes, yes, he did.

Was there a possibility that he could keep a secret, then?

Oh yes, yes, of course.

His head was shining in the morning sunlight, the reflection bouncing off the mirror hung by his wash bench, illuminating the skin to the highest sheen she had ever witnessed. The circle of gray hair looked thinner in the unforgiving light, not entirely like a squirrel, she thought. Perhaps just part of one.

"And on this land you own," Emma said, pursing her lips and drawing out her question, just enough to keep him on edge.

"Yes?" he asked, eager to help Emma accomplish her goals.

"There is a dwelling?"

"Yes. Oh, quite a presentable house. One built of log and bricks."

"And there is someone living there at present?"

"No. No. Jonas Fisher has inquired, but finds the rent too steep for his pocket."

"Well, then." And Emma launched into a vivid account of Hester's arrival, keeping Walter mesmerized, for he had truthfully never expected the sack wagon to hold anything quite that frightful. At worst, he'd imagined Billy to have pilfered some hay, which he figured only served that Simon down at the tavern right.

Emma wanted to move out there with Hester until these threats against the redskins died out. Billy would go with them, of course, and she'd school him at home. It was unthinkable for Hester to stay indoors in the town for such an extended period of time. When spring arrived, she would need fresh air and sunshine.

Oh, absolutely, Walter agreed over and over to Emma's plan, nodding his head so hard his chins wobbled and waggled as if they had entire lives of their own. Emma grabbed her own chin, tugged a few times before deciding, yes, definitely, she had only one.

When he walked with her to the back door, he briefly rested his hand on her back, which made her stiffen and lower her voice a few degrees in iciness, but he paid her no heed. She was very German, and he had his napkins, after all.

Hester was seated at the kitchen table, a small pile of rye straw in front of her. Emma noticed the new look of concentration, a purposeful demeanor, as she began the basket she would make.

"*Wunderbahr*!" Emma exclaimed, her spirits high, her cheeks flushed from the buckwheat cakes.

Hester smiled. "I learned from Clover and Beaver. You wait!"

Emma clapped her hands like a small overgrown child. "So exciting. Hester. Our house will be graced with your *kaevlin*!"

"You say *kaevlin* for 'baskets,' too?" she asked, her face alight with understanding.

Emma sat across from Hester, explaining her visit to her neighbor, then told her she had nothing to fear, that she would be taken care of, not just this day or even this winter, but always. She told her she would be the daughter she never had. Walter was willing to let them stay at his house, where she could roam the woods and adjoining fields among the Amish, who would never harm her. They could raise a sow, have a flock of chickens and a cow.

Hester's eyes glowed with happiness. She wiped her tears hurriedly and said she'd do her best to help make Emma's life easier.

Emma was so touched by Hester's declaration of loyalty that she patted her shoulder with her soft, puffy fingers and said she must never fear about the future from this day forward. She, Emma Ferree, would look out for her, same as Billy would, for as long as she needed their protection.

Over and over, she repeated herself, until Billy said he'd be the man of the house, but what was he going to do for excitement if they lived in the country? Without the tavern and the livery, and his band of friends to roam the streets, life was going to be dull beyond anything he could imagine.

Hester could easily explain the ways of the country. Water to haul, firewood to chop, animals to feed, garden to tend, the list went on and on.

Billy listened, his eyebrows drawn down as he thought about Hester's words. "Well, I know, but if *you* do all that work, there's not a whole lot left for me to do." Emma told him he needed his ears boxed.

Hester was happy to move to the country. She hoped her gardening skills were sufficient, as well as being able to keep house the way Emma required. The German Emma was always scouring floors, washing, and carefully smoothing out clothes and bedsheets, even linen towels and doilies, as if one speck of dirt would never be allowed to exist on anything washable.

Hester wove the rye straw expertly, drawing the rows tightly with strips of willow bark, a basket style whose origin was half-German and half-Indian. Emma was amazed. Billy fell silent, his bright eyes watching Hester's fingers like an observant hawk. Hester began to talk of her time with the Indians, about Naw-A-Te, Running Bear, Clover, and Beaver, the ways of the longhouse, their weapons and primitive tools. She spoke of her inability to stay, sometimes still not understanding the choice she had made.

Billy snorted. "Seems you didn't have much choice there toward the last."

Hester laughed easily, her eyes shining dark pools of appreciation. "No. No. I didn't."

"You were sorta dumped into the feedlot by the livery, and if I remember right, I found you, dead as a doornail."

Emma broke in, "Now, now, Billy she was alive."

"Barely."

Hester nodded, her face serious. "I would have died."

Billy told her if those men found her, he knew she'd been better off dead.

When a pounding on the front door exploded the homey atmosphere of the kitchen, they jumped, sat erect, then looked at one another with questions in their eyes, all fearfully recognizing that Hester might not be safe.

Emma was the first to think rationally. For someone of her size, she moved with lightning speed, opening the cellar door and beckoning Hester. "Into the potato bin. Cover yourself."

Hester knew she must obey. She asked no questions, merely slipped down the narrow, steep stairs backward, holding on to the railing on each side until her feet found the uneven, earthen floor. It was pitch black, but her hands fluttered in front of her until they found the stone walls, the shelves, the meat hanging on hooks. She stifled a cry as a large rodent scuttled across her woolen sock–clad feet.

CHAPTER 8

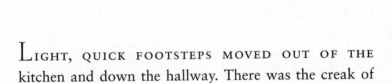

LIGHT, QUICK FOOTSTEPS MOVED OUT OF THE kitchen and down the hallway. There was the creak of the front door. Voices.

Hester moved blindly, her hands roaming the walls of the cellar.

Heavy footsteps, the solid clunking of big boots thundering down on the oak floor like an avalanche of boulders. Emma's voice.

Hester moved faster, her hands raking the wall. Where was the potato bin? It had to be here somewhere.

She heard the rough voices of men. She heard Emma say they could look all they wanted. She had seen no Indian running away.

She heard the steps of the men going upstairs. For one heart-stopping instant, she believed they were lowering themselves into the cellar. If they found her here, she had no way of escape.

The steps were muted, far away now. Hester imagined them upstairs, enormous, dark bodies, massive white faces outlined with black beards and filthy, smelly hats of fur and leather, glittering, greedy eyes, their single-minded goal to rid the town of Lancaster of the last of the redskins, the Conestogas.

Hester thought of the jailhouse, the hunger and filth she heard of there where she would be taken to join the small band of surviving Conestogas. When she heard the muted steps returning down the stairs, she moved frantically, the potato bin seeming completely unreachable. Surely it was along a wall. Perhaps not. She began swinging her arms wide, searching, when one hand slapped against rough lumber. Thank God.

With both hands, she found the square box. Bending over, she felt a large mound of potatoes. More loud footsteps sounded overhead. Her mind rushed faster. She had no time to cover herself with the small vegetables. It would take too long. Could she squeeze beneath the bin? She measured with her hands.

Emma was talking, talking, her words following a calm, relaxed march of ordinary words as she acted the part of a round little housewife, a *dumbkopf*, asking silly questions about the Indians that had nothing to do with this night or this mission.

Hester found enough space, she thought. Lowering herself, she flattened her body, wriggling and clawing with her hands. She felt the unhealed bruises on her head being squeezed. Dust and dirt slid past her cheek and filled her nose and mouth. Inch by inch, she pushed into the narrow crevice beneath the wooden bin containing the summer's potatoes.

The voices overhead continued. Hester could not understand the words.

She could go no farther. The floor rose in a mound beneath the potato bin. With every ounce of her strength, she pulled her hips and knees further into the opening. She stopped, guessing her skirt was hidden away. She had to leave the rest of her fate to God. If they came down the cellar steps and found her, then her life would surely be over.

It was hard to think of dying, but harder yet to imagine the hunger and torture of jail. As she thought of her life being in the hands of these swarthy, uncouth men, she inched her way into the crevice a bit more.

The dry, rasping sound of a snake. She stifled a cry as its heavy body slithered across her hand, then down across her knees.

The cellar door opened. A rectangle of flickering yellow light shone directly ahead of her. The men lost no time, coming down the steep stairway backward the way she had come. Hester heard the scurrying of the rodents.

She realized she had squeezed beneath the potato bin from the wall side, away from where the men had planted their feet. Had she come from the front where there was no opening beneath it, she'd have never found her hiding place.

She felt a cough begin in her throat. The veins in her neck swelled, her eyes squeezed shut, her mouth worked as she tried to abort the raucous sound that ached to be released. I will not cough. I will not cough. She swallowed over and over, finding with each contraction of her neck muscles that the sensation was receding.

Loud voices, footsteps on the packed earthen floor. "There ain't no Injun down here."

"Snake!" A bawling sound, a howl of mocking laughter and another one of glee as a man ran straight up the stairs.

She heard Emma. "I told you there ain't nothing down them steps."

"Potatoes."

"*Ya, wohl!* I work hard to dig them *Katufla*. You let them be."

Hester heard voices.

"You hear?" Emma shouted.

When there was no answer, Emma warned them once more, her tone strident but relaxed. After all, she was only an ordinary housewife protecting a summer's bounty, an important staple for the winter.

A rude reply rasped directly in front of Hester. She shivered and felt tears of panic begin to form. Now they were reaching into the bin, the candle held aloft, rolling the potatoes and laughing. They compared sizes, filling their empty pockets with the vegetables.

The men were so close she could hear their breathing. She smelled horses, stale sweat, deerskin, leather, tobacco. Hester's throat worked as she swallowed her fear.

Emma shouted down the opening of the stairway. "You leave them *Katufla* be. You let them down there for me and Billy. I'll tell the constable about you making off with my stuff. You hear me?"

There was only a rude mocking sound in reply. That, and a boot kicking the corner of the bin. A fine layer of dust from the potatoes filtered down on Hester's face. It felt cool, smelled like Annie's garden. Before she could think, a sneeze tore through her nose. She pushed her tongue against the roof of her mouth and willed the rush of air to be compressed.

A sound squeezed out, but it was overridden by another clattering of heavy boots on the stairway. Breathing rapidly, her nostrils filled with dirt, Hester lay beneath the potatoes and thanked her heavenly father for keeping her safe. The image of John Lantz, the Amish bishop, his hair white, his blue eyes piercing, saying, "*Gott sie gelobt un gedankt*," filled her mind. She repeated the saying over and over, the treasure of the words' meaning increasing fourfold now.

The choking dirt that filtered over her face took her back to the dust and heat of August, as she bent over a row of beans or hoed newly planted beets. She could see the flight of the butterflies above the purple blossoms, erratic little upward flutterings, only to zigzag sideways, or plummet ungracefully to hover over blossoms before moving dizzily on their way. Butterflies were beautiful creatures but without smooth flight patterns, which birds and other airborne insects had.

She could hear the clatter of the iron-clad wooden wheels of the wagon bouncing over the rutted field lane. Hans was driving the faithful, plodding team, while Noah sprawled on top of the hay, his hair as light as the hot, white sunshine, Isaac beside him, a darker shadow.

When Kate was alive, they would have waved, called out a silly saying. Hester would have straightened her back, waved, and answered, a smile playing around her perfect mouth, her spirits lifted.

When Annie became their mother, she spread her venomous jealousy to Hester's brothers, her staunchest friends, and they no longer acknowledged her presence in the garden or the barn at milking time. Nowhere ever. Hester carried that great and awful pain like a growth close to her heart that cut off her capacity to feel joy. Her brothers' love had carried her through the rough spots that occurred in her life, her grafting into the Amish community softened by their protection.

Lying beneath the bin of potatoes in Emma Ferree's house in this strange Lancaster town, Hester wondered at the twists and turns in the uncertain path of her life so far. Maybe sometime she'd be able to go back to Berks County, back to her childhood home where butterflies flitted blue and orange and black and yellow, and the dust was filled with the scent of honeysuckle and wonder.

Hester longed for that lost sweetness, savoring the sights and smells of that time when she had been filled with belonging, the serenity that came from knowing her place in the world.

All this flashed through her mind as Emma's staccato voice berated the men who had searched her house. She told them God would hold them accountable for stuffing their pockets with a poor widow's potatoes. She hoped their horses would all get hoof rot and their wagon wheels would fall off. She banged the door after them, then sagged against it. The color drained out of her face and a sheen of sweat appeared on her forehead as she yelled at Billy to bring the smelling salts. She was sure her heart was not going to take this.

She moaned about poor, poor Hester down in that cellar. Oh, what had she gone through? Tears puddled and dripped from her doughy cheeks as she rained down other wishes of deep trouble on those *schtinkiche men-na*. For what she felt responsibility for, she fiercely loved and protected and passionately esteemed as her own, sometimes to the point that Billy wished she'd stop saying all those flowery speeches. A fella didn't need to hear all that. But his eyes shone with the goodness of Emma's love and spread right out of his own heart to others, without him even realizing it.

The next day, all the Indians that were held in the county jail were murdered. Fourteen of them were hacked to death by a group of men that called themselves the Paxton Boys, led by a minister who was a zealot. The town of Lancaster and the area around it had effectively been freed of any Indians, they believed.

Hester heard the news, but her face showed no evidence of distress. She just folded in like a withering plant and did not speak the remainder of the evening. Emma watched Hester closely but decided to leave her alone to mourn, to sort out her feelings, to absorb this terrible deed done against her people.

For weeks, Billy arrived, breathless, with one gruesome story or another. Hester gave no sign that she heard one word, simply bowing her head to her basket-weaving without a single tear or acknowledgment of his presence.

Emma and Billy discussed the moving. It would be odd to move their belongings in the dead of winter. People would talk. They stoked the fires, cleaned the house, cooked their meals, always watchful as they went about their usual routines.

Every Sunday morning Emma dressed in her Lord's Day finery, combed Billy's rebellious mop of hair, pinned his high collar amid furious grimaces as she worked. Then they set off for First Reformed Church on Orange Street.

Hester had to stay behind for safety's sake. Emma was well aware that other Indians were still in the area, some of them hired out as slaves, serving wealthy families without wages, but she took no chances. Helen Denlinger told her there was talk of an Indian girl having escaped the jail the night of the massacre and that she was living with Emma Ferree. Then Helen looked at her with too-bright eyes and a knowing smile. Emma waved a hand, dismissing her entirely, then turned to speak to her neighbor, Walter Trout, who became so gratified by the widow Emma's attention that he began to stutter, something he hadn't done since he was eight or nine years old.

Hester sat by the crackling fire, enjoying its warmth, then got up to look out the many paned windows, watching the carriages and wagons moving up and down Mulberry Street. In winter, most folks were hidden inside their carriages, but frequently an open wagon would rumble by, the wagon's inhabitants blobs beneath layers of buffalo robes with even their faces obscured. Pedestrians walked off to the sides of the streets through the snow, ladies lifting their skirts daintily as carriages rattled by.

All going to church, Hester thought. She had never seen the huge brick church houses Emma described, or the stone ones. Everyone went to church. There were so many different ones, it was dizzying. Why, if they all believed in the same God and his son Jesus, were there so many different ways to worship? It was more than Hester could figure out, so she stood hidden by Emma's spotless, white curtains and observed the people. Always she stayed alert, her senses tuned for any peace-crushing blow delivered to the sturdy oak door that led to the street.

Hester turned away from the window, then sighed restlessly. Going to the small mirror above the hall table, she examined the wounds on her face in the light from the snow and sun. She found a redness, but very little besides. That pleased her immensely. She wandered back to the window and saw a tall, top-hatted man walking sedately, a lady's hand on his arm, her skirts spread below her coat like a yellow flower. What unthinkable finery! So out of the Amish *Ordnung*, the stringent rules that kept them obedient, that held them within the promise they had made to be faithful.

Hester had always been accustomed to wearing a huge cap and hat pulled well past her face with a heavy, black woolen shawl pinned severely over her shoulders. If she wore her Amish outerwear, she would not be taken for an Indian, but the Amish did not live in town, so that would be stranger still.

An oddity yet. An oddity all her life. Well, she wouldn't look too far ahead, which was like welcoming a whole nest of wasps into a kitchen. It did no good, brought a load of unnecessary anxiety, and in the end, a stinging pain that had to be daubed with care, same as memories that were painfully colorful.

She looked forward to spring, the time when they would take their belongings and move to the country, close to the Amish. Today was the Sabbath, so she would not work at her baskets. But she felt restless, a longing for something she couldn't name. If she had wings like an eagle, she'd fly above this house and all the others that looked exactly the same.

In row upon row of wooden houses with brick chimneys rising from their middles, gray smoke waved endlessly, coming from the heating and cooking fire in the *shuba,* the soul of each house.

Hester sighed again. She sat down, reaching for the *Heiliche Schrift,* the great German Bible Emma delved into constantly, reading out loud to Billy, who, like as not, was fast asleep or carving a small object from a stick of wood.

Hester looked at the intricate black and white pictures and tried to read in *Mattheu,* but so many of the words eluded her. Reading in English was difficult enough. Reading German was like climbing a tree without branches. Hans had taught all his children well. He brought out the catechism every Sunday morning as regularly as he milked cows. Noah and Isaac were brilliant. Hester could read only haltingly, but Hans had praised her nevertheless, his eyes warm and brown, staying on her face too long. She could never remember hearing him give a word of encouragement to Noah or Isaac. And they so deserved it.

In one quick, fluid movement, Hester rose, a fierceness in her change of position. Taking the German Bible in both hands, she dropped it on the floor solidly. Her breathing came hard. Noah and Isaac had been slaves, working—no, toiling—from the time the sun appeared above the mountain, till it sank below the opposite one. And always, always, she had received flowery words of gratitude for the smallest endeavor.

Well, she'd gotten what she deserved, she supposed. Reaped richly the suffocating jealousy of her stepmother, after, like a slow-witted opossum that's so easily trapped, she finally saw Hans for what he was.

For a moment she was tempted to compare herself to Joseph in the Old Testament who had been persecuted because of jealousy. But he was good and holy and found favor in God's eyes. She, too, had a coat of many colors laid on her shoulders, in the form of colored linen made into her Sunday dresses. And when other little girls had one Sunday dress, she had three.

Ah, but he had loved her—she tried to convince herself—in the proper way a father loves a daughter. It was she who had done wrong. Perhaps. But how?

She paced the confines of the house accusing herself, but for what? Her past was like rain—life-giving, sweet, and generous in its abundance of things that were good. But if she lingered too long in this rain, she became cold and uncomfortable and needed to retreat to a place where the rain could not touch her. And yet, it still did. The rain penetrated her heart, filling it with sadness for Noah and for Isaac. They were such noble young brothers, working endlessly to Hans's and Annie's specifications, until they built the farm from a lowly log house and a few cleared acres to the status of a homestead belonging to Hans and Annie Zug. They were regarded as the best managers in Berks County, owners of a large stone house and barn and of the finest herd of cows in that area (if not in all of Pennsylvania), plus a couple of Belgian horses and a blacksmithy.

Hans had it all. Hester's eyes narrowed. Yes, he did, but by his shrewd wife's manipulation and the sweat of Noah's and Isaac's brows.

Perhaps it was better that she wasn't alone too much, the way these thoughts rushed around in her mind, creating ripples of pain. Why did she remember her brothers so keenly now? If only she could talk to them and make things right. She wanted to tell them that they were the ones who deserved to be exalted, lifted up, encouraged. Just look at me. Please look at me. Talk to me. I need to tell you these things.

Hester was relieved when a quiet rapping sounded on the door. She quickly scooped up the Bible she had let fall, then hurried to slide back the bolt on the door, allowing Emma and Billy to enter. Emma's face was flushed, two purplish spots appeared on either cheek, her nose looked bruised from the cold, and her green hat was sliding to the back of her head. She resembled a frenzied bantam hen at home in the barnyard when a skunk raided her small, neat nest of eggs.

"We're getting company!" she said.

"Rufus and Helen Denlinger. And Walter Trout," Billy crowed, already divesting himself of the noose other people called a collar.

"But?" Hester was bewildered.

Emma was sliding the wool cape off her rounded shoulders, her eyes flashing beneath the folds of skin, now heightened to an alarming pink color. "Now, Hester, you don't worry. If Helen is nosy, then she's going to have the surprise of her life. You are my new maid from Virginia. A slave. Here." She stopped Hester, handed her a ruffled housewife's cap and an apron that was so oversized it was ridiculous, but since Emma didn't seem to mind, Hester didn't either.

Emma fried salt pork, the pan so sizzling hot it was only a miracle the kitchen didn't go up in flames. She peeled potatoes while Hester laid the table with a plain white tablecloth, serviceable ironstone plates, pewter utensils, and clay tumblers.

They served the sauerkraut with dumplings, the salt pork with pickled watermelon rind. The potatoes had a whole lake of brown butter on the mounded top. Like a volcano, the butter spilled down the sides, pooling around the edges of the serving bowl.

Emma served the chilled chow-chow in a glass dish. Pats of homemade butter gleamed and shone by the tall candles. Thickened elderberries sat alongside the butter, making a perfect marriage of fat and sweet to spread on thick chunks of crusty German bread.

Helen Denlinger was a bit stout, although she girded herself so severely that she appeared slender, at least in the proper places. As she ate and ate and ate, her face grew steadily more colorful, her eyes decreased in size, and her breathing became decidedly more labored, like a plodding horse pulling a plow in the spring.

She mentioned the delightful way the Germans served their bread, in a thin, gasping voice, before reaching for another thick, crusty chunk, spreading it with a greedy portion of butter and the marvelous berries. Her husband ate like a starving wolf, lowering his head and shoveling it in without the good manners of taking time to answer the smallest inquiry.

Walter Trout sat at the end of the table where there was plenty of room, cut his salt pork with knife and fork, poised like a perfect British gentleman, slowly chewing the neat squares of meat with his mouth closed. His small mouth, moving up and down in a grinding, circular motion, completely entranced Billy, who thought it amazing the way that small opening could be the only door for so much food.

To his knowledge, Walter had never tasted German cooking. He found the dumplings on the sauerkraut blissful, the salt pork heavenly, the turnips absolutely divine.

Billy rolled his eyes at Hester. "I can tell you come fresh off a sermon," he quipped.

Emma was so mortified she didn't know what to do, but when she looked at Walter and he was rolling from side to side, trying to repress his good-humored mirth, she spluttered, then gave up and lifted her hands, howling with unladylike glee that Helen Denlinger found ill-mannered. And since she had to struggle to breathe, she certainly could not waste precious air in laughing. That Billy Ferree needed to learn manners, to be seen and not heard.

Hester hovered over the Sunday dinner, the ruffled white cap hiding her sleek, straight hair, enhancing the simple beauty of her large dark eyes. She filled and re-filled water tumblers, filled the sauerkraut dish twice, and made sure the dumplings were moist and hot. She brought out a chocolate cake, loaded with walnuts ground to slivers and topped with crumby brown sugar. She served applesauce and golden pears, glazed with honey.

Helen looked up from her plate and watched Hester intently. "Emma, your Negro is light skinned. Is she a mulatto?" she asked, watching her friend shrewdly.

Emma's face was kind, soft, and benevolent, the steel beneath her skin well hidden. Her remark was courteous as well. "Why, yes. Helen, she is, in fact, of mixed origin. I believe they said Jamaican, when I bought her at auction."

"But," Helen spluttered, wrestling with curiosity, "I had no idea Enos was so well-to-do that you can afford a servant."

Emma batted her short lashes and lowered her eyelids humbly. "Oh, Enos was a man of means. Indeed he was. But so modest, so very unassuming."

This remark set Helen directly on the path of acquiring a girl to serve her food, no matter what the cost. Never once did she imagine that Emma had taken in an Indian, the way some people claimed. Why, she was so well-to-do she had her own servant. But then look at the way that woman has given, casting her bread upon the waters in more than one area. God rewards people like that, she told Rufus.

Walter Trout took one bite of the chocolate cake and figured it was among the best things he'd ever been fortunate enough to taste. He watched Hester's impeccable manners, her quiet serving of this delicious meal, and wondered if he could possibly be called to Sunday dinner more often. Even when they'd be living out in the country and all. His warm heart felt a great longing to erase the sadness from the young girl's eyes. He looked forward to being able to sit at Emma Ferree's table again.

Billy watched Helen Denlinger's face turn steadily darker, her breathing light and quick as she consumed her cake, and thought how much she looked like a catfish after you take it off the hook, gasping for air the way they did.

CHAPTER 9

It was in April, when every street in Lancaster had turned into a slick, brown quagmire, the showers replenishing the soupy mess almost every day, that Emma hired a boy from the livery to take them out to the country to see the new home.

She was worried about Hester, so lifeless and thin. She had no appetite and said very little. Even Billy could not get her interested in anything. When the carriage pulled to the door, Emma hustled both Hester and Billy out, shooting uncomfortable glances Walter Trout's way. He had hinted broadly that he could accompany them, seeing as how he owned the property and all, but Emma said there was no need, they'd be fine, and dismissed him easily. He watched them go through an opened curtain, then thought perhaps it was best that they go without him since the carriage looked pretty narrow.

Emma heaved herself into the carriage, taking the livery boy's hand as an aid. She meant to touch it lightly the way the younger ladies did, filled with grace, but she pushed down on the slight boy's hand so hard he had to hold it up with his opposite one. His face grew red with exertion, and he considered himself extremely fortunate to have any room at all beside her on the front seat. Emma did think that if the time ever came that Walter would accompany them to the country, they would need a sturdy wagon, not a weak carriage. They made them so flimsy these days.

She set her hat squarely on her head and tied the thin scarf down over it securely beneath her one soft chin, then sat back to enjoy the ride. The air was wet, filled with scents of rain and standing water and dripping new plants that seemed to be bursting with happiness. The sunlight was weak but getting stronger each day, holding the promise of heat and humidity, a coming season of plenty.

They passed the wheelwright's shop, a row of houses, and the livery. Soon they could smell the open fields, the forest, the clean new grasses that waved and bowed by the muddy roadside. Their progress was slow. The horse lowered his haunches and leaned into the collar, pulling the carriage through the ruts made by all kinds of traffic.

Hester sat in the backseat, her face hidden by the broad brim of a large, blue bonnet, an old one of Emma's, who had carefully adjusted it to hide the color of her skin. Beside her, his new straw hat pushed to the back of his head, Billy hooked an elbow over the back of the carriage, whistling and warbling and chirping to his heart's content. His blue eyes followed the soaring of the birds, the way they dipped and wheeled in the blue sky, smudged by streaks of white clouds.

Hester asked if he knew the fish bone clouds, the ones that appeared in the east when a good rain was coming the following day.

"You can't go by that," he said airily.

"Sure you can."

"Nah."

"So tell me how you can predict rain."

"Go out and see if it's raining. That's easy."

Hester laughed.

Emma turned, so glad to hear this sound.

Hester smiled at Emma and said there would be so much she could teach Billy about nature, the garden, the herbal medicines she prized. Emma said probably not just Billy, but her, as well.

Their first view of the house was a disappointment. It was in lamentable shape. A moth-eaten dress that looked suitable from a distance, but the damage clearly visible as they approached.

Emma almost fell out of the carriage in her eagerness, while the boy who brought them stayed sitting in the exact same spot. There was no way he was going to put his life in danger and help this lady down.

Emma rushed to the front door, her small feet pattering across the wet grass, giving the illusion that she was floating, as if wheels propelled her smoothly along.

The door was attached by only one hinge, allowing creatures access to the house. By the looks of it, plenty of them had taken up residence. The rooms were filthy, the kitchen black with smoke.

"Now, how can this be? Walter said there was a couple living here, but they couldn't afford the rent." Emma's voice was thick with despair, almost a whine. Billy had spied a snake already and was off across the wet grass. Hester stepped through the door, turned her

face left, then right, sniffed, wrinkled her nose, and pronounced it livable.

There was a fairly large kitchen in front, the first
room of the house. Half of one wall was filled by a vast
fireplace, a wide beam placed across the top, the stone
and mortar disappearing into the ceiling in the middle
of the house.

The floors were oak planks, wide and sturdy but littered with rodent's waste, bits of nutshells, grass, dead
flies, and other insects. The sitting room took up the
whole left side of the house, a tiny, circular stairway going out of a corner of it to the upstairs. There were only
two bedrooms. The ceiling was the underside of the oak
roof shingles.

Everything was covered with the remains of free,
scurrying mice and rats. Likely mink, otter, opossums,
and skunks, too, Hester thought.

"Let's just stay in town." Emma's voice carried genuine tears, ill concealed. "*Du yay. Du yay,*" she kept
lamenting.

Hester said nothing. She realized her position as
the person who was the recipient of this kind woman's
charity and didn't wish to appear bold. Her whole heart
longed for this space, the fields and grasses, the trees
and water, clean and fresh and free. She wanted to stay
here in this unused dwelling, away from the fear that
dogged each day, the feeling of being stalked, her spirit
repressed, unable to go outside and smell the scent of the
town. Without that, the very atmosphere seemed second-
hand, as if the air had already been breathed by someone
else, and her allotment had been spare.

Emma had started on her other excuses, reasoning that at her age, there was no sense in working like this, and she was fairly certain that fat Walter Trout wouldn't lift a finger to clean this place. Hester thought of Kate saying, "The pot shouldn't call the kettle black," but said nothing.

Quickly, Emma shot out, "Hester, what do you think?"

"I want to stay! Please, can I stay here? I'll clean, I'll do everything. I don't want to go back."

Emma's eyes widened, popping in surprise. "You do?"

"Yes! Oh, yes! I love it here!" She swung her arms toward the surrounding hills, the grasses heavy with good moisture, the soil beneath it so rich, so fruitful. She explained where a garden could be made, a horse and wagon kept in the adjoining barn, a fence built for a pasture, perhaps in time their own plow, more than one cow, a nice flock of chickens.

When the doorway darkened, Emma lifted a hand to her mouth, her eyes wide with fright. She squeaked helplessly. Hester stayed still, her back rigid, without looking. It was best this person did not see her face.

"Hello." The voice was deep with a demanding quality.

Emma's chin wobbled a few times before she could speak. "Yes, yes. Hello."

"I was riding across the field and saw the carriage parked by the barn. I was curious, is all."

"Oh, of course." Emma stepped forward, her natural goodness of heart shining as usual as she thrust her plump hand in the general direction of the tall, dark man.

He bent to take it and shook politely. "I am William. William King."

"Emma Ferree. Enos was my husband's name."

"The cheese peddler?"

"Why, yes, yes, he was a peddler. Cheese. Yes!" Delighted, Emma gabbled away like a silly turkey being chased by its peers, recognizing her words had no merit had she not been connected to Enos.

The tall young man was very good-looking, Emma summed up, and she was always a bit tongue-tied around *selly goot gookichy*. This one might be Amish, though, since he was wearing those wide suspenders and that flat-looking hat.

He lifted his chin in Hester's general direction. "And her?"

"Hester? You mean our Hester?" Too late, Emma realized her mistake. Hester moved swiftly. Like a wraith, invisible, she melted away through the half-open back door.

William King's face blanched. He looked as if he had, in fact, just encountered a *schpence*. "Who? What is her name?"

His eyes were terrible in their intensity. Emma's plump, pink hand went to her throat to still the fluttering. "It is Hester. Hester Zug."

"No!"

In a few long strides, he pushed Emma aside, tore through the door in the back of the house, and lunged down the steps. Hester heard his name. She heard his voice. All her own shortcomings, the color of her skin, Hans, her past, rose directly in front of her, roared and crashed and clawed their way past any hope of meeting him again. She could not look at him. He must never see her. She ran, lifting her skirts. The rush of air caught her hat, swinging it off her head. It hung by its wide strings, flopping, bouncing like a terrified bird, a parody of her heart. She increased her speed when she heard strong footsteps behind her.

"Hester! Wait! Wait!"

She looked back, wildly.

"Please stop. I just want to talk."

On she ran, determined that he must never see her.

He overtook her, then reached out and caught the flapping bonnet. She slid to a stop, her chest heaving, her hands balled into fists.

"Hester. Oh, Hester." The words were a caress, a coming home, a believing of the impossible, the accepting of a miracle.

"Don't. Don't." She whispered the words harshly, her eyes downcast. She would not lift them.

"Hester, it is you."

She felt his nearness, heard his breathing.

"Look at me, Hester."

"I can't."

"Try. Please try."

What kept her from allowing him to see her eyes? All the shame of her past. The greedy, clutching self-loathing that choked her and tamped down her eyelids.

She felt his strong, calloused finger reach out and lift her chin. "Hester?" he whispered.

Tears squeezed through her closed eyes. She caught her lower lip in her teeth to suppress the emotion.

"What is it?" he whispered.

"I am not who you think I am."

"Who are you?"

Her eyes opened, revealing black, liquid pools of pain and uncertainty. She saw the tall, dark form, the black hair cut squarely across his forehead, falling below his ears at the side. She took in the blue of his eyes, the chiseled nose, the perfect mouth. "I ran. I ran away. I am with the English."

The disappointment that darkened his face was hard to watch, so she lowered her eyes.

"Why?" he grated.

"You remember the wedding?"

He nodded, eagerly.

"Annie didn't like me. It didn't work out."

"If I remember, I warned you."

"Yes."

Emma was walking toward them, her calling reaching their ears. For a long moment, he drank in the face kept alive in his memory, so much as he remembered, and yet so different. Fear clutched at his heart. Why had she left? What had she done?

Emma's short form was so unwelcome William King had to visibly rearrange his features to accommodate her breathless appearance. Fat little *gwunder* nose.

"Oh, oh, oh." Emma's voice made puffing sounds, like a small, fussy locomotive.

"Hester. Hester, my love."

Stopping, Emma looked from one face to another, her sharp eyes boring into the mask of impatience across William's, the raw despair in Hester's, a vulnerability that brought sharp words of rebuke to her small, red mouth. "Mister, you are upsetting Hester. You should not have run after her this way. She has been through an ordeal. Now you just go easy on her. I mean it."

His anger was ill disguised. It rippled along the muscles in his cheeks, turning the brilliant blue of his eyes a shade darker, an orange flame appearing only one second before evaporating. "Oh. I didn't mean to upset Hester. I am not aware that I did."

Oily words. Emma was quick with her tongue. "Then, I would suggest you leave her alone."

William drew himself up to a magnificent height, his eyelids falling to a level of condescension he was accustomed to exercising over his peers. He cleared his throat. "Hester and I have met before."

"Really?" Emma's tone was flat and as uncompromising as a stone wall.

Hester became agitated. A hand went to her throat. "William King and I met briefly at my father's wedding. He does not know my story."

"If you will please allow me to continue my conversation, perhaps she can tell me in her own words."

"Oh, no, she ain't. You want to talk to my Hester, you ask her if you can come calling, like any gentleman. And for now, we will be busy, too busy, in fact, to have you around."

Before he could reply, Billy popped out of the high grass, his gray hat pulled down so far he didn't appear to have a face, only an opened collar and a chin. "Hooo!" he yelled. "Frogs ain't easy to catch."

He tilted the grimy hat back out of his eyes, releasing a curtain of copper hair, sized up William with his blue eyes, and blurted, "Who're you?"

William's smile was genuine, his white teeth lighting up his face as he bent to extend his hand to Billy's, grasping it firmly with a solid shake.

"William King. Nice to meet you."

"You, too."

Billy wasn't used to meeting men—strangers—that were ten feet tall, he guessed. His hand felt as if it left the wrist it was attached to, but he figured it was still in working condition, once William King let go of it. Together they walked back to the house. William did most of the talking with Billy injecting his flow of words with boyish remarks.

Emma's face looked like a thundercloud, her eyes snapping blue sparks, her mouth a compressed down-turned slash of disapproval.

Hester walked beside William, making no sound except for the gentle swishing of her skirts in the unkempt grasses.

"Hey! You know we're gonna move out here? Oops!" Billy's hat slid off the back of his head when he lifted his face to watch William speak. He grabbed it off the moisture-laden grasses and clumped it back on his head, shoving it down hard with both hands, then jerking on both sides of the brim, enlarging the tear on the left side of the crown.

"We hafta move on account a Hester bein' a Injun. You know they killed 'em all now. Lancaster County don't have any Injuns no more."

"Good. You can't trust them."

Emma jerked her right shoulder, walked faster, but kept her peace.

"Yeah," Billy said, nodding his head rapidly, unsettling the loose hat once more. He grabbed it with his right hand, pulled it down over his ears, bobbed his head a few times to ensure a good fit, then walked solemnly ahead, digesting this new way of thinking about "them Injuns."

When they reached the house, Emma turned to William. "Good day."

William searched Hester's face but found only hidden eyes beneath lowered lashes. "I'll be on my way then. If you need help, I'll be available. My parents' house is only a few miles across these woods as the crow flies."

Hester lifted her eyes to watch his retreat. She thrilled to the set of the shoulders, the way he loped easily. Like a wolf, effortless.

Emma fumed and steamed, fussed and stewed, worrying herself to the point of hysteria. She told Hester that man was up to no good, and if she knew her place, she'd have nothing to do with him.

Billy said, "Why not, Ma?"

Hester watched the figure on the horse, a striking rider, disappear into the row of trees. Confusion rode uncomfortably on her shoulders.

Well, first things first. Saying nothing, she left Emma and Billy to their own little war of words, slipped through the front door, and assessed the damage, the things they'd need. She made a mental list, then returned to the front door, preparing to leave. They did need a man to help them, certainly. Walter Trout was a bit dubious with his weight and all.

But Walter proved to be a wonderful help. His face was covered by the wide brim of a straw hat, his thick red suspenders holding up the homespun kneebreeches very well, the clean linen shirt bunching over the top of them as he wielded a hammer, pulled a saw, swung an axe. He whistled, sang, or talked, one of the three, all day long. He could only be described as a jolly soul. Hester found him to be a storehouse of amusement. It rolled out of him the way spring water bubbled out of the ground. Spring water was like that. It you tried to stop it, it squirted out the side, stronger than ever.

The May sun was warm. It heated the house with its fresh, yellow light. Even the dust turned into specks of gold, floating through the air like bits of magic.

Hester's hair was covered in an old kerchief, her dress smudged and torn, the gray apron tied about her waist layered with the dust that clung to everything.

Walter's whistling was infectious. She began a tune of her own, low, a sort of humming of an old song Kate would sing to the children. She slapped at the low ceiling with her broom, dragging a net of cobwebs with it, blinking and sputtering as chips of old whitewash fell into her eyes.

Walter straightened from fixing a hinge on the front door. "Mercy, mercy, child! You're raising more dust than the cavalry marching through town."

Hester laughed, swinging her broom in his direction. "You want to do this?"

Walter's eyes twinkled at her, the good humor crinkling them like a fan closing until they were mere outlines with lashes. "Good to see you so happy, girl! Never saw you with a full-size laugh on your face."

Hester laughed again, which brought tears of joy to Walter's eyes. They repaired, swept, whitewashed, scoured floors, and scrubbed cupboards and closets all through the mellow month of May.

Sometimes William King would appear, his offers to help always met with Emma Ferree's icy denial, which riled Billy considerably. He genuinely liked William.

Hester wanted him to help but would not step over the boundaries her benefactor had placed for her. Emma was the authority in her life now, and she respected her requests.

William caught her alone, scouring the wide oak planks of the small upstairs. She was whistling softly, the hot water reddening her hands as she worked on the floor with a wooden scrubbing brush. She held completely still when he whispered her name.

"Hester."

"Yes, William?"

"Why did you leave the Amish in Berks County? That question haunts me, keeps me awake at night."

"It's a long story." Hester placed the brush in the bucket of water, sat back on the wooden floor, her knees tucked beneath her.

"Tell me. Please. Emma is outside."

"She doesn't like you."

"I know. I can't say that I care much for her, either."

"My story is long, a bit complicated. Annie was not a good companion, as you pointed out to me."

"Yes, we are in *die freundshaft*. There is a cruel streak," William said, saying the words slowly, as if he handpicked them with great caution.

"The situation became unbearable. She didn't like Indians."

"Well, I don't either. They're savage. Wild men that deserve to be pushed west where they can live their un-civilized lives, roaming the wilds like the heathens they are."

Hester drew a deep breath to steady herself. Every fiber of her being rebelled against his coarse speech. Was this the same William who held her hand beneath the Amish wedding table, made her heart beat, sent shiv-ers of joy sluicing through her veins? How could he say these things?

"I am an Indian." Her words were firm, the syllables deliberate, as if she cast them in stone and held them up for him to see.

"You may have been born one, but the Amish saved you from being a dirty heathen."

William watched her chest heave with the force of her emotion. He watched as one work-reddened hand went to her apron front to still the upheaval she felt. Her eyes became blacker still, widening with the force of her words.

"The Amish had nothing to do with saving me, as you say. Hans Zug and his wife Annie have clabbered my spirit like soured cream, poured me out to soak into the cracks of their parched Berks County earth, leaving nothing but a smelly odor in God's nostrils."

William shivered beneath the dark truth in her eyes.

CHAPTER 10

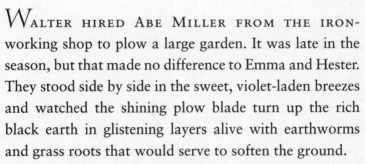

WALTER HIRED ABE MILLER FROM THE IRON-working shop to plow a large garden. It was late in the season, but that made no difference to Emma and Hester. They stood side by side in the sweet, violet-laden breezes and watched the shining plow blade turn up the rich black earth in glistening layers alive with earthworms and grass roots that would serve to soften the ground.

An Amish man by the name of Amos Speicher brought wagonloads of manure from his cowshed. Walter decided not to climb up on the wooden bed of the wooden-wheeled wagon because of his age. Emma rolled her eyes and held her hands in front of her own over-size stomach, making meaningful little dips with her eyebrows to show Hester it was his size, not his age.

Billy wrinkled his nose, but jumped right up and helped Amos fork the manure on to the harrowed ground. They dragged the harrow through the manure again and again, the sturdy Belgian plodding faithfully until they had a perfectly prepared plot of soil to raise the vegetables they'd need.

They placed onions into rows and sowed tiny carrot seeds in shallow trenches. They planted beans and then prepared poles for them to climb, once the bean shoots broke through the soil.

One morning Walter's face became an alarming shade of purple. He spent half the day with his straw hat tipped back, mopping his streaming head with a wrinkled, red handkerchief. Emma shook her head at his frequent lapses of effort, her own perspiration running freely down the side of her pink face. She swiped at it with the tip of her apron, discreetly, as if she could hide the fact that she did any sweating at all.

Hester heaped the good, loose soil over the seeds, her heart beating strong and sure, the love of the earth infusing her nostrils with a heady scent. She would search the surrounding forest and swamps for the plants in her memory—yarrow and licorice and comfrey, mullen, sorrel, and fennel. She worked ceaselessly, her bare brown feet treading the earth, her spirits soaring with the wings of an eagle.

Billy remembered nothing of living in the country before his life with Emma, but the small garden they dug by hand in the town of Lancaster had kept him occupied in spring. The house sat beneath two maple trees, squat and weather beaten, but as clean as a whistle, windows gleaming, floors smelling of fresh soap and lumber.

There was a front porch with a sagging roof that Walter had repaired, balancing his bulk on a seemingly inadequate ladder, until even Hester dreaded the approaching accident. Which, of course, never occurred. It was just his size, Walter said.

When moving day arrived, they hired the same man to drive and haul their possessions out to the homestead, still being careful about Hester's Indian blood. They left the china cupboard and some of the folderols they didn't need. The plank table and straight ladder-backed kitchen chairs fit so nicely by the fireplace, with shelves built along the low kitchen cupboard they brought, that Emma hopped up and down with excitement, spread a clean cloth on the table immediately, and brought out the *Schtick* she had painstakingly prepared for this long-anticipated day.

She sliced bread in substantial slices and spread them with pungent, yellow butter, freshly churned and packed into a small, shallow crock. She placed thick slices of salty ham on one slice of bread, topped it with more yellow butter and another slice of bread, then arranged the sandwiches on a pewter plate.

She fished hard-cooked eggs from the red beet brine that had turned them a delightful shade of red, placed them on a smaller plate with a salt shaker close by, a mound of pickled red beets among the eggs.

That done, she set out the square pan of gingerbread, the chilled bowl of clabbered cream to spoon on top, and the biggest treat of all, a sparkling jar of spiced peaches from Helen Denlinger, as a gift in appreciation of their Sunday dinner. It was very nice of Helen to present them with the peaches. Helen's gesture brought great relief to Emma, who had worried about Helen lapsing into heart failure, laced so excruciatingly into her corsets as she was during that Sunday dinner. Emma had given up trying to wear those torture devices as soon as she had snared Enos.

Now Emma poured hot tea into earthenware mugs and called Walter, Hester, and Billy to her table. Billy reminded her about the moving man and Amos Speicher, which sent her immediately to the door, yoo-hooing and making other ridiculous outbursts of sound, which served their purpose, bringing both men to the table.

Hester kept her eyes lowered but felt the curious eyes of both men on her face. Amos tried to engage her in conversation, which brought a quick look from the dark eyes, a nod of the head, but a minimum of words.

In the late afternoon, lazy, white smoke curled up over the stone chimney, the small cooking fire giving away its existence. The fresh white walls were clean and bright, the floors homey with bright rag rugs, the redware and pewter arranged on the shelves in straight sensible rows so they could be reached efficiently.

In the parlor, the corner cupboard stood sentry, a sturdy piece of furniture indispensable to their needs, holding anything from tablecloths and towels to buttons and thread. A few comfortable chairs, one armless, were pulled up to the window. A chest containing blankets and coverlets was pushed against the north wall.

The small bedroom along the back was Emma's. The sturdy wooden bedstead was loaded with a straw mattress and feather ticking on top. A tall handmade closet held her changes of clothes, high-topped shoes, and hats. Emma hung a serviceable white curtain across the window. You never knew, she said.

Billy shared the narrow attic with Hester. They strung a sheet of homespun cloth between them, down the middle of the room, for privacy. They set up a narrow rope bed on either side, plus a chest for Hester and a small wooden box for Billy. A window at each gable end let in sufficient light, but Hester knew the approaching summer would bring the stifling attic heat. First they learned to endure it, and then eventually accepted it as the summer days wore on.

Walter pronounced the reclaimed house and garden unbelievable. He praised Emma's work with lovely words of approval, holding his straw hat by the tips of his fingers, his freshly wiped head shining pink in the late- afternoon sun. Emma accepted his praise graciously, of course, but the thought ran through her mind that she'd probably like him so much better if he was not quite so pink. But then, bless the man, God had made him so. Or maybe not. All that eating was his own doing.

She remained unmoved about Walter Trout, being the stubborn, independent German that she was where men were concerned. Enos had won her heart, but it had taken him a while. Walter had always figured perhaps that was the reason for their childless state. Emma tended to be a bit brittle. Certainly not, though, to the poor and the suffering, the orphans and the destitute.

To Emma, men were an irritation, mostly. Take that William King. Now there was a winner. She'd as soon smack him as talk to him, with his making those sheep's eyes at Hester, his suave good looks, and a high-minded attitude that irked her every time he opened his mouth. But if Hester chose to allow him to court her, she'd have to let her go.

Walter rode home in the black buggy with the gold pinstripes, pulled by his fine, serviceable horse. He held the reins loosely in his pudgy fingers, his head bowed, the straw hat slightly askew, the breeze flapping up the front brim.

Emma Ferree was a hard worker who liked her things in order, but after all these days of labor (which had seemed but one sweet hour of devotion), she had not softened toward him at all. Ah, but wait. Had she made such a fine *schtick* for only hers and Hester's benefit?

He lifted one finger, holding it aloft, as he said out loud, "Now those were the finest, most hearty sandwiches I have ever come across." And who knew? Perhaps the peaches and the gingerbread and the pickled eggs were all prepared with him in mind. No, the battle to win Emma Ferree's heart was, indeed, not over.

Billy was milking the new brown Guernsey cow with Hester giving him instructions. In the adjoining stable, the brown mare gazed at them with her blue-brown eyes, the heavy black lashes blinking slowly as she watched. She was a small horse, but sufficient, Walter had told them, content to let them buy her from him at a low price.

Hester finished the milking. Billy stood nearby, flexing his fingers with overly exaggerated motions, his mouth open, his tongue hanging from it like a dog. "That hurts!"

Hester laughed. "I used to milk five cows at home."

"Don't see how you could!"

"You get used to it."

Hester straightened, then bent to retrieve the bucket brimming with frothy milk, when the soulful eyes of the brown cow caught sight of Billy's red hair. She kicked out with her right hoof, caught the edge of the wooden pail, and tilted it at an angle, spilling all of the good milk into the straw.

Hester shouted, but she was too late.

Billy yelled, then bent over double, howling with glee, slapping his legs over and over, as tears coursed out of his eyes.

The brown cow merely lifted her head, switched her tail from left to right a few times, before placing her cloven hoof in the center of the spilled milk.

Wiping his eyes, Billy chuckled the whole way to the house, walking beside Hester, who swung the empty pail by its handle.

They worked in the yard that evening, mowing the grass with a scythe, raking it with a wooden rake, and taking it to the barn for the animals.

They named the cow Flora, after Billy suggested Kicker or Thumper, laughing uproariously at his own cleverness. The horse they named Frieda. Emma said she'd always wanted a daughter named Frieda, meaning peace, but she'd never had a daughter until now, and she was already named Hester. She held Hester's hand warmly and thanked her for all the hard work she had done around the place.

Hester reminded her that they would not have had to move if she had not come to their house in town. Emma said it was high time Billy got away from that tavern. The coins he hoarded in the tin box weren't worth the danger he put himself in.

They slept in their clean, new beds that night, the windows opened to the sounds of night insects, the call of the owls, the whippoorwills, and the coyotes. A three-quarter slice of moon bathed the small house in the middle of the clearing in silvery shimmering light, casting black shadows on the north side and under the maple trees. The rectangular patch of newly planted garden needed a fence, but that would soon be done, Walter promised.

An opossum scuttled out from beneath the porch, poked its pointed snout into the ground, shoveled out a few onions, sniffed them, and let them alone. It moved to the barn, snuffling along the walls of the cow stable, its beady eyes taking in the night landscape, digging up tasty grubs along the back wall. Suddenly, it stopped. Like a stone, it held still, its nose twitching, then flattened itself against the wall of the shed.

A dark figure emerged from the woods, bent over, as if the person were aged or had an arthritic back. The person wasted no time in crossing the field, still crouched but running. The opossum stayed still, watching. The person straightened, flattening himself against the north side of the house where the shadows were thick and black.

The moon inched across the sky. A nighthawk screeched his unsettling call. The opossum stayed low against the wall of the shed, scuttled forward, stopped to listen, then disappeared into the thick grass. Still there was no movement from the deep shadow by the house.

In his sleep, Billy coughed softly. He groaned and stretched. The ropes beneath his straw mattress creaked in protest. Hester slept on, deep and dreamless.

They discovered a pear tree on the outskirts of the forest. Emma found wild raspberry bushes, then lamented her loss since the fruit had already been eaten by wild creatures.

"*Hembare! Oh, meine hembare!*" Over and over she wailed and groaned and recited the recipe for raspberry mush. They found *hulla* elderberries, but they were not quite the same.

Hester spent all her spare time in the garden. The onions popped out of the soil, succulent spears growing an inch every week. The wispy little tops of the carrots grew and sprouted like feather dusters, spreading their lacy tops across the fertile black soil. Red beets grew their tender green leaves, the red spines spread across them like blood veins. Emma cut the beets when they were new and heated them with butter and salt. They ate them with hard-cooked eggs and grated, cooked turnips.

Hester was in the garden one hot summer day as the afternoon sun was beginning to slide down the bowl of hot, quivering sky. Her hair was a mess, she was overheated, sticky, and a bit disgruntled at Billy's refusal to weed. Emma was too easy on him. She grabbed a stubborn dandelion and yanked, breaking off the root with the snap she knew too well, threw it aside with disgust, and stamped her foot impatiently.

A low laugh behind her made her jump. She whirled around, hating to be caught unaware. She always had thoroughly disliked the feeling of being exposed when she should have been able to discern the slightest movement.

It was William King. She watched him warily. She felt light-headed now, the way her pulse fluttered at the base of her neck.

"You don't like dandelions?"

She did not smile, just shook her head no, evasive, mistrustful.

"Why do you dislike me? Am I like the dandelion? A weed that threatens to take over your well-organized life?"

"I don't dislike you."

"Is it Emma?"

"No."

"What is it, Hester?"

"It's nothing."

"I have asked my father permission to court you."

"You didn't ask mine."

"May I come see you on Sunday evening?"

The toe of her right foot shoved into the loose soil. Her head was bent to watch the earth fall away from her toe's movement. "I don't know."

"What kind of answer is that?"

"Exactly what I said. I am not sure."

"My father said no."

"So why are you asking?"

"Hester, I have passed my thirtieth year. It is time I think of taking a wife."

"But if your father said no?"

"I'm past the age where he can dictate my choices."

Hester nodded.

"May I come see you?"

His voice was warm, eager, kind. His face was open and earnest, his black hair falling on either side, his obedience to the *Ordnung* so evident.

Hester's future stretched before her, an undulating plain of doubt, the road disappearing into a pit of fear and despair. With William, she could find happiness, she believed. They would take their time as they allowed the Amish community to accept their union. But did she truly want to go back?

"Yes."

Stepping forward, he caught her hands and held them to his chest. His blue eyes shone with the intensity of his feelings.

"Thank you, Hester. At last, I can say those words."

She smiled, a fluttering, shifting, stretch of her lips.

"I'll tell Emma. Do you want to come with me?"

She shook her head.

He walked off with an easy, loping gait, swung himself up on the porch, and rapped eagerly on the door. Hester watched as the doors swung inward and the stout form of Emma stepped aside. William bowed slightly, then began to talk. Emma's gaze hung over Hester like a two-edged sword, the way God's Word was described in the Bible. She felt as if Emma could see into her very soul and know her past. The part for which she was to blame.

Hans might never have had those thoughts and intents if she had been smarter. A dumb Indian. How often had she heard those words? She was dumb. As *Schtump* as a rock. She found the German language difficult, but English was like climbing a chalk cliff. And here she was, chasing dumbly after William King.

As she thought, Emma moped about the house, then unleashed a fury of words against William King, hurling them into the air so that they smacked against the walls and the sides of Hester's head.

Emma held her head and rocked back and forth, then cried copiously into her wide, white apron, spluttering and sniffing and saying it was all because she loved Hester more than she knew and she was so afraid she'd be mistreated by the Amish people. She didn't know these Amish from Adam, and she'd been in a bad situation before. What was Hester thinking?

"*Oh, du yay. Hester, du yay. Mein Kind.*"

A part of Hester wanted to obey Emma's dire warnings. But to live her life here for the rest of her days, never having experienced marriage or having someone close to her heart, without spending life together with a family, was unthinkable as well.

"Emma, I am not getting married now. I promise to spend only one Sunday evening with him. Only one. If I feel he is not the right man for me, I will end it then. I will."

Through her tears, Emma nodded her head, the chin wobbling, her cheeks wet with fresh pathways of more tears before wiping her face with a white handkerchief.

Billy stuck his head in the door and left again, shaking his head and muttering dire predictions about all women.

By August, the heat lay so heavy over Lancaster County that the cows stood in any available waterhole to cool themselves down. Heatwaves shimmered across the hot earth, pressed down on one's shoulders like a wooden yoke, causing Emma to sit gasping for air, her mouth opening and closing like a bluegill as she waved her apron in front of her face.

She sat on an upturned bucket, although very little of it was visible, beneath the still leaves of the maple tree. The air was thick and brassy. The bees' droning sounded tired, drained of energy: the cicadas clung to tree bark as they gasped for breath themselves.

"Hester! Get out of that garden!" It took all the reserve energy Emma could muster to raise her voice loud enough to yell.

"Why?"

"It's too hot."

Hester laughed the sound of a rippling brook, her white teeth flashing in her dark face. She laid down her hoe, lifted her head, and came toward the maple tree. Tall and little, she moved without sound, effortless, her Indian blood enabling her to travel great distances without tiring. Emma never got weary of watching her daughter's graceful, fluid movement.

Hester threw herself into the grass at Emma's feet. "I love the garden, Emma."

"If you stay out there, you'll melt like a lump of butter."

"No."

"I wish I had a springhouse."

"Oh, you should have seen ours in Berks County." Hester's eyes lit up with enthusiasm as she launched into a vivid account of the wet, cool, dripping stone house Hans had built so cleverly over the cold mountain spring water.

Emma watched Hester's face shrewdly, observing the animation. Did Hester miss her home so much? Obviously, there were good memories. There was a time when Hester had been happy, innocent, content.

"And my brothers? Remember I told you about Noah and Isaac? They loved to drag a bucket into the cold spring water, run ahead of me on the path I was on, quickly climb a tree, and then dump the cold water all over me."

Hester laughed at the thought, then became closed, pensive.

William had taken her to view the Amish community in Lancaster. They rode in his well-made wagon that was comfortable enough for a drive in the warm winds of

July. She had been intrigued by the Amish in this area, and interested, but in a halfhearted way, as if she were tasting soup and one important ingredient had been left out, but she didn't care enough to figure out what it was.

The farms were prospering, carved out of the woodland by swinging axes that bit into trees that were sacred to the Indians. They thought that a tree belonged to the Creator and not to any particular person. They couldn't conceive of owning tracts of land since all the land belonged to the Creator as well.

When the white men came and tried to impose their views, many of these peaceful, roaming tribes became furious, marauding in their defense without mercy.

Yes, she told William, the Amish and Mennonite settlers were amazing. They had a fierce work ethic. Like Hans, they thrived on hard, physical labor. Their goals were to make money, expand, get ahead.

They argued that time. He did not back down but kept his attitude, resolutely holding it within himself by the set of his jaw, the sparkle in his blue eyes a glint of determination.

She felt his superiority—and her inferiority and inefficiency. Her way of thinking lay fallow. It was dead, old.

He had what it would take to get this country going. It was called forging ahead.

CHAPTER 11

THAT LANCASTER COUNTY LAY DIRECTLY ON UN-usually fertile soil was evident in the growth of its crops. Its forests were also thick and green and dense, the oaks growing to majestic towers, their thick branches bearing a canopy of leaves so heavy it was like a roof.

Amish men cleared the land by the sweat of their brows, side by side with the Mennonites, the Dunkards, and the Quakers, to name several of the "plain" denominations who had settled in the area.

There were Scots, Irish, and English, too, many of them Roman Catholic. Churches sprang up in the town of Lancaster to accommodate the influx of people seeking to make a living on these fertile grounds and needing spiritual sustenance as well.

All her life as a child in Berks County, Hester had been used to attending services in Amish homes, with a simple meal served afterward. It had seemed odd to skip religious services on Sunday after she came to live with Emma. But because she was afraid to show her face in Emma's church, she simply did not attend any services.

She often thought about her childhood, riding to church in the wagon with her siblings. Hans would be practicing his songs, the way he always did, with Kate sitting soft and wide beside him, clutching yet another little one on her lap, the large hat pulled well forward past her pleasant face.

Going to church was a warm and comfortable ritual, like porridge for breakfast. There was an order to Sunday mornings that began with getting up from her bed in the chilly darkness. Kate would stand so close that Hester could feel her warm breath on the top of her head as she drew the heavy-toothed comb through the snarls in her thick, black hair, pulling it so tight her eyes felt slanted, like she was from Asia. She had once seen pictures of the Chinese with wide, flat eyes in a book that Theodore Crane, the old schoolteacher, had. In fact, she told Kate that her hair was so tight she was going to turn into an Asian. Kate's soft, rounded stomach had shaken up and down as she laughed quietly, then she'd held her head against Hester's for an instant, and said, "Ach, my dear daughter."

That she was loved was never a question. Love had been in abundance in that narrow little log house. It bubbled from rocks in the spring and hovered over the steaming bowls of oatmeal and corn and beans that Kate set on the table. Love was everywhere—in the sky and the birds and the distant mountains, the sights that made her heart swell and swell until she had to laugh or cry, she felt so much love. She missed it all now.

She sat on a chair she had carried outside, the rough, wide boards covered with a cushion, her bare feet hooked on one of the rungs. Already it was hot as the morning sun climbed into the bold, glaring sky. It was too humid to call the sky blue. Instead, it was white all over, shimmering with heat supplied by the orange sun.

In the pasture, the cow stood beneath an oak tree, her tail swishing endlessly back and forth, dislodging troublesome black flies that made her life a misery. The horse, Frieda, stamped a front foot, then a hind one, swishing her tail in the same steady rhythm as the cow's. Their heads drooped, as if they already had prepared themselves for the heat of the day.

Billy was off somewhere in the woods. Hester knew fishing was forbidden on the Sabbath, so Emma made sure he did not sneak off with his fishing pole. But Hester was almost sure that if she went to the barn to check, the pole wouldn't be there. She smiled.

Emma was inside taking her after-breakfast-Sunday-morning nap, her bare feet turned up, her ample hands crossed over her stomach, her breaths coming with quick, soft regularity. Her opened Bible lay beside her, a tribute to her Sabbath day's devotion.

Hester had read portions of her own Bible as well, but nothing seemed to satisfy her longing for a deeper knowledge of God's will. She skipped over verses, paging through the Old Testament and then the New. She read the words of Jesus but felt no sense of wonderment. Maybe she was too lethargic to be able to sustain her spiritual body, as if the heat and humidity stifled her desire to learn about God.

She reasoned and thought on these things. As she had been raised Amish, the days in her weeks were repetitive, an order to each one. Her clothes portrayed the *Ord-nung* or rules for living, agreed to by the Amish community. Her cap was a sign of meekness, symbolizing a subservient attitude toward the men in her life—Hans, her father, and if she should marry, her husband.

She had stopped wearing her cap. Her hair was now her glory, as the Bible said. Thick and black, it was so straight it resisted combs and hairpins, shining and so glossy it appeared to shimmer with blue. The feeling of being half-dressed had disappeared after a few months, until she felt no need to wear something on her head.

William had brought up the subject recently, allowing a sliver of guilt into her conscience. He told her God would not hear her prayers unless her head was covered, since she was a member of the Amish. She had promised to live, stay, and follow Jesus in that church, so who did she think she was?

Instantly, rebellion had raised its head, a hooded cobra ready to strike. Angry words filled her mouth, ready to fly forth. Her heart beat heavily, but at the final instant, she bit them back, her mouth wide, compressed.

She believed William wanted to marry her someday. Why would he be courting her otherwise? Yes, she thrilled to see him, but it was troubling, the instant, all-consuming resistance that rose in her when he spoke of so many things—the *Ordnung*, the Indians, Emma Ferree, almost everything.

Maybe the devil had control of her thoughts now that she had made a stand against Hans and Annie. Perhaps that had all been wrong. Should she have stayed and remained a true and honorable servant all her life? For now she was of the world. She was worldly. It was hard to always know if you were doing the right thing.

Had she picked up the heathen ways of the Indians, as William had said? But they were not heathen. They weren't. Would she say one thing and mean another all her life?

Oh, she'd stood up to William when his voice brought the usual uprising, the resistance that filled her. She'd told him how she felt about Hans and Annie. But what did she really believe about them, and what was right for her to do?

She leaned forward and dropped her dark head in her hands. She felt as if she were being torn in two directions. Two sides were pulling her in opposite ways, upsetting the peace and stability of her life with Emma and Billy.

She heard a sound that was not birdsong. It was a bit liquid and trilling, like the sound of birds, but. . . . Wait a minute.

Up came her head. She held so still she seemed built into the chair. Unmistakably, the whistle held a tune. Lightly, but it was there.

Now she heard the chirring of a gray squirrel, the call of the meadowlark she could see plainly, perched on the rail fence.

There it was again. Someone, somewhere, was whistling. Rapt, she remained seated, her senses keen, expecting the whistling to come closer. Instead, it faded away, leaving her feeling deprived, as if a wonder had occurred but been taken away before she could grasp it.

The feeling of melancholy, a lowering of her spirits, remained the rest of the day, until she realized it was almost time to prepare for William's visit.

Emma made no pretense about hiding her displeasure. She told Hester outright that she had no time for William King, but if she insisted on letting him court her, then she would stay out of the way.

Hester eyed Emma from her place at the oval mirror above the washstand, small and round as she was, her face beet-red with indignation, bristling with disapproval and something else. She wound her hair into a loose twist, held it fast with sturdy pins and combs, then turned to Emma, her eyes large and dark. She had no idea how beautiful she was, how pure and unspoiled, a magnolia in the midst of dandelions, Emma mused.

"Why do you dislike William so?" Hester asked breathlessly.

"I just do."

"I'm sorry if you feel bad about me spending the evening with him, but just let me try, all right?"

Emma's answer was a significant whoosh of forced air through her nostrils, a sharp turning on her heel, with her wide back floating across the room and out the front door, leaving the room empty of a spoken statement.

Hester felt as if she were violating Emma's goodness of heart. How could she be so set in her mind? Emma was the angelic figure who rescued poor children, wet dogs, and injured cats, who handed out food and money to dubious bedraggled recipients, who, more than likely, were not worthy of her generosity, spending it on cheap apple whiskey or frittering it away on senseless sins of a different nature.

William arrived in his shining wagon, the lap robe tucked beneath the seat, the horse black, his neck arched and his tail flowing, pawing the ground impatiently. Hester's heart fluttered as if a canary were caged inside her chest. A high song of happiness propelled her down the steps and out through the short grass surrounding the house.

His eyes found hers and stayed on them. He drank in the caramel color of her fine glowing skin, the black liquid stars that were her eyes, and vowed to himself that he would make her his wife. He would rescue her from the heathen nature of her origin and pull her out of the quicksand Emma Ferree had set for her.

Love beat strongly in his breast. He marveled that God allowed this wonderful creature, this child of sweetness and innocence, into his life. That outburst about Hans and Annie had all been Emma Ferree's poison, not Hester's own thinking.

Secure in the knowledge of his own intelligence, William lifted the reins, and they were off in a cloud of heat and dust. Behind them, a florid, sweating face peered around the corner of the brown house, and an arm was flung angrily in their direction. Her small feet carried Emma into the house, where she cut herself a wide wedge of custard pie, followed by another as large as the first, before she looked at the clock and wondered where that Billy was. It was getting late.

The wagon wheels made very little sound as they followed the country road away from the house. The magnificent horse trotted smoothly, its black mane flowing in the breeze. William's hands were strong and brown, with long, thick fingers holding the reins easily, skilled at the art of driving a fine horse. His profile was so handsome, his yellow straw hat set square and low on his forehead, the way she remembered Hans's.

He was kind and attentive, pointing out the Amish farms that dotted the cleared fields. The farm belonging to his parents, Elias and Frances King, had a stone house so much like her own in Berks County that she gasped. It was almost identical, including the grayish color of the limestone.

The windows were few, tall, and paned with many separate pieces of glass. The wooden sashes could be raised and lowered, allowing for breezes when the weather was warm and protection against cold winds and snow. The barn was built along the side of a hill, allowing easy access to the second floor. The animals were housed snugly against winter's frigid winds on the first floor. A vast orchard lay to the south, with apple and peach and cherry trees, sentinels of hard work and excellent management skills. The corn was tall and heavy, a deep green color that spoke well of Elias King's farming know-how. Hester imagined the hayloft bursting with mounds of loose hay and straw, the corncrib full.

Her heart beat firmly and steadily. Here in this fertile soil was her destiny. Here she could work tirelessly side by side with her handsome William. Finally she would be free of the creeping certainty that she was no one, always hunted because of the color of her skin. The Amish were held in high esteem, hard workers that tilled the land, and she would be one of them.

If William King wanted her for his wife, the Amish would come to accept her in time. She would prepare herself for the ridicule, which was as sure to come as rain. It was the nature of men, just as certain as the changing of seasons or the lightning that occurred by the powers of God. But she would belong. She would etch out a place for herself as William King's wife. Respect and honor would follow.

She would bake the lightest bread and the sweetest pies. Her garden would yield vast quantities of vegetables, enough to share with the neighbors. Like Kate's, the wooden cradle would always hold an infant.

Hester glanced sideways at William, noticing the neat angle of his nose, the perfect jaw, the set of his mouth.

"Here, Hester, is what I will inherit." William waved a hand in the general direction of his parents' farm. Hester's large eyes were round with awe.

"Of course, my father and mother will live in the *doddyhaus* on the same yard, but I believe, in time, my mother will come to accept you. She can teach you how to work."

"I know how to work. I was taught first by Kate, then by Annie. I doubt very much whether your mother knows more than I do."

"Oh, ho! The voice of inexperience, Hester! My mother is held in high esteem all through the valley. She is unequalled in just about every housekeeping skill. She makes her own *ponhaus* at butchering time, saying no one else's is fit." William laughed, a superior sound of exulting that eclipsed Hester's happiness and her plans for the future, turning her awe of the beautiful farm to a gray hue of uncertainty. Hester fell silent after that laugh.

William told her he would not introduce her to his parents just yet, adding that it would be nice if he had a magic potion that would turn her skin white like his.

Hester smiled, but it was a mere lifting of the corners of her mouth, a small, trembling mock of gaiety.

He stopped the horse by a tumbling brook, then turned to her in the glow of the evening light beneath a canopy of green leaves that made a soft rustling sound, as if they were settling themselves for the night. Somewhere a robin set up a short, raucous bedtime call, gathering her fledglings in. He let the reins dangle at his feet after loosening the horse's neck rein, allowing him to lower his head and pull at the thick green grass.

"Hester, I have loved you since I first saw you, so shy, so set apart among a group of girls at that wedding. I have never forgotten you. You have remained in my heart and in my mind. It is only by God's grace that he allowed you back into my life. I know this is very soon, but I hope to marry you by November."

"But." Hester was completely taken aback.

William held up a hand. "No, don't protest. I know I'm moving too fast. I love you, Hester. My love for you is a beacon of hope I carry in my heart. I want you for my wife. My mother needs to have me marry now."

Suddenly she was caught in his arms, held against him in a viselike grip. Clumsily, his lips sought hers, then found them. Hester had never been kissed. It was so sudden, so powerful. She had no time to resist, to attempt to loosen herself from his grip.

When she thought perhaps she would suffocate after all, he released her just as suddenly. His eyes shone with a new and triumphant light as he reached for the reins.

Hester wrapped her arms around her waist as if to steady the quivering in her stomach. So this is how it was. No one had ever told her. It was bearable. There were worse things. To belong, she could endure being kissed, held in that painful grip. It was good to feel as if she belonged.

Again William turned to her. "I love you, Hester. Will you marry me?"

Hester nodded. "I will."

Later, she remembered that she had not said she loved him. Or that he had not thanked her for accepting his offer of marriage. She did love him, she reasoned. Enough to marry him.

She spent her days without telling anyone of William's proposal. Emma clucked and worried when she left her soft-boiled egg beside the toasted bread at breakfast, then ate every morsel after Hester went to do the washing.

Billy started back to school that week, an unhappy red face spouting many bitter words of resistance beneath his new, scratchy straw hat with a decorative red band that matched the stiff collar on his starched new shirt. His riotous red curls were cut and plastered into subjection with hard strokes of wet palms against his head. Emma's threats to bring in a nice slab of wood from the woodpile were mere whistles above his furious little face.

Billy told Hester he was going to run away. He'd stay in the woods with the crickets and katydids like she had. Then he walked stiff-legged with fury the whole way out the lane—a grassy dent called a lane—turning right toward the schoolhouse two miles away, swinging his lunch pail angrily at a passing sparrow.

Emma chuckled and chuckled at her Billy. What a display! Like a bantam rooster, he was. *Ach, du yay,* she thought, shaking her head. Yes, and what good did school do for a bright boy like him? Why he made as much money down at that livery stable as some grown men. He was smart, her Billy. His brain was as quick as a whip. Oh, he'd grow into a fine man, but he needed schooling. It was the order, the discipline, that did him good.

All that week, every morning, she wet down his short red hair, packed his lunch pail with bread and butter, ham and cheese, stewed apples, and crumbly sugar-sprinkled cookies made with molasses. And every morning he stomped around like some dangerous little man, vowing to run away, making Emma chuckle and laugh, her round stomach jiggling with her efforts to restrain it.

When Emma served platters of beans with chunks of pork, roasted cabbage, and fresh mint tea, and Hester only picked at a few beans, Emma finished her third helping of roasted cabbage, wiped her mouth with the back of the tablecloth, sipped her mint tea, and turned to Hester. "Now, Hester dear, you're going to have to tell me what's wrong. You can't hide it. Tell me."

Silence hung between them, a curtain of irritation for Emma, a necessity for Hester, as she desperately searched for the courage to explain what was going on.

"I'm being married to William. In the winter. In November." Her voice was weak and whispery, but they were words, and Emma heard each one correctly.

"But, you can't!" she burst out immediately.

"He loves . . . me. He said so. He wants me for his wife."

"*Mein Gott. Oh, mein Gott. Oh, du yay, du yay.*" Up went the apron over her face as she rocked from side to side. "*Gook do runna, Mein Herr und Vater.*" Praying aloud in German, she beseeched her heavenly father to look down on Hester.

"Why? Oh, why?" Lamenting and exclaiming, perspiration forming rivulets of moisture down the side of her wide forehead, she rocked back and forth, as if Hester's announcement were too much for her rounded shoulders to bear.

"I told you, Emma. He loves me. He is taking me to live on his farm with his parents."

"Do you love him?"

"Yes." Firmly the word sealed her future. Surely now she would return to the fold and be welcomed with open arms, her life full and running over with purpose and belonging.

She would be exactly like Kate. Laughing, telling stories, her children about her like jewels, each one more precious than the last. William would love her as Hans had loved Kate. She would win Frances's love. She thought of Hans's mother, the abrasive Rebecca, who, like a stiff brush, had hurt Kate. But, that, too, would be the price she would pay. In exchange she would experience a great and wonderful sense of belonging.

Emma remained unconvinced that Hester could ever be accepted into William's family—and she said so. Not willing to hear Emma's tirade of words, Hester thought back to William's kiss. Was that how it was? She almost asked Emma, but she didn't want to listen to more agonized wails of wrongdoing.

Perhaps the tenderness would come later, like the way Hans would slip an arm around Kate's soft waist or whisper a word in her ear, making her face light up with happiness. No one had ever given her the slightest sense of romantic notions. Hans's tortured eyes and touch had been swept beneath the rug of denial now, where they belonged. It was nothing. It never had been. Whatever little bit that occurred had been all her own fault.

William would be like Hans was with Kate, filling the stone house to capacity with love. You couldn't separate love and belonging.

"Hester, you don't have to look for a place to belong. You belong here. With me and Billy." Emma began to cry, real sorrow running from her eyes so nearly lost in the folds of her round face.

Billy put up an awful fuss. He said William King was all right, he guessed, but not as her husband. She didn't need a husband as long as him and Ma were around, and besides, once he grew up, *he* was going to marry her. Which started Emma on another round of sorrow mixed with laughter, until her voice rose to a squeaky pitch and she became a bit hysterical, which served to turn her face into a purple color that stayed all evening.

Hester remained unmoved, stoic, steadfast. William talked to his parents and to Joel Stoltzfus, the bishop of the Lancaster County Amish congregation, who called a secret meeting with his *mit dienner*, and then met with John Lantz and his group of ministers, who said yes to the marriage. Hester grew up in Berks County, John confirmed, but why she suddenly ran away from her Christian home and joined the worldly people in the town of Lancaster they would never know. Hans and Annie Zug were prominent members of their district. They must be told that Hester had been found.

The leaders set about doing this, arriving late one evening at the Zug home to share this news. On the way home, Rufus Troyer told Amos Fisher that according to their beliefs, shunning Hester was right when she lived in the world—but why was Hans refusing to have anything to do with her now, when he should be wanting her to return to the fold?

Amos Fisher said likely Annie had something to do with it. What he didn't say is how he noticed blood draining from Hans's face. Something was a little mysterious there. Something you did not talk about.

Rufus said, yes, no wonder Noah went off to the war.

CHAPTER 12

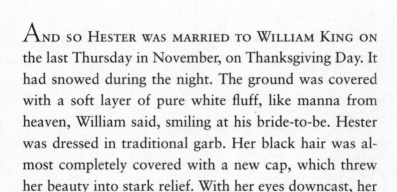

A ND SO HESTER WAS MARRIED TO WILLIAM KING ON
the last Thursday in November, on Thanksgiving Day. It
had snowed during the night. The ground was covered
with a soft layer of pure white fluff, like manna from
heaven, William said, smiling at his bride-to-be. Hester
was dressed in traditional garb. Her black hair was almost completely covered with a new cap, which threw
her beauty into stark relief. With her eyes downcast, her
mouth so soft and vulnerable, her whole demeanor one
of subjection, she fit the bill perfectly for Frances King
and her plans for her son.

The stone house was filled to capacity, the benches
set in long lines in rooms cleared of furniture. This was a
wedding, so everything that couldn't be sat on had to go.
The preparation had been a work of many hands.

Emma Ferree threw her hands in the air and said she
was having no part of this. She asked Walter Trout for
a group of helpers so she could move back to her house
on Mulberry Street in short order before winter came on.

She did not approve of William King and let everyone within earshot hear her opinion.

She went right back to Mulberry Street and began to minister to the poor. Billy went back to the livery stable and began collecting coins in his tin box. He found a straggly little terrier he named Hester, who lived beside the fireplace on a cushion, shivering with fright for weeks after they took her in. But they never quite got over the disappointment of losing Hester the young woman to William King.

The Kings' Amish neighbors gathered their cabbage and beans, beheaded their fat chickens, baked wedding cakes and pies and cookies, cleaned the house at Amos Speichers', and had a wedding.

Susie Fisher, a single woman, did the sewing for Hester. She had always hoped William King would ask for her hand, but had given up on that, seeing as she had already turned thirty. She liked *sell Indian maedle* and wished them the best. She measured and pinned, talking all the while in rapid Pennsylvania Dutch, exclaiming about Hester's dark hair and her skin.

Hester sat at her wedding table in the traditional corner with William's brothers and cousins as part of the bridal party. William ate great quantities of the festive wedding food from the fine china plates he had given Hester to be used on their wedding day.

He could not take his eyes off his lovely bride, a fact that was duly noticed by his mother, a keenly obser-vant woman, tall and spare, with the same loping ease of movement as her son. Good. That bode well for the future.

William's five sisters had all married before him and were quite happy to finally have him married off, even if it was to an Indian. They had been afraid he'd run off with an Englisher yet.

Hester's eyes shone with happiness—the excitement of the day, the headiness of being the center of attention. In a few months' time she had gone from being a refugee and living in the country away from prying eyes, to becoming a young wife of a handsome, older Amish *rumshpringa*, a youth who was overdue for a wife.

Far into the night, the wedding guests sang old German hymns, passed food and drink, and ate with great relish. Over and over again Hester and William shook hands with friends and family, accepted their blessings, and acknowledged their kind words and good wishes. Their wedding gifts were substantial, but then, everyone knew this poor Indian girl had no wooden hope chest piled with bedding and linens, towels, and other necessary items stored away for this day, the way other Amish girls did.

Hester was taken to the stone farmhouse and made her home there. William's parents were housed securely *ins ana end*, literally, "the other end," the phrase meaning, the apartment built on for the older folks on the homestead.

So many things reminded her of her home in Berks County. The hearth for cooking, the way the washing and cleaning were done—everything she had been taught came tumbling back.

With sturdy arms, she washed the whites to a shining clean that was almost blue. Her mother-in-law's approval rang in her ears like bells of much-needed esteem. She reveled in William's praise of her meals as well, as she turned out succulent roast beef, fluffy mashed potatoes, crisp corn mush, and creamy porridge.

She sewed carefully and scrubbed floors with speedy precision. She was accepted by William's family, which gave her the prestige she needed to be received well by the remainder of the congregation.

Two years went by. The wooden cradle stayed upstairs beneath the eaves, a beautifully carved work done by William's own hand. Often Hester would climb the stairs when William was in the fields. Today the weather was dreary, the rainwater running in rivulets down the mossy oak shingles. It dripped off the edge and splattered at the base of the house, creating thin indentations in the grass, soaking the scattered brown leaves and the acorns.

Hester shivered from the chilly dampness of the upstairs. She wrapped the thin shawl around her shoulders before reaching for the cradle. She dusted it with the tips of her fingers, then rocked it gently with her right hand. She prayed in broken whispers. She pleaded for the blessing of a child. She thought of Hannah in the Old Testament at the temple, lamenting for a child until onlookers thought she was drunk. Ah, poor woman.

As Hester threw herself on the unforgiving oak boards, sobs wracked her shoulders. No one could see or hear her. No one. "Let the rain pound the shingles. Let the water slide down the side of the roof. My tears will be like the rain," she said aloud to herself. For William and his mother and father were running out of patience. Their *gaduld* was wearing thin.

She often thought of Kate. If only she could have one conversation with her to ask her what had happened so that she was able to have children. Her table was filled, her heart and hands busy with the hundreds of duties of love that had brought so much enrichment to Kate's life.

Perhaps, Hester thought, it was her fault. William loved her well, but he never understood her shrinking away, her inability to welcome his ardor. She had finally admitted to herself that his kisses were an onslaught. It was a long time before she acknowledged the warnings of Emma Ferree.

But she was William's wife, and she loved him as best she could. She endured bravely, nodding her head in agreeable perplexity to William's question about her inability to conceive and answering Frances King's impertinent questions honestly.

Lying on the wooden floor, she cried until her spirit felt battered and brittle, as if it could easily break into thousands of pieces. Then she was finished. She got to her knees, folded her hands in supplication, and asked God to bless her one last time, before pushing the wooden cradle back under the eaves and making her way slowly down to the kitchen, where she dried her eyes, washed her face, and put on a bright smile for William's evening meal.

How she longed for him to fold her into his arms tenderly, carefully, whispering words of love and assurance. But that was not William's way.

Hester knew he had too much to do. He needed to hire a *Knecht*, a youth to help with the milking and the harvest, but he felt it was money unwisely spent. He often wolfed down his supper, barely noticing what he ate.

Tonight, though, it was raining, which allowed him some free time in the barn, repairing a harness and cleaning stables, jobs that had been pushed back during the harvest. Hester had prepared a special dish, the one he favored above all the hearty meals she set on the snowy white tablecloth. Lima beans and potatoes cooked together with milk and butter and a generous douse of black pepper, thickened to a creamy consistency, served with fried chicken and applesauce.

Before every meal he washed, combed his thick black hair, and then sat down at the sturdy plank table full of Hester's cooking. They bowed their heads. His lips moved in silent prayer. He raised his head, filled a plate, handed the dish to Hester, then served himself, usually without speaking, his thoughts on the cattle, the crops, or some other important matter. He would lower his head and shovel the food into his mouth, clearly hungry and sometimes ravenous. Hester learned to eat in silence, knowing he would talk later.

"The cake all gone?"

Hester nodded, her dark eyes lifted to his.

"You haven't had time to make another one?"

She spooned applesauce into her mouth. Swallowed. "Yes, I had time but thought perhaps I should spin wool upstairs."

"Upstairs? You go up there to moon about that cradle, working yourself into a frenzy about being childless. That's what Mother says."

Hester's eyes were black with rebellion when she raised them to his blue, mocking, appraising eyes. Her performance fell short. Unable to fill that cradle, she left William's quiver empty for the whole of Lancaster County to see.

"Hester, you need to read your Bible more. Get yourself in the *Ordnung* better. I see your cap tied loosely, your hair just a bit more worldly than I would like. You know God cannot bless us if we are inclined to rebel against the laws of the church."

"But I wasn't aware that I do!" Hester cried out.

"Oh, but you do. It's the Indian in you."

If William would have reached out and delivered a resounding blow to her face, it would have hurt less.

"The Indian in you." Always, she carried that flaw like a monstrous growth, a defect.

William got up, pushed his chair across the wide oak boards, and stood by the fire, chewing on a sliver of wood, his blue eyes waiting for her response.

When there was none, he watched her rake dishes off the table and carry them to the dry sink. To her back, he said, "Mother says to try pervinca."

Hester stopped washing dishes. As still as a stone, she stood facing the wall. When she turned, William flinched against the sizzle in the black depth of her eyes. "'Mother says. Mother says.' William, I am your wife. For over two years, I have been your wife. I bow to your wishes, as well as your mother's, which is my rightful place. But when you hurl insults, I do not feel it is my duty to keep bowing beneath them. Has not *Unser Herr* instructed us in the way of marriage? Should you not love your wife?"

"*Schtill!*" William's command was powerful. His voice rang out harshly as he flung the toothpick into the crackling fire. Two steps—long and deliberate—and his hand snaked out and spun her around to face him.

Lowering his face, his breath hot, he rasped, the words slow and methodic, branding into her conscience. "God has ordained from the beginning that your will is subject to mine. I am the head of the house. What I say is truth. You are to think as your husband. Your will is gone now. You are my wife."

Up came Hester's face, her eyes blazing. "Then you need to love me, William!"

"I do love you, Hester. I love you more than you know. But you are disappointing me in more ways than one."

As you are failing me, Hester thought.

"I do not believe pervinca has much to do with my needs. I have a storehouse of knowledge about herbs. When I was younger, I had the good fortune to meet an old Indian woman who wrote many cures for all kind of diseases in a book."

"Indians have no written language."

"She learned from Theodore Crane, the schoolmaster in Berks County."

"So you're saying you know more than Mother and I?"

Hester drew herself up, clasping her hands behind her back. "Yes. I believe I do." One eyebrow was lifted as William emitted a short, contemptuous laugh.

"I highly doubt it."

Hester returned to her dishwashing, the set of her shoulders giving away the fury that raged in her breast. She knew that continuing this conversation would prove futile. She would sin, pushing her words onto her husband, where they would only slide away from his hearing and disintegrate into the floor, contributing nothing to either one of them.

Frances dried and pounded the herb called pervinca, mixed it with whiskey, and brought it to Hester a few days later. Hester was folding wash. The sun shone through the small windowpanes, providing the light she needed to smooth out William's clean shirts before expertly folding the homespun fabric.

Today, there was a lightness in her heart, a song on her lips. The golden light streaming through the window, the November chill removed by the glowing fire, the dull gleam of the cupboard with the white agate pitcher containing sprigs of orange bittersweet, the white ironstone plates stacked neatly on the shelves above it all, pleased Hester, providing beauty and a sense of accomplishment. Imperfect she may be, but she was William's wife.

Frances never knocked on the door, saying that was for *die Englische*. Amish were family; there was no need to be formal, including knocking on doors. When Hester looked up, Frances was standing inside, startling Hester so that she jumped, surprised that Frances could open the door so quietly.

"Hester." It was Frances's way of greeting.

"Mam! You startled me."

"And you an Indian? You should be the one sneaking up on me."

Hester let that one go, squelching a retort.

"Here. Pervinca. One dram every morning and evening."

Obediently, Hester reached out, took it, and set it carefully on the cupboard by the bittersweet. She noticed the pale green color, how the light turned it to an olive shade, the orange bittersweet beside it.

"You will obey?'

"Yes."

"Good. You heard? Amos and Sarah Speicher have been blessed with their first child. A son. They named him Abner."

Hester's face softened, her eyes became moist. "Oh? That's good news! I must go see her. That's wonderful. God be praised."

"Yes. I am so glad for a successful birth. Always a sign of God's blessing."

Hester nodded, picked up the shirt she was smoothing, repositioned it, and prepared to continue.

"So, will you visit soon?"

Puzzled, Hester lifted her eyes to her mother-in-law. "Why?"

"Oh, you should go soon. Sarah is such a shining example of purity for you. She has obviously acquired the blessing that God is withholding from you."

This statement left Hester pondering, uneasy, exploring avenues of release from the condemnation in Frances's words. Why would God bless Amos and Sarah, when he would not fill William's and Hester's arms with a bundle so precious it would fill them with joy?

Kate had always told her that the moment when she first held Hester in her arms, she experienced a joy as great, if not greater, than when she held Noah less than a year later. God had not blessed Hans and Kate for nine whole years, then, unexplainably, he had. Who could fig-ure that out?

Had Kate submitted herself more fully to Hans' wishes? Had she drawn her cap well over her hair, covering her-self more convincingly with humility and subjection to Hans? But with Hans, subjection was not a hard yoke nor a dead weight slung on Kate's unwilling shoulders. Hans was easy-going. He had laughed, pulled her wide covering strings, and told her she was getting fat, but in an approv-ing way. His was an attitude lined with the comforting pillows of love on which Kate could rest and recline, her spirit exulting in the constant stream of his approval.

It was the approval. Hester smoothed the shirt over and over, long after the wrinkles had been rubbed out. Her thoughts turned to memories of longing, to a desperate hunger for approval, the kind that would allow her to be free, to move along with lightness like a dandelion seed, effortless, carried along on soft summer breezes of love.

She sighed. In the stillness of her kitchen, the bitter-sweet blurred into the waxy, dark green leaves as tears stung her eyes. For the first time in over two years, she longed for the safety, the haven of approval that was Emma Ferree. And Billy. Dear redheaded, mischievous boy. She should have listened to the words of warning.

But she had a whole life ahead of her. She would be brave. She was an Indian, fearless and stout-hearted, so she would summon her courage and live her life with William as she had promised the day she married him. Perhaps she could yet soften him, molding him into the kindness she longed for.

William was a good man. He was. She would try harder. She would be blameless. Then perhaps God would bless her and give them a son, another generation to till the fertile black soil of Lancaster County.

She swallowed the whiskey-soaked pervinca. She prayed, endured her husband's kisses, obeyed every wish. Often while he slept, she wondered at the ways of a man, that God had wrought such a difference.

William told her repeatedly that it was the woman who had sinned in the Garden of Eden. Not Adam. Eve had taken the fruit of that tree, that forbidden apple. Worse yet, she had enticed her husband into senseless betrayal as well. So it was her lot in life to suffer, to subject herself to her husband. Did he not do his duty, cutting trees, tilling the soil, keeping weeds at bay? The sweat of his brow was the price he paid to provide for his wife, the weaker vessel.

Yes, she said. Yes.

She threw the heavy harness on the brown driving horse named Fannie. It was Elias's horse, but hers to drive any time she wanted. Fannie was a small brown mare with liquid eyes the same color as her black mane, except for the green and purple lights in the irises. She was gentle and easy to hitch to the buggy so that Hester could manage the task by herself.

Fannie stood content and patient as Hester lifted the wooden shafts, then backed into her space with only a minimum of calling. Hester fastened the traces and then the backhold strap to the britching, gathered the reins, and looked up.

Frances stood, not ten feet away. It was uncanny the way that woman crept up on her, drawing irritation the way lobelia drew pus from a wound.

"You're off to see Sarah and the newborn?"

Swallowing her words of inflammation, she nodded. A semblance of a smile, to be polite, formed around her mouth.

"Where is your shawl?"

Hester threw up her hand and pointed to the buggy seat. "It's hard to throw a harness on a horse's back wearing a shawl."

"Not on Fannie. She's small."

"I'll put it on."

"Make sure you do. Some of the young girls have taken to wearing a coat without a woollen shawl. Serves them right if they freeze." With that remark vibrating in the cold December air between them, she turned on her heel and walked away, as stiff and formidable as an axe.

Hester climbed into the buggy, reached for the required shawl, thrust the heavy steel pin through the wool, then flung the corners over her shoulder, making driving easier. She flung Frances's words over her shoulder as well, then remembered her unacquired blessing of a child as the guilt piled onto her shoulders.

The road that led away from the Elias King farm was well traveled this December day. The ground was frozen, making the going easier. The first snow hadn't yet appeared, which was very unusual. William said the Bible spoke of the latter days when unusual weather would occur, and these were definitely the latter days, now, weren't they?

The earth lay cold and fallow, a time of dead, frozen cornstalks and wind-whipped grasses that grated together, brittle-brown, waiting for snow to cover their uselessness. Holes in the frozen road were covered with ice, broken where heavy steel-covered wheels had crashed through.

The sky was gray, the wind a bone-chilling blast from the east. It would begin to snow during the night if not before. William wanted to get more corn fodder into the barn before it fell, so he frowned when she'd said, over fried mush, that she wanted to visit Sarah and her new baby. He clapped his hat on his black hair and stalked out without further words.

She had opened her mouth to tell him if he needed help, she would be available, then thought, no she'd see Sarah today. Sarah Speicher and her little Abner.

Her heart sang in anticipation. *"Schlofe, Buppli, Schlofe."* She sang every verse of the old lullaby. She could see Kate, large and warm, her wide face serene and content, singing yet another baby to sleep. Oh, she'd loved her babies! Nurtured them, rocked then during the night, cuddled and loved and adored them.

Hester could still feel the warmth from her large body, feel her breathing above her head, the soft palms pressed on either side of her face, a reverence between them, a benediction. Kate's love, a remembered treasure, was still sufficient. But only sometimes, like now, did she really experience Kate again. Hester moved along the frozen dirt road with small, brown Fannie clopping along effortlessly, the cold wind tingling her nose and cheeks, her gloved hands expertly holding the reins. The fields of Lancaster County lay cold and deserted, waiting till God rolled the season along to spring, when the warm sun would wake up the dormancy of December.

Hester prayed that God would remember her body's own dormant December and would send the sunshine of his blessing into her life. Involuntarily, she set her hat forward with a well-placed grip of her gloved hand. Just in case William's words might be true.

CHAPTER 13

AMOS AND SARAH SPEICHER LIVED IN A LOG house built along a hill, about five miles from the large stone house Elias King had built. The road followed the Pequea Creek, the same route that led to the town of Lancaster.

Hester had traveled this road quite often, visiting friends or going to church, so she only needed a slight bit of pressure on the right reign to turn Fannie onto the small lane that led to the log house.

It was surrounded by pine and spruce trees, the larger deciduous trees having been hacked away. There was a small but serviceable barn, an empty corn crib and a henhouse with one door flapping on its broken hinges, squeaking desolately in the stiff, easterly wind.

Hester stopped the horse and looked toward the house. There was no yellow glow from the small window, but then, Hester reasoned, some people saved their candles or oil till darkness set in. Unhitching Fannie, she looked around uneasily. It was too quiet. The barn door creaked eerily as Hester swung it wide. The smell of raw manure made her nostrils tingle, the stench overwhelming.

A cow bawled. A horse gave a low nicker. A cat slunk around a corner, then slithered along a wall before disappearing. The manure was piled so high Hester could not find a way to open the gate of the empty boxstall, so she tied Fannie to the gate, leaving her in the walkway.

"Stay, Fannie. Good girl." Hester patted the moist neck beneath the heavy black mane before letting herself out, closing the screeching door behind her.

Uncertain now, she hesitated. The flapping henhouse door made shivers run down her arms. Resolutely, she walked to the front door. Wide planks were worn smooth around the heavy latch where many hands had struggled to lift it. The roof was gray, the shingles weathered and split. The chinking between the logs was drying out. Small pieces of it littered the unsown grass surrounding the walls.

The windows were empty of light like a lifeless person. Lowering her head, Hester tapped on the door. She waited, then tapped again. A thin voice called from behind the heavy door.

Hester struggled with the latch, then swung the door wide. A rectangular path of light appeared immediately. The gray shadows returned after she pulled it shut behind her.

"Over here. I'm over here."

Hester found her way to the rumpled bedstead, noticing the weak fire burning dangerously low in the small fireplace as she passed it. She was shocked to find Sarah beneath the covers, her husband, Amos, beside her, and the newborn tucked between them. A foul odor rose from the soiled diapers flung beside the bed, the sour stench of sickness hovering over the small bedroom like a yet undetected whisper of foreboding.

"Sarah?"

Hester's word brought a glad cry, a recognition of answered pleas.

"Oh, Hester. It's you! Thank God."

"Sarah, what is going on? Are all of you ill?"

"Our *maud* went home five days ago. Amos is very sick. Our little Abner is becoming so frail." Sarah began to cry, soft, hiccupping little sobs of shame and helplessness.

Hester was already shrugging out of her coat, flinging her large black hat aside. She rolled up her sleeves and went around to Amos's side of the bed, her mouth grim when the fevered brow burned the palm of her hand. Here was a dire situation. She needed onions. Lobelia. Bitterroot. Small milkweed.

Bending low, she asked Sarah for onions.

"Yes. We have plenty. In the attic."

When Hester found them, she put them in a kettle with water. She poked up the fire, adding the last few sticks of wood. She would get them comfortable, then look for the herbs later. The baby's thin cry sounded from the bed. Amos groaned, tried to rise, but fell back, breathing rapidly.

She found the crock of vinegar and heated it. She bathed their feet and foreheads with cool water, then with the vinegar. She applied an onion poultice and stopped to listen as Amos coughed, gasping and retching. Yes, it was whooping cough, the scourge of every settlement. The phlegm came up. Hester bent to examine it. She needed elecampane now. Also skunk cabbage, horehound, and pignut. She'd boil them together with brewer's yeast.

Her thoughts churned. She must go back home. She had all of these remedies stored in a wooden box. Adrenalin spurred her every motion.

For now, the onions would be sufficient. She brought fresh, cold water from the container on the back stoop. Both Amos and Sarah drank thirstily. She told them of her plans, promising she'd be back, with help.

Hester lashed the reins down on Fannie's back only once. The small horse, sensing the urgency, ran low to the ground, her feet churning with a pace so rapid she seemed to float. The buggy lifted and swung, shattering frozen clods of soil, tilted dangerously, righted itself, and followed the dashing horse.

She slowed Fannie before they reached the King farm. Hester knew she must be careful since Frances did not like to be told what to do. Calmly, she tied Fannie, slipped into the house, found the wooden box, and added potatoes, apples, a wedge of hard cheese, and a slab of bacon. Hurriedly, she put everything into a leather satchel and went back to the buggy.

Good. Frances had not interfered. Likely William was out in the lower cornfields.

Hester drove back at a slower pace, having mercy on Fannie. She gave her a nice pile of hay and a drink of water before returning to the house. The smell of onions, soiled diapers, and unwashed, feverish bodies was hard to bear when she entered, but there was work to be done. Suffering people needed help.

First, she put the herbs on to boil. Then she would mix the extract from the herbs with honey and give Amos and Sarah each a spoonful every hour. After she finished stewing the herbs, she made a warm pot of broth, added potatoes, and brought them to a boil.

She lifted the newborn and bathed him in warm water with vinegar, marveling at the strength in his lungs for one so young. He put up quite a howling, bringing anxious questions from the bed where Sarah lay beneath a plaster of boiled onions.

Hester dressed the baby in clean diapers and a white nightgown of soft homespun. She wrapped him in a heavy blanket and laid him in the cradle, bearing his indignant cries while she washed Sarah's feverish body and put her in a warm, clean nightgown. She draped the hickory chair with warm blankets, thought of Emma and Billy, then helped Sarah into it and put the baby to her breast for a good feeding.

Amos coughed and coughed, sucking in a desperate breath after each racking of his body. He tried to get up again and again. Hester moved among them, quiet, single-minded in her purpose. She would make them feel better. She would heal them with the old woman's wisdom of the earth and its fruit.

She heated water all afternoon. She washed clothes and hung them in the attic to dry. She fed them the fragrant soup, accepting Sarah's sighs of gratitude. While the baby slept, she washed diapers and floors, scrubbed dishes, and changed the rough, homespun sheets on the bed. She shook the dirt from the rugs, swept, and scoured the hearth.

Sarah and Amos swallowed the spoonfuls of medicine obediently, gladly. Hester was alarmed to find the light in the windows turning to darkness, subtly, as if a cloud had passed over the gray curtain that already hid the sun. Breathless now, she gave Sarah instructions, promising to return. She threw hay to the animals. She'd water them in the morning.

Fannie ran low and hard, but night had almost fallen before Hester had unhitched her and raced into the house, her shawl flying behind her through the deepening gloom.

Fortunately, William was late for his supper, so the bean soup was hot and the cornbread baked, golden and piping hot when he came in. He noticed his wife's heightened color, the snapping of her eyes, the renewed energy.

As usual, they bowed their heads. William shoveled large spoonfuls of the bean soup into his mouth and broke squares of cornbread into rectangles, loading them with freshly churned butter.

He asked her about her day, curious about the added energy that radiated like heat.

"Oh, I went to visit Sarah Speicher and baby Abner. Remember, they had a son about six weeks ago? Well, I found them in deplorable shape. All three were sick with what I think is whooping cough. So I stayed, helping them with onion plasters. And I cleaned and made soup."

For a long time, William said nothing. When he spoke, his works were measured, short, as if each one was contained in a very small cup. "That was nice of you. But I hope you won't go back. They need a doctor, not you."

"Oh, I had the whooping cough when I was six years old."

"You did?"

"Oh, yes, we all did. Noah and Isaac and Lissie and Solomon. Noah brought me cup after cup of cold water. Kate said I cried for it constantly."

Hester gave a low laugh, then lifted her eyes to his, seeking his approval, hoping he would agree that she had done the right thing. Instead, he forbade her to return.

"But I have to," Hester pleaded, floundering in the quagmire of his attitude. But he would not relent. He said he was afraid she would become ill, further removing his chances of producing an heir.

She bowed her head and submitted. When William went out to do chores, hot tears of frustration pricked her eyelashes, but not one drop fell on her cheeks. Anger replaced the tears. She gave vent to it by hurling a pewter candle holder into the wall and was pleased to find a nick in the plaster, a small spray of whitewash on the floor.

Word got around, though, probably by way of Elias King, who loved to help his neighbors—or at least organize a frolic, be the foreman of other men's labours, and acquire another pile of honor to his already elevated state. For Elias, like William, was highly esteemed by his fellow Amish. Fortunately, his goodwill included Amos Speichers, and a working bee was held. Hester was allowed to attend.

Hurriedly, furtively, she checked their supply of medicine. She was pleased to see they had swallowed every spoonful. Amos was on a chair, pale, trembling, still coughing, but visibly improved. Sarah's cheeks were pink, her eyes alive with interest. Baby Abner cooed on her lap.

Sarah wasted no time telling astounded neighbors about Hester's concoction of miracle herbs, as she called them. She related in minute detail the placing of the onion plaster, the vinegar baths.

"Ya, oh ya. Goot. Sell iss goot."

Old Hannah Miller nodded her head in agreement, her beady brown eyes going to Hester's face. But skunk cabbage? Pignut? She had never heard of it. Hesitantly Hester spoke. She told them of the old Indian woman. Suspicion hooded eyes and made tongues cluck with caution. These Indians were *behoft* with witchcraft. Perhaps the devil gave Hester the power. Women shivered, thinking of old wives' tales brought across the Atlantic's heaving waters from Switzerland.

The men cleaned the stables and repaired the henhouse. The community brought chickens and placed them in the newly repaired house. Wood was cut, as well as split and stacked beneath the eaves. The chinking between the logs was repaired, as was the fence surrounding the barn.

So much food was brought in the shelves in the cellar bulged with cheeses and hams, potatoes and onions and dried lima beans and cabbage. Honey, elderberry jam, molasses, and cones of sugar were squeezed in. People carried ground cherry pies, green tomato pies, and custards. Amos and Sarah stood side by side with little Abner and thanked everyone *gahr hoftich*. They felt unworthy, they said.

Elias and Frances rode home, confident of having shored up their foundation of good works yet again, followed by William and Hester, whose thoughts of the situation were completely opposite. William insisted that

Hester's *dumb gamach* with those herbs were over, for sure, when Reuben Kauffman said those Indians were all guilty of powwowing. Hester wondered how soon the next call for help would arrive.

She did not have long to wait. Exactly seven days later, in fact. Reuben Kauffman's daughter, Naomi, woke up burning with fever, coughing violently.

Hester cooked the herbs and mixed them with honey. She did not ask William or her parents-in-law. She merely went about her business, hitched up Fannie, and set off to Reuben Kauffmans through the cold, dry countryside. It was almost Christmas, a few days before, in fact.

When the first snow came from the north, the flakes were small and hard, driven by a relentless, moaning wind that howled under the eaves like ghostly wolves. The big oven glowed with heat. The massive fireplace in the kitchen crackled and popped with a lively fire, yet the corners of the house made Hester shiver. She rubbed her arms as she went upstairs for onions and hovered by the fire as chills raced across her back.

She was making medicine again. After the herbs had boiled down, she lifted out the sodden mass, then mixed the extract with honey, bottled it, corked it, and waited for the next household to come down with the whooping cough. By the time Christmas arrived, she was becoming weary of all the sleepless nights and the days spent nursing the sick, cleaning, cooking, and washing.

On Christmas Eve, the snow lay thick and heavy like whipped cream layered over the stone house and barn, the pine trees, and bare branches of the forest. The yellow glow of the downstairs windows made William and

Hester's house appear warm and inviting, a cozy haven of rest for travelers or acquaintances. The people who traveled by on sleighs turned an appreciative eye to the big stone house, so well built that it would last for hundreds of years, a beacon of true workmanship. The son was so like the father. Yes, they were something, weren't they?

William was in a secretive mood, his blue eyes alight with pleasure. He invited Hester to sit beside him on the deacon's bench by the fire. She put a cork slowly onto the last bottle of medicine, washed her hands, and dried them on a flour sack towel before turning to William, who caught her hand in his, so unlike him. Bewildered, suddenly ill at ease, she drew back, hesitating.

"What, William?"

"I have something for you."

"A gift?"

"Certainly. For *Grishtag*." He scuttled to the walnut corner cupboard, boyish in his anticipation. Hester turned to watch as he opened the cupboard door, then extricated an oblong box awkwardly. How had he been able to hide that in such an obvious place? Hester felt the weight of the box.

"Don't drop it!"

Slowly, she unwrapped it, the white paper falling away to reveal a wooden crate containing a set of the most beautiful dishes Hester had ever seen. Blue. A pattern of indigo blue on a white background. Eight plates, eight saucers and teacups. A soup tureen and a serving platter. The china was so delicate, so beautiful, Hester was afraid to touch it.

"Go ahead, Hester. Put it on the big cupboard in the kitchen," he coaxed.

Hester gasped, her eyes wide with wonder. "Oh, I can't, William. It would be too showy. *Hochmut*, you know. I'll place it very carefully in the corner cupboard where no one will see it."

William was clearly puzzled. "But why would you do that?"

"I don't know. Wouldn't it be *grosfeelich* to display the expensive china in my kitchen? Perhaps one of my women friends would become jealous of me."

"That would not be your fault." Sighing, Hester placed the dishes on the cupboard in the kitchen, then felt William's arms about her as he stood behind her. Together, they admired the lovely dishes. They drank spicy eggnog and popped popcorn over the open fire, staying up late to talk about their pasts.

William was attentive, drinking in Hester's rare beauty by the light of the flickering fire. His beautiful wife intrigued him even now, three years after marrying her. She had needed a stern hand at first, but he had taught her well the ways of an Amish wife. He eyed the bottles of herbal medicine. Warily he approached her, bringing up the subject.

Hester listened, then drew away from him. "You do not approve, even after so many people have been helped?"

"What do you mean, 'helped'?"

"The. . . the medicine helps them through the coughing."

"Really? You think so?"

"Yes. It makes a big difference."

"It's only you that thinks so."

Hester shook her head.

"Do you charge them for your trouble?"

"No. Should I?"

"Of course. You could make a tidy profit. The herbs are free. So is the honey."

"But would it be right to charge poor young people like Amos Speichers? They have so little."

"We don't have a lot either. We have land to pay. To my father."

Hester nodded slowly. "How much should I charge?"

Quickly, William calculated the amount Hester could profit, named a sum, and told her to charge that for each bottle.

Hester thought of Lissie Hershberger and the endless hours of devotion she gave to the families around her, for which she received potatoes, a slice of salt pork, some cornmeal. Her payment was more than cold, hard coins. Hester knew love could not be measured. It couldn't be valued the way land or money could. Love kept flowing and flowing until it created a wide river that carried others along with it, straight into Heaven's door.

But William would think her silly if she tried to tell him that. He would say she talked like a woman. *Weibsleitich*. So she agreed. He was surprisingly pleased as he gathered her in his arms, his words of love effusive.

Long into the night, Hester lay awake, pondering her life. So many things were good, and for this she was thankful. For William, for the ability to use her knowledge of herbs far beyond anything she had imagined. So many short years before this, she was only an Indian in hiding.

She was thankful for Emma Ferree. And for Billy.

Quick tears sprang to her eyes, sliding down the sides of her face, but she let them go unhindered. Pillows held secrets well. No one could tell how often they were wet with the heart's sorrows and longings, the sighs of repression.

Sometimes she imagined her life being large and healthy with real love, the way her childhood had been sustained by it. Emma and Billy kept it alive in their good-natured way, as much as any strangers could fill in for real family.

The Indians contributed to the meaning of life and love in their own special way of living.

And now. Was she still blessed with the knowledge of acceptance? Yes, she was. Yes. She told herself this over and over as the warm trail of her tears kept a steady course into her silent, secretive pillow. It was just the way of it, after Kate died.

She was blessed. For a scavenger, a seeker of whatever she could find, she had a good life with William.

She knew, also, that she would gladly break every piece of lovely expensive china to be free of his highly esteemed authority. Always, it was William's way. The belief that a woman should have an opinion never crossed his mind. Did all women feel like she did, whether they'd admit it or not?

On Christmas Day they attended church services at Ezra Fishers, a brother-in-law to Elias. The sun shone with a blinding brilliance. Hester's tears had cleansed her spirit, leaving her with a warm glow that radiated from her dark eyes.

She held little Abner Speicher, whispering with Sarah while the congregation sang the old Christmas hymns from the thick leather-bound *Ausbund*, and was thankful for a home and a husband, the empty cradle beneath the eaves forgotten for the moment.

Frances outdid herself, cooking and stewing, baking, and serving huge platters of festive foods to the extended family. The stone house brimmed with relatives Hester had never met. They spilled over into William and Hester's house, where they admired the dishes. Goodwill and merrymaking poured from every window, the men and women singing lustily, their faces red and perspiring.

The great pink hams were adorned with holly and berries; the turkey lay in a bed of parsley with a display of red apples. The sweet potatoes were lavished with walnuts; the pies were high and sweet and creamy. William's older brothers brought chestnuts, which they roasted over the fire.

Hester glowed in her red dress and moved among her relatives with a renewed sense of belonging. Every man in the room was enchanted with her but remained circumspect, distant, blushing, and bowing when she spoke to them in her perfect, low voice. She possessed a husky quality in her speech, which one brother-in-law found extremely endearing. He was nipping the fermented apple cider in the cellar when Hester opened the door, turned her back, and lowered herself down the steep stairs, the way she would go down the rungs of a ladder.

CHAPTER 14

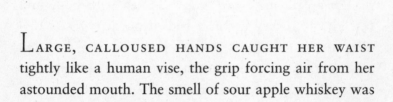

LARGE, CALLOUSED HANDS CAUGHT HER WAIST tightly like a human vise, the grip forcing air from her astounded mouth. The smell of sour apple whiskey was hot and rancid, flowing past her ear, as she was pulled against the person who held her in his grip.

Instinctively, she began to struggle and pull away, her hands going to her waist, clawing at the disgusting hands that held her.

Slurred words of affection accompanied the sour stench of his breathing. When Hester saw how dire the situation was, she drew up a foot, and kicked backward, the sharp heel of her leather Sunday shoe catching her brother-in-law's shin with a splitting blow.

She was released so suddenly she fell headlong onto the caked red earth of the cellar floor. Before she had a second to recover, the door creaked open and a shaft of light shone on her as she struggled to her feet. Her dress was covered with loose dirt, her eyes were wide and filled with fear.

"Hester! *Vass geht au?*"

It was William, her husband. Before she had a chance to brush off the dirt, he was down the cellar steps, his long legs lowering himself as swiftly as possible. Breathing hard, he grasped Hester's shoulders, his eyes boring into hers from the light of the flickering oil lamp.

Before she could open her mouth to explain, William found the brother-in-law, his hands hanging stupidly by his side, his mouth working as he wrestled with his shame.

The result of that fateful encounter in the cellar were lies the brother-in-law told William in smooth, pious words, punctuated by sighs of righteousness as he explained Hester's descent down the cellar steps and into his unwilling arms. She was an Indian, after all.

Hester remembered very little of the Christmas evening, her eyes large, afraid, furtive.

Nothing was wasted on Frances.

William did his duty, bringing his errant wife to task. Simply, it was her word against Johnny's, the brother-in-law.

Over and over, she repeated her story, her words falling on ears stopped with indignation. William was furious, disappointed. How could she?

Hester sat beside the immense fireplace, the deacon's bench empty except for her quivering form on one end, the soiled red dress in stark relief against the white-washed wall like a Christmas poinsettia someone had trampled upon.

For the hundredth time, she shook her head. "I didn't, oh, William, I didn't. It was him."

William stalked the kitchen floor, his hands behind his back, his head thrust forward in the throes of his anger. "I would believe you if it wasn't for the Indian in you. Indians lie. They don't care, godless heathens that they are."

She stopped then. She gave up trying to tell William the truth. She watched with eyes that were dull and lifeless as he hurled every bottle of herbal medicine into the roaring fire, forbidding her to travel the community with her witchcraft, her Indian powwowing.

He grasped her shoulders, her forearms, leaving dull blue marks that lasted for weeks. He told her that if it ever happened again, the ministers of the church must be alerted, and she would be forced to make a public confession. Perhaps the bishop would then decide to excommunicate her for her sins. He, William, would carry out the required shunning afterward, for the extended period of time the *Ordnung* called for.

The threat drove a numbing fear into her heart. Anything, anything, except public humiliation. So she bowed her head, telling William she was sorry to disappoint him, that she would repent, do better, become more vigilant.

He slept beside her as she lay bruised, her eyes open, tears pooling on the pillow, darkening the dried blotch again where they had fallen before. This was the way of it then. The lineage of your blood, the nature God gave you the day you were born, handed down from generation to generation, was what made you who you were.

Ah, William. So much like Annie, Hans's second wife. What had he said the day he met her at her father's wedding? Be careful, be careful of that family. And he a cousin of Annie's.

Folks went to church, counted themselves Christians, followers of Jesus Christ. Amish, Mennonite, Baptist, Lutheran, all following this man called Jesus. In Hester's battered spirit, she pieced together remnants of her past, filled now with guilt made from the unfairness and cruelty of good Christian people. Each one a dark square of abrasive wool fabric that hurt her fingertips as she threaded the steel needle up and down. She wanted to add a square of color and light, to give William and Annie the benefit of the doubt.

Jesus had been nailed to the cross, and he prayed God to forgive the Roman soldiers as they pounded the rusty nails through his palms. She would try to do the same. Everyone who believed in the man called Jesus was called upon to forgive.

Perhaps William did not know how he hurt her. He was well steeped in the laws of the church, like a pot of tea come to a dark green color of perfection after just the right amount of time, the required amount of tea leaves added at the right time. So important to him, this perfection.

She sighed, prayed to God, begged his forgiveness. Like the petals of an unfolding flower, the beauty of God's love was revealed to her. The luxury of his grace and forgiveness arrived in waves of peace, filling her heart, enfolding it in a kind of pureness, almost like the purity of an angel's wing.

For who could know? Perhaps she had behaved immodestly. Had she fueled Johnny's desire for her? First, there was Hans. And now the brother-in-law.

She cringed, then, with shame and humility that quite effectively eliminated the fresh breath of God's love. Over and over she blamed herself, heaping measures of self-loathing on her own head as she remembered moments with Hans. Now, here again she was to blame.

How much better it would have been if Kate had left her to starve as an infant. Death would have been merciful. Quick. Better. She was forever torn between two cultures, and now, two voices, one enveloping her in the security of God's love, one accusing her of her own heathen ways, the Indian in her, the thorn in her flesh.

Suddenly she remembered a time with Noah when Kate was still alive. They were playing together, brother and sister, one as dark as the other was blond and light-eyed. They were swinging in the barn on the long rope swing Hans had attached to the rafter for them. She could smell the dry hay and see the slivers of light that sifted between the barn boards, carrying tiny pieces of dust, catching the gleam of her straight, black hair.

She had just completed a wide arc, flying high above the hay, lithe, strong, and supple, her hands around the knot at the end with a tight, well-placed grip. Strangely, Noah had reached out, touched her hair, and said she was like "a *schöna* Indian, so dark."

She remembered looking into his pale blue eyes, afraid to blink. She knew then that Noah was special. He was so much like Kate, who found it hard to confront anyone, to demean them with words of rebuke.

Ah, but Noah and Kate had accepted her. All of her. Being Indian had not been a loathsome trait, but an honor.

She would try harder yet again. William might come to appreciate her if she continued with the work of being a healer. She remembered, then, his destruction of her medicines. How like Annie and her goal to destroy the book of herbal remedies.

A stabbing thought about Emma Ferree's premonitions of William suddenly pierced Hester. In one moment, she was face-to-face with the thin film of resistance she had allowed to cover the truth from this astounding little woman. Emma's goodness of heart was sweeter than anything Hester had encountered since she'd left her childhood home. She knew now that Emma had been right. The truth was like a branding iron. If only Billy had let her die in the granary of the livery stable.

Long into the night, a mixture of peace and despair, truth and unacknowledged lies, spilled and rolled around Hester's heart. Her weary eyes were swollen when William heaved himself from bed and went out into the cold, dark, snowy morning to begin the day's milking.

At breakfast Hester was silent and downcast, her white cap pulled so far front on her head that very little of the beauty of her dark hair was revealed. She had drawn the strings up beneath her chin in a large bow of humility.

She had fried the mush crisp and thin, cooked the eggs sunny side up, and finished them with boiling water cooking up furiously beneath the lid, just the way William liked them. The porridge was firm, the tea dark and piping hot. They ate together in silence, the new set of dishes like mocking sentries, a show of love and affection.

William broke the silence only when he poured the steaming tea onto his saucer to cool it. "Hester, I forbid you to leave the house for six weeks now. I expect you to think upon your sins, read your Bible, and repent. It is because of my love for you that I require this. I do love you, Hester, and am glad you are my wife.

"I just need to train you well in the ways of a devoted Amish housewife. I believe Kate was a bit loose with you. My mother always talked of it, wondering how the household would ever turn out with her lack of discipline."

He gave her a sad look of righteousness, a sniff. "I guess this latest episode answers my mother's concerns and questions. You ran away from home and lived English for a while. Noah has gone off to the war, I hear. They say Isaac got on a river barge with a man named Lee who worked on the river."

Hester successfully hid any sign of caring or having heard. She acknowledged his words with a mere dipping of her head, a sipping of her tea. A fierce gladness welled up in her before she could quell it. Let Hans reap what he sowed. Let all his neglect come home to roost. He had never cared for those two boys, and now they apparently did not care for him.

"Why don't you answer me?" William's voice was harsh. He leaned forward, his blue eyes intent, his mouth compressed into a slash of discipline.

"Oh, no, I mean, yes. I hadn't known about my brothers."

"They are not your brothers. You have no ties to them."

"No. I don't."

"Did you know this riverman named Lee?"

Rigid, with eyes downcast, Hester tried to decide quickly. If she shook her head, he would catch the lie, as sharp and perceptive as he was. If she said yes, he would see the past in her eyes.

"Well?'

"Yes. He poled us across the river a few times."

"Is that all?"

"Yes."

Miraculously, he believed her.

Her hands shook as she held the cup, stirred the tea with a spoon.

"I want Mother to teach you quiltmaking."

A sickening thud of her heart was followed by nausea roiling her stomach, churning the food she had eaten. "But I am not skilled with a needle."

"Till the winter is over, you will have learned."

The thought of spending time with his mother, her hands clumsily plying the needle through fabric cut in exact squares and triangles, brought on a cold sweat, an acceleration of her heart.

On the very next afternoon, Frances suddenly appeared in the kitchen like a dark ghost of discipline. Hester was sweeping the hearth and looked up to find her standing by the table.

One eyebrow was elevated, one lowered. "Dishes not done yet?" was her way of greeting.

"Yes, well, not all of them. I overbaked a cake. It's soaking."

"What kind of cake?"

"A molasses. William's favorite."

"He likes *gelbkucken* best."

"He does?"

"Why of course."

"I'll make him one next time."

"He wants me to teach you quiltmaking."

Gripping the back of a chair, Hester nodded.

Out came the tumble of scraps. The scissors flashed in Frances's capable hands as she sliced expertly around the templates, cutting exact triangles and rectangles. Bits of fabric grew into tall stacks as her scissors raced along, keeping time to the staccato words from her thin mouth.

So Hester had overstepped her bounds with Johnny. That's what happens when a woman has no children. Like a cavorting heifer. William was so disappointed. Very generous of him to forgive her for such a wrongdoing.

She, too, could forgive. It was her duty. A Christian was called upon to do this. In time, she was sure that Hester would make a good wife.

Hester acknowledged her words with a humble dip of her head. When she spoke, her eyes were clear, glistening with truth. "I am not to blame for Johnny's overtures. He was drinking apple whiskey. I went down to the cellar, and he caught me about the waist. I struggled."

When Frances met Hester's eyes, the truth in them found its mark, accurately piercing the false lies in her own. But expertly, in the same way she plied the scissors, she cut off the truth and flung it away with contempt. "Puh! They all say that. Every loose woman always comes up with an excuse."

Calmly, her eyes glowing, Hester spoke again, her voice clear, low, and husky, like bells enhancing her words. "Then you must live with what you choose to believe."

When Hester struggled to thread her needle, bending over the triangles she was laboriously bringing together, Frances noticed her long, uneven stitches. Patiently she showed her how to shove only the tip of the needle into the fabric to make one tiny stitch, which immediately helped Hester improve.

Frances soon noticed Hester's eye for color, the way she alternated the blue with the golden maize fabric and the red with the green like a holly bush or a cardinal in a fir tree. But she was careful to withhold praise, careful to keep Hester from becoming *schtoltz*. Words of praise would only serve to give her more free rein than she already had.

Till the week's end, Hester had acquired a new level of quiltmaking. She endured Frances's words of rebuke and her criticism like an unwelcome cold. She dealt with her inability to please, stayed patient, and was rewarded with a perfect quilt top that contained a star pattern, its symmetry so pleasing that her eyes lit up with delight.

Frances almost warmed to her beautiful daughter-in-law.

William was happy beyond Hester's expectations. He praised her work and told her about the verses in Proverbs that lift up a woman who pleases her husband by the work of her hands, then takes her goods to market. She cooked his meals the way he liked them, stayed at home for the required weeks, went to church, and held

little Baby Abner. She whispered senseless bits of news
and gossip with her friend Sarah, evading her questions
about the tinctures and the herbs, saying in winter it was
hard to find them. Amos was doing better, but could not
stand to do a full day's work yet. Hester said the sun in
spring would help.

The snows came often, piling around the stone house
and blowing across the Lancaster landscape in great,
white, stinging clouds, whipped up by a relentless north
wind that created drifts higher than a man's head. Horses
floundered up to their bellies in packed snow. Sleds over-
turned, spilling loads of firewood into deep white drifts.
The men shouted and shoveled through the snow, their
faces red with cold and irritation, clapping their gloved
hands down on the crowns of their black felt hats as the
wind tugged at their wide brims.

William came into the house for a scarf that he tied under his chin, tucking his beard beneath it as well. Hester
laughed, thinking him very handsome without the long,
bushy black beard, and told him so, blushing. He smiled
at her, then held her securely in his arms, kissing her
soundly before he went outside to join the shoveling crew.

At times such as these, Hester believed she did love
him. She did. Perhaps she expected too much from the
word "love." Obedience, having no will of her own,
brought good times. Weren't her quilts a visual display
of her obedience? Wasn't Frances's teaching a blessing?

When the news of sick children reached her ears,
a longing welled up in her so intense that she felt she
had to go somehow. When a four-year-old succumbed

to *lunga feeva* and a ten-year-old to seizures because of an escalated temperature caused by the same disease, she battled with her will to go nurse them, to be allowed to administer the herbs of her foreparents. She fiercely believed that the old Indians carried a wealth of information that they passed down from one generation to the next, and she knew many of these remedies.

Miserable, she stood in the snowy graveyards, her black hat hiding her sorrow, her black shawl wrapped around her desperate longing to save these children. She cried with parents remembering her mother, Kate, and her sister Rebecca. She listened to mothers, looking on helplessly as their children choked on swollen tonsils and thrashed feverishly on soiled beds, the doctor unable to save them.

She baked pies and bread and took them to houses with William by her side. She bent to view yet another child lying white and lifeless, its eyes closed, dressed in white, a life cut off before its time by the dreaded diseases of winter.

One cold winter evening, when the stars hung like little individual icicles, the wind moaning around the eaves, the blowing snow whispering the sadness of the little children's deaths, Hester could bear it no longer. She laid aside the pattern of triangles she was sewing, gathering the ends to fold them into the rye grass basket at her side, breathed in, and turned to her husband. "William, must these children die?"

Astounded by her words, William raised his head from the German Bible he had been reading. "Why, Hester, I am surprised at your question. Have you not heard Bishop Joel say so clearly that their time was up? God needed these children in heaven. They are angels now." His eyes were heavy-lidded with the patience he needed to exercise over his wife's childish question.

Hester shivered and drew the corners of her light shawl around her neck. "But if God put all these herbs on the earth for our use, then gives wisdom to. . . to, um, to people in how to use them, surely there is wasted knowledge somewhere."

"The doctors did all they could."

"The doctors don't know enough!" Hester flung the words into the room with unbridled desperation and the repression that suffocated her spirit.

Instantly, William was on his feet, towering over her with the strength of his anger. "Are you telling me, Hester, that you know more than the doctors? That thought is so preposterous it's laughable."

"No, I don't know more. Just a better way."

"You don't know anything." William grated out his words like a rasp on an oak board.

"But I do, William. I want to help the sick children, just for the love of these suffering little ones."

"Your Indian knowledge is witchcraft."

"No, William, it is not. I believe that viper's grass made into a tea would help these little ones' lung fever."

William was breathing hard now, his eyes containing desperation. Here was his wife rising up again, displaying her own will, just when he thought that the winter months, tempered with the tutelage of his mother, had finally cured her of this nonsense. "Viper's grass! You speak of your medicines in terms of serpents even."

"Ach, William. No. It is merely a grass. It grows in low places by the water. Hence its name."

Frustrated, angered, and without a thought other than the contesting of his will and the need to stop it, he brought back his hand and administered a sharp crack to the side of her face.

Hester's head snapped sideways. The shock in her eyes made William flinch, but only for a moment. He gathered his wits hurriedly and said she must never speak of these things again, ever, in his house.

Hester's face stung, but she lowered her eyes. He gathered her limp form into his arms, whispering words of love, saying that if she rose up against him like a re-bellious child, he would have to treat her as one. It was all done out of his great love for her.

Never again did Hester contest her husband's will. That one blow finished any thoughts of changing his opinion about the herbal medicines and her ability to use them.

She spent the remainder of that winter learning the art of quiltmaking. William praised her choice of colors. He built a small wooden frame for her, a clever device to hold portions of a quilt so that she could stitch the pieced top to the bottom layer of homespun fabric. Her needle flashed in the light of the oil lamp, her dark head bent to her work as she immersed herself in the skills her husband and his mother asked of her.

Elias, her father-in-law, was a man of few words, a distant man who kept to himself, minding his own busi-ness. He was tall, like Frances, and spare, with the same loping gait as his sons. One evening he asked Hester why she no longer made tinctures. Sam Riehl had asked him the question in church.

Flustered, Hester could not find words to fit the situation properly. William came to her aid immediately, however, telling his father that she had seen the error of her ways, recognized the powwowing of the Indians, and did not wish to continue.

Slowly then, Elias King cracked a chestnut with the nutcracker, popped a portion into his mouth, chewed, swallowed, and then met Hester's eyes. For only a second, a love like Kate's shone from his eyes, warm, soft, and so mellow and approving it was like a balm to a broken heart. He said, evenly, "Well, William, some of these old Indians know more than we do. And I personally don't think the devil has anything to do with it."

No one but Elias saw the look of warm gratitude Hester bestowed on him. And no one knew how Elias yearned to help his daughter-in-law, seeing how caught she was in the net of marriage covered by the deceit of piety, the same as he was.

CHAPTER 15

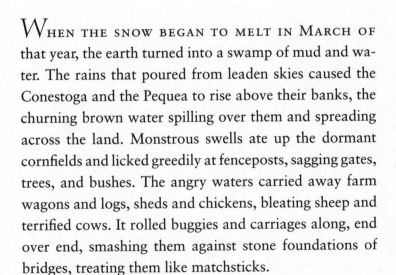

When the snow began to melt in March of that year, the earth turned into a swamp of mud and water. The rains that poured from leaden skies caused the Conestoga and the Pequea to rise above their banks, the churning brown water spilling over them and spreading across the land. Monstrous swells ate up the dormant cornfields and licked greedily at fenceposts, sagging gates, trees, and bushes. The angry waters carried away farm wagons and logs, sheds and chickens, bleating sheep and terrified cows. It rolled buggies and carriages along, end over end, smashing them against stone foundations of bridges, treating them like matchsticks.

The men were called to fill sandbags to keep the town of Lancaster safe. Elias and William rode horses through the fields, skirting flooded, low-lying areas, answering the call for assistance.

Frances and Hester were left alone to keep the animals fed and the cows milked. Normally, Hester did not milk cows. William said it was better for his parents and for him to continue doing the milking by themselves, that it was better for the cows to have familiar and experienced hands working with them. So now, when Hester dashed through the pouring rain, a kerchief tied around her head, she looked forward to milking the cows. She had always milked at home in Berks County.

Frances was beside herself with worry. She was terrified of flood waters. So many people miscalculated and took risks, driving their buggies through waters that appeared to be shallow but were deceptively high, rolling them over and over after the churning waters caught the bottoms of the carriages.

Hester shook the water off her head and shoulders, grabbed a wooden, three-legged stool, and set to work, expertly pulling and squeezing the cows' teats. Thick streams of creamy milk poured into the bucket held firmly between her knees.

Frances was amazed at Hester's ability. She did not allow one word of praise to escape her lips, but her eyes were approving. She asked Hester to spend the evening with her; she was afraid that her worry would undo her if she was alone.

They walked back to the house along the sodden path, the rain pelting them with its fury. Hester looked up at the gray sky as if to calculate the duration of the rain, but had to admit that the heavens appeared the same as they had for three days.

It was awkward, sitting in Frances's kitchen. Hester was required to call her Mother, but had never felt any motherly love coming from her, ever. Only discipline and rebuking. Still, she was William's mother, so she made every effort to be respectful. She helped her set the table for the two of them. They ate slices of homemade bread with good, yellow butter and ladled vegetable soup into big pewter bowls.

Again and again, Frances's eyes appeared wild with terror. Repeatedly, she opened the door, peered out into the cold and the wind, and asked Hester when she thought the rain would stop.

Hester told her the only bit of information she knew. If the wind continued from the northeast, there would be no change.

That seemed to send Frances into despair. "Hester, do you think the men will be safe?"

"Oh, I trust William to be careful. They are riding with a group of men. Surely they'll stick together and use sound judgment."

Frances nodded. But she became increasingly restless. She paced the kitchen. She added sticks of wood to the fire. She shivered when a gust of wind sent hard pellets of rain against the windowpane. She got down her Bible and began to read, her lips moving as she formed the words.

"Hester, do you think the water will come up to the barn?"

"I wouldn't think so. We're up pretty high."

When Frances nodded, Hester was reminded of her stepmother Annie when her hands lost their strength, creating a vulnerability and a loss of power that was hard to watch. It was pitiful, in fact. Clearly this rainstorm exposed a hidden weakness, a lack of faith, in Frances.

"Hester, don't go home to sleep."

Surprised, Hester looked at her. "Where should I sleep?"

"Here."

"Do you have a spare bed?"

"No."

"But."

"Oh, go then, I know you don't want to sleep in my bed with me."

"I suppose I could."

"No, you don't want to. Go home."

Quickly, Hester ran the short distance to her own door through the rain. She let herself in, poked up the fire, washed, and got into her long, warm nightgown. She crawled under the quilts and fell asleep to the rhythm of the rain on the shingled roof, tumbling down the steep incline from one hewn-oak shingle to another, dripping onto the crumpled brown grass that had been covered with snowdrifts all winter long.

She was awakened by a sobbing, wild-eyed apparition that struck terror to her heart. A half-dressed Frances, holding her navy blue dress front together with one hand and gripping a sputtering candle with the other, was calling her name between hoarse cries, a dry, sobbing sound that would not stop. "Hester! *Komm! Komm!*"

Hester sat bolt upright, alarm drying her mouth and her tongue. "It's William. Amos Fisher just arrived. William's horse fell, and he struck his head against a bridge."

Dumbly, Hester voiced, "The horse struck his head?"

"No. William!" Frances was screaming now, hoarsely. "Where is he?"

"They brought him back. He's lying in the barn."

"Is he alive?"

There was no answer, only the slamming of the door, the rain on the roof, the sound of footsteps as they splashed through the rain.

William's inert form was brought to the house and laid on their bed. His heavy black hair clung to his skull, forming a cap that allowed his ears to show. They were white, bloodless, a sight that seemed alien to Hester. She had hardly ever seen his ears since his hair reached to chin-level. Now he was strangely defenseless, even sensitive, somehow.

Frances moaned and cried, making strange, choppy little sounds of fear and foreboding. Her hands shook as she helped Hester put William into dry clothes, roll him over, and cover him. The doctor would come as soon as the floodwaters receded. Smelling salts brought no response.

Hester worked as the morning light crept into the room, gray, ghostlike, ominous. She glided from the bed to the fire, stroking William's forehead with cloths soaked in vinegar and camphor. She sat by their bed, watching his face for signs of awareness, trying to endure Frances's wet sounds of lip-smacking and crying.

Elias and Ben Hertzler came, peering under William's eyelids and pinching his nose to see if he would gasp.

The doctor came from Lancaster, held William's hand, and said there was little to do except wait to see how soon he would awaken. His heartbeat was good and strong, his pulse lively. He was a young man and healthy. He would probably be fine after he woke up.

The doctor left, and still the rain continued to pound on the roof. Hester was left alone with William. How could she begin to sort out her feelings when so many emotions crashed into her senses, leaving her with no clear direction?

Sad, yes, to see her husband, the William she knew so well, lying inert, unable to move. She was surprised by an overwhelming kindness she suddenly felt toward him. He had been so capable, always following his father's pattern of managing the farm. His profile was so handsome, yet still. His dark lashes lay on his white cheeks, his nose perfectly shaped and adding to his good looks. No wonder she had been visually attracted to him.

The pinched lines between his eyes and his dark eyebrows gave away his capacity for raw and unseemly fury.

The thought of his demise forced its way into her mind. No, he would live. She would be able to bear his children. The farm would prosper, their children would till the soil, and their children after them. God would smile down on her, bless her yet, in spite of her troublesome ways, her uprising against her husband. William would live. It was necessary that he did.

The rain stopped when the northeasterly wind changed to the west. Unbroken gray clouds tore in two on the western horizon, allowing a darker gray, rolling cloud to emerge, followed by churning white ones.

Raindrops skittered from the eaves, were blown sideways, and then fell to the ground with a defeated sigh.

By the time a brilliant blue sky showed behind the gray clouds, the wind was already teasing the tree branches, ruffling the grasses, swaying the weeds that seemed dead.

Hester listened. What she heard was more than the wind. A low roaring swept over the landscape. The wind crashed against the stone walls of the house, seized the windowpanes, and rattled them in its teeth. It lifted loose shingles and let them fall. Floppy gates swung back and forth. Barn doors flapped. Windows shivered as men dashed madly, clutching their hats, their beards split in two. They pushed rocks against barn doors, latched windows and half doors.

Slowly the Conestoga Creek went back to its borders, grumbling and leaving a residue of disease in its wake. Horses pulled carriages through the mud. Mud glued to their wooden wheels, making their load twice as heavy.

Neighbors hopped down from buggies, knocking mud from their boots in the brown yard. They brought biscuits and dumplings, stews and soups. So many remedies from kindly, well-meaning faces. Rub a potato and bury it at midnight when the moon is full. He will awaken. Use burdock root for the palsy or for fainting.

Old Hannah Troyer, bent and feeble, her teeth gone so long her gums were tough as nails, put a gnarled hand on William's forehead and repeated the Lord's Prayer five times in German, the wart at the end of her nose sliding up and down with each word.

Hester met each visitor at the door, thanked them for coming, then took her place beside William on the chair by his bed.

Frances talked and talked, giving each of the visitors a full report of his fall, about the night they brought him home, what an exceptional, well-behaved son he had always been. Each visitor heard an account of his abstinence, how he never touched hard cider or apple whiskey, and how, unlike his father and brothers, he had never smoked a pipe or chewed tobacco.

William was becoming so thin. Hester repeatedly tried to feed him and give him a drink. Still he slept on. She felt almost crazy at the end of seven days. So many visitors, so many good wishes. They flowed and swirled about the room like incense, leaving a blessed odor of love and kindness, along with pies and cakes and loaves of bread.

Everyone agreed that no one could be blamed. It had simply been an accident. The group of men had been riding. Their horses were lively and well behaved when they neared the bridge where the water was churning and roiling only a foot below. But when the henhouse floated down the swollen creek and crashed into the bridge, William's horse lunged to the left, away from the terrifying crash, and unseated William so that he flew through the air. His head hit the side of the bridge.

Amos Fisher said reverently that it sounded like a ripe melon when he hit the ground.

Phineas Stoltzfus said, "*Ach, du lieva.*"

They came and cried with Frances, wrung Elias's hand, shook their heads in sorrow at the sight of his beautiful young wife sitting so stony-faced, so unmoving. A good thing she was barren. The little ones need not see their Dat like this. An *shaute soch*.

The brothers-in-law and sisters came, their voices hushed, their footsteps muted as they rocked back and forth, their hands clasped behind their backs, unable to voice the emotion they felt.

Johnny would not enter the room, saying it gave him the shivers. Hester knew better.

They ate their meals together. The Amish women of the community cooked and did the washing. They spoke of it that the young wife would not cry. Had not cried, ever, that anyone could tell. It was the Indian in her. They didn't feel the things white people did. Death was different to Indians.

Hannah Troyer's voice rose. The wart on the end of her nose jumped when she spoke emphatically, "He's not dead yet."

Eliza Bert's eyebrows jumped, and she said he may as well be.

All of this was only a buzz in Hester's ears. Unable to sleep well, afraid he would wake and call her name, she never slept deeply, which finally caused her days to take on a dreamlike quality. She was finding it hard to separate the real from the unreal.

When gentle souls clasped her hand in both of theirs and cried great quantities of tears, her face remained serene, calm, dry-eyed. Her large black eyes were rimmed with gray shadows. Her skin was dry from the lack of fresh air and much-needed moisture.

Toward the end of the ninth day, after everyone had gone home and Frances had swept the floor, she stood over her son, crying and smacking her lips in the odd way she had. As she bade Hester good night with a touch on her shoulder, the door opened and Elias entered alone.

"Go on home, Frances." He spoke the words with unaccustomed authority. Frances went without a backward glance.

Elias came slowly toward Hester and stopped directly in front of her chair. "Hester."

She looked up, questioning.

"He won't live, you know."

Hester said nothing.

"Not anymore. Tomorrow is the tenth day."

Hester nodded.

"I came to tell you that in spirit, I have stood by you. William is so much like his mother. I don't believe you've always had a good life with my son." In the light of the fire, a teardrop, like silver, appeared, trembled, and dropped, creating a glistening rivulet of moisture on one brown cheek. "God has mysterious ways, but sometimes they are not so mysterious. You will be free to love again, and I believe that is his will. You are a special woman, and I also believe he has plans for you."

He hesitated, then placed a thin hand on her shoulder. "*Herr saya.*"

Silence laden with kindness whispered its way into the room. "You will always have a home here. You may always stay if you want to, my daughter."

His presence and kind words were hard to grasp as a great knot of fear and self-condemnation formed in her throat. "But, I am not worthy of your blessing. I have not always loved William, nor bowed to his will in the way he required. God is punishing me for rising up against him."

"As I have not always loved my Frances, Hester. You and I have done the best we could. I have full trust that we will someday hear the words, 'Well done, thou good and faithful servant.'" The silence was unbroken as Elias laid a hand on Hester's shoulder once more, as if the touch could assure her of his words. He offered a solid, warm caress to comfort and fill her with the same faith he carried deep in his heart, covered only by his humble demeanor.

Then, in a broken cry, Hester breathed. "He must live. He must. So I can have a chance to do better."

Elias sighed, a ragged sound of pity which grew from his own agony of living out his years with a woman devoid of compassion. "You could do your best, and it would fall short every time."

"But God must give me another chance." Her words were heavy with desperation.

For a long moment, Elias stood close to his son, watching the slight rising and falling of his chest. The oil lamp flickered, sputtered, and then resumed its steady glow. The shadows on the whitewashed wall crept after Elias's form as he stepped forward, bending slowly to brush back a lock of William's dark hair. The corners of his mouth twisted as he struggled for control.

"I think *unser Herren Jesu* understands William. I think he knows his nature. He was born with one much like his mother has. He took Jesus as his Savior and tried to follow him, but his exacting nature often got in the way. He did the best he could. I trust God understands this when he reaches the other shore. William loved you, Hester, in his own way."

Why did those words bring her comfort when his previous ones did not? Was she somehow responsible for William's salvation?

"Thank you, Elias, for your kindness."

He nodded once, wished her a good night, and then moved out the door and into the night.

It was only then that Hester lost all reserve. The stone in her heart was smashed to tiny fragments as she bent over, pressed down by the weight of her disappointment. It could have been better. Their marriage had fallen so short of her expectations. She had longed to be cherished and loved for who she was, not for who he wanted her to be, as he tried to mold her into a more devoted, strict, and spiritual wife.

Sobs tore from her throat, dry, rasping sounds of grief and unfulfillment. She rocked back and forth, her hands covering her face, her eyes closed tightly against the awful battle in her heart. If only he would live, she would tell him all this. She would pour out words of love, help him change, teach him compassion somehow. Oh, somehow she would find a way.

As the oil burned low, the smell of the rancid wick stopped Hester's keening. She brought up the corner of her black apron, swabbed her face, and then bent to extinguish the flame, throwing the room into darkness, except for the dying fire in the great fireplace. It was enough.

Hester sat back in her chair and turned her face to William. He was but a slight bump in the white bed, his hair etched dark against the pillow.

"Why must you go now, William? Why did we ever meet on my father's fateful wedding day? What plan did God see?"

Getting up, she placed a hand on his chest and stroked the fabric of his nightshirt, her hand stumbling on the row of buttons. She felt his forehead and his lips, which were dry and parched. Going to the bucket on the dry sink, she poured a small amount of water on a cloth, wrung it into the dishpan, and wiped his mouth lightly. His cheeks were so sunken, so white. She wiped his face all over as if to instill life.

She knew that beneath the caked black hair there was a large, angry bruise that had spread almost the entire way across his skull. She touched it now with her long, delicate, brown fingers. Her lips moved in prayer. Turning down the white quilt, she brought his hand, the large calloused hand that held her so many times, tenderly to her lips. "I love you, William." Her voice was low, whispered, calm.

The storm of her grief had prepared her for God's will. Whether he lived or whether he died, he was the Lord's.

The windowpanes let in a small amount of the night sky. Hester moved to the door, lifted the heavy iron latch, and stepped outside, closing it softly behind her. The air was cold. The chill crept up her arms and across her shoulders. She wrapped her arms around her thin waist and lifted her face to find the familiar constellations. A sliver of a moon hung low in the sky, the remainder of it like a veil trying to appear invisible, but it was there.

Unbelievably, she heard Kate's low laugh. "You know, Hester, the moon thinks it's clever, showing us only portions of itself, but we know it's there," she had said.

Tears of longing rained down Hester's face. She wished to bury her face in Kate's old blue dress, her shoulder warm and soft and forgiving, to feel her soft hands pat her back, her voice crooning, making a terrible world into a perfectly beautiful one.

The shrill cry of spring peepers came up from the creek. It was the seasonal ritual, this beckoning of spring, along with a call for purple violets and yellow, round-faced dandelions. Turning, Hester lifted the latch to go inside. She hesitated at the high-pitched warble of the screech owl. Another one replied, a melodious sound of two of God's creatures.

She slept fitfully, too exhausted to stay awake or to sleep soundly. Just before morning, when the clock's hands on the mantle crept toward five, William breathed his last. Hester didn't know. She had fallen asleep for only an instant. She woke with a start, went to William, and felt the difference immediately. There was no movement; the rising and falling of his chest had stopped. His face was slack, gray.

Quite simply, Hester did not know what to do. The tears that should have come, the grief she should have felt, were replaced by a familiar shroud of indifference, a separation from reality.

When Frances pushed her way in, her eyes wide with fear, her face white beneath the black kerchief on her head, she stopped at Hester's chair, a question in her eyes, her mouth working.

Hester looked up. "He's gone."

Frances nodded and went to William's bed. The familiar sighs and sobs of grief, the wet smacking of her lips, began all over again. She keened, lifting her face, then fell on her knees, her cries reaching levels of hysteria.

Hester stood, helped her up, and patted her shoulder clumsily. She spoke words of encouragement, but nothing could stop the rushing torrent of Frances's sorrow. A mother's grief, Hester reasoned, is a desperate hurt, the tearing away of a child before his time.

And so she comforted, answered questions, shouldered accusations. Yes, she should have stayed awake. She should have, certainly.

But the curtain of death was drawn, and Frances could find no way to push it back.

CHAPTER 16

COVERED COMPLETELY IN BLACK, HER HAT PULLED well over the sides of her face, Hester stood alone by the casket. It was a plain, wooden box where her husband lay, waiting to be lowered into the wet soil of Lancaster County, in the graveyard where mounds of fresh earth were heaped over the graves of the children who had not survived the winter.

The singsong voice of the minister reading the *leid* failed to bring any response from the grieving widow, while Frances blew her nose copiously behind her. Elias bowed his head, wept quietly, but remained calm, his face a harbor of peace.

The horses and carriages tied along the fence were in a neat row, the group of mourners all in black. The trees had not yet begun to push their buds, their branches stark and black as well. The grass was olive green mingled with the dead brown of winter, bent over, waiting to be pushed out of existence by fresh, lively, new shoots.

After the Lord's Prayer, Hester stayed by the grave as Frances and Elias turned to go. She felt a tap on her shoulder. Hester turned.

"You can ride back with me." It was Johnny, the brother-in-law. Without Naomi, his wife.

"No."

Without another word he turned away, a deep crimson spreading across his face, his eyes blinking with humiliation at the low-lying fury in her one word of refusal.

The funeral dinner had been prepared by members of the Amish community. Long tables were set in William and Hester's house, then filled with great platters of sliced beef, mashed potatoes and gravy, along with cheese and applesauce. Hester sat humbly with Elias and Frances, William's brothers and sisters, and the family's large, rowdy group of children. She spoke when she was spoken to and acknowledged well-wishers, but nothing seemed real.

She did not want to be noticed. She wished they'd all go away and leave her alone. Yet she did not want to be alone with her thoughts this first evening, with William's passing so close. It seemed as if he should be there sitting by her side, laughing, always glad to be among his brethren.

She was so weary, so bone-tired, and yet she still needed to spend the remainder of the day with William's family, the dreaded Johnny among them. She sighed a small breath of defeat. She was seated on a bench beside the fire, William's sister Amanda holding her infant daughter beside her, surrounded by children, aunts, and cousins. She didn't notice her at first. It was only when a narrow black form sat on the bench beside her and a hand reached over to clasp her brown one firmly in her own that she turned her head to see two bright-brown eyes, like polished stones, peer up at her like an inquisitive sparrow.

"Hester." The word was spoken solidly, well placed, like bricks, square and useful and sensible. The voice was low, accompanied by a dip of heavy eyelids held there, shutting away curiosity, as if she wanted to share a moment of silence, of companionship. Then the eyelids bounced back and the curiosity resumed, brighter than ever.

"I am Bappie Kinnich."

Hester smiled, a slow, hesitant widening of her perfect lips.

"Barbara King, in English. Every old maid in Lancaster Country is called *Bappie*. Don't ask me why." She chuckled, then quickly covered her mouth with her hand, clenched tightly around her chin as if to squelch any humor or unseemly words.

"You are Hester. The wife of my second cousin, William. We have never met, likely because I have been teaching school in Tulpehocken Valley, about twenty-five miles away as the crow flies. As the crow doesn't fly, it's a long arduous trip, hard on the backside."

Hester wasn't sure if she had heard correctly, so she didn't say anything.

"So, Hester, what are your plans?"

Hester shrugged her shoulders, a gesture revealing the blankness she felt, the complete absence of anything called a plan.

"You don't have any, right?"

Hester shook her head.

"I didn't think so."

Bappie leaned back to allow a large uncle to pass. Her eyebrows were lowered in annoyance, but only for a short time. "You don't want to stay in this stone house by yourself." It was a statement, not a question, and not a gentle inquiry either.

"I guess not." Another statement. "No, I don't plan on it, but I hardly know where else to go." Hester spoke so softly Bappie had to lower her head to hear her.

Bappie's head swiveled in both directions as if she were waiting for a passing team or a pedestrian, the way Emma Ferree did in town. Then she lowered her head. "You don't have family, do you?"

"In Berks County."

"Not Amish."

"Yes, they are Amish. Hans and Annie Zug."

Bappie's mouth dropped open. "You're . . ."

Clearly speechless now, she drew back, her eyes wide open, her small mouth open in disbelief. "You're that Indian baby!"

"Yes, I guess so."

"Oh, *siss unfashtendich*!"

Again, Bappie clapped a hand over her mouth and closed her eyes to stares of disapproval. When the coast was clear, she launched into a loudly whispered account of everything she had heard about Hester over the years. She knew Annie, all right. Couldn't stand her. Mean as a wasp. No apologies were offered after each blunt statement, so Hester took it the way Bappie said it—as an honest opinion that didn't bother to be clothed in masks of righteousness or pride.

"Well, here's my offer. I don't want to teach another year. Those people in Tulpehocken Valley are about the limit. I'm tired of their *gamach*. So would you want me to live here with you? I have my own place, but it's small."

Hester rolled awkwardly into a pit of despair. She searched for words, her eyes large and frightened.

Bappie saw immediately the need to reserve her proposition and said so quickly, grabbing both of Hester's hands and holding them warmly in her own, as her brown eyes filled with quick, glistening tears of sympathy.

"Ach, Hester, I'm not fit. No wonder I don't have a husband. Forget what I said. You barely know who I am."

Quickly, Hester grabbed back Bappie's hands and hung on as if they were a branch in floodwaters. "No. Oh, no. Let's just. . . Bappie, please come visit me on Sunday. I have no one and no place to go. Elias, Father, wants me to stay, but Frances." Her voice faded away.

"Frances? She's a regular scarecrow. Meaner, too."

Hester smiled and lifted her own hand to cover her mouth as Bappie clapped a hand to her chin again. The eyes above the hand sparkled and danced mischievously, rolled in Frances's direction, then closed as she laughed quietly.

"I'll be back Sunday." With that, Bappie got up and made her way quickly through the room, stopping to talk to a few relatives before heading out the door.

Hester held babies, talked to the bashful children, and listened to Frances's account of William's accident and his life with Hester. She acknowledged kind words of sympathy, shaking hands with so many people they seemed to be an endless line of faces and figures dressed in black.

Her head spun with weariness. She longed to lie down anywhere. She seriously thought of sitting against a wall somewhere, wherever she could close her eyes, but knew she could not until the last well-wisher had gone through that door.

The night did come, as it always does, but never was the veil of darkness more anticipated. She refused every offer from kind folks who wanted to stay the night, saying she would be safe here with Elias and Frances.

She fell into bed and remembered drawing the quilt over her shoulders before falling into a deep and restful sleep, the sound of the tree frogs and barking foxes going undetected.

The bedroom was pitch dark when Hester opened her eyes. The soft sighing of a spring rain against the windowpanes reminded her of William's passing, a gray mourning that filled her heart, dripping from the battered portion that remained.

She had never imagined the despair his death would bring, the solid weight of guilt mixed with disappointment, the life-draining inadequacy of her spirit. If only she had done better. She had been unfit to be the helpmeet she had promised to be on the day she spoke her sacred vows. God had not blessed their union with children, heirs to William's family, and it was her fault. Yes, he had been harsh at times, but that was his right. He was the husband, she the lesser vessel, and she had never succumbed fully to his will. Now she must live with the punishment God had wrought. He had taken William, and that, too, was her fault.

Wave after wave of humiliation accompanied the falling rain that blew softly against the dark windowpanes, until the thought of William became a torment. She must never think of marrying again. In her wildest imagining, she had not thought of marriage as the burden it had become, unable to bow fully to the will of her husband and his family.

She had spoken out boldly, accusing him of his lack of love, when all the while it had been her own stubborn will refusing to bend. It was the way the Indians in this Pennsylvania forest refused to bend to the demands of the white man who hacked down their sacred trees, who bought and owned the land they assumed belonged to the Creator they worshiped.

She would never be a white woman.

Somehow, before Barbara King came back to visit, she must leave. She would find her way to the western frontier, to her people. She would speak to Elias and Frances. Perhaps they would understand her sorrow.

The gray light of dawn brought fresh resolve. This time she would ask for a horse. She would plan better now that she was aware of the dangers, the thirst, the hunger that had been her constant companion when she left Hans and Annie's homestead. She had one wish—to see Emma and Billy Ferree. She had never thanked them properly, or enough, for what they had done.

She was surprised to find herself weak, her joints aching, her head spinning dizzily, as she got out of bed, found her clothes, and stoked the fire. Her hands shook as she swung the kettle over the new flames. The room tilted as she brought the cold water to her face at the dry sink.

She was bringing the steel-toothed comb through her heavy, black hair when the latch was lifted with a resounding crack of steel, the door creaked open, and Frances stood in the gray, early-morning light.

"You're up."

"Yes."

"Have you eaten?"

"No."

"Then come eat breakfast with Elias and me. Johnny and Naomi have spent the night. It would be nice if you ate with us."

Hester kept her back turned, her shaking hands twisting her hair into a bun on the back of her head.

"Well?"

"All right. I will come."

There was no reply. Only the creaking of the door and the latch falling into place behind Frances.

Hester finished inserting the steel hairpins. She reached for the white muslin cap, placed it on her head, and tied the heavy strings under her chin. She made her bed, tucking the white quilt beneath the pillows, stroked the top to smooth out the creases, then turned to the corner for the bellows. She clapped them up and down to fan the small flames licking out below the chunk of wood she had placed on the dying embers.

She swept the hearth and carefully replaced the chairs. She would clean the house properly after the men had moved the wooden benches to the attic, where it was customary to store them until the next church service.

The act of carrying out normal, mundane chores was healing and allowed her a sense of well-being, if only in sparse amounts. She threw a thin black shawl over her shoulders and stepped out into the fine, misty rain, then made her way to the addition built onto her own stone farmhouse, hesitating at the door.

She dreaded the breakfast table with Johnny's mocking eyes. Taking a deep breath, she knocked lightly, then pushed up the heavy latch to find the family seated around the table, candles on the mantle shelf illuminating the room, the smell of bacon and fried cornmeal mush hovering thickly around the room.

Frances cleared her throat. "We have been waiting."

"I'm sorry." Quickly Hester shrugged out of her shawl and slid quietly into a chair, her hands clasped in her lap, her eyes downcast.

All heads bowed instantly in silent prayer. Then Elias lifted his head, cleared his throat, and looked around the table. "Everyone help yourselves now."

How could Hester know her own stark, tragic beauty in the flickering yellow light of the candles? If anything, the experience of sadness only enhanced the dark luster of her large, almond-shaped eyes, the thick, black lashes drooping in remembered sorrows. She bowed her long, slender neck in humility, her mouth vulnerable with the sense of past mistakes, a sight that left Johnny's eyes glued to her as he tried unsuccessfully to tear them away.

Naomi, a small wren of a woman, bright-eyed and quick in her movements, helped the four children with their breakfasts, cutting the slabs of fried mush, tying a bib around the one-year-old, completely oblivious to her husband's wandering.

"You have slept well?" Elias asked, his eyes kind.

"Yes."

"That's good. I was afraid you wouldn't sleep after everything was over."

Frances blinked, once, twice. She opened her mouth as if to speak, hesitated, then closed it. She took up her spoon, toying with her bacon. Suddenly she spoke, her words cutting through the kind words of her husband. "I told you, Elias. Death is different to the Indians. They do not feel loss the way we do. Neither do they treasure life."

Naomi looked up, her birdlike eyes darting from one face to another.

Hester's heart leaped within her. She recognized the opportunity to present her case. It took all of her courage, but she folded her hands on her lap, lifted her head, and began. "Yes, Frances, you are right. I am an Indian. I have failed you in many ways, as I have failed William."

Elias raised his hand to silence her. Frances drew in a sharp breath, then laid down her spoon, poised to hear. "If you will be kind enough to give me one good horse, I will leave today. I will ride away from Lancaster County to find my people. I am not fit to be an Amish wife and mother."

Frances hissed, "You can't!"

"Why not?" Hester was calm and composed, drawing strength from her own words.

"How would that make us appear in the eyes of the Amish community? Our son's wife! Riding off to join the. . . those heathen Indians? We would be the ones who failed then. They would excommunicate you." Shrieking now, her voice high-pitched in desperation, her head bobbing in agitation, Frances was clearly horrified.

Elias sat as a stone, unmovable.

Johnny snickered self-consciously.

Naomi broke out. "Hester, why do you say that? You have been a good wife. By all appearances you have been an excellent housekeeper and a learned quilter. William seemed happier than I have ever seen him."

Elias began nodding his head in approval. "I told Hester she can always stay here. She is now the heir to the farm rightfully. She is William's wife."

"*Schtill!*" Frances's command slashed across the table. The children sat up and stopped chewing, their eyes wide with interest.

"I don't know why you would say such a thing. Elias, how can Hester own this farm? An Indian? I certainly hope you have not gone to see a lawyer, unbeknownst to me."

"It is the law, Frances. The wife inherits the husband's share."

"William had nothing!" Frances spat.

Hester listened. She could think of nothing she wanted less than this farm or the great cold stone house that held William's austerity. His rules clung to the whitewashed walls; the shadow of his superiority stained the wooden beams of the ceiling. The wide oak floorboards sounded the echoes of his displeased footsteps; the marriage bed spoke of her inability to conceive. Every corner of the house was rife with the ghosts of her shortcomings.

"I don't want the farm." Soft and low, Hester stated the fact.

Johnny's eyes pierced her face. Naomi saw the look of her husband. "I'll take it," he said quickly.

Elias looked to the eager, flushed face of his son. Frances trembled, then a slow smile spread across her face, the pleasure erasing the anxiety. "Why, of course. The most perfect solution! God be praised!"

Seeing the happiness on their grandmother's face, the children smiled and resumed eating, content.

Elias blew on his pewter mug of tea. For a long while he said nothing. He looked first at Naomi, whose eyes were bright with anticipation, then bowed his head to the turn of circumstances he knew were out of his control. "It is done, then."

Those words sealed the ownership of the farm.

Triumphant, Johnny's eyes seared into Hester's, conveying victory over her. She lowered her eyes. Otherwise, the contempt would have flashed, and Naomi would have seen. Best to let her revel in her husband's acquisition.

"Although I cannot allow you to have a horse. It is simply not safe for you to travel on your own with robbers and highway men about as thick as fleas. Johnny and I will build a cabin for you here on the home place. You can be *maud* to Naomi. We will pay your living expenses."

Hester shook her head before Elias stopped speaking. "No."

Frances breathed out, so obvious was her relief. With shaking hands, she lifted her tea and sipped a tiny portion, blinking rapidly.

"Where will you go?" Johnny's eyes begged her to stay. She was a necessity for him like she had been for Hans.

"Barbara King is coming to make me an offer. But I would rather travel to Ohio, to go back to my people where I belong."

Elias shook his head, his mouth grim. "Hester, you are one of us. You do not belong with the Indians. They are being steadily pushed farther west, becoming more savage and more hostile as time goes on. Or so we hear.

You have been raised among the Amish, you have promised to keep the faith. How could you turn your back to us now?"

Stony-faced, Hester lifted her eyes. "It would be out of necessity that I do this."

They allowed her the good little mare, Fannie, and the top buggy that day. She had only one wish, and that was to visit Emma Ferree, which they agreed to.

Hester's face was flushed with anticipation as she took up the reins, clucked to the little mare, and rode away from the farm in the gray mist of a spring rain. The wheels turned, picking up mud and old withered leaves of winter. Fannie's hooves made a sucking sound in the low, wet places, but Hester saw neither the mud nor the gray drizzle. On this one day she was doing something she had wanted to do for years—return to Emma and Billy.

The surrounding fields were still unplowed. Old wet cornstalks bent low, driven into the earth by the heavy snows of winter. The hayfields were drab, but new growth was sprouting in low places, the promise of an abundance of grass to cut into hay.

An oncoming team of horses made her pull on the right rein, drawing Fannie to the side, allowing the team to pass. Inquisitive faces peered out from the open front of the buggy. Hester nodded, glad when they continued on their way.

On the outskirts of town, the road widened and hardened. The stones from the lime quarry made traveling easier. Fannie pricked up her ears as they passed the blacksmith shop on the right, a low stone building with a wide chimney. Smoke poured from it, created by the hot coals used by the smithy.

She remembered her excursions with Hans, the smell of the horses' hooves as his trimming knife cut expertly into them. His strong, muscular arms pounded the shoes into shape. There was the anvil, the hot coals, the odor of hay and corn and manure. From her perch on the wagon, she would take in all of this, cultivating a love of horses that Hans had taken away when he forbade her to ride. Still, it was an enriching part of her childhood, listening to Hans's voice as he told her stories, bouncing along on the seat of the spring wagon beside him. He had been a good father to her.

Many carriages passed her now. There were poor farmers in clumsy wagons with wide wheels, covered in mud. Drawn by thin mules, their ribs strained against the wet, brown coat covering them. Their necks were too thin, their heads enormous and bobbing, unsightly ears above them.

There were also ornate hacks, polished to a high gloss and drawn by high-stepping black horses, their coats gleaming in the rain. Their drivers were top-hatted and mustached, with long, thick sideburns down their cheeks like squirrels' tails. Ladies protected themselves from the rain with fancy parasols as they cast superior glances at the Amish woman clad entirely in black, her plain, serviceable buggy drawn by the squat, little mare.

A group of children dashed across the road, their hats and bonnets slick with the rain, the girls' skirts like striped flowers, the petticoats beneath them ruffled and sewn by loving mothers.

A lone boy strolled through the rain, rolling a hoop expertly, his white shirt front in stark relief against the gray of his opened coat. For one instant, Hester thought it must be Billy, then remembered that Billy would be fifteen years old now, close to sixteen, and no longer a child.

She drove up the narrow passageway called Water Street, turned left on Orange, and then right onto Mulberry. Everywhere she looked, there was a construction site. Houses were springing up like mushrooms.

The homes were all made of wood. Even the chimneys were slapped together with mud, the way Hans disliked. He said more houses burned to the ground because of shoddy chimneys than for any other reason. Hester knew the wealthy lot owners erected these wood dwellings cheaply, charged a goodly sum for rent, and made a hefty profit. It was only when yet another fire broke out that they saw the error of their ways.

She drew Fannie off to the right and tied her to a lamppost when she neared Emma Ferree's house. Better to walk the last distance, then knock on the door to see if she was home.

Her breath came rapidly as she blanketed the steaming Fannie. She patted her forehead, promised her return, and walked across the street, a lone, black figure, the corners of her shawl spreading out behind her.

There it was. The sturdy house made of stone and wood, the steps going up right off the street as if to welcome any person who wanted to enter.

Hester drew in a deep breath, steadied herself, and lifted a hand to knock. She tried once, then twice. Disappointed, she raised her hand again and knocked harder. When no one answered, she drew back to gaze through the window. On a day such as this, Emma would be burning her oil lamp and perhaps a few candles.

Obviously, there was no one home. She turned to make her way back down the steps when she thought of Walter Trout. It would be better to see him than no one at all.

She made her way to his front door, resolutely, remembering his kindness, his effusive words of praise. Seeing him was the closest thing to meeting Emma Ferree, and it would have to do for today.

CHAPTER 17

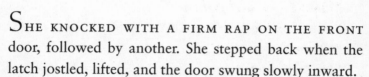

SHE KNOCKED WITH A FIRM RAP ON THE FRONT door, followed by another. She stepped back when the latch jostled, lifted, and the door swung slowly inward.

Hester's mouth dropped open when a ruffled white housecap appeared around the edge of the door, below which shone two beady blue eyes and a florid pink face. Emma Ferree opened her mouth to speak, closed it again, gave up, and threw both hands in the air, her eyes wide and full of recognition. "*Ach, mein Gott im Himmel!*"

Hester started to laugh, but a sob cut it in two. She fell into Emma's soft, plump arms, bending over to lay her bonneted head on her warm shoulder and to let her tears and hiccuping flow for a long moment. Emma's plump hands patted and soothed, her voice crooning as if Hester were an infant.

Somehow Hester was drawn into the dim hallway, the door was closed behind her, and she was enveloped in warmth and the heavenly scent of ginger and molasses and cinnamon and sugar.

"*Ach, du yay, du yay. Meine Hester. Meine own Hester.* How often my prayers went to heaven because of you, *meine Liebchen, miene* Indian girl, still so beautiful." Exclaiming nonstop, Emma reached for Hester's hat strings, yanked on them and removed the hat. Her brilliant gaze swept over the white cap, taking in the severe cut of her black dress, cape, and apron.

"You really are Amish!" she said forcefully.

The back door swung open. The gray light from the doorway was darkened as Walter Trout hove his large frame through it.

"Emma?" he shouted.

Emma held up one finger. "Yes, Walter?"

"Where are you?"

"Here in the hallway. Come look who's here, come quick."

Walter Trout filled up the width of the hallway with his presence, his reaction much the same as Emma's. He began with a polite handshake but pulled Hester into a gentlemanly embrace with one arm, looked down on her face, and proclaimed her his long-lost daughter.

Hester let herself absorb the luxury of their welcome, the love that flowed unhampered by pride or judgment. Her soul expanded with the knowledge that so much kindness was available and that God had not forgotten her after all.

Walter's shirt smelled of ginger and cinnamon, his breath like sugar.

She found herself seated at the kitchen table, a checked cloth covering it. Walter arranged cookies on a platter. Emma put the tea kettle on the stove, and brought out china cups, talking all the while. "Tell us, please tell us,

Hester, how is your life? Does he treat you well? Are you happy?"

"My husband is dead." When she spoke the words, they crowded her consciousness, blotting out the moments of love and acceptance mere minutes before.

Walter became very still. "Oh no! Oh no! What happened?"

Emma sat down heavily, her hands to her face. "The rain? The flooded creeks?"

"Yes. Yes. He rode with a group of men here to Lancaster to reinforce the lower part with sandbags. His horse shied going across a bridge and threw him against the bridge's stone foundation."

"Dead instantly?"

"No. He lived for eleven days. He never woke up."

"Oh, *mein Herr*. An act of God. An act of God."

Hester nodded. Guilt flooded her eyes.

Emma spoke on, freely and openly. "God took him. He did. That's good. He was not for you. It was not his will that you marry him."

Walter came to stand behind Emma's chair. He reached out a hand and patted her round shoulder. "Now, now, Emma, my dear."

Hester's mouth opened in surprise when Emma reached up to clasp the round fingers placed on her shoulders and kept them there. "What?" Hester could not put words to the question, so she gestured toward the clasped hands.

"Oh!" Emma and Walter said with one voice and a great display of merriment. Their pink faces were wreathed in smiles, all the aging lines and wrinkles turning into little trails of happiness. "You don't know! Why, of course not. Walter asked me to marry him after Billy ran off to the war. Oh, and you don't know that, either," Emma burst out.

And so began a long tale, a story spun into emotional clouds of longing for Billy, newly discovered marital bliss, the blessings received from the Lord for their marriage, and spending their days together in gratitude.

"But, you didn't like Walter," Hester stated, laughing.

"Indeed, indeed, were it not for Billy's leaving, I would not have my darling Emma." Walter, always the well-bred gentleman, patted her arm reassuringly.

"That and my washline," Emma chirped. "How I hated the fact that Walter could see my nightclothes flapping on the line! It was downright immodest. And it never failed, I'd hang them out, and there he was like a nosy gopher, up over the top of that fence."

Walter laughed, and his tears ran copiously as he held his rotund stomach. "Now, Emma, I never looked at your washline."

"Puh! That is a *schnitza*!

"Billy got himself in trouble down at the livery. He punched a drunken man in the stomach, then let his horse loose. He had fines to pay after his arrest and couldn't go back to the livery, ever. He almost landed in the stocks on the square." Emma shook her head as sorrow filled her deep-set eyes.

She clucked and lamented, but he was gone now. "Old enough, he was, and fit as a fiddle, that boy. Strong in the legs like a draft horse, he could run for miles without being winded. He'd make a good soldier, but any day, he might be killed." Emma could hardly live with that.

Walter added solemnly that as long as the French supported the Indians to the north, and they fought the English colonists this way, the war would continue. It all boiled down to the lust for land. The Indians had been driven to Pennsylvania from the south, and here they had been wiped out, driven west to Ohio and beyond.

Then Hester began her story. Her marriage to William, her failure to give William children, his stringent rules and exacting nature.

Walter and Emma allowed Hester to continue unhindered, giving no indication of their opinions. They drank cup after cup of tea, snipping off so much sugar with each cup that the solid, white cone was disappearing rapidly, which seemed quite wasteful to Hester. But she must remember, these were English people, not frugal Amish. So she allowed Emma to place a large piece of white sugar in her own tea, sipped it with relish, and pronounced it very good. Frances would have a fit.

The last of her story was her plan to travel to Ohio to look for her people. She presented her case well without seeking pity, stating her inability to be a good wife to William because of her Indian heritage.

The loud ticking of the clock was the only sound in the homey kitchen. The candlelight cast the whole room into the warmth of its yellow glow. The kettle purred on the lid of the cast iron stove. The checked tablecloth was covered with molasses cookies and tea, the cone of sugar, and a white milk pitcher, so much like Kate's kitchen. The only thing missing was children, a baby in the cradle. There had always been babies. And Kate's devotion to them.

Walter sighed, and his great bald head swiveled from side to side. He stood up. "I'll tend to your horse, Hester. She must be thirsty."

Hester nodded. Her eyes were bright with unshed tears, her mouth soft and trembling.

Emma was careful with her words. She chose them deliberately, while letting Hester know that she had done nothing wrong. In fact, she had done well. God had chosen to take William, yes, but not by her sins. Or because of them.

And there was no way on earth she could allow Hester to travel west, a young woman alone. She wouldn't last two weeks before some ruffian would make off with her horse and perhaps even herself.

"Hester, my dearest heart, you must finally make peace with who you are—an Indian, yes. There is nothing wrong with being one. And you were Amish-raised by a loving Kate. And you've lived with Hans, Annie, William, and Frances, all created by God, too, living here by the grace of God. Imperfect, yes; perfectly lovable, no. Blaming yourself has got to go. None of this is a fault of your own. But if you want to hang on to that whole misery, then go right ahead."

Hester cowered beneath Emma's forthright manner.

"Stop running away."

"But I'm not."

"Yes, you are."

"But it's for the best."

"Do you really want to go?" Emma's beady blue eyes shot darts of truth. When they hit their mark, Hester's shoulders sagged and her face relaxed, as warm, healing tears appeared in her black eyes. They hung like silver jewels on the thick, dark lashes, trembled, and then splashed on her cheeks and down the front of her black dress, where they soaked into the fabric, turning it darker than it was.

What followed was a shock to Emma. She had never heard weeping become so forceful. The sobs of anger emitted from her open mouth, the hoarse heaves of sadness and misery propelled by the power of her guilt and misplaced blame, were frightening. In simple language, Emma urged Hester to grasp forgiveness and draw on God's unlimited supply of grace. Slowly, she dismantled all the explanations and resolve Hester had created to explain what she had experienced.

Emma held her, letting her sobs enter her own heart, and cried with her. Walter's small eyes filled up as he came through the door, and he cried as he filled the teacups. He cried as he sliced ham into the frying pan, sniffed as he seasoned the beans, and wiped at tears that plunked into the water in the dishpan as he peeled potatoes. For he loved Hester so much.

She went home in the fading gray light, the rain splashing on the buggy top and the little brown mare named Fannie. She told Elias and Frances of her plans to move into Emma Ferree's house, the empty one beside Walter and Emma Trout. Quite simply, she wanted to be with them.

No, she would not attend church every time, but she would remain true to the Amish faith. Emma thought it would be best.

Barbara King came to visit on Sunday, early, before the hordes of others arrived who would come to wish the young widow well. She came in on the stiff April wind, the kind that bent tulips double, flopping them against the side of the stone house, brushing their delicate petals. She whirled through the door and banged it shut behind her, latched it with a loud ring of iron, and turned to the fireplace, rubbing her hands furiously.

Hester rose immediately, her black dress swishing about her narrow hips as she used the bellows to stir up the fire.

"Chilly out there." Barbara handed her stiff black hat to Hester, loosened the long steel pin so she could slide the black shawl off her shoulders, folded it expertly, and gave it to Hester as well. "How's it going, Hester? I think of you every night."

"Good, Barbara, it's—"

"Call me Bappie."

"Bappie, I went to visit an old friend, Emma Ferree, and her new husband, and she helped me out of a few *dumbkopf* decisions."

"Don't you know the old saying? 'No decisions for a year, when a spouse passes away.'"

"What? A year? A whole year to live here with Johnny and Naomi? I can't," Hester whispered her defeat.

"Why not? You've got it made. Big stone house. Money. Frances at your beck and call."

Hester told Bappie about Johnny and Naomi, and the farm.

"You're not thinking straight, Hester. Take the farm."

"I don't want it."

Bappie looked thoughtfully at Hester, her bright brown eyes polished with understanding. Then she nodded firmly, signaling her empathy. Hester's heart relaxed in the strength of knowing that Bappie, Emma, and Walter all stood with her.

"You're right. You shouldn't accept the farm."

"I'm going to live with—well, not *with* Walter and Emma, but in the empty house beside them. In the town of Lancaster on Mulberry Street."

Up went Bappie's eyebrows. "What will you do for a living?"

"They won't charge me rent. I'll make quilts." She kept her love of herbs and doctoring hidden from Bappie.

"I was hoping you would consent to live with me." Bappie spoke softly, so unlike her.

Hester saw the disappointment in her eyes, the dejection in her shoulders. Hester wavered in her decision. Should she accept her offer first? Indecision cracked the shaky new foundation Emma had placed beneath her so firmly only a few days ago.

Suddenly Bappie sat upright, shrugged her shoulders, and said it was all right, she'd always done well on her own and would continue to.

"I go to Lancaster's curb market, selling garden things. I'll see you on Friday and Saturday sometimes, maybe?"

In that moment, Hester told her of the herbs, her plans to grow them, to bottle tinctures and teas, and to go wherever there was a need. And how William had not wanted her to do this.

Bappie was enthralled. She asked dozens of questions, saying the need for a service such as she spoke of was large and growing.

"Is there room for a garden in the back lot of Emma Ferree's house?" Bappie asked finally.

Hester considered, mulling over the fact that she did not really know this Barbara King, a distant relative of William's. She watched the woman, warily. Reddish hair, a nose like a hawk, observant eyes, a long and lean and narrow face like William's and Frances's. The only thing soft about Bappie was her eyes, bright like polished stones, but guileless, and yes, soft. She was all sharp angles, no womanly curves anywhere, her black dress hanging as if from a coat rack, loose, empty, almost rectangular.

Finally Hester decided the best way was total honesty. She had been betrayed too often. "Are you a cousin of Frances?"

"First cousin not to her, but to Elias."

"So how do I know you're nice, like him?"

At this, Bappie hooted a strange laugh, almost like a screech owl at night or the clumsy squawk of the nighthawk. "Hester, you're odd. You can't go tiptoeing through life afraid everyone is not nice. Very few people are. Don't be so serious. You wear your cap so far over your ears, every bit of your hair is covered. Who made you do that? Or were you always so plain, or whatever?"

"William was very conservative."

"May he rest in peace," Bappie said softly but her eyes flashed without piety. "I can bet a nickel that man was very much like his mother." The words were out of her mouth before she could grab them back. Up went the hand, sideways across her mouth, her brown eyes like glistening river pebbles. "Sorry."

Hester shook her head, a smile curving her lips.

"You know how beautiful you are, don't you?" Bappie asked.

Hester frowned and her eyebrows fell, a straight black line over brooding eyes. "Beauty is a curse."

Bappie stared at her, unblinking. "You really do believe that."

"Of course I do."

"Why?"

"Someday I'll tell you."

"Someday? Does that mean you're asking me to live in Emma Ferree's house in town?"

"Are Amish women allowed to live in town? Does our *Ordnung* forbid it?"

Bappie's eyes turned bright with humor. "We'll never know until we try it, will we?"

When the spring rains turned to the heat of summer, Emma Ferree's house was newly whitewashed, the windows polished, the floors scrubbed. There was new ticking in the mattresses, the fireplace was cleaned and whitewashed. Walter Trout repaired the front door, his face red and streaming in the summer sun.

Hester accompanied Bappie to her house in the country, a low dwelling built of logs, fashioned in a peculiar style without an upstairs. It was extremely small, but sufficient for one person. It was built on the south corner of her brother Samuel's farm, a former hut built by an earlier owner to house slaves.

Bappie had beautiful furniture for a single woman. Fashioned in the old German style with intricate scrollwork, the blanket chests and cupboard doors were painted with delicate motifs carefully preserved from the old country.

Bappie put Hester to work cleaning the furniture with oil soap, then polishing it with sheep's wool. They packed it well with heavy blankets on a farm wagon Johnny loaned them. The massive Belgians stood, their heads drooping patiently as he helped them load the valuable pieces. He remained a gentleman, so impressing Bappie that she became quite flustered when she spoke to him.

Hester sat perched on a wooden chest. The sun had climbed high at the noon hour. Heat shimmered across the cornfields. Bright butterflies hovered among the columbine, delicately feeding on the thin nectar of the lavender flowers, bobbing in the stillness.

A meadowlark sang its lusty song, opening its bill like a pair of scissors. Chimney swifts wheeled in the hot, cloudless sky, dozens of them dipping and wheeling as one.

Today there was a song in Hester's heart, an old tune Kate used to sing while doing the wash. It welled up until Hester was humming softly so no one would hear. She lifted her face to the sun, glorying in the summer scents of the earth and the verdant crops, growing so lush and green. Here men's axes had laid the heavy trees to the ground; then they'd used the lumber to build barns and houses for their growing families, a way of life Hester knew well.

Foreign to her was the way of the nomadic Indian, she recognized. Over and over, gratitude for Emma Ferree's sound advice lifted Hester's spirits.

Elias and Frances sent her away, wishing her the blessing, "*Herr saya*," as they clasped her hands warmly in their own. Frances was glad to be rid of her, she knew, but still Hester admired the effort she put forth to stand beside her husband and wish her the usual German blessing.

Naomi said she must come often to visit. Johnny shook her hand, holding it longer than necessary, but she endured his touch, shaking off the repulsiveness. To forgive, to let go, was the Amish way, and the way of all Christians who chose to follow Jesus's teaching.

Bappie turned. "You still back there?"

Hester acknowledged her words with a wave.

Walter and Emma awaited them, motioning them to the back alley. Walter helped Bappie guide the horses carefully to the back door, and the work of unloading the furniture began.

They filled the house with the beautiful German pieces. They scattered bright hooked rugs of blue and purple, yellow and red, across polished oak floors.

Hester put her wedding gifts—the towels and table-cloths, doilies and rugs that were made of rushes—with Bappie's things. She placed the set of china with the blue pattern on the cupboard shelves alongside Bappie's set of white dishes.

Frances gave her William's desk and his rocking chair, tears streaming as she presented them to Hester, her mouth compressed piously when she asked her to take good care of them. They put the desk in the living room with the rocking chair beside it. Hester placed one of her glass vases on the desk top, then picked a bouquet of white daisies to remember William. She could picture him rocking by the fireplace, content after supper, his dark head bent over the massive Bible on his lap.

Bappie laid a small fire in the fireplace and made tea for her helpers. Walter and Emma sat side by side on the bench, watching with eager eyes as she cut a strawberry pie. Shoveling huge wedges onto the pretty blue dishes, Bappie winked broadly at Hester as Walter and Emma began enjoying the sweet dessert. Hester smiled, bending quickly to fold a tea towel into the cupboard drawer. She had the distinct feeling that life could become extremely interesting with Bappie, Walter, and Emma.

Every week they drove Bappie's team out to the homestead, as she called the house that was barely more than a hut. There they weeded and hoed the huge vegetable garden, toiling side by side in the blazing sun. They picked the vegetables that were ripe, set traps for marauding raccoons and opossums, then loaded the weeks' supply of vegetables for the downtown market. On the curb they set up wooden crates, then piled the freshly picked beans, red beets, and cucumbers in pleasing mounds, the tops of the beets dripping with fresh water, the way the townsfolk wanted them, Bappie said. Customers came, looked, and voiced their pleasure at Bappie's fine vegetables.

"No," she'd say, "I'll have cabbage next week." Lifting her thumb and forefinger, she squeezed her eyes shut to mimic how very close the cabbage heads were to being the perfect size, but not quite yet.

She was noisy, her voice rising above the cart wheels, the hooves of the horses, the other sellers hawking their wares. She flung her cap strings over her square shoulders. Her coppery hair gleamed from beneath the wide expanse of muslin, her bright eyes never missing a potential buyer.

She sold peas in the pod for exorbitant prices, and raspberries fat and black and luscious with moisture. Wealthy, fair-skinned ladies fought for her smallest cucumbers, her ruffled heads of lettuce.

Hester helped to set up and kept the piles looking fresh and succulent, her large, dark eyes taking in the way Bappie did business.

The men came, staring at Hester, then looked away respectfully, bending to the wishes of their wives, although many discreetly glanced backward at the beauty of the new Amish girl.

Bappie howled with unashamed glee as she loaded up the empty crates. Passersby frowned at the raucous sound, unable to believe their eyes and ears at that unmannerly vegetable seller. But Bappie sold every morsel, every leaf she brought.

She and Hester counted the money at the kitchen table after the sun had gone down. Bappie leaned back in her chair, a pleased expression spreading across her features. "We're all set, Hester. We'll put enough by to hold us over the winter. I never sold so many vegetables. All you have to do is perch on a crate and look at the crowd." She leaned forward, slapped the table, and said Frances would have a fit, now, wouldn't she?

CHAPTER 18

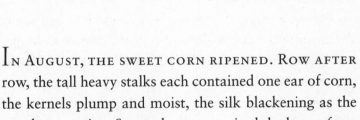

In August, the sweet corn ripened. Row after row, the tall heavy stalks each contained one ear of corn, the kernels plump and moist, the silk blackening as the ears became ripe. So much corn required the heavy farm wagon and two Belgians, which took Bappie immediately to Johnny and Naomi's front door in spite of Hester's disapproval.

When Hester refused to accompany her, Bappie drove off in a tiff, her cap strings flying out behind the back seat of Walter Trout's one-seated buggy. Leaning forward, she rapped the silver mare to a fast trot, muttering to herself about stubborn Indian blood.

Hester watched her go, her arms crossed tightly about her waist, her eyes flashing black heat. If Bappie insisted on hiring that offensive Johnny to haul her corn to market, she'd have to do it alone. Hester was not prepared to work freely in his presence. The moving had been bad enough. That Bappie certainly did have a mind of her own.

The dew was heavy. So heavy, in fact, that by the time Bappie and Hester made their way down the first and

second rows of sweet corn, they were soaked. Their ker-
chiefs clung to their sodden hair, the corn tassels dusted
their heads with clinging, yellow pods. The cornstalks
were wet and itchy, scraping their necks and faces like
rasping claws. They made sacks out of their aprons,
holding up the bottoms by two corners until they bulged
with ears of corn, dew-laden and heavy. Bappie was frenzied in her movements, yanking the corn off the heavy
stalks and filling her apron twice as fast as Hester.

"This corn may as well be made of gold," she crowed,
her breath coming in gasps.

"It's about as heavy," Hester called. She was happy,
working in the early morning. Johnny had not showed
up, thankfully allowing them the use of the wagon without his assistance.

Up and down the rows the women toiled, loading the
large green ears on the bed of the wagon. The sun was a
pulsing red orb in a yellow sky that already reflected its
heat. Not a cloud was in sight, not so much as a small
breeze moved the wet cornstalks.

Hester figured that if the wet heat continued, they'd
have a thunderstorm. She eyed the perfectly staked tomatoes, the heavy, prickly vines of the cucumber plants,
then lifted a hand to shade her eyes as she looked toward the sun. There it was. To the left of the sun was
a brilliant flash of light like an uncolored rainbow, the
harbinger of rain. The sun dog. Well, if the rainstorm
came, they'd dig the vegetables out of the mud, the way
Kate used to.

Her thoughts were not on the mundane task of ripping off ears of corn, when suddenly a solid form ahead

startled her so that she drew back, her eyes wide with alarm. "Oh!"

His grin spreading widely, Johnny stood at the end of the row, his thumbs hooked in the side pockets of his broadfall trousers.

"Hester! Didn't mean to scare you." His teeth flashed white in his dark face, the straw hat pulled low, his hair as dark as midnight, so like William's.

Hester said nothing, bending her head to her task.

He refused to move, to allow her to step out of the row. His dark eyes glittered, black coals shaded by the filthy straw hat.

He opened his mouth to speak, the black coals turned to slits. "You can't always hide," he sneered.

"Johnny!" Bappie's joyous greeting rang from a short distance away. He turned and patiently hailed Bappie, warmly lifting a hand in greeting. Bappie stumbled over her words, so effusive was her welcome. Johnny grinned, praised her growing of the vegetables, and said he'd never seen nicer corn. She'd get a good price today.

Hester turned down another row. Her apron was bulging with the heavy ears, her dress was soaking wet, and she had no plans to step out for that man's inspection. Discreetly, she emptied her apron in between the rows of corn and kept pulling ears, moving away from their voices.

"Hester!"

Bappie's sharp call stopped her short. Slowly she emptied another apron-load of corn, straightened, and resumed picking furiously. The color in her cheeks heightened; her eyes were dark and brooding.

"What are you doing?"

"Picking corn."

"You're dumping it on the ground!"

"So."

"What ails you?"

Angrily Bappie came stomping down the row, bending to pick up the corn Hester had unloaded. "What got over you?" she hissed.

"Get that Johnny away from here," Hester hissed back.

"Why?"

Hester's face was terrible, her eyes boring into Bappie's with an intensity she had never seen. "Just do what I said. I mean it."

Bappie rolled her eyes, but she obeyed. Quickly she loaded the last of the corn onto the wide bed of the wooden wagon, told Johnny to drive, and hopped up behind him, saying Hester would bring the team.

Shrugging his shoulders, he could do nothing other than obey. He lifted the reins, hiyupping to the big, quiet Belgians. Only when the creak of the heavy wheels sounded in her ears did Hester emerge, watching the wagon until it disappeared behind a curtain of overhanging willow branches. Then she stepped out, smoothed down her apron, untied Bappie's gray horse named Silver, and sat heavily on the open seat of the buggy.

Johnny had already taken the team of Belgians home by the time Hester had changed into dry clothes, the blue dress and black cape and apron, topped by the muslin fabric of her cap, her face freshly washed.

At the curb market, the corn was piled in a high, beautiful bin, green and white at the ends, dewdrops clinging to its dark silk. Carrots lay in bunches, bits of black soil clinging to their thick orange roots. Beside them, the first tomatoes, red-cheeked and inviting, added color to the green, lacy carrot tops.

Immediately the buyers came, pushing, shoving, and carrying away great armloads of corn, wooden crates of it, and cloth bags stuffed full. The coins clinked into the cash box as Bappie yelled and made hand gestures, smiling and dipping her head when the praise became too effusive.

Hester talked to perfect strangers, smiling and handing tomatoes and carrots to fat, overdressed housewives and stick-thin women in ruffles, all sweating profusely in the sweltering heat.

"De corn! De corn!" Beckoning excitedly, her face flushed to a high color, a German housewife plowed through the crowd, elbowing her way through the more well-to-do.

"Step back. Watch it there," came snorts of disapproval and words of rebuke, all to no avail. On she came.

"De corn! De corn! Oy, so fresh! So yellow! Just picked!"

Hester found herself laughing freely, the sound like water rippling over smooth stones. She lost herself in the mad, colorful crowd of pushing people. She heard Bappie's words rising and falling, selling her vegetables. She wasn't quiet, nor circumspect, and certainly not humble.

But Hester was carried along by the gaiety, the high spirits that caused Bappie to talk constantly to her customers. Hester smiled without self-consciousness. She spoke to strangers. And she was surprised to find that they weren't strangers after she had spoken to them. She learned from Bappie to be tolerant, happy to let go of her suspicion, her dislike of certain people. To Bappie, they were all the same. They bought her vegetables.

Too tired to cook supper, and the house holding the heat like a tea kettle, Hester and Bappie collapsed in the backyard beneath the shade of a wilted lilac bush at the end of the market day. Bappie lay flat on her back, her knees bent upward, poking into the sky, all sharp angles and dark colors. She had thrown one arm over her forehead and was saying they made enough money to buy a house today.

Hester lay on her stomach, her chin in her hands, her shoulders shaking as she laughed at Bappie's ridiculous expansion of the coins in the wooden box.

A low rumble of thunder grumbled in the distance. The evening sun shone on.

"It'll rain," Hester said shortly.

"Nah! What's wrong with you? The sun's shining as bright as ever."

"It'll rain."

"Hey, what is up with you and Johnny? You act like he's as lovable as a snake."

"He is."

"Oh, come on. He's much nicer than William was. Sorry. May he rest in peace."

Hester rolled onto her back, shaded her eyes the way Bappie did, and outright told her about Johnny's misdeeds at Christmastime, the lies that followed, and her own bowing to his wickedness.

Bappie pulled a blade of grass, chewing it slowly as she listened. She spit it out, plucked another one, and chewed it the whole way through, then spit it out, too. Finally, she said, "Well, Hester, you in a red dress were probably a sight to see. I'm surprised William allowed it."

"It was his mother's."

Up went Bappie's eyebrows. "Hm. Ain't that something? Well, just goes to show, you never know how men's minds work. I sure never had that problem. No one ever tried to, you know." Her face turned as red as her largest red beet.

"I guess I was too dumb to see."

"Stop blaming yourself. That's why I'm unmarried. You can't judge a book by its cover. You never know if a man is sincere—a good, kind, Christian fellow—or a genuine traitor."

Hester nodded.

They both fell silent. Another rumble of thunder worried itself on the horizon. The red glow of the evening sun disappeared, leaving them in an eerie, grayish-yellow light.

Bappie sat straight up like a jack-in-a-box. Her eyes turned dark and wide with fear.

"Rain's coming," Hester said.

Walter Trout's perspiring face popped up over the fence.

"Emma says we have a few corn cakes left. And some molasses and applesauce. If you're hungry, she has a muskmelon cut open for you."

By the time the storm hit, Hester and Bappie sat cozily by candlelight, eating Emma's good food, washing it down with many glasses of cold, sugared, spearmint tea.

The lightning flashed blue, followed by great rolls of heavy thunder that shook the wooden frame of the house. The wind screamed around the corners, howled under the eaves, and lashed the windowpanes with sheets of water. A high sound of pinging ice soon followed. Bappie held her hands over her ears and squeezed her eyes shut tightly. "Oh, my garden, my poor garden," she said swaying back and forth as if mourning the demise of all her vegetables.

"Gott is unhappy with us," wailed Emma.

She believed a storm was God's fury on humankind and all its sins, to bring everyone to repentance.

Hester sat, tired and relaxed, rocking quietly on the armless rocking chair. Her dark eyes watched the rain and ice punish the glass windowpanes. She heard the howling of the wind. Unafraid, she knew all humankind was subject to storms, to the ways of the sky, the sun, the moon, the earth. It was all a part of the universe, so much greater and so much more than one mind could begin to grasp.

Like the eagle's flight, the storm spoke to her soul. All the earth and the things of the earth could not be separated. Like the weather, everything was controlled by the almighty creator. He chose to send storms and heat, cold and wind and drought. If the garden was ruined, they had enough to get by.

The harder the hail bounced off the windows, the more agitated Bappie became, mournfully shaking her head and muttering about the green tomatoes and cucumbers, the green beans and squash. "It'll be gone. All of it ruined. What will we do?" she wailed, rocking back and forth, misery turning slowly to hysteria.

"It'll be all right. Hail is never widespread." These words came from Hester on the rocking chair, her dark eyes untroubled pools of calm.

"How can you say that? You have no idea!" shrieked Bappie, her eyes large and dark with the fear of losing her vegetables and of the wooden box becoming empty of coins before the coming winter was over.

A deafening clap of thunder followed sizzling white light as jagged streaks of lightning erupted from boiling black clouds above the town of Lancaster. Winds increased as the storm moved directly above them. Hail rattled the wooden shingles, attacked windowpanes, jumped on the streets, and nestled in backyard grasses.

Then the rain increased its fury. The wind's force soaked every hand-hewn shingle and brought the rain to seep beneath them, then drip steadily onto attic floors. Meticulous housewives squawked, grabbed wooden buckets, and raced pell-mell up their steep attic stairs to find the dripping leaks, placing the buckets at the proper places.

Rain seeped down mud and stick chimneys and ran down whitewashed walls. Horses whinnied in alarm, kicking and pounding against the sides of their stalls, their eyes rolling in fright as the sizzling lightning became more constant.

A sound reached Hester's ears. She held completely still. A shingle? A loose shutter? Again, the repetitious knocking. She sat up straight.

"Someone is at the door."

"Ach, nay, nay!"

Emma, quite distraught, looked to Hester for assistance. Bappie, forgetting her ruined vegetable garden, sprang into action, tearing open the latch. From the narrow hallway came a shriek of surprise and then an exclamation of sorrow, a sort of mewling edged by the beginning of a sob.

"Hester!"

The command was so forceful she sprang into action, peering around Bappie's narrow shoulders. There in the blinding white flashes of lightning stood a very small boy, holding a bundle almost as big as himself. Drenched, and his sodden bundle dripping water, he turned calm eyes to the incredulous women but said nothing at all.

Behind her, Hester felt the floorboards raise and lower as Walter and Emma lumbered toward them.

Bappie turned, unsure.

Hester reached out and drew the boy in, as water ran off him in rivulets, pooling at his small feet. She took the bundle amid shrieks from Bappie, the usual half prayer, half exclamation coming from Emma. Quickly she unwrapped the sodden blanket, not surprised to find an infant. A baby.

Bappie was squealing about the offensive odor and the rain in puddles on Emma's clean floor and rug.

Walter cleared his throat as he shuffled back to the kitchen for rags, shaking his great pink head with the crown of grayish hair circling his ears. He never could expect a normal day since marrying his Emma, not even during a summer thunderstorm. But that was all right. Anything was better than the life of crippling solitude he had led before he met the boisterous Emma. And she was so loving.

They carried the children into the heat of the kitchen and dried them with the towels. Their smell was like a mixture of manure, sour grapes, and spoiled cream, the stench thick and cloying.

Bappie's anger forced a few surprising words from her mouth. She moved fast, getting down the agate washtub, then starting a fire in the washhouse. Above the howling wind and stinging rain, her voice could be heard commanding and giving instructions. The end result was two shivering children, both like lost kittens, their skin scrubbed, their heads scoured with kerosene, then soaped, rinsed, and soaped again.

Wrapped in rough towels, the boys were terrified of the smell, the powerful soap, the water, Bappie's less than gentle hands. The women threw the stained and torn clothing in the backyard. Bappie said she was taking no chances with the likelihood that those clothes had to be crawling with lice.

When darkness closed in around the wooden house on Mulberry Street, the storm had moved on. Eaves still dripped. Branches and leaves, torn from sturdy trees by the powerful gusts, were strewn across the streets. Small rivers roiled by, then pooled in low places, filling large holes that set drivers' teeth on edge as the steel-rimmed wheels of their carriages hit them.

The quietness that eventually came was a blessing. Bappie rinsed the tubs and set the washhouse in order. Hester wrapped a towel around the baby, who seemed to be about a year old, weighing a bit more than she had thought. The older child was perhaps four. Emma reached for him, rocked and crooned, sang and stroked the small back. Tears came, puddled, then ran down her shining cheeks.

"*Oh, meine liebe Kinner. Meine liebe,*" she repeated over and over. "What the *deifel* does!"

She never blamed any person in circumstances such as these. It was always the devil's fault. He stalked around the town, seeking who he could devour, that cunning *deifel*, Emma would say. Why, just look at the women who were slovenly, the men who chose to waste their wages on liquor and became drunkards, leaving their children to starve and eventually be turned into the streets when irate house owners put them there.

When the devil had his way, there was no money for rent, food, or clothing. The women, in despair, turned to the orphanage and left their children there, half-mad with fear and anger and hopelessness.

None of them could get the four-year-old to speak. His tears had dried up, but his light-colored eyes remained fixed, stone cold. Those once glittering eyes went to a place none of them could follow. His face was triangular, with a wide forehead, sunken cheeks, and a pitiful, pointed chin. His mouth, too wide, held decaying teeth that looked like wormy corn kernels.

Hester spoke to him gently in English. She spoke in German, then tried the more common Pennsylvania Dutch.

The smaller one continued to wail, sobbing and sniffing. Walter heated a pan of milk, added molasses, and stirred. He put a small portion in a cup, spread butter on brown, crumbly bread and brought it all to Emma, setting it quietly on the oak washstand beside her rocking chair like a well-trained servant.

When Emma patted Walter's arm, her eyes going to his face, her "*Denke schöen*" was so filled with love that

Hester resolved to someday, if she lived to a ripe old age, feel a love such as they had.

Emma offered the milk to the young boy, who grabbed the cup from her hand, sucking and slurping greedily, straining at the sweet milk. It dribbled down the sides of his face and splashed on the towel as he lifted his face to drain every drop. His eyes begged for more, even as his chest caved in, his shoulders tensed, and he leaned forward to purge every ounce of the nutritious liquid.

There was a sudden flood on the clean floor. Walter and Bappie turned as one. They found a rag and mopped everything clean.

Hester spoke. "That's what happened to me when I was starved on my journey from Berks County. The child is starving like I was. Allow him only a teaspoon at a time. Give him the bread in small bites."

Bappie looked at Hester with a rueful shake of her copper-colored head, the hard, gleaming pebbles that were her eyes disappearing behind lowered lids.

Emma gave the boy small pinches of bread and butter. She waited until he leaned forward, his mouth open wide, before she allowed him more. His translucent eyes were glittering with desperation, the urge to fill his stomach, to rid himself of the torment that was hunger. Small sips of warm milk, more bread. A bowl of porridge. More porridge.

Bappie did not know anything so terrible existed. She was born and raised among the Amish, who lived frugally, and whose food was plain and simple but sufficient. Real hunger had never entered her life. She was incredulous, asking question after question. She pondered the answers. She said that even the Indians, who were supposedly ungodly, provided for their own little ones. This was a shame.

"It's the liquor. The homemade stills, the rye whiskey, the fermented apples, and hops and all the other stuff—they use it to make the devil's brew," Emma said, emphatically.

Both boys' heads dropped, their eyes lowered, and sleep overtook them. The room became still. Occasionally there was a drip of rain, a sighing of the wind, as if the earth was relieved the storm had moved on. Candles flickered. Deep breathing sounds assured them of the boys' slumber.

Emma said quietly, "We'll let them sleep in our bedroom by our bed. Just in case they wake up."

Reverently, as if Christ were in the room, Walter clasped his hands over his rounded stomach and shook his head up and down.

The two women left the hush of Walter Trout's home, returning to the dark, damp interior of their own. They poured cool glasses of tea, and Bappie plied Hester with dozens of questions. Why had she left her family in Berks County? How could she travel all that way? Why wasn't she dead?

Far into the night, Hester recounted her story. She left some of the truth out. She told Bappie it was Annie's dislike of her that finally severed the familial cord.

"Like a birth." Bappie nodded.

"In a sense it was like that. I was free. And yet countless times I have longed to return to the stone farmhouse. To Noah and Isaac and Lissie and Daniel, Solomon, and the baby. I still miss the children."

"Were Noah and Isaac good to you?"

Hester gazed past the candlelight, her eyes drawn to the black corners of the room, as if secrets were hidden best in the dark recesses. Her eyelids grew heavy with sadness as her mouth became soft with remembering. Her voice was husky with fettered pain, a torture that constricted her will to speak.

"Before Annie, they were. They were my brothers. She destroyed the loyalty, the ties that bound us."

"Then they didn't love you for real if they allowed that woman to come between you."

Hester nodded, her eyes somber. "I guess not."

Bappie nodded back, drained her tea, set the glass on the table, and got up a bit stiffly, putting a hand to her back. "It's been a long day. I'm off to bed. Ah, life is crazy, Hester. Don't look back, or your plow will go way off course, the way the Bible says. Not that I'm much of a Bible reader, but that one thing is true." She yawned, stretching like a long, skinny, black cat.

Hester watched and said, "I'm glad you live with me, Bappie."

"Hope you'll say the same thing a year from now," Bappie said, grinning.

CHAPTER 19

THE GARDEN STRETCHED BEFORE THEM, GREEN and flourishing and unharmed. The late-morning sun slanted through the washed tomato plants. The red fruit was mud-splattered, their stalks tossed and showing the lighter dusty shade of green underneath. The corn all lay at an angle, its short roots partly exposed but the ears of corn intact.

They stood, two women shading their eyes with their hands, palms down. One, dressed in dark navy blue, was taller, sharper. The other, dressed in green, was tall and willowy, but possessing the figure of a woman. Their skirts rippled. Cap strings lifted, moved, and fell across their shoulders, the clean, fresh breeze of summer playing with them.

Hester turned to Bappie, her eyes conveying her pleasure. "What did I say?"

Reluctantly, Bappie answered, "Hail is never widespread."

They laughed.

Together, they weeded that day, the cool mud
squeezing up between their toes, the hems of their aprons
becoming brown with it. The sun shone hot but pleasant. Doves hurried across the blue sky, propelled by their
triangular wings. Crows wheeled and flapped, their raucous cries grating and unpleasant, on their way to rob
other birds' nests if they could.

Sometimes, Hester broke into song, with Bappie
joining in. Mostly though, they remained quiet, pulling
weeds, tossing them aside. They spread a blanket in the
shade of a spruce tree and opened the lunch basket between them. Bappie cut a ripe tomato into slices, then
laid them warm and sun-kissed on squares of new brown
bread, spread with plenty of yellow butter, and sprinkled
the slices with salt.

They drank cool tea and glasses of buttermilk. Side
by side, they reclined on the blanket, resting their backs.
Above them, suddenly, a deep laugh, a joyous welcome.

"Well, surprise, surprise!" A lilting slick tone, lifting
and falling in all the wrong places.

Without thinking or caring, Hester sat bolt upright,
her privacy invaded, her happiness destroyed. Black,
hostile lights filled her eyes, and her voice sounded like
an assault. "Does Naomi know you are here?"

Johnny recoiled, looking quickly at Bappie for support.

She shrugged her shoulders and kept quiet.

"Go home to your family and leave us alone. You
have no business out here with us." Hester did not flinch
when Johnny's eyes became bright with anger. She met
the light head on, unwavering.

For one wild moment, she thought he was going to hit, to lash out with his fist, helplessly flailing the air between them. Instead he tried to frighten her with his anger, held in check by the regulations of his religion. Still she did not back down. He turned on his heel, sharply throwing his shoulders back, and stalked off with exaggerated steps like an irate schoolboy sent to stand in the corner. Hester would not have been surprised to see a rock come hurtling in their direction.

"Hoo-boy." Bappie shook her head.

"He doesn't need to follow us around. He has wrong intentions."

"But still, Hester. He may be trying to make amends."

"He's not."

"How can you tell?"

Hester shrugged her shoulders and went back to work without another word, pulling weeds like someone possessed, without one backward glance in Bappie's direction.

The child would not speak. Walter and Emma had tried every available resource to get him to at least tell them his name, some sense of where he had come from, who a relative or parent was. But the boy sat, his eyes giving away nothing, only the greenish-yellow light ringed by brown flecks, impossible to decipher.

Both children ate every morsel of food given to them. They were clad in a set of Emma's "necessaries," meaning a small shirt and pants for the four-year-old and a girl's dress for the baby, all made from flour or feedsacks. Emma always kept a wooden trunk well stocked, just in case a hungry or homeless person had need of clothing. The baby crawled, but slowly, pulled himself up by his thin little arms and stood, his thumb in his mouth, his eyes wide and frightened.

Emma showed Hester the stripes on the older child's back and across his legs where a switch had bitten through the flesh. It had healed, then been cut open, time after time. He had angry flea bites and rashes on his elbows and his knees. In the candlelight, they had failed to notice.

Emma sighed. One little victim saved for now.

They gave up trying to find their home after Walter walked to the constable's office, where he was waved away. Repeatedly he talked to the clerk at the desk, who fixed an impatient stare of resentment on his perspiring face. Finally he lifted his hat and wished her a good day, losing no time in getting out of that office.

Hester and Bappie took it on themselves to try to find the children's home. Taking the boy by the hand, they asked him to come with them. They were going for a walk. His terrified eyes glowered at them. Turning, he zigzagged wildly through the house, finally coming to a stop beneath the table, where he curled into a trembling fetal position, his eyes tightly closed.

The baby began wailing, its sobs turning into screams of hysteria. Leaving Emma to comfort the distraught child, they walked out onto the street, more determined than ever to find the source of the children's mistreatment.

The town of Lancaster was newly washed, the storm having given the dusty streets and buildings a thorough rinsing. The evening was warm but not humid, making their stroll a pleasant one.

Naturally, they turned toward the more common section of town where the separate dwellings turned into huts that housed miners, coal-shovelers, and migrant workers. Here the streets were a soup of mud and water.

Tired, unkempt mothers peered suspiciously from doorways, swatting at clouds of mosquitoes that swarmed up from the liquid streets. Yelling children clad in mud shot across the roadways, all thin arms and legs with big feet and hands and bellies.

A youth sagged against a crooked doorpost, smoking a homemade pipe made of a reed and a corncob. He blew a jet of brown smoke in their direction, coughed, squinted, and spat into the mud before lifting the pipe and inhaling deeply.

"Hello?" Bappie said, a question more than anything.

The youth nodded in their direction.

"Do you have any idea if anyone on your street is looking for their children? Two boys?"

A shrug of the shoulders. His too big shirt slid off one shoulder, leaving his thin, white neck exposed, childlike, too vulnerable.

"Is your mother here?"

"Aren't got no ma."

"Your father?"

"Died two days ago. At the foundry."

Bappie perked up, her eagerness bringing her through the puddles of water, the mosquitoes, and the green-tailed flies that buzzed around the filthy doorways.

"Do you have two brothers?"

"A course not."

"Did anyone else die? At the foundry?"

"Two more."

Clearly they were on the right path. They asked him to take them to the men's families. He said no, they didn't have no families.

Defeated, they looked at each other. Feeling dismissed by the disinterested youth, they retraced their steps, lifting their skirts to avoid dragging them through the mud. There were many more streets, but the evening sun was already low in the sky, and both of them had no wish to be here in this corner of Lancaster when darkness arrived. Better to go back home.

The squalor, the odor, and raw poverty of the miners' homes kept Hester awake. She thought of the Indians, their uncanny ability to flourish with nothing except what the earth provided. With the gift of trees, they erected their lodges; with stone they fashioned arrowheads to find food that sustained them. From the wild animals, they fashioned their clothes. They made their tools, in fact, an entire way of life, with nothing except the knowledge handed down from generation to generation. They roamed the land, never hungry, always resourceful.

So who had gone wrong that intelligent white people should let the poor fall along the wayside? Had the liquor and its alcoholic content become a tradition as well?

She considered the Amish, the Mennonites, the Dunkards, the conservative groups who cared for their own. They had the poor among them always, but not like this.

Constantly they gave, they *fa-sarked*, they cared for any less fortunate than themselves.

She supposed she had always been sheltered from the depravity of humankind. The ignorance and unfairness. How could a row of shacks come to be? On that street? What kept the people in poverty? Over and over her mind mulled, searching for a reason that all of God's children were not the same. Perhaps God does love unequally. Otherwise, how could he allow these little ones to suffer untold terrors?

Hans seemed so much better, his shortcomings so different in the way he loved her and ignored the boys, Noah and Isaac. In spite of all that, he provided shelter and food and instilled a work ethic, teaching them to be self-sufficient, to work the land, fell trees, milk cows, and train horses. The list went on and on.

So much of Hans' weakness was her fault. Hadn't she always thought so? As time went on, that idea became firmly entrenched within her. It was easier to handle the past if she lived as the one who had done wrong somehow.

The same with William. She had failed miserably.

Her own sense of unworthiness unrolled like a scroll, the writing not quite legible, but unmistakably there in black and white.

To stay alert, to stay away from men, was her new and immediate goal. It was the only way to fix her past, to stop making mistakes. She would grow herbs and make tinctures with Bappie's help. Together they would tend to the sick, erase the miserable huts, and teach the men and women to clean and cook, to grow vegetables, grind corn, and make their own bread from wheat kernels.

Hester flipped on her side and punched her pillow. She was awake completely now by the passion that drove her thoughts, the tumbled possibilities, the lessons she learned from Emma, good, kind soul that she was. Together with Bappie they would roll up their sleeves and make a big difference in the lives of the poor.

For starters, Bappie did not need to throw away the leftover cabbage leaves or the few tiny carrots half hidden in the loose soil in the bottom of the wooden crate. Red beet tops were very good cooked with salt, pepper, and a dash of vinegar. Bappie threw them away, which Hester found extremely wasteful. But so far she had kept quiet.

Kate had used every last wrinkled pea pod, every little nubbin of corn. She packed away late green tomatoes to roll later in flour and fry in lard. "It'll taste good in the cold winter," she would say, her eyes merry as she shucked that last pitiful ear of corn. This week after market, Hester would crate all the outer cabbage leaves, the red beet tops, anything she could salvage.

She saw the rowhouses every time she closed her eyes. She felt the hopelessness.

Why was the boy lolling about in the late afternoon when he should have been at work the way farm lads were? What caused these people to live in desolate clusters of shacks, when less than a half mile away, wealthy families lived in opulence, black servants seeing to their every need?

She thought again of the Amish and their stringent work ethic. They, the Mennonites, the Dunkards, and many of the more liberal English worked hard to establish farms, clearing entire forests to make room for roll-

ing fields of crops. Maybe no one had taught these poor
families how to garden or save money. Hester's heart
beat faster. Her pulse quickened with the daring plan
that formed in her mind.

Yes. She would start, one family at a time. The summer would soon be over. This is what she would do.
With her store of herbs and the wisdom she had learned
from the old Indian woman, she would heal the sick
children and teach the destitute women to cook, clean,
and wash clothes. She hoped Bappie would agree to
help her.

Outside in the warm summer night, a figure crept
past Hester's bedroom window, tiptoeing stealthily, bent
over, a dark figure with his face hidden. He stopped, then
slid his hand along the German siding as if to test the
sturdiness of it. For a long time he stood, his face lifted,
white and featureless in the dark night, with only the
ineffective light from the stars overhead.

Hester turned, her dreamlike edge of sleep disturbed
by a sound she could not place. A sliding or slithering.
A brush against stone? If she were in the forest, she would
have known, but here in town, she could not place it. She
sighed, untroubled, and let sleep overtake her.

Back in the verdant garden the following day, Hester
straightened her back, met Bappie's eyes, and said, "This
fall when cold weather approaches, we will go to the
poor houses, you and I."

Bappie's elevated eyebrows rearranged her freckles.
"We will?"

Hester nodded. She lifted a hand to tuck a strand of
hair beneath her cap. "I think God wants me to do this.

This might be why I was led to this town. I have all these herbs and the knowledge of how to use them."

Bappie's face turned a shade darker, obliterating the freckles. Her eyes snapped with anger, black and abrasive. "Hester! You think you're going to solve poverty once and for all with a musty box of stinking herbs? Don't you know the reason those people live like that? They're lazy. The men don't care. They sit down at those taverns and drink away any wages they earn. It's hopeless." Bappie sniffed and mopped her brow with her gray handkerchief.

Hester's mouth turned down. Her nose tingled as her breathing became fast and shallow. "You say that because it leaves you free and blameless. The Amish are soaked with that attitude. You sound exactly like Frances and William."

The words were out before she could think of their consequences. Bappie straightened to her tallest height, her eyes wide and bulging with the scratching truth of Hester's words, an uncomfortable affront to her own righteous life. She stamped one bare foot.

"You! You are such a . . . such an *Indian* in your strange way of thinking!" she burst out, her cap strings flapping, then coming to rest across her shoulders.

Hester faced Bappie squarely. "Yes. I am an Indian. After seeing the squalor and destitution of poor white people, I am glad. Glad. The Indians have no money, only a priceless heritage handed down to them from their forefathers. That's just like the Amish. They are self-sufficient in so many ways, making a good way of life with only the things God has created. I am proud of my Indian blood for the first time in my life, and it feels good."

Bappie's mouth hung open in surprise.

"You can think what you want. I defend my ancestors and the way they live."

Bappie snorted. "I guess you defend the Ohio massacres, the scalping, the savages plundering and burning homes. Those Indians are worse than animals."

"Because they were driven to it by the white men's greed for land."

This Bappie could not truthfully deny.

"The Indians roamed these Pennsylvania woods peacefully, and you know it."

Bappie nodded.

Hester continued, "All my life, I have worn my Indian heritage like an abnormal growth. Ashamed of it. No more. Seeing the little boys, realizing the cruel, depraved way they were beaten . . . ." Hester shook her head.

Bappie looked off across the garden to the woods beyond. She shaded her eyes with a hand, the palm turned down, watching the flight of a meadowlark. Suddenly she turned. "Let's not quarrel about something so unnecessary."

"For you, maybe. But not for me. I know for the first time that I do not have to go through life feeling ashamed of who I am. I want to be able to use the knowledge handed to me by an old Indian woman. Many herbs that grow in these fields and swamps and forests are priceless. They heal. They are good for so many things."

Bappie held very still. "Listen."

From the edge of the woods, by the meandering little creek, came the sound of whistling. At first the women thought it was an unusual bird, till Hester shook her head. Somewhere, she had heard the whistle before. It was more than blowing air through lips, the way Hans and Lissie would whistle. It was a sad, captivating tune. It brought tears to her eyes so many years ago, and it did again.

"Someone is down there," Bappie said, her eyes wide, her hands knotted into fists.

"Sounds like it," Hester agreed.

Warily, they stood still, their ears straining to hear the unusual sound coming from below them.

"Wish we had some sort of protection. Like a gun," Bappie murmured.

"No one dangerous would whistle like that," Hester said, clearly moved by the sound.

They waited, then bent to the task of weeding the heavy pumpkin vines. Soon the green growth would die, leaving the orange pumpkins to ripen in the late autumn sun, one of the last crops to be sold at market before it closed for the season. A few late beets, some lima beans and potatoes, and the days at market would be over.

They worked in solitude, their argument forgotten, each one bent to her own task and her own thoughts.

New life flowed in Hester's veins, filling her with a re-newed sense of purpose. She had found her place on earth. She embraced the reason Kate had found her, the reason she left the farm, even the fact that Billy had found her and brought her to Emma Ferree, who had ushered her into the path of the town's needy. The penniless. The weak.

She knew how they felt, the feeling of being an outcast. Hadn't she felt that way all her life? No more. Her soul sang within her. Over and over, the waves of a new understanding lapped at the edges of her own lack of self-worth, wearing it away, creating a sense of peace, of purpose.

Everything—her marriage to William, his death, her senseless servitude and lack of trust in herself and her husband—had prepared her for this venture. Freed from self-blame, she began to whistle, to hum, to break into song, as tears dripped off the end of her nose.

She froze when a figure stood directly in front of her. Straightening slowly, she found a tall Indian, his black hair parted in the middle, a heavy braid down his back, his skin darker than her own. His nose was prominent, his eyes quick and black and restless.

His clothes were the same brown, made of skins, as any white frontiersman. A knife was thrust through the wide leather belt, and he carried a rifle and a gun powder horn slung over his shoulder.

"Hello." He addressed Hester in perfect English.

She met the eyes that were blacker than her own and recognized a part of his face. This was the Indian youth who had moved through the trees like a wraith. She had seen him, heard his whistle. Cold chills crept up her back. The blood drained from her face, leaving her dizzy, light-headed.

"Who are you?" she whispered.

"I am of the tribe of the Lenape. I believe I know who you are. I have watched you for many years. Only now do I make myself known. Your mother was of my tribe. We played together as children. I have come to ask you to go with me to the Ohio River where my people dwell on its banks. I will give you time. I am on my way to the Great Waters and will return in the spring when winter has gone."

Hester could not stand alone. She sank to the ground, slowly folding under this unexpected arrival from her past. Instantly, the Indian brave was beside her, extending his hand to help her to her feet. She shook her head, keeping her eyes lowered to the restless hands in her lap.

"I do not want to disturb you. You have the winter to decide if you will accompany me. You will consent someday to be my wife, I have hoped for many years."

Hester lifted her face to meet his eyes. They were black but kind, gentle, and alive with interest in her alone. A magnetic force rose from his eyes, and she stood, unaware that she had risen to her feet.

The meeting of their eyes could not be broken with so much they recognized in each other. He placed his hand on her arm, taking her trembling hand in his own. She was close enough to see the texture of his skin, the strong cords of his neck. He smelled of animal skins, dust, gunpowder, and sweat. His hair glistened with grease in the ways of her people.

"Thank you for allowing me the winter to decide," she whispered, after long moments had elapsed.

"That makes me very happy," the Indian said. Then, "My name is Hunting Wolf."

"I am Hester King. I was Hester Zug before marrying."

He nodded. "Your husband died."

"Yes."

"Your mother's name was Corn Maiden."

Hester gave only a weak wave of her hand, a dipping of her dark head to acknowledge what he said. She was thankful for his words, but confusion veiled her ability to understand why he had waited all this time, why he had suddenly made himself known.

"You are Lenape."

"Yes." Hester smiled then, directly meeting his eyes.

His face softened, his eyes became black velvet, the longing true, forthright, and honest. "I will return. Think on my words, dearest one. I will take you to my lodge so you can meet your cousins, your brothers. But not without your consent."

"Thank you."

Without another word, he turned and disappeared, blending into the waving grasses and the thick line of trees, as if to hide the sight of her confusion.

Bappie lifted her freckled face to the bright sky and gave a low whistle. "Whoo-ee!"

That was all she said before turning to face Hester with a look that was undecipherable in her brown eyes. Finally she placed a hand on Hester's back, gave a small pat, and said, "Isn't life crazy, my friend? Just when you thought you had it all figured out, along comes a new direction, huh?"

She gave Hester another small pat. "Remember, all your troubles come from men."

Bewildered, Hester turned her face to Bappie, a frightened look widening her eyes. "Are you sure?"

CHAPTER 20

THE CURB MARKET OF LATE SUMMER WAS A SPEC-
tacular sight. Every member of the township, and those
who lived inside the town and did not have room for a
garden, hurried to the market to purchase the last of the
produce to store down cellar.

Farm wagons rattled by, men urging their horses to a
fast trot, their straw hats clamped low on their brows,
bringing in the potatoes and squash and apples. The
smell of cider hung in the air as the steam-driven press
clapped and sputtered while juice ran from a pipe into
wooden buckets.

Carriages that shone like glass, drawn by high-stepping horses, their necks arched like proud swans, their
manes and tails braided with red ribbon, moved slowly
through the crowd, enjoying the attention they received.

Amish farmers sold potatoes and turnips, pumpkins
and squash. But no one's vegetables were arranged quite
like Bappie's. The largest crowd always surrounded her
colorfully displayed goods.

Hester wore a light black coat, just enough to fend off the stiff breeze. She moved as if in a dream, her thoughts certainly not on her duties as she arranged the heavy orange pumpkins, counted the yellow squash, and shooed away a few bees that kept droning around the beet tops.

She stopped working when the hulk of a man named Reuben Troyer threw a look in Bappie's direction as she hawked the merits of her fine vegetables, as usual.

"Someone should tell her to go home to the kitchen where she belongs. No woman should be allowed to sell things in that manner."

Hester smiled. "Oh, she's very good at selling vegetables." She looked at him directly, humor flashing from her dark eyes. His mouth slid up into a wobbly smile, his eyes becoming soft as they caught Hester's goodwill.

"Ach, yes. So she is. Yes, yes."

He moved on, graced by the most beautiful smile he had ever encountered. He told his wife that Hester was like an angel, so beautiful was she. Luckily, the large, big-boned Rachel agreed with him, and he whistled the whole way to the barn to do his chores.

Hester mollified any displeased customers with pleasant words and a frequent smile. When her teeth flashed white in her dark face, two dimples appeared in her cheeks. Her eyes laughed pleasantly as she spoke, universally warming everyone who saw her.

She stored the beet tops in a crate out of Bappie's sight. At the end of the day, she told Bappie she was going to the poor section of town to take some of the day's leftovers. She didn't say what she was taking, just leftovers.

Bappie was exhausted and drained after her long day's work, hunched over her money bag, counting coins, so she waved a hand, and Hester went on her way, triumphant.

For once she did not need to make a decision. For once she could pursue the passion she had so often dreamed of. She carried the crate on one hip, balancing it with an arm flung over top. She walked fast, her long strides taking her down Market Street, then left on to Vine where the street became more narrow. A row of squalid houses sat at the bottom of the incline like blobs of mud someone had thrown.

Strangely, there were no children racing around in the mud, no youth lounging in doorways. An eerie quiet pervaded the street. Hesitant now, Hester set the crate beside the first house, where the door swung crookedly on leather hinges, its wood darker and smoother from so many grimy hands pulling it shut and pushing it open.

Placing her fist on the door, she rapped, loudly.

Immediately, a white face appeared beside her, a mop of tangled brown hair above it, the mouth covered in dirt, the neckline of her dress torn, exposing painfully thin shoulders. The small child glared, her eyes as alert as a chipmunk.

"Hello. May I come in?" Hester asked.

Like a flash, she disappeared.

Hester waited.

Another white face appeared, almost level with her own, blotched and with swollen cheeks protruding below sunken dark eyes. The woman wore a dark dress, matted hair clung to her head, and a thin baby rode on her hip, sucking on a questionable item.

"Vot? Vot you vont?"

Hester smiled, which brought a black look of suspicion from the woman. "I have some greens here from the vegetable seller at market. I thought you might want to cook them for your supper. They don't cost anything."

"We don't eat that stuff."

"Oh, it's good, cooked with salt, a bit of vinegar."

"Couldn't eat it."

Hester sighed. How could she begin if they wouldn't accept her offer? From inside the house, the sound of crying rose to a crescendo until Hester thought she must break down the door to find the cause. "Is something wrong?"

"Oh, my boy stepped on a rusty nail, and his foot swole up so bad I don't know vot to do viss it."

"If you'll allow me, I'll take a look at it."

Reluctantly and offering no other welcome, the woman stepped aside, leaving only a narrow passage for Hester's entrance.

The smell was the worst. Always, from her first step into these dwellings, the odor of grime, spoiled food, unwashed bodies, and earthen floors was the hardest. Breathing as lightly as possible, her head bent, Hester entered the dark room. On a wooden pallet in a corner, she found the source of the agonized wailing. A small boy clutched both hands around a grotesquely swollen foot, angry red streaks reaching almost to his knees, his mouth open in wails of pain and anger.

Hester fell to her knees beside him. She gripped the foot and uncurled the filthy little hands as his wails turned to terrified screams.

"Don't. Don't. Here, don't cry. I just want to see if I can help you. I won't hurt you. Sshh."

The small boy lay back, attaching his gaze unwaveringly on Hester's face.

"I need a light," she said, crisply.

"Don't haf von."

"Yes, you do. Get it." Hester was angry now. She knew they had some source of light, even if it was only the stub of a candle.

Sullenly, a sputtering candle was placed in front of her. She held it to the foot. Instantly the screaming started anew. She had seen everything she needed to know. An angry, festering wound with pus pushing against it, desperately needing to be lanced, drained, and then treated with a fresh poultice of scabious.

She could see the plant, its heavy, soft, whitish-green leaves, their edges ragged, the clumps of pale blue flowers. It grew in meadows and old fields left untilled. She knew where a fine clump of it grew close to the road leading out to Bappie's patch of vegetables.

She rose, her eyes seeking the mother's face. "I will return tomorrow, if you will allow me. The wound needs to be opened and crushed leaves of the scabious plant applied to draw out the infection."

"You aren't no doctor."

"No, but I know about healing with herbs."

"If you come, make sure it's not when my husband is home."

"Please don't tell him if he will become angry."

"No. No." Agreeable now, the woman's eyes sought Hester's face. "Vill my Chon die?"

Hester looked at the sniffling child, his flushed face, and wondered if another day would mean his condition would deteriorate to the point of no return. "No," she said.

The woman nodded stoically, as if any emotion would be her undoing. Life was what it was, and she could do nothing to alter it. To stay alive, to keep her children alive, took all the energy she could muster.

Hester looked around the dim room. Two small windows let in a minimum of light. The small fireplace was black with smoke, soot, and damp air. Cold ashes were piled in a wet-looking heap.

Bits of string, twigs, and pieces of stone lay scattered across the floor. A table, small but sturdy enough, with benches pulled up on each side, a few more pallets covered with colorless blankets, a cupboard, several washtubs hanging on nails, and odd crates containing what Hester guessed were towels or rags or extra clothing, furnished the room.

Where was the food kept? Was there food?

She sat down quickly when the door was flung open and a large dust-covered man entered the room. His heavy eyebrows were drawn down over his eyes, which were only slits in his face. A bulbous red nose stood above a mouth that held a constant snarl. He walked over to Hester and told her to leave, now, in a voice that was both grating and wheezing.

"Heinz, no. The lady vants to help our Chon." The voice of his wife seemed to hold surprising authority. He looked at her, and only for a moment, Hester saw the glint of acknowledgment.

"How is he?"

"Not goot."

Hester spoke. "If he does not get help, he will die of the infection. Do you see these red streaks?"

Going to the child, she lifted the leg, pointing to the angry red marks. "That can turn into poison of the blood. If he turns feverish overnight, he will die."

The big burly German named Heinz turned his eyes on her, mere slits of blue, flashing now.

"Git. Git out. If we need a doctor, we will fetch one. Git." He raised an arm, his long, thick finger pointing in the direction of the door. The ragged edges of his filthy sleeve shook with the force of his anger.

Hester looked at the threatening hulk of a man, then down to the boy, who had curled into a fetal position, whimpering like a hungry puppy. The sound brought an explosion of unnamed emotion in Hester.

She faced Heinz squarely and told him in a level voice ringing with authority that she would be back, and there was nothing he could do about it. His son would die if he did not allow her to help. They had nothing to pay a doctor.

She had heard Emma's tales of the town's doctors treating the less fortunate without pay, perhaps a sack of potatoes, or a chicken, at best. But after years of going into the squalid conditions of these streets, they would no longer venture there. In turn, all sorts of strange practices, old wives tales, myths, mysterious chantings and wailings could now be heard among the sick in this part of town.

Heinz's shaking finger stayed. He shifted his gaze to her face. Slowly he lowered his arm and turned away. The boy on the pallet moaned.

Hester left the red beet tops and the bits of potato, as if she'd forgotten them. She lost no time hurrying home, looking neither left nor right, her long steps taking her to the stable in the back yard.

Bappie called out the back door.

Hester waved but quickly disappeared into the small stable. She yanked a surprised Silver from his stall and without bothering to brush his matted coat, flung the harness on his back, adjusted the buckles, put the bridle on his head, and backed him between the shafts of the serviceable black buggy. She was unwinding the reins when the back door clunked shut and Bappie strode across the yard.

"Hester! Stop! Where are you going?"

"To the meadow to get scabious."

"Can I come, too?"

"Suit yourself."

Bappie attached the britching and traces to the shafts on her side, then climbed into the buggy. She sat forward tensely as if Hester's driving made her nervous, as it should have, the way Hester guided poor Silver. She was requiring the utmost speed from the dependable animal who was never given to fast trots, only a contented clopping along, a regular old farm workhorse.

"What do you need?" Bappie asked finally.

"Scabious."

"What is that?"

"A plant."

"Why?"

"A boy will die if I don't have the chance to treat his infected foot."

"Just one plant?"

"No, if I can find nettles, I'll use them, too."

"Nettles are all over the place."

"Good."

Hester watched the fast sinking sun. She shivered in the cool evening breeze. She hoped the scabious plant would be where she thought she remembered seeing it.

Bappie's lips were grim. For Hester, the knowledge of herbs and their uses was a direct golden thread to her past. A redemption. Proof that her history was retrievable, worthy. She was not only the illegitimate daughter of an outcast young Indian maiden, she was shamed many times afterward, abused by her step-mother, lowered by her husband and mother-in-law. Lowered until she had no idea who she was. More than ever, the passion to pursue the dream of healing rose within her.

Hester turned her face to Bappie. "I want to do this. I know it works. You would, too, if you had met the ancient old grandmother, her face like wrinkled leather, her eyes containing an inward light, so brilliant was she. She knew every plant, every tree, she could name all the barks of the trees, all the mosses, all the mushrooms.

"Every plant has been put on God's earth because of its vital use to us. An important part of life is vanish-ing as Indians flee Lancaster County. You don't have to agree, Bappie. Just give me a chance to honor my ances-tors. It's all I can do."

Bappie was shocked to see Hester's chin wobble, then observe a quick dash of her hand across her eyes, as if when the emotion came, it was unwelcome.

Bappie looked straight ahead, blinked, and swallowed, then cast a sidelong look at Hester, lifted her nose and sniffed. She blinked furiously, before she said, "If you let me, I'll help what I can. Not that I know very much."

"Whoa!" Hester drew back on the reins. Silver lifted his head to release the pressure of the bit on his mouth, lowered his backside, and slid to a stop.

"There. There it is," Hester breathed, handing over the reins. In a flash, she was off the buggy and across the overgrown grasses. Her foot caught on the undergrowth, and she fell headlong, fell flat into the waving grasses as clumsy as on ox.

Bappie lifted her face and howled with glee.

Hester didn't look back, just waved a hand above her head, got up, and kept going. Her face was alive with energy, an inner light radiating from her dark eyes as she held up a clutch of strange-looking mint-green plants with red roots, a passel of limp pale blue flowers on top. "Perfect."

"I thought you needed nettles."

"I have some."

They drove back wordlessly. Silver lifted his head and trotted briskly, as if he got the message and meant to do them proud.

Walter Trout was watching across the backyard fence like a great nosy dog, his liquid eyes filled with love and trust, his face shining pink in the glow of the setting sun. His great slabs of arms lay across the top of the fence, his fingers entwined like sausages below his face. Bappie and Hester both knew he was a cauldron of unsatisfied curiosity. They winked at each other, smiled, and ducked their heads.

Silver, loosened from the shafts, walked obediently away, the sweat staining his silver hair to a dull gray. He lowered his head to drink thirstily from the long cast iron trough that rested on a stone base.

"Hello, ladies." Shrill and energetic, Walter voiced his presence.

"Good evening, Walter."

"Nice evening, now, isn't it?"

"Indeed."

Silver lifted his head, water dribbling from his mouth. He smacked his lips, making the funny sound horses do when they have almost drunk their fill, usually returning their mouths to the water for a few more swallows.

"Too nice for you ladies to stay home, then?"

"Oh, yes."

Hester led Silver through the barn door and into his small box stall, as Bappie turned to close the door to the harness cupboard.

"Market went well, I gather."

"Yes, we had a good day."

"That's good."

Hester reappeared.

"You were off in a bit of a hurry, I saw."

"A bit."

"You got what you were after?"

"Oh, yes."

Without further words, Hester and Bappie headed for the back door, leaving the herbs in the safety of the buggy.

"You'll be over later?" Poor Walter was slowly accepting that he could not extract a sliver of knowledge about where they had been or why.

"Maybe."

With a wave over her shoulder, Bappie opened the back door and held it, allowing Hester to go before her. They laughed freely, deliciously, knowing they would relieve poor Walter's insatiable curiosity later.

Their presence in the Trout home was lauded with many grand bows of welcome. Walter all but ran back and forth, bringing them cups of tea and fresh slices of custard pie sprinkled heavily with nutmeg. He brought a plate of cheese, yellow and pungent, a bowl of popcorn, salted and buttered lavishly.

The two boys, their faces freshly washed, and wearing thin homemade nightclothes, sat up to the table, their eyes bright and alert. The oldest one nodded and shook his head now, Emma informed the women proudly. He did not speak, but at least he was communicating something.

Clearly Emma was in her element. Her eyes snapped with sparks of energy; her face was as pink as Walter's. She bent to the boys, crooning, placing the palm of her hand on their cheeks, brushing back locks of hair that had never been out of place.

She cut their custard pie in small pieces. Walter placed a tin cup of buttermilk at each plate, then watched joyously as each child lifted it carefully and drank thirstily.

They talked of market, about going to church on Sunday. They spoke of William's passing, the time that had already elapsed.

Walter hovered, refilled teacups, inquired whether one small slice of custard pie was enough. Yet his English manners would not allow him to ask them where they had gone earlier.

Emma spoke around a mouthful of custard pie, which Hester could see made Walter cringe to the point of carefully wiping his own mouth daintily. "We have named the boys now. We called them One and Two for so long, until we decided a pet would be named long before these dear ones."

Proudly, Walter said their names were Sebastian and Vernon. Sebastian began to cry, a weak mewling sound at first, which rose to sobbing and hiccupping, sending Emma to his side in great distress. "What? What?" She kept repeating the word, seeming to try to relieve her own guilt, yet taking the blame for his crying entirely on herself.

His voice was only a croak, an unoiled piece of machinery, but they heard his words clearly, in spite of it. "My name is Richard."

Emma's face turned a shade darker, and her small eyes seemed to grow from the folds of her cheeks. She clapped a hand to her rounded bosom, where the row of tiny pearl buttons creased the gray fabric, and said softly, "*Mein Gott! Das kind schprechen.*"

Walter put a heavy arm about his shoulders, smiled into his face, and praised him effusively. Richard looked up into Walter's reddening face, the beginning of a smile forming at the edge of his mouth.

Hester got up. "I must go. I have a few herbs to prepare for the morning."

Walter looked at her, his curiosity buzzing. "Where are you off to?"

"Home." She went around to Richard and hugged him. "Welcome to our family, Richard. We're so glad you are with us." She kissed the small cheek, which brought a definite widening of his mouth.

"Good thing. Good thing." Bappie meant Richard's speech, Hester knew, and accepted her lack of social skill, her inability to convey feelings.

Then Hester nodded to Walter, thanked him for the tea, finally telling him about the herbs in the meadow and that she'd be making poultices, tinctures, and a liquid medicine as well. "I have a sick little boy to tend to in the morning."

Walter was grateful for that bit of information. He sat down heavily and cut a large wedge of pie, thanking his stars that Emma was a talkative woman and gave forth her information readily, unlike these strange Amish.

Back in their own kitchen, Hester stoked the fire while Bappie retrieved the herbs. They boiled the roots, chopped the scabious plant, and bottled some of it in the strong corn whiskey Hester kept for this purpose. They boiled the nettle roots separately and bottled them, too. Darkness had fallen by the time they were finished.

Hester paced the kitchen, straightened doilies, and fiddled with the candle wax. Finally she told Bappie she would never be able to sleep.

Bappie became quite huffy, saying if she was even thinking of going down to that dirty place in the dark, she was going alone.

Hester said she would then. "I have to see him tonight. He may be seriously feverish till morning."

"You are risking your life. It's too foolish. You can't go down there."

Hester nodded. That was all. Already she was putting on her black shawl and hat and pulling on a thin pair of gloves, her jaw set in a line of determination.

Bappie watched her, staying silent as Hester gathered the jars, herbs, and a small knife, some white muslin, and a scissors, then put them carefully into a cloth satchel and let herself out into the dark street.

Bappie called after her. "If you're not back by ten o'clock, I'll come looking for you."

Hester waved, her long strides separating her from Bappie's voice. At midnight she had not returned. Bappie lay cowering in her feather bed, alternately praying and being angry at Hester and her foolishness. Hadn't she warned her?

She tried to summon the courage to get dressed and go find her but could not bring herself to do it. Better one person dead than both of them. At this thought, her heart began banging beneath her ribs until she thought she would surely be torn apart, rib by rib.

When the gray light of dawn finally lightened the dark windows, she got up, tired, miserable, and vowing to herself that she would not go down to those stinking rowhouses, she didn't care if Hester was dead or alive.

As she combed her flaming red hair and scrubbed her freckled face, she considered going to the town constable to tell him about Hester. But as she ate her steaming bowl of cornmeal mush, she figured it would be better to go see for herself what had happened to Hester. She would wear her high-topped boots this time and carry a large walking stick, just in case.

CHAPTER 21

HESTER STAYED ALL NIGHT IN THE PITIFUL HOVEL after lancing the wound, draining the thick, greenish infection, and applying the poultice.

She spooned up a decoction of the bark of the white oak and the bud of the acorn from the same tree and heated the mixture to a soothing warmth. The child resisted at first, then willingly drained the liquid from the spoon.

Heinz lay rolled in a blanket on a pallet in the corner, his rasping snores settling themselves inside Hester's head until she thought she could no longer keep her sanity intact. At least he was not interfering, snoring like that, she told herself, as the weary night ticked toward morning.

At the first gray light of dawn, she lifted the cover from the sleeping boy and turned his foot toward the flickering candle she held to it. She lowered her head and sniffed the wound. The absence of the sickish sweet smell a revelation, she lifted her face, closed her eyes, and whispered a direct, *"Denke, mein Herr."*

When Heinz rolled out of his pallet onto the earthen floor like a great animal, Hester stiffened and kept her face averted. He rose to his knees, then to his feet, and began scratching his armpits and his filthy hair. He thrust his feet into the shabby torn shoes made of leather, belched, coughed, and let himself out the door without a word to his wife or acknowledging Hester's presence.

His wife's name was Josephine, but her pronunciation of it was funny. She told Hester to call her Finny. She could not speak English well, her German permeating every word, so that they each had a flat sound, mingled with all the wrong consonants. She was sincere, though, and she cared about her boy, Chon.

Heinz worked at the tannery on Water Street, Finny informed Hester, which explained the loathsome odor that followed him like a cloud. The dead animals and their hides piled in stinking heaps to dry, and then be made into leather, were odorous. There seemed to be nothing to do about it. It was a thriving business in the town of Lancaster, a necessary evil, if anything.

Some horses hitched to carriages refused to travel past the tannery, balking and rearing. Others lowered their heads, took the bits in their mouths, and ran at breakneck speed, the buggies swaying and clattering over the stones, the drivers' hats crushed low on their heads, their hands occupied solely by handling the reins.

More than one schoolboy took to loitering about the tannery, gleefully swooping in on an airborne hat and racing off with it before the harried owner could return to retrieve it.

When the first rays of the sun enlivened the street outside, Hester swept the floor and helped Finny stoke the fire. She boiled water, poured some in a wooden bucket, added cold from the crock by the back wall, and asked for soap. Finny shook her head, spreading her hands, palms up.

Hester nodded and set to work with one of the muslin patches in her bag. She scrubbed the table first, then the benches. She swept and scoured the meager hearth while Finny brought out a loaf of coarse brown bread, bought from the fat baker on Queen Street.

Hester's eyes narrowed. For two pennies, Finny could buy a sack of meal, a bit of lard, and some salt. She could make her own bread.

There was no milk, no eggs, no porridge or butter. Only the coarse brown bread torn into chunks. The children sat to the table in the same clothes they slept in, reaching for their share of the bread and stuffing it hungrily into their mouths. Their eyes were wizened far beyond their years, their thin faces colorless and translucent.

"Where is Heinz? Does he not want his breakfast?"

Finny made a sound not unlike an irate horse.

"Nothing to eat?"

"Of course. He eats good down there. But a man has to have his food."

Hester shook her head, brought in the beet tops, washed them with the small amount of potatoes, and put everything in a pot. "Salt?"

Finny shook her head.

When Bappie's anxious face appeared at the door, Hester did not waste any words explaining her night. She sent her straight back to the house with a list of items they would need. Bappie muttered and complained, dis-

gruntled, but did as she was told, returning with a wagonload of supplies.

And they went to work. The scoured the house with
strong lye soap. They washed the thin blankets in tubs
of boiling water out in front of the house, by the street,
where all the neighbors came to watch, their eyes hooded with suspicion and mistrust. Children threw sticks
and called them names.

Bappie lifted her hands from the hot, soapy water and
ran after one especially bold child, caught him by the
suspenders, and tweaked his ear. That brought a loud,
surprised squawk and a scattering of the rest of the by-
standers.

Hester grinned and kept scrubbing the filthy blanket
up and down on the washboard. Leave it to Bappie!

They nailed the scrubbed wooden crate to the wall,
then filled it with meal, a tin of lard, a bag of salt, flour
ground from fresh wheat kernels, a jar of tomato preserves, and a bag of potatoes.

They brought towels and sheets and two extra quilts.
They brought crockery dishes and pewter spoons. Emma
and Walter cried, wiped their tears, and contributed
soap, dried corn, bread, and a hunk of bacon.

Bappie said she was one solid mess of chills climbing
up her back and down her arms. Her nose burned all
day and all she wanted to do was cry. It was the spirit
quickening her, she said.

Embarrassed, then, she lowered her head and asked
Hester what in the world was she thinking, washing these
blankets if they had nowhere to dry? She said it gruffly,
as if that would prove that she was not turning into a

soft-hearted person. Hester remedied the clothesline situation by having Walter string a heavy rope from his and Emma's house to Bappie's, a sturdy line that would hold many clothes for years to come.

Finny held her sickly baby, fed him, then sat on the lone rickety chair and stared into space. She did not offer to help or hinder them. She allowed them to clean and wash, her eyes veiled with an expression of mystery.

When Walter contributed the armless rocking chair, they told Finny to sit in it. She sank onto the seat obediently and began to rock, stiffly at first, then at a slow, steady, relaxed rhythm. She lowered her head as the tears began to fall, dripping steadily, until her arms and hands glistened in the firelight where they gathered.

Little Chon ate his bread. Hester brought him a tin cup of buttermilk and a bowl of salted vegetables. He looked at Hester's face, his large eyes asking her if it was all right to eat it. She nodded, so he bent his head, lifted the spoon, and ate every bit, greedily licking the bowl to get every last bit of salt.

His recovery was imminent now. Pink highlights appeared in his face, and he smiled and talked to his younger sisters. Hester kept the plaster of the scabious plant tied firmly in place, and he had to remain on the pallet.

Hester and Bappie asked Finny's permission to bathe the children, wash their hair, and then dress them in the clothes Emma had given to the family while they washed the ones they were wearing. Tearfully, she nodded.

First, they doused their heads in strong smelling coal oil, with peppermint added to the lye soap, to rid the children of lice. They did not cry out, sturdily bearing the hot water and strong fumes, squeezing their eyes shut as they allowed Bappie's furious scrubbing.

The day was waning into evening when the two women stopped. Enough had been done.

Finny said she knew how to make bread. But she had no lard and no money to buy it. Patiently, they explained about the butcher's back door and the vats of rendered lard available for taking. She could bring home a large tin of it that would last for months, for one penny. Finny shook her head, overcome.

The goodwill that radiated from the cleaned hovel was infectious, and Bappie and Hester were radiant, fulfilled. They walked home in the golden glow of early autumn, pulling the emptied wagon, chattering together like magpies dressed in dark Amish colors, their muslin cap strings lifting and failing with the rhythm of their steps.

Bappie was duly impressed. She'd never seen anything work like that crazy plant, that weed that grew all over the place. You'd think the child would die, drinking that stuff in the bottle. What was it? Purple wine?

She fussed and waved her arms, quite forgetting to help pull the cumbersome wagon up the hill to Mulberry Street, until Hester stopped for breath, leaned against a lamppost, and exhaled.

Bappie never took notice. She merely stopped with Hester, lifted her hands, and asked how in the world she knew this stuff, and what else grew all over the woodlands and meadows that she knew had the ability to heal?

Hester laughed, told her she'd see, and went straight to Walter and Emma's house. Little Richard opened the door, peering around it like a shy deer mouse, and every bit as cute.

"Do come in," he said, for all the world like a little butler.

"Thank you, Richard," Hester said, smiling, then scooped him up and planted a kiss on his cheek. She was rewarded by a clenching of his arms around her neck like a vise.

With so much happiness and so great a purpose in her life, Hester spoke with energy and enthusiasm, completely forgetting her steaming cup of tea. It turned cold as she related her rewarding day of giving to the poor and helping Finny to climb out of the pit of despair where she had no longer cared whether she lived or died, so great was the burden of staying alive.

Emma lifted a finger. "Hester, I don't mean to lower your banners, but don't be surprised if Finny returns to her old ways. Remember, you two women did all the work. She may not want to continue."

As it was, Heinz proved to be the biggest obstacle. He swore, tore down the wooden crate, said no two Amish do-gooders were ever going to tell him what he could do and what he couldn't, and they were not going to tell him how to raise his family either.

But Finny remained steadfast and calm, going about her days with renewed purpose. Seeing little Chon on his feet, alive and healthy, his eyes shining, was enough inspiration for her to continue to cook the limp vegetables, make her own bread, and buy lard and salt.

Regularly, Hester or Bappie, sometimes both, would visit, encouraging, praising, and bringing her a squash, a pumpkin, some turnips, or potatoes.

One week before the market would be closing because the vegetables were finished, Heinz left the tavern in a drunken rage and smashed all the tannery windows with a club. He was caught, fined, which of course he could not pay, and was thrown into the worst cell in the dank, rat-infested cellar of the town's jail.

Finny was quite unperturbed. "He vill driggle up [dry up], vonct now," she said firmly, pounding and kneading the bread dough as if it was Heinz himself being punished roundly for all his drinking. She stopped, then gave the bread dough one last pat. Like a wise owl, her eyes large and round, she said bitterly, "My Heinz was not always so. It iss the ale. He can't let it alone."

Her words were so infused with the German, her "O's" a total other sound. "Alone" became "aloon;" the "is" a sharp "iss." But the strength of her words was enough to let the women know she loved Heinz still, but he needed to get better, and jail was a godsend.

Hester held the baby, her eyes dark and alive with interest, listening as Hester talked. Finny was strong, an amazing woman, keeping her children from starving in the rawest conditions.

When the winds of autumn became chilly, the leaves of the trees blew through the town and filled the gutters. Rains pounded them into a slimy, brown soup that lay in every ditch.

Finny needed firewood. She burned every stick she could find, her pride keeping this problem from Hester until she was forced to speak to her. The children were coming down with the chilblains, rashes, and angry blisters on their lips.

Soberly the women rode to church, Silver running along sedately as if he knew this was the Lord's Day. In their black shawls and bonnets, they rocked together comfortably in the roofless buggy, the road wet and puddled, brown streaks of water spitting from the wheels as they traveled.

They did not speak, for Hester's thoughts were muddied and clouded over with the knowledge of winter coming and the decision she would soon have to make. She thought of the handsome brave named Hunting Wolf and his true, honest love for her. She believed he came from the Lenape as he had said. He was not someone who repulsed her. A part of her longed to see her mother, her cousins and sisters, perhaps brothers. But that was all.

Having been married before, she knew the tremendous effort it would take, the constant work, the drawing on every reserve of love and affection, just to make it through her days and nights.

She had truly fancied herself in love with William, but was it love? Was what she experienced all that she was capable of? Perhaps with her own kind, with Hunting Wolf, it would be different. She had failed William and would likely fail the Indian. The thought of marriage was as burdensome as lugging a wagon behind her, up a hill from the rowhouses to Mulberry Street. Yet his eyes had held her, made her feel alive.

To his lodge, he had said. One separate lodge, or a communal longhouse?

The decision was too monumental, too formidable today with the sky the color of the Indian's turquoise, the clouds large and puffy like whipped cream, the air brisk and invigorating, alive with swaying branches and the smell of black walnuts hidden in wet brown grasses. Squirrels were romping and collecting hickory nuts which still clung to their summer branches, reluctant to fall and become the squirrels' winter staple.

The women were headed north from town on the level road, passing homesteads that were turning into well organized farms, each year making a difference in the amount of buildings and the cleared land.

Hester was grateful, as they drove by the well kept farm where she had spent her years with William, that Johnny kept up the tradition of tidiness. The fields were clean of corn fodder, the woodpile was stacked neatly, the cows looked well kept in the barnyard. Well, you had to give him that credit. He had, by all accounts, forgotten about pestering them, the silly man. He simply had never grown up. Despite having a wife and children, he acted like a youth.

How could he have grown up in the same house and have had the same parents as William? Her sober, conservative, meticulously versed William? A great tenderness rose in her, a memory of William's face and his touch.

"You better get him going or we'll be late." Bappie's voice broke in on her thoughts.

"How far is it to Jacob's?"

"At least another three miles."

Dutifully, Hester brought the whip from under the seat and flicked it lightly over Silver's back. The air whizzed past as he lunged forward. Hester shivered, tugging at her hat.

The women that stood around the kitchen of the stone house shook hands with both Bappie and Hester. Their lips met in a brief kiss of holiness, the traditional greeting among the women.

Jacob Stoltzfus's wife, Veronica, was flushed and "nerved up," the way women were when church was at their house and they were responsible for the comfort of the congregation. Was the house too cold? Too warm? Was there enough food for the dinner table? How many *freme* would show up?

Having made their rounds of greetings, Hester stood to the right of the fireplace, her arms crossed at her waist in a familiar stance, the way most of the women did. She looked around at the typical whitewashed walls, the shelves built on top of the sturdy cupboard that contained all Veronica's dishes.

She admired the embroidered artwork on the wall and noticed the heavy pewter of the candle holders. The curtains which hung on the one window in the kitchen appeared to be very worldly, crocheted along the edges like Emma Ferree's. But then Veronica was said to have a hankering for fanciness, she'd heard from Bappie.

In the center of the heavy oak table was a brown pitcher filled with sumac and goldenrod mixed with foxtails. My, it was so beautiful. Who would have thought that an assortment of plain weeds could be so pretty?

Wistfully she thought of her own blue dishes, more expensive and prettier than anything Veronica owned. The same with the hooked rugs Frances made, too. At the thought of her mother-in-law, she looked for her among the circle of women, remembering now that she had not greeted her. Was she sick?

Leaning toward Samuel Zug's wife, she inquired about Frances's absence in quiet tones. Taken aback, Lydia opened her eyes wide, then leaned close to whisper in her ear. "Hadn't you heard? She requested to be put out of the church."

Hester could not believe it. They had missed church two weeks ago, so they hadn't found out, nor had Hester been to any quiltings or other social events. It would have been far too much like gossip to inquire about Frances's reason for doing this, at her age—a highly unusual happening—but then, she had always been a bit strange, like a . . . Hester tried hard not to think of which reasons her highly critical mother-in-law might have cited for leaving the church, because, well, it was the Sabbath, and she should do her best to live right.

She suppressed a giggle and kept her face hidden from Bappie, striving to keep her thoughts and intentions pure. She sat with the women, singing with a clear and rousing soprano, then listened carefully to the words of Bishop Joel Stoltzfus.

He warned of worldly lusts and the hellfire that would surely rain on their heads, were they to disobey. He spoke of the need to live wholesome lives, upright and honest in all business dealings, to work the land by the sweat of their brow, the women bearing children as was commanded by the Lord.

Oh, how glad, how glad I would be to have children of my own, Hester thought, with a longing so intense she felt a physical ache in the pit of her stomach. Lowering her head, she pictured black-haired, naked little Indian children playing with bones and dogs, running among dusty intestines as the women butchered the wild animals.

She shuddered. She knew she did not want to be alone for the remainder of her years here on earth. But . . .

Joel Stoltzfus's face reddened, and he lifted his fist along with his voice, as it rose and fell in a singsong chant, carried through the generations like a ribbon from the Catholic Mass, their ancestors.

The sound made Hester feel a part of these people, these darkly clad, sincere, spiritually hungry and thirsty people who longed to do what was right. Everyone, in their own ways, did the very best they could, given the nature they each had. Often the children were raised with stringent rules and punishment, so they became their parents, passing the traditions and views on to their children, resulting in a tightly knit group of conservative people.

On her knees in silent prayer, Hester brought a heartfelt petition to God, asking that he show her the way, in Jesus's name.

The second and longer sermon was preached by a fiery old minister named Eli Fisher. His head was bald and shining, his beard in lustrous health, perhaps because he had no hair on his head. The gray beard seemed to come alive, jumping and swaying as he lifted his head, opened his mouth, and expounded on the word of God in all its power. That two-edged sword sliced right through the middle of the congregation and revealed their sinning souls.

Brother Eli clapped a skinny, work-roughened hand to his bald head, then wept and pleaded. He slammed himself back against the wall when the immensity of the seriousness of life became almost more than he could bear. His hands shook. He swayed on his feet. He swung his thin arms and called each person to repentance.

Babies cried and were carried discreetly from the room. A young child was pinched by a frustrated father, the ensuing wail bringing a clap to the face with a handkerchief. Somewhere was the sound of soft snoring. The men looked at one another with shamed smiles surfacing. Eyebrows lifted, a resounding punch was administered, and then a loud snort echoed through the room.

Women craned their necks. Who was snoring? Shame on him. Aha, young Willie Zug. Out too late last evening with Fannie.

They sat at the dinner table then, eating bread and dried apple pie, cup cheese, pickled cucumbers, and spiced red beets. There was cold water to drink. Hester longed for a cup of hot tea, but that would be too much work on the Sabbath day.

Bappie approached the ministers about helping to cut firewood for the Heinz Hoffman family. She was told they would not get involved in those lazy Germans' lives, and if she knew what was good for them, she wouldn't either.

Then Joel Stoltzfus told her in authorative tones that Hester and she would better start considering moving back to the country. Some of the *gleeda* were not satisfied with the way they lived in town, hawking their vegetables, perhaps being less sober and reserved than the world expected of the pious Amish. They would be better off as keepers of the home, quiet, devout, and not walking the streets of Lancaster, often with their caps untied. Someone had seen them wearing coats without the required shawls and hats. If they did not conform, they would be subject to a visit from the deacon.

It would be better for them to marry, bear children, and look after their husbands, he informed Bappie, not unkindly. He wished her *Herr saya*, and his eyes softened when he looked at Bappie's plain, freckled face. He walked away, aware of the ministers' duties that were not always so pleasant. But he did agree with the lay member that Bappie's voice at market was anything but chaste and humble.

Bappie was furious. She leaned forward and slapped both reins down on Silver's rump until the poor horse flew along the road, the buggy tipping and careening, bits of water, mud, and gravel spitting out from under his hooves until their faces were peppered, and Hester couldn't tell which were mud splatters and which were freckles all over Bappie's face.

Bappie talked as fast as she drove. She said, couldn't he see how homely she was? Ugly as a mud fence and God had made her that way. Was it her fault that no man wanted her for his wife? How was she supposed to go about making a living? Huh? How? She scraped the back of her hand repeatedly across her cheeks, then blew her running nose into the edge of her back shawl.

"And not one of those men will help gather firewood for them!" she shouted into the wind, a strand of brilliant red hair loosening and waving above her black hat like a torch.

Hester assured her that she was not ugly. She just had never met the right person.

Bappie snorted so loudly that Silver broke into a gallop. "You can say that. You with all your beauty."

"I'm not married."

"Puh. Well, I'm going to get a load of firewood, if I have to chop every piece myself. I don't understand. Evidently you have to be Amish to receive any help. Puh."

Hester placed a comforting hand on Bappie's arm. "You won't have to chop firewood alone. I'll help."

Bappie sniffed and looked straight ahead.

Chapter 22

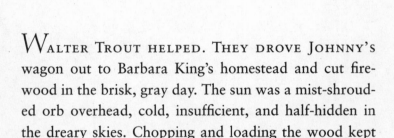

WALTER TROUT HELPED. THEY DROVE JOHNNY'S wagon out to Barbara King's homestead and cut firewood in the brisk, gray day. The sun was a mist-shrouded orb overhead, cold, insufficient, and half-hidden in the dreary skies. Chopping and loading the wood kept them warm, their breaths coming in short, white puffs as they worked.

The great Belgians stood patiently, dozing in the still November air as the wood clunked into the sturdy oak wagon bed.

Walter worked alongside, grunting, puffing, and perspiring. At precisely ten o'clock, he announced his wish for "the luncheon" Emma had prepared. "Ah, yes, a bit early, perhaps, but to the working man, having a full stomach is of great and utmost import."

Bappie grinned cheekily and gave the axe a good whack into the chopping block. She dusted her hands by clapping them together and said loudly, "Where is this picnic?"

Walter was already arranging a blanket on the lee-
ward side of the wagon. Giving it a final pat, he happily
dug through the large wicker basket. He brought out a
loaf of bread first, cut into inch-thick slices. Chunks of
fried ham were laid between the slices, after a thick layer
of yellow salted butter was applied with intense concentration. Every corner of the bread was covered precisely.

There was cold buttermilk, spicy little cucumber
pickles, hard-boiled eggs, spiced peaches, sugar cookies,
and wedges of squash pie with cinnamon, brown sugar,
and nutmeg sprinkled over the top.

Walter was in his glory, his eyes shining with the pur-
est delight as he ate. Such large quantities disappeared
from the spread on the blanket that perhaps even Emma
would have become concerned.

He dabbed delicately at his mouth with the cloth
napkin, belched quietly behind it, arranged the belt of
his trousers more comfortably, and humming delicately,
cut a slice of pie that was very nearly half of the whole.
"Fuel for the soul," he crooned, after swallowing
every bit.

"I thought preachers supplied that," Bappie said.

"Oh, they do, they do. But if I had my choice, I'm
afraid the squash pie would prevail, indeed." His shoulders shook with merry giggles.

Word spread among the rowhouses. Something had
happened at Heinz Hoffmans. Finny was working. The
children were clean. They ate green things. Chon survived the infection. Their house was warm.

When, a few houses down, a young girl was tak-
en sick with pleurisy and bleeding in her lungs, Finny

reported this to Hester, who had merely come for a visit, eager to hear how Finny was doing.

Instantly, Hester thought of the red Beth-root, bayberry root, and witch hazel leaves which she boiled in wine, and then stirred in a teaspoon of honey. This was the ancient treatment for pleurisy that she had learned from the book.

Bleeding of the lungs? Or consumption? These were deadly viruses that spread like wildfire. She shivered, with Finny beside her, as they walked to Bessie's house. Bessie was the wife of Joe Reed, a Scots-Irishman who had fallen on hard times, having broken his hip in a farm accident. He was able to walk, but only by leaning heavily on a cane. His wife Bessie was at least twenty years younger and bore him a child each year, with little or no means to provide for them.

The house was bigger than the Hoffmans', if only by a few feet. It was decidedly cleaner, but so bare of even the most basic necessities it was hard for Hester to grasp the Spartan conditions the family lived in.

Joe was a gentleman, proud, kind, and so polite. He bowed over Hester's hand and thanked her for coming in an Irish brogue so thick she could not understand his speech.

Bessie was English, her words spoken precisely. Toothless, thin, and her brown and curly hair riotous, Bessie looked out of eyes that were flat and strained with the impossibility of her days. She was barefoot, her too short dress showing puffy ankles criss-crossed by bulging blue veins.

A baby slept in a broken cradle close to the hearth. A group of thin toddlers were lined up on a bench, either sucking on a thumb or a finger, or holding a corncob as if it were a doll.

The girl with the sickness was propped up against the outer wall by a rolled up blanket, her chest heaving as she struggled to breathe. Her eyes were sunken in her face, her lips apart, cracked and bleeding, a gray pallor spread across her features.

"This is Dulcie."

Hester bent to her line of vision.

"Hello, Dulcie."

A rolling of the eyes and a slow drooping of the tired lids were the only signs that she had heard. One thing was certain. Dulcie was very sick. To Hester, it looked as if she had an ongoing case of consumption, likely well seated, which was, in fact, not curable. Why the smaller children had not come down with it, she didn't know. Perhaps it wasn't the dreaded illness.

Elecampane, pignut, sage, horehound, yellow parilla, Solomon's seal, golden seal, all boiled in rainwater. She had the tincture at home.

Again Bappie accompanied her, cleaning and giving the family food and clothing. When the women had no more extras to give, they went door to door, asking for clothing, food, whatever they had to spare. Bappie said there was no difference between that and peddling wares. Lots of the Amish peddled vegetables, bread, pies, and cakes.

They approached gabled brick houses with ornate white trim, where the front doors were opulent, and there was a brass ring to lift and let fall without smashing your knuckles. Servants, mostly black-skinned housekeepers in immaculate white caps and aprons, opened the doors, shook their heads from side to side, and spoke in low velvety voices. "No, ma'am." "Sorry, ma'am." "Not to-day, ma'am."

When Dulcie breathed her last, Hester cried. Bappie rubbed her shoulders and blinked rapidly, saying she didn't think she would die. They buried her in the common graveyard where the town's poor laid their children. Hester stood in the biting December air, hung her head, and raged at the rich who lived inside their protected brick walls, surrounded by wealth and plenty, their consciences and their money secured by brick walls as well.

She kicked pebbles the whole way home, her nose red from crying, her soul withered within. "I'm going to go with Hunting Wolf. I can't stand another day of this. We did all we could for the Hoffman family, and what happens? He's in jail. Dulcie dies. What's the use?"

Bappie inserted the key into the lock. They let themselves in, shivering and rubbing their hands. Hester poked up the fire, laid small pieces of split wood on the burning embers, and watched it flame up before swinging the kettle over it. They stood in their black shawls and hats, staring morosely into the gray, joyless day, their spirits trampled, as if a giant hoof had staggered all over them.

"I guess there's not much to say, except that the Lord giveth and the Lord taketh away," Hester said softly.

"They have too many children anyway," Bappie said gruffly, slamming her gloves against the stone wall of the fireplace. "Will they all get the consumption?"

"Likely. It's a bad thing. They can cough and spit blood for years. It's hardly ever curable."

They put a handful of beans in the boiling water and added a bit of salt pork from the attic. The rich smell moved through the rooms of the house, warming and cheering their battered feelings, giving them a small degree of comfort.

They made their rounds of the shopkeepers and came away with a wagonload of potatoes, turnips, beef tallow, lard, and cornmeal, heaped on until they had to be careful not to throw anything off.

Joe and Bessie were grateful, the children overjoyed.

Two of the toddlers were coughing, so Hester left some of the same tincture, with instructions for Bessie.

A week before Christmas, when the women were knitting gifts, and green boughs and holly berries decorated the mantle, there was a sharp rap on the front door, then another. Bappie moved quickly down the short hallway.

A gust of icy air moved across the floor. Hester heard Bappie's low voice. When she closed the door, she sighed, relieved the visitor had gone. But then she held her breath as heavy footfalls followed Bappie's lighter ones.

She looked up. A white-coated livery man stood in their kitchen. Tall, dark of face, his eyes light with a greenish flash like a trout in a forest pool, his face was trimmed by a neat beard, a mustache above his lips.

He saw Hester in the gray afternoon light, the crackling fire casting her face in an ethereal, golden glow. Her eyes were large and dark, her mouth slightly open, revealing her perfect, white teeth, her long, slender neck reminding him of a swan.

He forgot where he was and his errand.

Bappie cleared her throat, which severed the spell efficiently.

"I . . . I beg your pardon. You must be Hester Zug."

"King."

"Hester King. Yes. I am employed by the Breckenridges on King Street. Their daughter is indisposed. They have heard of the Amish women and the herbs they have knowledge of. Would you be so kind as to accompany me?"

Immediately, Hester was on her feet.

The livery man was amazed at her height. He had never encountered such charm, such innocent beauty.

"Allow me a minute for my shawl." Her voice was like the call of the whippoorwill, a babbling brook, the trill of a bluebird, the wind in the fir trees.

Hester had acquired a black bag, which she filled with labeled bottles, all in order side by side, along with clean strips of muslin, scissors, a knife, and any small utensil she thought she might need.

As she followed him down to the grand carriage, her heart swelled within her, recognizing this venture for what it was. A dream. A passion.

When he opened the door for her, he saw her face was completely hidden by her large black hat. He wanted to grab the wide black strings and rake it off her head. He mourned the loss of her face.

He sat outside, up high, while she sat alone, Bappie having opted to stay indoors and finish her knitting.

Hester stayed hidden, afraid someone from their church district would see her being borne away to the wealthy section of town. With the stern reprimand of Bishop Joel Stoltzfus still weighing heavily on her conscience, she shrank back against the luxurious cushions.

The carriage stopped. Hester waited. When the door opened, the white-coated man stood directly in her line of vision, his eyes intense, eager. She shrank from his too-familiar look. She lowered her eyes and brushed past him, seeming to skim the steps in her haste to reach the front door.

He mourned the loss of her. She mourned the fact that some things never change.

The brass ring slipped in her hand and crashed against the red door with a splintering sound. Quickly, the door swung open from the inside. A short, buxom woman stood aside, her graying hair piled on top of her head in artificial poufs, containing so many glittering combs her hair seemed to be alive.

"Oh, you've come! You've come! Miranda!" She called quite loudly for a lady of her stature, but was quickly rewarded by the heavy pounding of steps from the wide, oak staircase directly in front of her.

Hester gave Miranda the black shawl and hat. Hester's fingers moved restlessly on the black handle of her satchel; her heart beat loudly in her ears as her eyes took in the sheer grandeur of this house.

The stairway was almost as big as Heinz Hoffman's whole house. The foyer, the hallway with the adjoining library and receiving room, would hold five or six of the poor hovels.

She had not known that wallpaper existed. Flowers and leaves and birds on a wall were unthinkable. How did they get there on that paper? How did the scrolls of paper get stuck to the walls?

"Are you listening?" The woman's voice came from far away.

"Oh, yes, yes, of course."

"I am Cassandra Breckenridge. I am pleased to make your acquaintance. I gather you are Hester King."

"Yes."

"My daughter is very sick. The doctors are puzzled."

Hester nodded.

"You may follow me."

Hester followed at a polite distance, the brilliantly flowered skirt bobbing up the stairs ahead of her, the ruffles sweeping the dust carefully as she moved. A white hand with four short fat fingers trailed along the gleaming banister, each one circled by jeweled rings either gold or what she supposed were diamonds. She had never seen diamonds, or any precious stones, so how would she know?

The room they entered was a vision of pink tulle and huge puffy roses on the wallpaper, as if someone had dreamed of this room and placed it here. The bed was high and deep and wide, the coverlet of white as pure as snow.

The girl reclining on the pillow was short and round-faced, like her mother. Her hair resembled spun gold, with waves that reminded Hester of a pool of water when the wind disturbed it. Her face was flushed, her blue eyes bright with fever, the lids drooping with the weariness of the sick.

A tall glass of water stood on the round-skirted table by her bed, next to a box that held what Hester supposed were confections, a new sweet Bappie had spoken of, which the English brought across the ocean from their home country.

"Cynthia, this is Hester. She is a plain lady from the Amish. She has herbal decoctions to make you better."

A look of sulphuric, hissing blue was cast in Hester's direction. The pink lips blossomed prettily into a pout of steely rebellion. "I won't take it."

Instantly, a fluttering and whining began, a tearful pleading that led to hysteria, the mother hovering and bowing as she begged.

"Won't do it."

Hester stood, waiting till the mother settled down.

Finally, she said, "Tell her where it hurts."

"No."

"Darling girl, oh, please, please, please obey your mother."

"I want to talk to her," Hester said.

Dipping and swaying, perspiring effusively, the mother settled herself on a chair, moaning softly to herself.

"Can you tell me?" Hester ventured carefully.

"My stomach."

"Top or bottom?"

The girl widened her eyes, her eyebrows lowered, as she pouted prettily. "It just hurts."

She allowed Hester to feel the swollen abdomen.

What had the book said? The old grandmother? Hester felt the stomach, which was swollen a bit, but not hard. She needed to summon the courage to inquire of this wealthy woman questions only a doctor should be asking.

Hester drew down the girl's soft, pink nightgown, replaced the covers, and gave her a gentle pat and a shy smile. Turning to the still moaning mother, she crossed her arms tightly below her chest and coughed lightly, self-consciously biding her time. She would not be able to ask of her a question so dubious, so personal.

The delicate apparition on the chair had ceased to moan and had taken out a well-used crocheted handkerchief. Flinging it over her nose, she began a wailing that made Hester decide to speak before she brought more sickness to her poor daughter.

"Mrs. Breckenridge, please don't."

From the bed, the fever-bright eyes turned toward the mother and a sour expression came down over her face like a gray, mottled cloud. "Oh, Mother, shut up."

The words were spoken wearily and without respect, her spoiled face turning into a caricature of her mother's weeping one before a triumphant smile stretched across her face.

"Does Cynthia have . . ." Hester hesitated. "Does she, are her, um, are her bowels loose?"

Hester's face flamed with embarrassment. These things simply were not spoken for anyone to hear, except perhaps a doctor.

Immediately the mother ceased her wet, sloppy crying and dabbed indelicately at her eyes, her head held to one side, alert. "I don't know."

From the bed came the angry, "How would you? You never empty the chamber pots. Miranda does."

"Honey, do you have, um, what she asked?"

Indifferently, Cynthia shrugged her shoulders. "Ask Miranda. She knows."

With that, she flipped on her side. Up came the covers over her fever-red face as she burrowed beneath them like a squirrel.

Whimpering, the mother bustled out of the room, her shrill voice preceding her, calling the servant.

She reentered with the fast-breathing, portly Miranda in tow. Hester spent a few awkward moments, unsure of what she should do—go to the bed and question the sick girl herself, or leave it to the housekeeper?

She viewed the beautiful room with appreciative eyes again. She stroked the glossy top of a dresser to be sure it wasn't wet. How could anything wooden shine like that? Her hand dropped to her side as the mother disappeared out of the door with Miranda, and then just as quickly returned with her, urging her to speak.

"Yes, yes, she do. She have the looseness. She sick. Her stomach not right. Course not. The doctor? What those doctors do? Nothin'. They don't do nothin'. They don't know what wrong with her."

Hester stood still. She saw the old Indian woman, her hand going to her stomach. She spoke of the pains, the things to take. So many different ones. So many herbs, and the matter of finding the right one.

She was feverish, this young girl, which spoke of infection. Hester had listened closely as the old Indian woman spoke of the fermented juice of apples, mixed with the salt she gathered at the salt licks by the "waters." Her black eyes had snapped with enthusiasm, and she laughed, a cracked, rough sound of triumph about the taste, but, she had whispered to Hester, the healing would not fail. She had never seen it fail.

Going to Cynthia's bed, Hester gently peeled back the covers. "If I bring some medicine, will you take it, even if it doesn't taste good?"

"No!" The scream was high-pitched, defiant, sure.

"If I mix it with juice?"

"No! The doctors all do that!"

Again, Cassandra, the hovering mother, began picking at the pink coverlet, her voice pleading, cajoling, promising her sick daughter anything her heart desired, if only she would take what Hester asked.

"No!"

Miranda plucked at Hester's sleeve and led her out of the room. "What you need?"

"Vinegar and salt."

"I have both. Come with me."

Together, they moved down the wide staircase, back the wide, gleaming hallway, down another flight of stairs, and into a kitchen that seemed to have no end. A huge fireplace, two cookstoves, a deep sink with a drainer board on each side, and so many pans and pots and dishes, Hester could not imagine the uses for all of them.

Miranda moved to the far wall, opened a wide door to a pantry lined with shelves, and got down a jug. "Vinegar."

Hester found the salt, measured it, then poured in the vinegar, enough to make a liquid.

Miranda's round brown eyes searched Hester's face. "You'll not do the young miss harm?"

"No, this will not harm her."

Miranda lowered her voice, held a palm against the side of her cheek, and whispered, "That little miss is full of worms, that's what. She eat sugar all the time. Breakfast, cookies. Dinner, pie. All day long."

Hester smiled. "This will help."

"How you getting it in her?"

"I think she'll take it."

"Hmph."

They passed two African girls lugging baskets of clothes, their hair done with dozens of colorful ribbons within their braids. They were pretty, their faces wreathed in smiles as they met Miranda.

When Hester and Miranda entered the room, the scene had not changed except for Cassandra's elevated hysterics, her daughter a lump beneath the covers, unresponsive.

Hester felt her patience snap. "Everyone leave the room," she barked in a voice that carried well, brought the mother's face, astonished, toward her, and sent Miranda scuttling from the room, her black eyes rolling in her head, the whites showing her fear and respect for this tall, dark woman.

"I will not leave," Cassandra said, her face a solid mask of resolve.

"Your daughter will not live then." Hester placed the bottle and spoon by the bed, picked up her black satchel, and prepared to leave.

Instantly, two fat, white hands fluttered in her direction. "I'll go, I'll go. Only please, please don't hurt my darling. Don't make her do anything she doesn't want to."

Hester's answer was a steely gaze. Slowly, the mother backed from the room, a hand to her heaving chest, another going to her trembling mouth.

As soon as the door closed behind her, Hester turned, flung off the covers, and said, "Sit up."

"No."

Firmly, Hester grasped the girl's shoulders, turned her, and sat her up. Keeping her hands on her arms, she lowered her face, her dark eyes compelling, and said only one sentence in a voice to be feared. "You have a badly infected stomach."

Cynthia nodded, wide-eyed with fear.

"Take this." Pouring out a measure, she put it to the girl's mouth. Keeping her hand on her forearm, she held it against her lips. When Cynthia turned her head away Hester turned it back. Quietly, and not ungently, she remained firm until Cynthia obediently opened her mouth and swallowed all of it.

"I don't like it," she cried.

"You'll get used to it. I'm staying here to give you this every two hours all night long. You will get better if you obey."

Hester did not praise, neither did she scold. She merely did not relent. And Cynthia took the medicine two hours later and cried again.

The mother and Miranda stayed out of the room, although Hester had to have a conference with them in the hallway, telling them Cynthia would not live if they interfered and the medicine was not taken.

So steady was Hester's trust in the voice of the Indian grandmother, she never doubted the ancient remedy. Not once.

Chapter 23

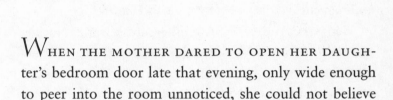

When the mother dared to open her daughter's bedroom door late that evening, only wide enough to peer into the room unnoticed, she could not believe her eyes.

Hester sat on the bed cross-legged, leaning forward in the soft, yellow light from the oil lamp. She was holding both hands up, her long, tapered fingers spread with a length of string wound through them. Cynthia was following Hester's instructions—right then left, over then under—giggling. Her face was alight with the interest she felt. When the string was pulled and every intricate loop loosened in perfect symmetry, Hester clapped her hands. Cynthia squealed, bouncing up and down on the bed.

When Miranda tapped on the door, the girl told her to come in, her eyes going to Hester's face, questioning.

Hester nodded.

The glistening dark face of the housekeeper was followed by the anxious white one of the distraught mother.

They stood side by side, short and buxom, their arms pressed to their stomachs, their eyes wide with the wonder of the scene before them.

Hester stayed the night, sleeping only a few hours on the chaise lounge in the opulent bedroom. Precisely every two hours, she gave the child the bitter mixture, followed by an offering of milk or custard or thin sugar wafers, all of which she petulantly denied.

In the morning, the fever had lessened noticeably, Cynthia's glassy eyes had returned to their normal blue, and her flushed cheeks were pale and smooth.

With strict orders to the mother and Miranda, Hester warned of a recurring infection if the girl's earlier diet was not changed. She could have sweets only occasionally and only after other substantial fare.

Cassandra Breckenridge pressed a wad of bills into Hester's hand. The mother's gratitude was as outsized as the floral wallpaper, resulting in words of praise and flattery tumbling over themselves. Hester quickly put on her large black hat, as if to protect herself from the vanity that could so easily strip her of the humility and submission she was committed to. She was, after all, of the Amish faith and not given to vain words that blew oneself out of proportion, larger than truth.

She pinned her black shawl securely about her shoulders and prepared to be driven back to the safety of Mulberry Street.

"You look like a witch." This observation came from the bed where the child lay propped up.

Laughing, Hester untied her hat, went to the bedside, and kissed the girl's cheek. "I'm not a witch. I just dress Amish."

"I know." As if to make up for the blunt speech, Cynthia threw her arms about Hester's waist, clinging to her as if she'd never let her go. "Come back to see me, please?" she whispered.

Hester stroked the silky, flaxen hair, her hand going to the smooth roundness of her cheek. "I will. I'll come see you soon. And bring you carrots and turnips and parsnips."

Cynthia wrinkled her nose.

Bappie was anxious but resigned to the fact that Hester's comings and goings would eventually be a routine part of their lives.

"After the Breckenridges, who knows what will happen? You better hope the bishops allow this. You know there are quite a few of our members who look on these old healing remedies as witchcraft."

"Ach, Bappie." Hester shook her head as if to erase the threat of being unable to practice the use of her medicines.

"I mean it. Look at the warning *I* got."

"But I'm not on the town square, hawking my wares."

Bappie cast her a level look beneath lowered lashes. "No, you just ride in fancy carriages with lovelorn grooms."

"What does that mean?"

"Exactly what I said."

Hester's face flamed with shame. Her fault again. How could she ever stop this? "I'm sorry," she whispered.

"Sorry for what?"

"That the groom was . . . like that."

Bappie rose from her chair, her movement too quick, too calculated. She went to the window and peered between the wooden panes to the gray, windswept streets of the town. For only a moment, the longing, the dissatisfaction of being an older, single woman, barren and unnoticed, crossed her face.

"Ah, Hester. Dear girl. Of course it's not your fault. You can't help that any more than a dandelion seed can help being torn from its stem and whirled away on fickle April winds. Only God knows where that seed will go and what will become of it."

"I wish I was like you, Bappie." Hester spoke harshly and fast.

"No, you don't. You don't. You will never have to know what it's like to never be noticed, to never be asked to be someone's wife."

"And you, Bappie, will never know what it's like to shrink within yourself when men look at you with that leering expression. I hate it."

Bappie only nodded.

They sat together in silence, each protected by the solitude of her own thoughts. The fire crackled and burned, the steam rose slowly from the bubbling pot on the hook. Outside, a branch scraped against the wooden siding of the house, a brittle leaf was hurled against the windowpane.

"Think you'll always be a widow?"

The words frightened Hester. Like being pushed off a cliff, she was being confronted by the yawning, unknown depths ahead of her. It was much too complicated to answer Bappie's innocent question.

Failing to be a good wife, failing to provide William with sons and daughters, angering Francis, Hans, and

Johnny, and their intentions gone awry, the puzzle was too difficult to figure out.

And yet. She longed for something she didn't fully understand. She wanted the same kind of union she observed with Hans and Kate. That easiness. That toughness, the comfortable happiness. Was that kind of union possible only for special people like Kate? Likely.

In answer, she shrugged her shoulders.

Bappie nodded. Sighing, she said quietly, "Well, Hester, what say we cover the garden really well with about a foot of good horse manure."

"And where do you plan on getting it?"

"From that cranky old Levi."

"You mean Levi Buehler? Surely he'd want to spread it on his own fields, which are lying fallow at this time of year."

"His wife is sick."

"What's wrong with her?"

"Wouldn't know."

Bundled into heavy shawls, scarves, and gloves, they hitched faithful Silver to the courting buggy and drove off down Mulberry Street, past the livery, the wheelwright, and the candle shop, into the open road that led away from the town. Everything was bare and brown and windblown. Every crevice was filled with leaves, every tree branch, etched against the gray sky, moved back and forth, tossed by the stiff November breeze.

Pieces of torn cornstalks whirled across the road, but Silver merely pricked up his ears and hopped across them. The straps on his haunches lifted, then fell with a flapping sound as he ran.

An oncoming team pulled abreast. They both lifted their hands to wave at Frances and Elias. Frances's white face was hidden well by the sides of her great hat. Elias sat stiffly, his black hat positioned squarely on his head, the brim wide and flapping, his hair cut well below his ears.

"Shoo!" Bappie whistled. She looked at Hester. "Your cap tied?"

Hester meant to nod without acknowledging the pious severity of William's family, but a smile played at the corners of her mouth, tugging it into a reluctant smile, and then a wide grin. Finally she burst into a startling laugh that ended up being flung into the air, joined by Bappie's lusty guffaw, and whirled away.

When they turned Silver into the uneven driveway that led to the Levi Buehler homestead, they had to duck their heads to avoid being smacked in the face by pine branches.

"He needs to clip these off. I'm going to tell him," Bappie said, swatting forcefully at the low-hanging branches. Hester had never seen a more beautiful pine forest. Thick and green and dotted with healthy brown pinecones, the evergreens were breathtaking. Redbirds flitted away from the women and horse with their saucy cries.

Hester and Bappie came on to the set of buildings, all weathered and gray, but sturdy and not without charm. The house had a porch on two sides and dormers in the roof, which were quite ornate features for an Amish-designed house. The barn was built into the side of the hill, a sturdy bank barn made to accommodate wagonloads of hay and straw into the top bay. There was a neat henhouse, reliable-looking fences in good repair, and a corncrib with a mended roof, filled to the top.

Silver flicked his ears and arched his neck when a sound, not unlike the baying of wolves, erupted from the barnyard. Immediately, a passel of skinny hounds came around the corner of the barn, their red tongues lolling, their eyes squinting from the effort of the incessant howling. They were so thin every one of their ribs could be counted beneath their scruffy hides.

"Puh. Anyone that keeps those hideous-looking dogs can't be too smart." Bappie snorted her disapproval as her eyes made a sweeping survey, sizing up the management of the farm, or the lack of it.

She reached under the seat, pulled out the sturdy whip, and flicked it in the hounds' direction. "Go on! Shut up! *Schtill*!"

Hester shrank back as the tall form of an Amish man came from the house, his gait easy and lanky, as if he had all day to meet them. He snapped his fingers at the hounds, and they slunk away, looking balefully back at the visitors.

"What do you want with those ugly critters?" Bappie called. Only Bappie, Hester thought.

Amazed, she watched the Amish man adjust his hat, shift his toothpick, and smile broadly, looking directly into Bappie's eyes like a schoolboy, and every bit as guileless. "I make more money with them than I do with my cows," he announced flatly in a deep, rumbling baritone.

"Puh."

"Sure I do."

"How?"

"Coonhounds. Good ones, too. I sell pounds of good-quality furs. They tree a coon, he ain't gonna get away."

"Ain't he?" Bappie said, punching Hester's side with her elbow.

"Nope."

Bappie changed the subject immediately. "We want your manure. The horse manure. We need it for the garden. You told me we could have it."

The toothpick changed directions again. "I did?"

"Yes, you did. Remember? You were at market."

"Can't recall."

Frustrated, Bappie said too loudly, "Yes, you can."

Still he had not noticed Hester, obviously enjoying Bappie's tantrum. Hester was delighted by the unusual banter.

Levi was of medium height and wide, with a good, solid look about him. In a crowd, he would not have stood out. His looks were not striking. His hair was the color of dry brown grass, his eyes clear, his skin medium brown and a bit freckled, his beard unkempt, the way most Amish men's were in the middle of the week.

"How's Martha?"

"The doctor's been out." A cloud passed over his face, turning the clear eyes a stormy gray.

"And?"

Out came the toothpick. He lowered his face, threw it on the ground, and rolled it with the sole of his shoe. "I'd rather not say."

"Why not?"

"You'll find out soon enough."

Hester swallowed. She sat forward, eagerly. "May I visit her?"

Finally, his attention shifted to Hester. His eyes appreciated her beauty in a friendly, offhand way, the way he'd view a pretty child or charming kitten. "You may."

"Hester, no. We have work to do."

Whistling, Levi led the way to the barn. He hitched up two brown mules, attached the flat-bed wagon, put Silver in a box stall, and fed him a generous amount of oats. Then he showed them the pitchforks. "Do what you can today. I'll help you when I can. Martha needs me much of the time."

They pulled rubber boots over their shoes, rolled up their sleeves, and set to work, forking out the acrid, rotting manure, slapping it down on the sturdy, flat bed of the wagon. As soon as they had a load filled, Bappie hopped up on the wagon. Hester followed, standing beside her in the cold air as the mules lowered their heads and tugged dutifully at the wagon they were attached to. The gigantic ears flopped up and down as their heads bobbed. The traces jingled where the chains were attached to the singletree.

Hester braced her legs, shifting her weight with the way of the wagon, breathed deeply of the cold, fresh air, and watched the flight pattern of a flock of snow buntings, flushed from the tall, brown briars.

"What's wrong with his wife? Why doesn't he want to talk about it? Why did he say we'll know soon enough?"

Bappie shrugged. "She's pretty sick. I think it was Enos Troyer's wife, Salome, who said she heard she has cancer."

"What's that?"

"Incurable. Nothing you can do." Bappie's words were hard.

"How do you know?"

"Well, you can't. I don't want you to start with your potions and tinctures and herbs. All that craziness."

Startled, Hester's eyes flew to Bappie's face. She was alarmed to see an expression so painful it changed her features, twisting them into a caricature of Bappie's normally plain, unflappable demeanor.

As if to ease the pain, Hester tried to change the direction of her inquiries. "I don't remember ever seeing Martha in church."

"That's because she hasn't been there."

Suddenly, Bappie turned to Hester. "He . . . he told me, she's not going to make it. God only knows what that man has suffered. They had three babies. All of them died within two years from German measles. They say it got the best of Martha. She's never been right since." Bappie's words were brittle, short, and thrown into the cold November day like rocks pelting against a tree, quickly, one by one.

Ashamed then, Bappie turned her head to watch the brown grasses and the dead cornstalks trampled into the cold, brown earth. A corner of her black scarf flew up into her eyes. Bappie grabbed it, stuck it inside her shawl, coughed, and cleared her throat.

"Looks like we have company," Hester observed.

Sure enough. In the grove of trees by the large garden stood a team of Belgians. The grinning Johnny sat on the oak boards of his wagon, swinging his legs, his hands tucked beneath him. "Well, well. Imagine meeting you young ladies out here."

Bappie leaned back, pulling the mules to a stop. "What are you doing?"

He didn't hear Bappie. His concentration centered completely on Hester, his brown eyes alive with interest, his teeth flashing white as he smiled broadly. "Hester! How are you?"

"I'm fine." Her words were clipped, firm, and without a trace of warmth. Bappie climbed down. Quickly Hester took up the reins, chirped to the mules, and moved off to the center of the garden where she stopped the horses. Then she proceeded to pitch the manure off, flinging it across the garden with monstrous strokes.

Johnny shook his head. "She still doesn't like me."

"Why should she?"

Suspicious, Johnny turned his head and found Bappie's eyes boring the truth from his own. So she knew. Cranky old maid. "It wasn't my fault," he muttered.

Bappie's snort was loud enough to startle the sleepy Belgians.

Johnny sighed, gathered up the reins, and drove away without a backward glance, his shoulders slumped in defeat.

Bappie marched over to Hester's wagon, leaped aboard, and began heaving manure as if her life depended on it.

The baying of the coonhounds heralded their return. Levi helped them load another heaping wagonload. They moved off through the pine forest, back to the garden, bringing more of nature's best fertilizer for next year's vegetables. They worked steadily without speaking. Hester felt the beginning of a painful blister on her third finger, so she shifted the position of her hand and kept forking manure.

A line of dark clouds was forming on the horizon where the setting sun should have been. Like a curtain, it hid the sun's light. Hester shivered as the wind picked up, bending the grasses and rattling the dry branches overhead.

"Too early for snow," Hester observed.

Bappie nodded.

"You want to try for another load before dark?" Hester asked.

"We could finish."

Together they increased their speed, cleaning all the manure from Levi's horse stalls. He came out as they were spreading fresh straw. Hester led the horses back to their cozy pens, clean and sweet-smelling.

Levi whistled his admiration in one long exclamation. "You did good!" he said simply.

Bappie's face was red, as was her hair, strewn about like flames of fire. Her black kerchief had slid off her head, so she let it lie around her neck. Hairpins straggled from the roll of hair on the back of her head. Pieces of straw were caught in the unruly curls that stuck out everywhere. Her breath was coming fast and she was laughing, obviously enjoying the challenge of getting the last load out. "Yes, well, Levi, we can't visit. We have to go. Looks like a storm's coming in the west."

Hester smiled at him, but he missed it completely. He was watching Bappie grab the leather reins and expertly maneuver the mules out of the barnyard, and at a competent pace down the rutted driveway, until they disappeared out of sight beneath the pines.

He stuck his toothpick back in his mouth, called to the coonhounds, and went to the house to tend to his ailing wife before he began the evening's milking.

Bappie kept the mules at a quick trot, the traces bouncing up and down, the wagon lurching over the ruts in the road. Hester's eyes scanned the low bank of black clouds, tumbling and tossing now, as they climbed higher into the sky.

When they reached the garden, they shoved most of the manure off the side, then leaped off the wagon to scatter it efficiently. Overhead, the black clouds boiled and rolled. The first ping of ice hit Hester's nose as she lifted her head to watch the approaching tempest.

"We're in for it!" she yelled, as the wind slammed against her back.

"We'll live!" Bappie yelled back. She lifted the reins, then brought them down on the mules' rumps with a high "Yee-ha!"

The mules lurched into a mad dash. Hester hung on to the makeshift boards that separated her from the mules' pounding hooves, her eyes wide as she watched the fury overhead. Ice pounded the galloping mules, bounced off the wagon bed, pummeled the women's heads, and pinged against their faces. Hester squeezed her eyes shut and held tight. She slanted a look at Bappie, astounded to see her standing upright, her eyes wide with delight, thrilled to be part of this dangerous adventure.

"Ouch! Ow!" Bappie laughed as the ice hit her face, but she stayed on her feet, goading the mules over the rutted road.

Hester was just about to warn Bappie about the steep incline when there was a cracking sound, as loud as the shot of a rifle. The mules were hurled to a standstill as the front axle broke, throwing both women from the bed of the wagon and into the wet, icy grass beside the road. Bappie screamed.

Hester flew through the air, landed on her shoulder with a sickening crunch, rolled on her back, and lay in the cold, wet grass, the ice still pinging on her upturned face. Her shoulder felt as if fiery darts were being shot into it. She squeezed her eyes shut and trembled from the pain.

Gently, she twisted her head, shocked to see the mules standing still, obedient, the only movement the quick flicking of their ears. The wagon was slanted to one side in front where the axle had broken, severing the wheel. It lay in a heap of metal, the ice making dull pinging sounds as it fell against it.

Hester heard a cry. She turned her head farther to see Bappie hobbling toward her, alarm bleaching her face to a chalky white.

"The mules, the stupid things. I never met a mule I liked. Hester, are you all right?"

Hester sat up and gingerly moved her shoulders. She winced, then grinned up at Bappie. "I'm all in one piece."

"It's these *dumbkopf* mules, that's what," Bappie spluttered.

Hester pointed. "Look at them, Bappie. Just look. They're standing there in the pounding ice, hitched to a broken wagon, dutifully waiting until we get ourselves together. You drove them too fast, Bappie. It was your reckless slapping that broke that axle.

"Don't you go on about stupid mules, either. You should have seen Hans when our wagon upset when I was little. The horses ran off for miles, with him floundering in deep snow after them. We walked all the way home without him. I still remember my mother dragging the blanket, with Noah and Isaac wrapped in it, while I watched the redbirds."

Bappie's face changed color again, back to its normal deep pink. "Well, how are we going to get Levi's mules back to him?"

Hester was already walking calmly toward the mules. "Unhitch them and walk them home. The next time, I'm driving." A gust of wind and ice tugged at her long, heavy skirt, but she kept on, resolutely unhitching the traces, remembering a time before when life held only the wonder of a redbird in the pure white snow.

CHAPTER 24

THE HAVEN OF THEIR HOMEY KITCHEN WAS BLISS-
ful as the ice bounced off the windowpanes and water
sluiced alongside, dripping from the eaves and running
down the sides of the sturdy German siding.

The fire leaped and crackled. Sparks exploded up the
chimney each time they added a chunk of wood. The room
was warm, enveloped in a yellow, fire-lit glow. Sputtering
candles on the table enhanced the coziness of their domain.

They had put up Silver first, bedding him comfortably with fresh straw and giving him a good feeding of
oats and corn, then putting down a forkful of hay. They
latched the barn door carefully before checking in on
Walter, Emma, and the boys.

They found them in good spirits, chortling over a
game of marbles as chestnuts roasted on a pan in the
oven, filling the house with the nutty aroma of fall.

"*Keschta*!" Bappie had cried.

"Oh, indeed, indeed. The finest nut of the forest. A
delicacy!" Walter agreed happily, a tankard of warm ale
at his elbow.

The boys lifted their shining faces, elbows propped on the table, their shoulders hunched as they watched the game Emma and Walter were playing. With round cheeks, clean, smooth hair, and warm clothes, the boys were barely recognizable as the forlorn waifs who had appeared on their doorstep months before.

Emma was as round as a pumpkin still. If anything, marriage only served to increase her enthusiastic appetite for good food, which was certainly not lost on her ample partner. Together they bestowed all their generosity of spirit on the two lonely orphans who seemed to blossom like well-tended flowers.

Hester wanted to stay. Walter and Emma's home never failed to fill a need, a certain yearning she had for the goodness of Hans's and Kate's home, and for her childhood, which they had supplied well with the nurturing that children require.

But Bappie wanted to get home. She was cold and wet, with the same temperament as a hen in a similar situation. So Hester got up reluctantly and followed her back to their house.

A hot, steaming bath, a pot of bubbling stew made of salt pork, potatoes, and dumplings, and the warm, cozy firelight, all made Hester sleepy. She was content, thankful for all God had given her.

She looked at Bappie reading by the fireplace, the German *Schrift* opened on her lap, her eyes dark and brooding, her thoughts a galaxy away.

Conversation was not necessary at this hour. They were at peace. The hard labor of shoveling natural fertilizer onto the large vegetable patch had been rewarding. It was good to know, when spring came, that the rich, brown loam would be full of nutrients, enough to feed the tiny plants shooting from the dropped seeds into tall cornstalks, heavy cucumber vines, hardy tomato plants.

"It's not right!" Bappie's pain-filled voice shattered the peaceful atmosphere, slicing it in two like the thrust of an axe.

Hester lifted her face, her eyes wide with surprise. Warily, she watched as Bappie rose to her feet, her movements swift. She slammed the Bible onto the table with a resounding thump, then propped her open palms on top of it as if to derive strength from the bound volume of God's Word.

Hester opened her mouth to speak, but closed it when Bappie's anguished voice rose as she talked. "He's too proud. If he would only talk about her. I don't see how he can keep his wits about him. That's so often the way of our people.

"As long as he can make things appear normal from the outside, no one is going to inquire. I can't understand where his relatives are. He's so alone, looking after that farm and caring for her. I don't know if the doctor has ever been to see her."

"Who?"

"Levi."

"Oh, you mean Levi's wife."

"Yes."

A silence fell, with only the tiny hiss of a flaming candle to break it.

"Should I go see her sometime?" Hester asked finally.

"Of course not. It's not that she has cancer, which your greenery couldn't heal anyway. It's that her mind is . . . Well, she's like a child. Her good *fashtant* is gone. He has to feed her and dress her as if she were a child. I don't think very many people know how bad it is.

"She hasn't been to church for years. Hardly anyone goes to visit them. Now he has those coonhounds slinking around his buildings. I'm just afraid he's slowly going, as well."

Hester winced at Bappie's mocking word, "greenery." Quickly then, she shook it off, knowing it was only her forthright manner. "Could *we* go visit, do you think?"

Bappie shrugged her shoulders, her eyes dark, hooded. "I'm afraid to," she said, soft and low.

"Why?"

Again Bappie did not answer. The lifting and falling of those angular shoulders was her only response.

Hail continued to ping against the windows. Hester shivered as she watched the rain run down the dark windowpane. She got up to put a log on the fire, stepping back quickly as the flames shot upward.

"I just can't stand to think of Levi going through his days, never complaining or asking for help." Hester eyed Bappie keenly. She had never seen her like this. She was always noisy, sure of herself, knowledgeable, voicing opinions without holding back, and joking easily and lightly. But now, quite unexpectedly, this miserable brooding.

So taken up in the mystery before her, Hester did not hear the gentle tapping on the sturdy front door, closed securely with a large padlock against intruders.

When the tapping turned to raps of a more solid nature, she held very still, her head tilted to one side.

Bappie was so engrossed in her own thoughts she did not suspect anything. Hesitantly, Hester partly rose, her hand on the plank table, her long, tapered fingers trembling slightly.

Bappie looked up unaware.

This time the rapping was harder, more urgent.

"You go," Bappie said.

Biting her lower lip, Hester felt tingling in her nostrils, the acceleration of her pulse. Very unusual to have a caller at this time of the evening in weather like this. With a hand at her throat, and a few light, soundless footsteps, she reached the door, inserted the key, and drew back the latch.

The figure on the doorstep was tall, wide, and dark. Hester did not recognize him until he spoke in the deep, guttural voice of her people. The words were thick, as if he spoke through the swelled linings of his throat.

"May I come in?"

Quickly, Hester stepped aside. "Oh, of course. Forgive me."

As he walked in, the smell of wet deerskin was overpowering. It was the rancid smell of the longhouses, nearly lost to her fading memory of her past. Her heart sank.

His profile was startling. He was every inch the proud brave, the lineage of his ancestors, the Conestoga Indians, running in his powerful veins. His hair hung sleek and thick, parted in the center of his head and braided with thongs of rawhide. Not a hair stood away from his forehead, so well had he applied the rancid bear fat.

Hester swallowed. A choking sound rose in her throat. She put four fingers to her mouth to suppress the cough that would follow.

Bappie stood, startled, as she placed a hand on the chair back in front of her. "Good evening," she stammered, clearly at a loss for further words.

"Good evening."

Turning to Hester, the Indian's deep, unfathomable eyes evaluated her. "I have returned," he said.

"I see. I hope you are well," Hester said, her voice low.

"I am."

Silence crept its uncomfortable way between them. Ill at ease, Bappie spoke too quickly and much too loudly. "Well, you're soaking wet. You're dripping all over the floor." Puzzled, the Indian bent his head to see what Bappie meant.

"It will dry. The fire is warm." He stood closer to the fireplace, his back to the hearth, his silhouette a stance of power, of rigid restraint. His eyes sought and found Hester's face.

"I, Hunting Wolf, have come before I planned. I can wait no longer. Before the snow comes, we will be in Ohio on the banks of the great river. Here, there is much danger for me."

Hester put out a hand as if to stop his words. "But . . ."

"You cannot decline my proposal."

Bappie stepped forward. "Now just a minute here. You can't do this to Hester. She isn't ready to decide."

Like a rock, Hunting Wolf was immovable in his intent.

Hester sank to a chair. The only sound was the crackling of orange flames as they licked greedily at the logs. She watched the candle flame dance, shiver, then resume its steady glow. In it she saw the hills and fields of Berks County. The log house nestled beneath the maple trees, the barn below it, the pathway, the split rail fence beside it. She could smell the pies and the bread that Kate baked in the outdoor oven, the homemade lye soap she used for washing, the air-dried clothing that she brought in off the clothesline.

The sun played with the ever-moving shadows of the trees surrounding the cabin. The rain plunked on the cedar shingles of the roof when she lay, warm and drowsy, beside Lissie, with Noah and Isaac on the low pallet on the other side of the attic. The scrubbed wooden floor, the sweet smell of raspberry jam on Kate's fluffy biscuits. The hard benches she sat on during church services, the beautiful rising and falling of the German plainsong. All of this was part of who she was.

The smell of the Indian longhouse, the daily slaughter of small animals, the endless pounding of corn, sitting in dust, squatting by the fire, a stone for an oven, a turkey feather for bellows. The communal sleeping arrangements. Hester winced.

To stand beside this noble brave, a proud specimen of her people, would be an honor, had she been raised by her blood mother in the ways of her people. She was approaching her thirtieth year of living among the Amish, except for the brief time with the Conestogas.

To live as they did was too foreign. Too distant. A river that flowed too deep and too swift for her to ford. She knew the decision had already been made in her heart, for she belonged to the Amish, the plain way of life, the German heritage she had adopted as her own.

In spite of the trials, here was where her heart found a home. Here in Lancaster County, working the fertile soil with Bappie, working among the poor and the wealthy, but using knowledge the Indian grandmother had passed on to her.

The look she bestowed on Hunting Wolf could only be described as tender, sorrowful, perhaps, but certain. "I cannot go. My heart will remain with my people."

"Your people are the Conestoga."

"The Lenape."

"You belong to us. The red man."

"In blood only."

"I want you for my bride. I desire you as my wife."

Hester lowered her eyes, her head drooping in shame. "I have been a wife. You do not want me."

"Yes. Yes. I do."

"No, I am not a good wife."

"You will be among my people. We will teach you the way of the Indian woman."

Hester knew the ways of the Indian women. She had learned the communal ways, the squabbling, the boldness, the crude laughter. It was good in many ways. There was affection, love, and strength. Yet the culture divided so widely from her own.

"I would be honored to be your wife. But you will find an Indian maiden worthy of your love. I was raised among the Amish and wish to remain with them. I have no intention of marrying."

Hunting Wolf sighed audibly. He opened his mouth as if to speak, then changed his mind. In true Indian fashion, he moved softly away from the fire. Going to Hester, he lifted her chin with his fingers and looked intently into her eyes. He spoke quietly with great respect. "Then I can only wish you the best in the trail you have chosen. I have lost my heart to you. But I will not force you to leave your people."

Like a wraith, a wisp of smoke, he moved away from the kitchen, soundless. The only sign he had even been in the room was the cloying scent of wet deerskin and bear grease.

Quickly Bappie hustled to the door, shoved the latch into the clasp, turned the key in the padlock, and leaned against it. "Whew!" she sighed, heavily.

Hester said nothing. Her hands were in her lap, her fingers intertwined so tightly the knuckles were white. The set of her shoulders gave away the turmoil of her emotions, the pressured burden of making the decision in so short a time.

"Buck up, Hester. You did the right thing."

Hester's smile was only a minimal lifting of the corners of her mouth, but it was a beginning. Slowly the smile widened until it reached her eyes. When Bappie returned to the fire, their eyes met, and Bappie shook her head. "You did good, Hester. For a while, when you sat there like a rock staring at that candle, I declare you were every inch an Indian. Quiet, stern, commanding. I had a notion to get up and wave my hands in front of your face."

Hester sighed, a long sound of expelled tension. "I guess my childhood with Kate as my mother is planted and rooted so deeply in my heart, it's there as sturdy as an oak tree. I will love her always. Everything I am, everything I do, I want to be like her."

Bappie nodded. "As it should be. My mam is dead and gone, but she is the whole axis on which I revolve."

The silence that followed was very deep and comfortable as the icy rain slanted against the cold, dark windowpane.

In the spring of that year, Hester was filled with an unnamed feeling of sadness. In spite of the earth's renewal and the wonder of new life around her, darkness clung to her spirits as if her soul was mired in an unrelenting muck of despair.

The dogwood trees flowered at Easter, and the daffodils and tulips lifted bright, happy faces to the strength of the warming rays of the sun. Everywhere the grasses turned a deep green. It hurt her senses to lift her eyes to the hills as she dropped seeds in the rich, brown earth.

Her feet were bare in spite of the cold, damp soil. A blue shortgown swirled around her ankles, a dull gray work apron flapping above it. She wore a kerchief of off-white muslin, knotted beneath the thick coil of glossy black hair. Tendrils of it blew in straight wisps around her forehead and down the nape of her long, slender neck.

Her eyes were large and luminous, glistening with the strange melancholy that had deepened the light in them.

She dropped one wrinkled pea seed at a time, her heart still, her lips compressed and songless. The butterflies and other insects failed to attract her attention. She didn't hear the birdsong.

Bappie was whistling, breaking into a ribald song occasionally, one that angered Hester. It was simply not a proper tune for an Amish woman, and one who was close to middle age, for sure.

Hester opened her mouth to speak her mind, straightening her back as she did so. Lifting one hand, she shaded her eyes against the strong sunlight and said, forcefully, "Bappie."

Bappie stopped, straightened, and lifted surprised eyes to her friend. She tilted her head at an angle, her eyebrows jumping in the most annoying manner.

"That song is. . . ."

"Oh, get off it, grouch. Just because you aren't happy doesn't say I can't be. Stop pitying yourself."

Hester returned Bappie's glare, the black fire in her eyes popping and crackling. "I'm not pitying myself."

"Yes, you are. It's a beautiful day and a beautiful spring. God has granted us good health through the winter, and are you thankful?"

"Of course I am."

"Then act like it."

Hester dropped the seeds she was holding, turned on her heel, and stalked out of the garden. Blindly, she walked away, faster and faster until she was running, her feet swishing through the tender new grass, her skirts swirling about her ankles, hampering her speed.

Behind her, Bappie watched, lifted her angular shoulders, then let them drop. She shook her head from side to side and went back to dropping the pea seeds precisely. Hester would get over it, whatever it was.

Hester ran effortlessly like a deer, up a slope and through a grove of trees until she reached the top of a rounded hill. She threw herself down in the old growth of grasses, her breath coming in ragged gasps.

She didn't cry. She had no tears within her, but only an ever-widening void, a darkness she could not hold at bay. She felt as if her life held no purpose, and the summer stretched before her as a long, dark tunnel of endless heat and hard work.

Had she made the wrong decision? Should she have accompanied Hunting Wolf to his people? Her people? She tried to pray, but no words would form. She wasn't sure God would hear her prayers if she managed to speak to him.

Alone, bewildered, she rolled on her back and opened her eyes to the intensity of the brilliant sunlight, the blue of the sky interrupted by clouds of white cotton. A shadow passed over her face. Startled, she opened her eyes wide. An eagle was flying so close she could see the white feathers on its head, the distinctive curve of its beak, the great majestic wingspan, and the soaring motion as it propelled itself higher with the graceful lifting of its wings.

Cold chills washed across her back and down her arms. Unbidden, tears pricked at her long, black lashes. She caught her breath as a sob tore at her throat. Leaping to her feet, she lifted her face to the eagle in flight. Flinging out her arms, she sensed the knowledge of God's love swelling inside her, filling her heart and soul with its warmth.

So long ago, it had seemed, and now, a mere heartbeat ago, she had stood on the outcropping of limestone rock and felt God's presence as the eagle soared above her. God was here on this Lancaster County hilltop. He was real, alive. He remembered her. He cared for her.

Over and over, she spoke her praise, her face lifted to the eagle's flight, tears streaming down her face, her arms lifted in supplication.

How long she remained, she didn't know. Finally, like a graceful swan, she folded her arms and sank to the ground. She rested in the peace that had eluded her earlier.

Quiet, her soul anchored once more, she was filled with a new acceptance of her place in life, and gratitude for Bappie, for Walter and Emma, for her home and her work.

Slowly, she got to her feet and began the trek back to the garden. She stopped abruptly when a figure emerged from the grove of trees, hesitated, then swung to the right toward Bappie working in the vegetable garden.

Hester quickened her pace. She had no idea who the man might be, and it was better that Bappie not be alone when she saw him. Turning left, she broke into a run, taking a shortcut by slicing through the woods, so she would reach Bappie before the man did.

Breathless, she slowed herself to a walk. The pounding of her heart was stifling her.

On he came. Tall, immense, his shoulders wide, his body thick, straining at the seams of his clothes.

Hester stopped to watch, mystified now. His gait was heavy, purposeful, the long strides covering ground effortlessly. Where had she seen this gait? The set of those shoulders? Hester stopped, her eyebrows lowered in concentration.

He was in full view now. His hat was brown and pulled low on his forehead. His face was barely visible, so low was the hat's brim.

Hester was motionless, watching, her eyes taking in the familiar walk. Why was this man's gait etched into her memory, branded into her remembering? And yet she could not name him.

He was a stone's throw away. She could not move. When he came on, she stood like a statue, her hands hanging loosely at her side, her skirts blowing gently about her ankles. Her eyes were wide with bewilderment, her graceful neck held taut like the Indian princess she was.

Did he smile first, or take off the hat that hid his features? She didn't know.

When he removed his brown leather hat, thick, straight, blond hair tumbled to his shoulders. His blue eyes were wide and filled with a light that was so glad. Hester lowered hers, shyness overtaking her.

She began to tremble. Her knees shook as if a strong wind was threatening her strength. She drew a sharp breath.

The plane of his cheeks, with weathered lines around his wide mouth, was so even, nearly perfect. He stopped. His eyes were fringed with lashes she had seen before. The cleft in his chin had been there before.

She tried to speak, but could not utter a word. A hand went to her mouth.

Slowly, he came closer. As if in a dream, he reached out, gently grasped her hand, and pulled her toward him. His eyes devoured her face, her eyes, her mouth, still as perfect in their symmetry as he had remembered. Her eyes were the dark jewels he had carried in his heart all these years. Their luster filled the emptiness in his heart. Twice, he opened his mouth to speak. Twice, he failed.

Their gaze locked and held.

When he spoke, his voice was low, filled with years of longing. "I am Noah."

The End

GLOSSARY

Ach, du lieva.—Oh my goodness.

Ach du lieva. Grund a velt!—An old, High German exclamation of amazement. Translated literally, it means, Oh, you love. Ground of the world!

Ach, du yay.—Oh, my, my.

Ach, mein Gott im Himmel!—Oh, my God in heaven!

Ach, mein Herr Jesus, Du Komm.—Oh, my dear Jesus, please come.

Ausbund—The hymnbook that the Amish sing from during church services. The old German book was written by their foreparentss during a time of persecution and imprisonment.

Aw-gnomma—Adopted

Behoft—Has, or has to do with.

Dat—Name used to address one's father.

Deifel—Devil.

Denke, mein Herr—Thank you, my Lord.

Die Englische leid—Anyone whose first language is English.

Die freundschaft—The extended family.

Doddy haus—An addition to the main house, built as living quarters for the grandparents.

Du, yay—Oh, dear.

Dumb gamach—Chaos, or chaotic.

Dumbkopf—Dumbhead.

Ein maedle ein shoe maedle. Oh, du yay, du yay.—A girl, a beautiful girl. Oh, my, my.

Faschtendich—Sensible.

Fa-sarked—To take care of.

Fashtant—Sense.

Freme—Visitors.

Gaduld—Patience.

Gahr hoftich—Very much.

Gamach—Chaos.

Gelbkuchen—Yellow cake.

Geeda—Members.

Gook do runna, Mein Herr und Vater.—Look down here, my Lord and Father.

Goot. Sell iss goot.—Good. That is good.

Gott sie gelobt und gedankt.—God be praised and thanked.

Grishtag—Christmas.

Grosfeelich—Proud, vain.

Gwundernose—Curious nose; nosey.

Hembare! Oh, meine Hembare!—Raspberries! Oh, my raspberries!

Herr, saya—God bless you.

Hochmut—Pride.

Hootsla—A bread and egg dish.

Hulla chelly—Elderberry jelly.

Ins ana end—A small addition built onto a homestead to house the older generation.

Katufla—Potatoes.

Keschta—Chestnuts.

Kinner—Children.

Knecht—A young hired man.

Leid—Verses.

Lunga feeva—Lung fever.

Maud—A helper, usually in the house, to the wife and mother in a family.

Mein Gott! Das Kind schprechen!—My God! The child talks!

Mein Gott im Himmel.—My God in heaven.

Mein Himmlischer Vater, Ich bitte dich hilf mir.—My heavenly Father, I ask you to please help me.

Mein Kind—My child.

Meine Liebchen—My dear one.

Meine liebe Kinner—My dear children.

Mit-dienner—Fellow ministers.

My grund! Die fees. See Fa-freer.—"*My grund*" is an old High German exclamation of amazement. "*Die fees*" means "the feet." "*See fa-freer*" means "they freeze."

Ordnung—The Amish community's agreed-upon rules for living, based upon their understanding of the Bible, particularly the New Testament. The *Ordnung* varies some from community to community, often reflecting the leaders' preferences and the local traditions and historical practices.

Ponhaus—Scrapple.

Rumschpringa—A young man who is overdue for a wife.

Sage mihr.—Tell me.

"*Schlofe, Buppli, Schlofe*"—a lullaby; "Sleep, baby, sleep."

Schnitza—A lie, a falsehood.

Schöna—Beautiful.

Schpeck—Fat.

Schpence—Ghost.

Schtick—Piece.

Schtill!—Be quiet!

Schtinkiche menna—Smelly men.

Schtoltz—Proud.

Schtump—Dull.

Schtup—Room, or living room.

Seck veggley—Sack (or bag) wagon.

Sell Indian maedle—That Indian girl.

Shaute soch—A pitiful thing.

Siss unfashtendich!—It makes no sense!

Unser Herr—Our Father, referring to God.

Unser Herren Jesu—Our Lord Jesus.

Vass geht au?—What's going on?

Vass sagsht?—What do you say?

Vesh pettsa sock—Clothespin bag.

Weibsleitich—Having to do with women.

Wunderbahr!—Wonderful!

OTHER BOOKS BY
LINDA BYLER

*Available from your favorite bookstore
or online retailer.*

"Author Linda Byler is Amish, which sets this book apart
both in the rich details of Amish life and in the lack of mel-
odrama over disappointments and tragedies. Byler's writing will leave readers eager for the next book in the series."
–*Publisher's Weekly* review of *Wild Horses*

LIZZIE SEARCHES FOR LOVE SERIES

BOOK ONE   BOOK TWO   BOOK THREE

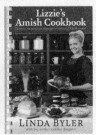

TRILOGY   COOKBOOK

Sadie's Montana Series

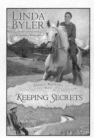

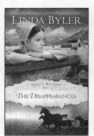

BOOK ONE   BOOK TWO   BOOK THREE   TRILOGY

Lancaster Burning Series

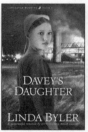

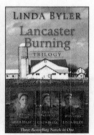

BOOK ONE   BOOK TWO   BOOK THREE   TRILOGY

Hester's Hunt for Home

BOOK ONE   BOOK TWO   BOOK THREE

THE LITTLE AMISH MATCHMAKER
A Christmas Romance

THE CHRISTMAS VISITOR
An Amish Romance

MARY'S CHRISTMAS GOODBYE
An Amish Romance

ABOUT THE AUTHOR

Linda Byler was raised in an Amish family and is an active member of the Amish church today. Growing up, Linda loved to read and write. In fact, she still does. Linda is well-known within the Amish community as a columnist for a weekly Amish newspaper.

Linda is the author of three series of novels, all set among the Amish communities of North America: Lizzie Searches for Love, Sadie's Montana (whose individual titles are *Wild Horses*, *Keeping Secrets*, and *The Disappearances*), and the Lancaster Burning series.

Which Way Home? is the second novel in a new series, *Hester's Hunt for Home*, which features the life of a Native American child who is raised by an Amish family in colonial America. The first book in that series is *Hester on the Run*. A third volume yet to be released, *Hester Takes Charge*, will complete the series.

Linda has also written three Christmas romances set among the Amish: *Mary's Christmas Goodbye*, *The Christmas Visitor*, and *The Little Amish Matchmaker*.

Linda has co-authored *Lizzie's Amish Cookbook: Favorite recipes from three generations of Amish cooks!*